THE OVERCOMER

EUGENE H. STRAYHORN JR.

ISBN 978-1-966540-41-0 (softcover)
ISBN 978-1-966540-42-7 (hardcover)
ISBN 978-1-966540-43-4 (ebook)

This book is a work of fiction. Names, characters, places, and incidents are the product of the author's imagination or are used fictitiously. Any resemblance to actual locales, events, or persons, living or dead, is purely coincidental.

Printed in the United States of America.

TABLE OF CONTENTS

1

THE ORIGINS OF SELF

May 2050

"My father was a violent man. He could fly into a rage at the slightest provocation and at the most unpredictable times. There was no telling what might set him off. One minute he could be calm, even laughing. The next, his face would turn dark red, and the veins on his forehead would stand out like ropes. As a child, I learned to dread those warning signs because what followed was often humiliating and always painful."

That should get the point across, I told myself, *but it could be better.*

I studied my reflection in the full-length bedroom mirror, noting each gesture, each nuance of expression. Later that afternoon, my grandson, Casey, was supposed to stop by. I had invited him to pay me a visit. My intention was to share my life story. Hopefully he would permit me to do so.

Over the course of several months, I had devoted serious thought to what I hoped to accomplish. My fervent desire was that my grandson would benefit from hearing my narrative. For that to happen, he would need to pay attention, and for that reason, it seemed imperative that my delivery be compelling.

I squared my shoulders and inspected my reflection again. In a measured voice, I continued, "How ironic it was that between bursts of rage, my father, your grandfather, was a quiet and unpretentious man. His mercurial nature made for a difficult childhood, to say the least."

It wasn't perfect, but it would have to suffice.

* * *

Outside, it was a balmy May afternoon in the year 2050, though I had spent most of the day indoors, rehearsing. Only once had I left the house, and then only for a quick trip to the grocery store to pick up the supplies I would need to fix dinner. Having prepared as best I could, I felt that I was as ready as I was ever going to be.

My grandson arrived precisely at our agreed time of 4:00 p.m. One thing about Casey, he was punctual. After welcoming him to my home, we migrated to the library, one of the homier rooms in the house. It would provide a comfortable environment for our conversation.

From across the room, I regarded Casey as he sat on the leather couch opposite where I was seated. I had chosen the padded armchair. It was where I preferred to do my reading at night. Over the years, it had conformed nicely to the shape of my body. To a guy seventy-one years old like me, creature comforts are something to be esteemed.

To break the ice, I asked, "How are you doing these days? How's school?"

My grandson's full name is Casey James Masters, and he just recently turned twenty-one. Casey is a bright personable lad, and I'm very fond of him. I enjoy his company. In some ways he reminds me of me.

"Going well—can't complain." There was a tightness in Casey's voice that made me wonder if he was under more stress than he wanted to reveal.

I suspected that I knew what his stressors were. "You have your final exams in, what, a month?"

"Six weeks. I'll be ready." As a senior at the University of Montana, Casey was enrolled in the prelaw curriculum. Always a good student, there was no reason I should fret about his education, none whatsoever. Without a doubt, he would pass his exams with flying colors.

With sincerity, I agreed, "I know you will. By the way, I want to thank you for agreeing to meet with me. I realize that you have more interesting things to do on a Sunday afternoon."

"I will always have time for you, Grandfather."

My name is Adam T. Masters, and I live in Missoula, Montana. When I had issued my invitation, I had foreseen that I would be the one doing most of the talking. However, my hope was that my grandson would have many questions, which was actually the point of our encounter.

With a thrust of my chin, I indicated the empty wineglass on the end table at his elbow. "Can I get you anything? How about a refill?" I had intentionally offered wine in celebration of his having just come of age.

"No thanks. I'm not used to the stuff. I already…"

"Have a slight buzz on?"

"I guess that's what it is. It's a weird feeling."

"You'll get used to it—unless you become a teetotaler. You know, it's good having you here."

"I'm glad you invited me."

"About that, perhaps I should explain my motives." I paused to take a deep breath. "I've spent months thinking about my life, seeking to analyze its ebb and flow, its ups and downs, but now I've come to the point where I need your help. With your permission, I would like to tell you my life history—straight through, from beginning to end. I believe that in sharing my story, I'll be reminded to be precise in the telling, and if I can keep the proper perspective, I should be better able to identify cause-and-effect relationships. My goal is to make sense of it all and to come away with a greater understanding of why things worked out the way they did. For some time now, I've had this feeling that obscure factors have acted to guide my journey. My aim is to explore that dynamic."

Casey nodded thoughtfully. "I think I understand what you're trying to accomplish, but why do you need my help?"

"When I try to review my history on my own, my mind tends to drift. Frequently, I wind up going off on a tangent. I'm hoping that with an audience, I'll be more inclined to relate events in their proper order. Also, you may be able to pick up on subtle congruences that I miss.

"If you agree to aid me in my quest, I trust that you too will profit from the telling. Perhaps you can learn from my mistakes and be inspired to make better choices than I did.

"If we do this, keep in mind that I'll be recounting my experiences from memory, which means some of the narrative may be colored by the perceptions of an old man, though I'll do my best to describe events as they actually happened. Still, the distortions of age may creep in from time to time. Feel free to ask any questions that come to mind. So, what do you think? Would you be willing to help me?"

"Of course, Grandfather, whatever I can do."

"Excellent. Are we good to go?"

Casey nodded with a look of anticipation. "Absolutely."

"One final thing. To maintain a certain degree of objectivity, I'll be telling my tale from a third-person point of view, which might seem impersonal, even awkward. Nevertheless, keep in mind that the events I'll share actually happened to me, not to some abstract character. Do you understand?"

"Bring it on."

"Very well then. I suspect the best way to move forward is to jump in at the beginning. That would mean starting with my earliest childhood memory. I was two years old, and it was a bright, sunny day, much like today."

*　　*　　*

June 1981

A smattering of fluffy clouds drifted across a sapphire sky. The grass felt spongy under Adam's feet. For an hour he had been toddling around the backyard, exploring with the inquisitiveness of a two-year-old. For the last fifteen minutes, he'd been pushing a bright yellow dump truck to and fro, as if motivated by some purpose other than a random expenditure of energy. A tinny song rattled out of a portable radio sitting on the ground near where his dad was working. Adam was too young to recognize the song that was playing. Later he would come to think that it might have been "Bette Davis Eyes," one of his dad's favorites.

To a two-year-old, the whole world seems gigantic. This especially applied to the three-bedroom cottage on Springwood Lane where Adam and his family lived. In future years, Adam would come to appreciate just how small their house truly was. The wooden fence that enclosed the backyard also seemed huge—insurmountable. Its dark brown slats matched patches of dark earth where the grass refused to grow.

Above the music rolling out of the radio, Adam listened to the sounds of his father working.

Adam's father's name was Lloyd Masters. Everyone called him Dusty. Straight out of high school, he had begun a career in the construction trades, eventually qualifying as a journeyman carpenter. With such an appropriate skill set, it was understandable that he would undertake rebuilding the back steps, rotted from years of exposure to the elements. For Dusty, the project was akin to a busman's holiday.

Sunlight glinted off the saw's bright metal as Dusty ripped it through a plank of wood, turning a length of board into a tread for the stairs.

Having grown bored with pretending to be a dump truck driver, Adam looked around for a new adventure.

Dusty stood beside the sawhorses, measuring the next tread. With his father preoccupied, Adam toddled over to the back stoop where he found an assortment of tools lying around. His natural instinct was to try and match his father's carpentry skills. He picked up the hammer and retrieved a nail from the battered coffee can, just as his father had done.

Raising the hammer high, he brought it down with as much force as he could muster, which, still being in diapers, was hardly any at all, which was fortunate. The hammer missed the nail and landed squarely on his thumb. The flash of pain was excruciating. Initially too stunned to react, when the injury finally registered, he let out a bloodcurdling scream that might have been heard by all of Missoula, or perhaps all of Montana.

Dusty turned his head to see what all the ruckus was about. Rather than rush forward to investigate, he quipped, "That was a stupid thing to do. You must be retarded. That's what I get for having me such a sickly child."

Adam had been born three weeks premature and then had suffered a failure to thrive until his doctor had switched him from breast milk to formula.

"Maybe you should put off playing with hammers till you're older." Dusty went back to marking up his board with a T-square and a carpenter's pencil.

Adam's mother, on the other hand, wasn't quite as cavalier. Alerted by the screams, she burst through the back door, her face distorted by a look of alarm. Her name was Mary Elizabeth Masters. Everyone called her Lizzie. In high school, she had also been known as Lizard, a nickname she thoroughly despised. Years later she would still bristle with indignation whenever anyone would dare address her in such a fashion.

When Lizzie saw her son holding his thumb and wailing, she rushed to his aid. "What happened, sweetie?" She swept him into her arms and then glowered at her husband. "How could you let this happen? You were supposed to be watching him."

"Hey, the kid's all right. Any fool can see that all he did was bruise his thumb."

"You should be ashamed of yourself," Lizzie blurted out, but then blanched, as if having belatedly realized that she was on the verge of sparking a confrontation.

"Hold your tongue, woman," Dusty growled. "I told you the kid is all right. Leave it be." With that, he turned away and reached for his saw.

Lizzie ushered Adam into the house. In the kitchen, she gave his thumb a thorough inspection. Satisfied that no bones were broken and that the trauma would heal, she suggested, "How about some ice cream? Rocky Road, your favorite."

For a two-year-old struggling to comprehend what had happened, all Adam knew was that something unexpected had radically altered the course of his day. Beyond that, he was hard-pressed to make sense of his misadventure. In any event, the Rocky Road did its job. In no time at all, he had forgotten the incident—well, almost. For months, his thumbnail's blackish discoloration would serve as a reminder.

*   *   *

"I can imagine how much that must have hurt." Casey grimaced. "That's your earliest memory, smashing your thumb with a hammer?"

"It is," I replied.

"Must have made an impression."

We both chuckled.

I responded, "As I've grown older, I've come to regard that trauma as especially significant. In thinking it through, it's taught me several lessons."

"Oh yeah? What lessons, other than making sure to keep your thumb out of the way when pounding nails?"

"Well, for starters, it showed me that if you're not careful, you can seriously damage yourself. After all, that was the first time I'd experienced a self-inflicted injury, though it certainly wouldn't be the last. As a corollary, it demonstrated that the world can be an unfriendly place. Without warning, you can fall victim to its hurtful situations. That truth laid the foundations for a certain wariness I have maintained through the years. The third lesson was realizing that I had just stumbled upon a new though somewhat dubious way of getting Mom to serve me ice cream. Of course, intentionally injuring myself would be inherently stupid, but then again, depending upon the flavor, the reward might justify the agony."

Casey raked his fingers through his chestnut-colored hair. In recent months, he had been letting it grow till it had reached a length that kept falling into his field of vision. He said, "I'm curious. You've obviously put some thought into what you want to say, but why make the effort? What do you expect to gain? Aren't we supposed to avoid focusing on the past? Isn't the future where we should direct our attention?"

"You can't shape the future if you don't understand the past. If you're willing to hear me out, I think you'll come to appreciate that there is value in teasing apart old memories. Socrates said, 'Man know thyself,' which I believe is sage advice, no pun intended. The process is akin to mentally assembling a jigsaw puzzle, fitting memories together until the big picture comes into view. Wouldn't you like to discover who you truly are?"

"I'm not sure," Casey admitted with sincerity. "Honestly, there are times when I can't stand myself."

"I hear you, but isn't that one of the best reasons to explore the past, to sort out the reasons we are the way they are and learn to live better lives?"

"I'm not sure men can change. Anyway, I'm listening. Please go on with your story."

I leaned back in my armchair and crossed my legs. "The next memory that comes to mind happened three years after getting hammered. Once again, it was a beautiful day in the middle of July, not to mention that it was my fifth birthday. Mom, who happened to be pregnant at the time, had planned a surprise birthday party, the surprise being that she hadn't told my father…"

*   *   *

July 1984

A half dozen kids sat at the picnic table in the Masters' backyard. All were under the age of nine. Collectively they created quite a commotion. Several munchkins still had on their pointed party hats. Nearly all wore smears of cake and ice cream on their faces. They all seemed to be having a good time.

On a collapsible table near the back door, six neatly wrapped birthday presents awaited Adam's attention.

As the hostess, Lizzie Masters went from child to child, assisting with this or that as needed. She might have moved more gracefully had she not been nearing the end of a long and difficult second pregnancy.

Lizzie had planned the party for weeks, but had deliberately neglected to inform her husband. Dusty was at work and was not expected to return for several hours. Had he known of her plans, he would have forbidden his wife to spend even a penny on cake and decorations, not to mention the special gift she had covertly purchased. Paying for it had depleted her meager savings, the secret stash to which she added each week's unspent grocery money. Nevertheless, she felt certain that the joy the gift would bring would justify its expense.

When everyone finished eating, the time had come to open presents. Needing no encouragement, Adam rushed to the collapsible table. The other children followed. With zeal, he tore the paper wrappings off all six gifts. With each new plaything, he dutifully expressed his appreciation, but with little enthusiasm. The gifts were nice but uninspiring: a half-sized rubber football, crayons and a coloring book, a polystyrene glider, and such. After opening the last gift, he looked up at his mom. One gift was missing.

Lizzie grinned and pointed to the gray tarp thrown over a large carton unobtrusively stationed in a corner of the backyard.

Adam whooped with excitement as he rushed to see what was hidden beneath the tarp. Tugging on one edge, he pulled the tarp away, revealing a large cardboard box decorated with birthday-themed wrapping paper.

Olivia Gardner, the fifteen-year-old girl who had agreed to help with the party, whispered in Lizzie's ear, "Judging by his reaction, I'd say you did good."

Lizzie smiled in return.

For a moment, Adam seemed unsure how to proceed until he discovered that the box had no bottom, only four sides and a top. "Come on, Theo. Give me a hand," he said to the boy standing at his elbow.

Theodore "Theo" Lane was eight years old. Being small for his age, he fit right in with younger children. Theo and his family had moved to the neighborhood six months earlier. He and Adam had hit it off from the start and were well on their way to becoming fast friends. Both were inquisitive by nature with above-average IQs. The difference between them was that Theo was a happy, easygoing child with an inherently optimistic attitude, whereas Adam was reserved, standoffish, and frequently inclined to play on his own. They were like oil and water, but their friendship worked.

"Sure." Theo stepped forward.

Together, the two boys hefted the large cardboard box and set it aside, revealing a pedal toy modeled after the cargo van the A-Team drove. Adam let out a holler and began jumping up and down.

"What the hell!" bellowed a voice from the back door. Dusty stood framed in the portal. He threw an empty beer can at the metal trash can by the stoop but missed.

Adam froze. His first thought was that he was in serious trouble, though he was uncertain why.

"I thought you had to work?" Lizzie said with alarm.

"The lumber we'd ordered wasn't delivered, so I took the afternoon off. What's going on here, and what is that?" Dusty pointed at the pedal toy.

"A birthday gift for your son," Lizzie said self-consciously.

"How much did that cost?"

"Don't worry, I paid for it out of my savings."

"What savings?" The edge to Dusty's voice threatened that there would be an accounting later.

"Keep your voice down," Lizzie pleaded. She tilted her head to indicate the children.

"Screw them—I want to know. How much?"

About to respond, Lizzie grimaced as a rush of pain drew her breath away. "Oh my," she groaned. Sitting down on the picnic table's bench seat, she motioned for Olivia to come closer. "Quick, go next door. Get Maggie Sullivan. Tell her it's time, and I need her—right now."

Lizzie looked to her husband, who had just crossed the yard.

"Maggie and Olivia can watch the kids until their parents come to pick them up. You need to get me to the hospital. We're having a baby."

"Fantastic" was Dusty's surly reply.

"Help me into the house." Lizzie held out her arm.

Dusty looked away rather than respond to his wife's request. "You sure this ain't some false alarm like last time?"

Lizzie glanced at the wetness spreading across the front of her dress. "My water just broke. I'm pretty sure this is for real."

Adam watched his parents disappear inside the house. When he turned toward the backyard again, he saw that Henry Phillips, a fat six-year-old, was sitting in the pedal toy and preparing to steer it around the yard. "Hey!" Adam yelled. "That ain't yours. Get out."

Henry refused to budge.

Adam surged forward. Grabbing Henry's arm, he tried to yank him out of the van, to no avail. When he realized that Henry wasn't going to budge, he drew back his fist and punched the interloper squarely on the shoulder. The other children responded by ramping up the racket they were making.

Alerted by the commotion, Dusty stepped out onto the back stoop and bellowed, "What's with all this noise?" He advanced to where the children were gathered. "You're going to piss off the neighbors if you don't keep it down."

"He won't get out," Adam declared as he pointed at Henry.

Dusty laughed. "Is that right? Well then, hit him again."

Adam delivered another punch to Henry's arm.

Wary of being hit a third time, Henry apparently decided it was time to fight back. After climbing out of the van, he took a swing at Adam's head, but Adam ducked aside.

"That's the way," Dusty said, egging his son on. "Just like I showed you, hit and slide, hit and slide."

Lizzie also stepped out through the back door. She waddled across the yard to stand behind her husband. "Stop this immediately," she demanded. "Make them stop."

Dusty turned his head to glower at his wife.

Instinctively, she retreated a step.

Adam launched a straight jab that smacked Henry in the face.

"Good job," Dusty declared as he returned his attention to the fight. "Do it again."

"How can you encourage your son to act like that?" Lizzie's voice rose above the clamor the children were making.

Dusty squared his jaw. "He's going to have to learn how to fight sooner or later. Now stay out of this. It ain't your concern."

With surprising agility considering her condition, Lizzie moved to grab both boys by their upper arms. "You will stop this now. Adam, apologize."

Dusty balled his fist, but then noticed that the children were watching.

"He started it," Adam proclaimed.

"No, I didn't," Henry protested. "You hit me first."

"You wouldn't get out."

"I was just sitting in it."

"You were about to drive it."

Lizzie gave both boys a shake. "Stop this, both of you. Adam, say you're sorry. And as for you, Henry Phillips, maybe you should ask before you play with other people's toys."

Maggie Sullivan, with Olivia in tow, entered the backyard through the side gate. "We're here." The middle-aged woman hurried forward.

Lizzie let go of the boys' arms and, moving to greet her neighbor, began explaining what was happening.

Adam watched his mother cross the yard. He then looked up at his dad, who had drawn near. With an air of finality, Adam declared, "I don't want a baby sister." A troubled pout drew down the corners of his mouth.

Dusty nodded. "Yeah, I know what you mean. I don't much like the idea either, truth be told, but it is what it is. Look, I have to take your mom to the hospital. Mrs. Sullivan will look after you while we're gone. If that fat kid gives you any more trouble, you let him have it. Do you hear me?"

"Yes, sir."

"Good. We Masters have to defend our things. Ain't nobody else going to. Look, I ain't staying at the hospital. After we get your mom settled in, I'll be coming home. So I should be back soon. Don't do nothing dumb like you usually do. You hear me?"

"Yes, sir."

When Dusty stepped away to speak with his wife, Adam turned to cast a threatening scowl at Henry Phillips. Needless to say, as soon as Adam's parents had departed, the two pugilists resumed their unfinished business.

*   *   *

A wry smile formed on Casey's face. "Who won?"

"Who do you think?"

Casey seemed troubled. He rolled the sleeves of his lightweight cotton shirt halfway up his forearms. Summers in Montana could be rather warm, and he had dressed appropriately. After pausing to gather his thoughts, he said, "I've always wondered what my great-grandfather was like. I've often thought I would like to have known him. Now, I'm not so sure."

"He was a troubled soul. That's what makes understanding how he impacted my life so difficult. I wish you had known him. In a number of ways, you two are a lot alike."

"I'm not sure that's a compliment, from what you've said so far."

"Oh, it is. My father had many fine qualities, and I believe you've inherited the best of them."

"Really?" Casey steepled his fingers, as if having given the matter some serious thought. "He sounds like a tyrant and a tightwad."

"If that's your assessment, it means I've captured the essence of the man, but there's another event I should mention. It was difficult to endure at the time, and it's equally difficult to bring to mind now. Many times, I've sought to forget what happened, but I can't, not if I'm going to faithfully tell my tale. Besides, like I indicated, there should be value in working through the past—"

Casey interrupted. "Before you continue, you mentioned a boy named Theo. He helped lift the cardboard box off the pedal toy. You were referring to Uncle Theo, I presume?"

"One and the same. He's going to put in an appearance from time to time."

"Good. I like Uncle Theo."

"You are aware, I presume, that uncle is merely an honorary title, aren't you?"

"Of course. You two grew up together. I didn't know that."

"Theo is three years older than me, and he was two grades ahead in school, but we managed to spend a fair amount of time together getting into trouble, which we still do on occasion. But enough about Theo. I need to relate this next event before I lose my nerve."

"Sorry, but you said to ask questions if I had any."

"That I did." I smiled an acknowledgment.

A queasy feeling arose inside me when I reflected upon what I was about to impart.

Ignoring my distress, I said, "Moving on, it's time to tell you about the worst whipping I ever suffered…"

*   *   *

May 1987

Adam was seven years old when his father came home late one evening. Both Adam and his mother had gone to bed at their usual times, but then Adam couldn't sleep. With nothing better to do, he made his way to the kitchen. The house on Springwood Lane was quiet. A three-quarter moon poured pale yellow light in through the kitchen window.

Dinner had been a meager affair, hot dogs and beans, and Adam was feeling bored and hungry. So he decided to fetch a bowl of cereal, sugar-coated flakes. Being one of the more uncoordinated children in the neighborhood, he had spilled nearly a full bowl on the floor. He was starting to clean up his mess when his father entered the kitchen.

It readily became apparent to Adam that his father was falling down drunk, undoubtedly having stopped off at Woody's Bar after work. As Dusty passed through the doorway, he stumbled and landed on his hands and knees. Now at eye level with his son, a look of embarrassment colored his cheeks, but as he thrashed about trying to get up, an angry scowl spread across his face. The more he struggled, the madder he became. He glowered at his son as if his predicament was the boy's fault. "What are you looking at?" he snarled.

"Nothing, sir." Adam averted his gaze and began backing away.

That would have ended their encounter except for what came next. With a grunt, Dusty clambered to his feet and headed for the refrigerator to grab another beer, no doubt to soothe his bruised ego. When his foot began making crunching sounds against the linoleum, his anger flared into rage. The veins on his forehead signaled a red-flag warning.

"You idiot!" Dusty screamed. He glared at Adam with bloodshot eyes. "Can't you ever clean up after yourself?" His speech was thick and hard to understand. "Or are you too stupid to know you've made a mess? Why don't we build you a fucking pigsty out back? You could live in it. It would suit you fine." The tirade that followed was laced with additional expletives.

With each harangue, Dusty's fury fed upon itself until he was nearly frothing at the mouth. Then he growled softly as he moved toward Adam with loathing in his eyes. "You need to be taught a lesson."

Adam's first impulse was to bolt and run. Yet from experience, he knew that were he to flee, his plight would get horribly worse. He stood his ground.

When he had advanced to within striking distance, Dusty balled his fist and cocked his arm, but then seemed to change his mind. He stripped off his belt instead.

Adam felt a nearly irresistible urge to flee. Perhaps he might have escaped. Who could know? For whatever reason, however, he remained rooted in place.

With the belt gripped tightly in his fist, Dusty reached back and then lashed forward. He had aimed for Adam's buttocks but missed and struck the middle of his son's back instead. Adam nearly cried out. The blow stung horrifically. It would leave a welt that would take a week to fade, as would the second, the third, and the fourth. After five, Adam lost count. Each additional blow magnified the pain. Silent tears streamed down Adam's cheeks. Still, he remained unmoving. With his jaw clenched, he uttered not a sound.

After what seemed an eternity, Dusty appeared to grow weary, or perhaps, swaddled in his alcoholic haze, he simply forgot why Adam deserved such a beating. Either way, without comment, he walked away, dragging the belt behind him.

As Dusty was about to exit the kitchen, Lizzie blocked the doorway. She stared at her son's tearstained face. When she noticed the belt and it became clear what had transpired, she declared, "I'm going to call the police."

"No, you're not." Dusty's reply was delivered with surprising composure.

"Oh yes, I am."

Lizzie turned toward the telephone hanging on the wall, but her husband reached out to grab her by the hair. He spun her around until she faced him. He then hit her in the mouth, splitting her lip. She fell to the floor on her backside, too stunned to get up.

Looking down with his hands on his hips, Dusty said, "You'll leave it be if you know what's good for you." With that, he stumbled off to bed.

On hands and knees, Lizzie crawled to her son. Together, they hugged each other as if willing their pain to go away. Adam was near to passing out. He spent the next three days in bed, and it was two weeks before he could return to school. They never told a soul about what happened.

*   *   *

"Until now, that is," I whispered. I tilted my head back and covered my face with my hands. I had watched a look of revulsion settle in behind Casey's eyes. His loathing was precisely what I had anticipated seeing.

Casey sat for a long time, staring at nothing. At length, he said with disgust, "My great-grandfather was a child abuser. Did he do anything to Rachel?"

"He did."

"I meant, did he…?"

"I know what you meant. The answer is yes. He did."

A flush of anger spread across Casey's face. "Why didn't Lizzie follow through and call the authorities?"

"Many reasons, I suspect."

Casey shook his head slowly. "That's a horrible story."

"Agreed, but it was even more horrible at the time." I winced at the memory of the pain. "I was laid up for two weeks. It took even longer to be able to sit down without flinching. Yet as terrible as that beating was, I learned several lessons: First, if a small voice inside your head tells you to run, you might want to do as it says. Second, when it comes to pain, most people can endure far more than they think they can. And third, for the most part, people can't help themselves. We are who we are. All of us are slaves to our own demons. Deep down, he was just being himself."

"An abusive alcoholic!" Casey blurted out accusingly.

"True, but that's who he was programmed to be."

"You're not excusing him because he was drunk, are you?"

"Partially. My father would never have beat me like that if not for the booze."

"You can't be serious. He chose to drink. In my mind, that makes him responsible." Casey arched his back and flexed his shoulders. "Man, we're talking heavy-duty stuff. You know, rather than wine, maybe I will have a cola or something—whatever you've got."

I rose and stepped to the built-in wet bar. After looking in the mini fridge, I announced, "I've got club soda or ginger ale."

"Club soda, please," Casey responded.

As I refreshed my glass of wine, I said, "Those were interesting years. Computers were just becoming a thing. The first word processor was invented. People were beginning to worry about global warming. And yet, life went on much as it does today."

After handing Casey his soda, I sat down.

"One thing I've worked out is that my father was a control freak. He had a deep-rooted need to manage every detail of his life. The irony was that the tighter he squeezed, the more things slipped through his fingers. When you think about it, there's very little we can actually control. We influence things, sure, but outright control is an illusion. That was the lesson my father never learned."

"I like that, what you just said, that control is an illusion. What else have you discovered?" Casey leaned forward with interest.

"Not much. Instead, all these questions keep popping up to trouble me."

"Such as?"

"Why do some people have a proclivity for violence? Is it genetics? A learned behavior?"

"There are probably different reasons for different folks."

I jabbed an index finger in Casey's direction. "I'll tell you the question that really haunts me: Are some people violent because it satisfies an unspeakable sadistic need? Do they take pleasure in other people's suffering?"

"That's fairly freaky." Casey's eyes narrowed. "You're not worried that you might have his tendencies, are you, him being your dad and all?"

I laughed. "You'd think that at age seventy-one, I'd know if I'm a sadomasochist."

A flush rose on Casey's cheeks. "Hey, I didn't mean—"

"I know."

Still blushing, Casey said, "I can see why these memories would trouble you. Let me ask you something. Why did you choose to share your story with me? Why not my dad?"

"Charlie is a good man, but he's not a critical thinker, as I'm sure you know. Also, our relationship has never been particularly close, which will become obvious as we proceed. Besides, you're young, and so far, you're relatively untainted by the ways of the world."

"So far?"

"It happens to all of us." I checked my watch. It was dinnertime. "Say, are you hungry? When I invited you, I promised you a meal. How about a turkey sandwich with Boston baked beans, potato salad, and chips?"

"With mustard and cheese?"

"If you wish."

After agreeing on the menu, we headed into the kitchen.

2

SURVIVING MY FAMILY

When my grandson and I finished dinner, we returned to our previous seating arrangement with Casey on the couch, me in my familiar armchair. During the meal, we had talked mostly about Casey's college experiences. I had watched him closely as he spoke. As he described campus life and how he fit in, a disturbing fact had come to light: upon graduating, my grandson would be saddled with more than $43,000 in student loans. Such a large debt was a heavy burden to lay on a recent graduate's shoulders. It could take years for him to earn enough to pay off his obligation.

Touched by his predicament, I had silently resolved then and there to cover his debt. I mean, what else was I going to do with all the money I'd made?

Another concern had cropped up during our meal. When the conversation had touched upon Casey's plans for the future, he had tensed up. It had seemed clear that whatever was bothering him was unrelated to his financial worries. Although curious as to why he was so uneasy, I had elected not to press for an explanation. I figured if he wanted me to know, he would tell me. Also, it was important that he feel relaxed so he could focus on my narrative.

Now, as I observed him seated opposite me, my grandson looked to be comfortably at ease, for which I was grateful. Not only did I want him to hear what I was saying, even more, I wanted him to appreciate the message behind the words.

I cleared my throat and began. "I believe we were discussing my father's persona and why he was who he was. To this day, I consider it a loss that I never really got to know him. His tendency to hold people at bay, to keep them at arm's length, it's a trait I recognize in myself. Perhaps if I'd been older, or if I'd had more time with him, I might have overcome his standoffishness. As it was, I never got the opportunity."

*   *   *

September 1992

The three-bedroom cottage on Springwood Lane was eerily quiet. A somber mood pervaded every nook and cranny. Outside, it was a dreary day. Dark low-hanging clouds obscured the sun. At two o'clock in the afternoon, Lizzie and her children were getting ready to attend a funeral.

Lizzie was in the master bedroom adjusting the fit of her black dress and arranging her shoulder-length walnut brown hair. For the first time in years, she had elected to wear makeup—well, at least lipstick and eyeshadow. The effect was remarkable. Not only did she look younger, but less haggard as well, though perhaps her serenity came from no longer having to fear that she was about to be battered.

Adam's sister, Rachel, was in her room playing with dolls. Her meager collection often received a disproportionate share of her free time. Even for a seven-year-old, she had an active imagination and would spend hours entertaining make-believe friends. The simple black dress her mother had picked out for her lay on the bed. Rachel was still debating if she would put it on. She could be extremely recalcitrant when it suited her.

Likewise, Adam was in his room, trying on his new shirt and dress pants. Neither were black, but they were close enough—dark blue and charcoal gray. The striped necktie his mother had selected hung over the back of a chair. Adam eyed it with dismay; he couldn't remember how to form the knot. At thirteen years of age, he figured he ought to know how. After all, some of his friends were wearing neckties to church. *If they can do it*, he asked himself, *how difficult can it be?*

When the family finished dressing, they assembled in the living room, and Lizzie began preparing her children for what was to come. She explained that Dusty's body would be lying on a table in the Blackford Mortuary's viewing room. But then rather than talk about death, she left it at that. Since this would be the first time either child had seen a corpse, she didn't want to distress them any more than necessary. After explaining the rules of etiquette that would apply, she finished up by issuing the usual instructions: behave yourselves, and act like a lady and a gentleman.

"I don't want to go," Rachel declared with an edge of defiance.

Lizzie responded by focusing on the anxiety behind her daughter's declaration. "There's nothing to be afraid of, not anymore. He's gone. Nothing is going to harm you now."

A sinking feeling settled in the pit of Adam's stomach when he realized his mother wasn't referring to the fact that they would be in the same room with a dead body.

For her part, Lizzie seemed more animated than she had in months.

The kitchen clock chimed the half hour.

Lizzie straightened up. "Come, children, it's time to go."

The drive to the funeral parlor took less than ten minutes. To Adam, the building resembled a drab, unpretentious warehouse. Located on the outskirts of town, it served a poor neighborhood.

Less than half a dozen cars were parked out front. A hearse waited by the side entrance.

As the family passed through the front door, the funeral director stepped forward to greet them. He was a tall thin man with bushy eyebrows and a conciliatory tone of voice. He welcomed his clients and asked if there was anything they needed. Briefly, he explained the order of service. In closing, he said, "Now, if there is anything you require while you're laying your loved one to rest, please don't hesitate to ask. Also, I imagine you might wish to spend a few minutes with the departed before we begin the service."

"His name was Dusty," Lizzie stated flatly.

"Of course," the funeral director replied. "Dusty. A truly unique name."

When the family entered the viewing room, Adam paused just inside the door, gathering his resolve. His father lay in a nondescript brown casket. The top half was open, exposing his father's head and shoulders. The funeral home had dressed him in his only suit, a pinstripe more than ten years old.

Adam lingered, but then approached slowly. For a brief, interval he wondered if his father might be asleep rather than—he couldn't bring himself to even think the word. He looked closer. His father's face was tranquil. The ridges and wrinkles that had plagued him in life were gone. One feature stood out because it was impossible to ignore. Dusty's ashen complexion had an orange tint, much the color of a rotting pumpkin.

Adam thought of the doctor who had treated his father. The man had explained the cause of death listed on the death certificate. The document declared that Dusty had died from cirrhosis, a poisoning of the liver caused by alcohol consumed over many years. In later life, Adam would come to believe that his father had in fact died from a form of slow suicide.

After a decorous interval, the family returned to the gathering area outside the meeting room where the memorial service was to be held. Lizzie looked around. Nobody else had arrived, though a notice had been published in the local newspaper. The funeral director signaled that it was time.

Lizzie led her children into the meeting room. A place had been reserved for them in the front row. The funeral director removed a partitioning ribbon so they could sit down. When they were in place, he signaled that the service should begin. A local preacher stepped up onto the dais. After surveying the nearly empty room, he frowned at the funeral director, as if to say that he really should wait. Pointing at his watch, the funeral director indicated that he should get on with it.

Adam heard a noise behind him and turned his head to identify its source. Two men had entered the meeting room. One was Dusty's construction foreman, and the other was Mr. Robinson, a local banker. Adam hurriedly looked away before making eye contact.

The pastor braced himself against the pulpit and began speaking.

Abruptly, Adam became aware that several minutes had elapsed. The pastor was preaching about walking with God. As far as Adam could recall, that was the first time God had been mentioned in connection with his father's passing. The man was saying that God is love and that Dusty was now in heaven and would be forever, young and healthy, free from all earthly cares and worries.

It can't be that simple, Adam protested inside his head. *There has to be more to it.* The pastor's message sounded enticing, but something was missing. Adam felt deeply unsettled as he pondered the issue. A new thought rose up to bother him. *Had God ordained his father's death? More to the point, had God directed the course of his life? If so, what about me? Does He control me as well?* These and similar uncertainties would haunt Adam in the years to come.

For another ten minutes, the pastor droned on and then closed with a four-minute prayer. And that was that.

In the hallway outside the meeting room, the job foreman approached Lizzie to express his condolences. When Lizzie asked if he would be attending the graveside service, he murmured an apology and moved away. Likewise, Mr. Robinson, the banker, stepped forward to speak with the family. He too offered his condolences, but then delivered some alarming news. Apparently, Dusty had borrowed $5,000 from the bank, and Mr. Robinson was wondering when the bank might expect the loan to be repaid.

Lizzie explained that she knew nothing about any loan, but promised she would look into it. Mr. Robinson seemed displeased with her response. He began to press the issue, but Lizzie stood her ground. She reminded the man that they were at a funeral, and she was ill prepared to do business then and there. Frustrated, the banker turned away and departed, but not without first raising an index finger and declaring that he would have his money sooner or later.

It subsequently came to light that the bank loan was one of many debts Dusty had left behind.

Adam fervently hoped that his mother would choose to go home rather than visit the grave site, but such was not the case. The three members of the Masters family were bundled into a sedan that followed the hearse to the graveyard, a depressingly unkempt plot of uneven ground located just outside of town. It was where the community's indigent poor were buried.

The funeral director delivered a three-minute eulogy full of platitudes. Although brief, his sermon troubled Adam, not because of its content, but because the director kept referring to his father as Lloyd. Nobody ever called his father by his given name.

The grave had previously been dug, and so without delay, the undertaker and his team lowered Dusty's casket into the earth. Lizzie tossed in a handful of dirt, as did Adam. Rachel refused. In no time at all, the gravediggers covered the casket over. They worked swiftly, as if dinner was waiting for them at home.

And then suddenly, the ceremony was finished. Lloyd "Dusty" Masters was officially dead and buried, God rest his soul.

Another thing bothered Adam when he became aware of it. Tears had formed at the corners of his eyes and were rolling down his cheeks.

Why am I crying for a man I never liked? he wondered.

*   *   *

Casey shifted his position on the couch. "Can I ask a personal question? You don't have to answer if you'd rather not."

Reluctantly, I nodded in anticipation of what was to come. It pleased me that my grandson was taking on the role of inquisitor. That's what I had hoped for. At the same time, I would rather have avoided the subject altogether.

Just as expected, Casey asked, "How did you feel about your father's passing?"

"Honestly?"

"No, you can lie to me if you want. It's your story. How would I know the difference?"

Glancing at my grandson to see if he was serious, I noticed the wry smile that was forming. I chuckled. "You could say I was conflicted. I'm sure you can guess the reasons why. I both loved and hated the man. I suppose that's why I felt both glad and sad when he died. He was a violent child abuser, and he put our family through hell. On the other hand, he was my father."

"When he died, did you experience a sense of relief?"

"Yes," I blurted out, and then added after a moment's reflection, "I also felt true sadness."

"Were you sad for yourself, or were you sad for your father?" I noticed that Casey was eyeing me intently.

"That's a perceptive question. When did you get to be so smart?"

"I have taken a couple psychology classes."

"Well, kudos to your professors. You know, I have thought about this. Mainly I was sad because my father led such a diminished life. He was unfulfilled and generally unloved."

Casey looked at me as a barrister might interrogate a witness. "Is there anything you can say good about the man?"

I considered my reply and then said, "He supported his family for more than twenty years, and he was a decent carpenter who took pride in his work. More than that, as I've mentioned before, there were moments when he displayed what for him must have been genuine affection, primarily in the form of buying us small toys or ice cream or such. You know what's weird? Even after all these years, when I think about him, I feel guilty."

"How so?"

"It's perverse, but it's true. I have this unshakable feeling that I was responsible for the beatings, that I deserved them. It's totally irrational, I realize that, but it's how I often feel. That's one of the horrors of child abuse. The victim sees himself or herself as the one to blame for what happened."

I noticed that the hands of the antique grandfather clock beside the door were not moving. I rose and crossed the room. Using the key hanging beside the clock, I wound the mechanism and then reset the time.

Casey leaned back and closed his eyes. Keeping them shut, he said, "Did you ever get your questions about God answered?"

"Not then, but later," I said over my shoulder. "In fact, I've learned a lot about God's role in my life. But that's a topic we should put aside for now."

I returned to my armchair and sat down again.

Casey opened his eyes and inclined forward. "Come on. I'm curious. What did you discover?"

"Another day."

"If you insist." He seemed truly disappointed. "Well then, tell me this. If you could go back, would you? And if so, what would you do different?"

"No, I don't believe I'd go back. I mean, what could I have done differently? I was thirteen years old."

"Good point. One thing we haven't mentioned is Rachel. How did she respond to losing her father?"

"Rather than answer that question directly, maybe I should share another event."

*　　*　　*

December 1992

After a fitful start, winter had finally settled across Montana. Three months after Dusty's funeral, the howling wind was hurling sheets of snow and sleet against the Masters' house on Springwood Lane. Eight inches had already accumulated in the front yard, obscuring the walkway that led up from the street. The outdoor temperature hovered around seventeen degrees Fahrenheit with a wind chill that made it feel like thirty below. Huddled inside the house, the family had gathered in the kitchen, trying to stay warm. It was Christmas morning. Lizzie had just turned thirty-nine and was coping with a midlife crisis, compounded by having lost her husband.

The national news wasn't that great either. The economy was slowing down, people were getting laid off, and although the Gulf War had ended months earlier, the world's oil markets were still reeling from its effect, which explained why gas prices were high and going higher.

Except for the roaring of the wind, an uneasy quiet had taken hold. Lizzie stood by the stove. Adam and Rachel sat at the kitchen table. A heightened level of tension filled the room as they looked at one another without speaking. To Adam, it felt as if they had silently agreed not to mention Dusty or the life they had shared before his passing.

Lizzie had made hot cocoa and was pouring herself a cup, having already served her children.

In the living room, a scrawny six-foot spruce stood huddled in a corner. Strings of popcorn graced its branches. Tiny ornaments made out of cut-up soda cans glinted in the pale-yellow light cast by the standing lamp beside the couch.

Lizzie joined her son and daughter at the table. "Well, my children, Merry Christmas." She seemed on the verge of saying more, but was fearful of broaching a topic that was off-limits.

The children had arisen early that morning, excited to see what treasures Santa had delivered. Given the family's financial status, their expectations had been realistically low.

Lacking a fireplace in the house, their stockings had been settled into the corners of the couch. Upon inspecting them, they found that each stocking contained an orange, an apple, a handful of nuts still in their shells, a dozen pieces of hard candy in colorful wrappers, and a dime store trinket. Adam's trinket was a whistle. He had also been given a toothbrush and a new pocket comb. In her stocking, Rachel had discovered a good luck charm, a collection of barrettes, and a pair of new shoelaces. No presents were to be found under the tree.

While her children rummaged through their stockings, Lizzie watched, sorrow in her eyes. But then her expression shifted. A tight smile declared that she was determined to make the best of an impoverished Christmas.

"So what shall we do today?" Lizzie rose from the kitchen table. "I think it should be something special."

Rachel was first to respond. "I'm going over to Mary Jane's. Her mom promised to take us ice-skating." She spoke with finality, as if permission had already been granted. For an eight-year-old, she could be dogmatic when the occasion demanded.

"I'm staying home." Adam smiled at his mother. He had already determined that she should not be left alone on Christmas Day. At thirteen, he was already beginning to bear some of the burdens of adulthood. "We'll play rummy."

The front doorbell chimed. Rachel was startled.

"That would be William." Lizzie rose to answer the doorbell.

When Lizzie opened the front door, a blast of cold air roared through the house. William Rutherford stood on the front stoop with a stack of presents in his arms. He was Lizzie's new male companion. She considered him more friend than boyfriend. They had been dating for nearly three weeks. Thus far, their relationship was entirely platonic. Dusty had been in his grave for only three months when Lizzie had explained that she needed to get on with her life—put her husband's passing behind her.

William was a cattle rancher. His hundred-acre spread sat nestled up against the foothills twenty miles outside of town. He and Lizzie had first met when he had stopped by the diner where she had just begun waitressing. He had an easygoing manner, and she had been attracted to him from the start.

"Come in, come in," Lizzie said cheerily.

William entered. Standing on the throw rug just inside the threshold, he stomped the snow off his boots.

Without being asked, Lizzie reached for the presents. "Here, let me help with those. Let's put them over here." She carefully arranged the gifts in front of the Christmas tree.

With a shiver, William declared, "The wind is really whistling out there." He dusted snow off his stocking cap and off the shoulders of his heavy winter coat. When they were reasonably free of wetness, he hung them in the entryway closet. He then indicated the presents. "They're not much, just a few sundries. I thought it would be nice for you guys to have something to celebrate." When he grasped the implications of what he had just said, he stammered, "I mean—"

"Thank you," Lizzie interjected hastily. "Come in and get warm. I'm making cocoa. Would you like a cup?"

"Absolutely."

Twenty minutes later, after the chill had dissipated from inside the house, the family migrated to the living room to open William's gifts. Being middle-aged and somewhat portly, William resembled Santa Claus without the beard and the red suit. He picked up the first gift and handed it to Adam. "This one's for you."

When Adam accepted the long narrow box, he was surprised at how heavy it felt. Receiving gifts from a man who was a virtual stranger troubled him. Nevertheless, he laid the box crosswise on his lap. Tearing the wrapping paper away, he discovered a Winchester .22-caliber pump-action rifle, precisely the model he had dreamed about owning. Surprised by his benefactor's generosity, he blurted out, "Hot damn."

"Watch your mouth," Lizzie scolded.

"Sorry." Adam hefted the box. "Thank you, Mr. Rutherford. This is fantastic. How did you know?"

"William, please. I just sort of figured you'd like it. I thought we might go shoot together. I have a hundred-yard range out on my property. By the way, your ammunition is out in my truck, but I wanted to get your mom's permission before bringing it in. You know how it is."

Lizzie responded with a tight smile. "I think we'll leave it where it is for now."

"This is really great," Adam declared with unbridled enthusiasm.

William gathered up the second gift and handed it to Rachel. "This is for you." He stepped back to see how she would respond.

Rachel took the gift, but rather than open it, she let it lie on her lap as if wanting nothing to do with it. As time passed, her reticence became a source of uneasiness.

"Open it," Adam whispered, but his sister remained passive.

"Here, let me help you." William stepped forward to render assistance.

Rachel abruptly shrank back with a shriek. She hugged her arms close to her chest, as if attempting to draw in upon herself.

William backed up several paces and stood with his hands open in front of him. "I didn't mean to startle her," he said in his own defense.

Lizzie, standing near the Christmas tree, crossed the room to comfort her daughter. She sat down next to her on the couch. "It's okay, sweetheart. Don't be alarmed. William isn't going to—"

The color drained from her face.

"I mean—"

Fighting back a rush of embarrassment, she wrapped an arm around Rachel's shoulders.

"You needn't worry. It's all right. Come here." She drew her daughter closer.

Rachel did not protest, but instead allowed herself to be enfolded in her mother's embrace.

Adam leaned over to take the present off Rachel's lap. Gently, he said, "Why don't I open this for you.? I'm sure you want to see what it is."

Rachel hesitantly nodded her consent.

Adam tore the gift wrapping away, exposing a lovely foot-high doll attired like a royal princess. The gift looked rather pricey. Adam wondered why William, a man they hardly knew, would buy them such expensive gifts. To make a good impression? Probably.

"I hope you like it." William seemed uncertain as to what had just occurred.

Adam regarded his mother as she sat with her arm around Rachel's shoulders. Without warning, his pleasant mood was shattered by an upwelling of contempt mixed with anger. Unbidden, an ugly thought had come to mind. *You could have prevented this!* he yelled at her in silence. The candor of the accusation startled him. Even thinking such an allegation caused him pain. What hurt even worse was knowing that the sentiment was true. *You knew what was happening. You knew Dad was molesting her. Didn't you? You had to know, but you did nothing. Why didn't you protect us? Where were you when we needed you?* This was the first time he had admitted his mother's culpability for the traumas he and his sister had endured. The feelings of rancor and bitterness would stay with him for years to come.

"Well," Lizzie said, still flustered by her daughter's reaction, "why don't we all go back into the kitchen? It's warmer there, and I've made a special treat."

When William and the children were seated at the kitchen table, Lizzie served a plate of assorted cookies: chocolate chip, peanut butter, macaroons, and crispy morsels sprinkled with powdered sugar. "Merry Christmas, one and all. I hope you like them." She set the plate down on the kitchen table and then smiled brightly, as if nothing distressing had happened.

"Merry Christmas," Adam whispered under his breath as his thoughts were being torn in competing directions.

"Merry Christmas," William echoed.

Rachel said nothing. Instead, she stared into her cup of hot cocoa. The royal princess doll was still in its box on the couch.

*   *   *

Casey seemed genuinely distressed. "How did you survive such a dysfunctional family?"

"It wasn't easy," I replied. "In many ways, it was worse than you can imagine. Frankly, I wouldn't wish such a childhood on anybody. Well, maybe this one guy I know, but we'll get to him later."

Casey stood up and began pacing the floor. He had the look of a man wrestling with an unacceptable reality. I let him pace without intruding on his ruminations. After several circuits, he halted midway across the room and turned to look at me. "You're right, I can't imagine how bad it must have been, especially when you suddenly recognized your mother's accountability for having turned a blind eye. Had that insight not occurred to you before?"

"Not really. You see, one of the truly ugly facets of child abuse is that children are too inexperienced to think critically. They internalize whatever accusations are thrown in their direction. For them, everything is their fault. They don't consider the accountability other people must bear."

"Did you ever forgive your mother?"

I had foreseen that my grandson might ask such a question. Even so, it caught me off guard. Old memories came roaring back. In their wake, they left a jumble of unpleasant emotions. "Yes, I did," I declared flatly, "but not while she was still alive. It took years and a great deal of introspective analysis."

"It had to have been a struggle. How did you finally manage it?"

"Bottom line, I had help."

"What kind of help?"

"First you need to know more about my formative years. There was a situation that developed when I was a senior in high school. I had just turned seventeen and was still coping with the dross of my childhood."

"Before we get into that, I have one more question."

"Shoot."

Casey's eyes narrowed. "Whatever happened to William Rutherford?"

"Mother dated him for another couple months, but then grew weary of having him around. After my father's passing, she had several such relationships. None of them ever went anywhere."

"And Rachel? What about her?"

"That's two questions. Let's say she had a hard time adjusting. She was pretty messed up, more than we knew at the time. I sincerely regret that we didn't get her the professional help she needed when it might have done some good. It's not a happy story, as you'll see."

"Go on then. What other traumas came your way?"

"There were a few, some worse than others, and a couple near misses. One close call happened in the spring of my senior year, three months before graduation. Clearwater High School was hosting a regional track meet. I had just finished running 1,500 meters and had come in third…"

*   *   *

May 1997

The sports complex where Clearwater High School held its track and field events was crowded with athletes. The bleachers were full of spectators. Three visiting teams had journeyed to Clearwater to participate in the regional track meet. Noise and commotion reigned wherever Adam looked. Yet there was a method to the apparent chaos.

Adam, now seventeen years old, had just finished running the 1,500 m race, the last race of the day. Having run nearly a mile, he was still trying to catch his breath. His heart was pounding in his chest. He had crossed the finish line with a time of five minutes twenty-eight seconds, but had come in third, which was a huge disappointment. He had expected to win.

Adam stepped off the cinder track and headed across the infield to where he had left his gym bag. Opening the bag, he removed the towel he habitually carried and used it to dry his face, neck, and arms.

Although evening time was approaching, it was still a warm day, and he was sticky with sweat.

For Adam, running track was a novel experience. Now seventeen years old and in his senior year of high school, on a whim, he had elected to try out for the team. To his amazement, he had discovered that he had a fair amount of skill as a long-distance runner. His coach had pushed him hard, and his times had been getting progressively faster.

Hefting his bag, Adam headed across the grass toward the gym where he intended to shower and change clothes before heading home. However, he had not gone far when he noticed a fellow senior about to pass in front of him. Being near his own age and having long blonde hair and long legs, Jenny Vaughn was widely considered one of the prettier members of the cheering squad. Adam had been hoping to speak with her but, thus far, had been unable to catch her alone.

Rushing forward, he positioned himself to block her path.

Jenny halted, but then tried to go around him. She had on a short pleated skirt and a lightweight sweater that bore the Clearwater logo. Even though it had been a long hot day, both garments looked to be fresh and clean. She carried a pom-pom in each hand.

Adam confronted her. "Why?" he said. "That's what I want to know."

Jenny ignored the question and again attempted to pass by.

Adam responded in kind and again blocked the way. "I need to know, so tell me."

With a sigh of exasperation, Jenny punched her fists to her hips. The pom-poms shimmered in the late afternoon sunlight. "Why do you think?"

"I haven't a clue. Why would you do such a thing?"

Jenny's face melded into a mask of hostility. "Nobody disses me. Nobody."

"Is that what this is about? You lied about me attacking you because you were pissed off? You want to ruin my reputation because I wouldn't have sex with you?"

Jenny looked around to see if anybody was listening and then said, "Like, yeah. You're one of the untouchables. You're smart, athletic, and not bad looking. Also, you're a virgin. I made a bet with the girls in my squad that I would snag you. When you said no, you humiliated me. Nobody does that."

Jenny's words stunned Adam. All he could think to say was "What you did is wrong. You need to tell the truth."

"And admit that I lied? No way. That ain't gonna happen." With a burst of speed, Jenny ducked around Adam and continued on her way, shoulders back, head high. Her hips swayed as she walked.

Adam could not believe what he had just been told. To be falsely accused, with no way to rebut the lie, he felt helpless. Feelings of impotence gave way to an overpowering sense of gloom. He was about to head for the gym again when he noticed his faculty advisor standing near the shotput ring. He began walking in that direction.

"Coach Green!" Adam called out when he was still five yards away. "Do you have a minute?"

Richard Greene was also Clearwater's math teacher. He turned around at the sound of Adam's voice. When he realized who had spoken, his mood became more somber.

Adam said as he drew near, "Have you heard about what's going on?"

"You mean pertaining to the charges leveled against you?"

"That's right. They're false. I was at home."

"Can you prove that?"

"No. I was alone."

"That's a pity. Look, I'm on the Sexual Misconduct Committee, so I can't discuss this with you. You'll have to wait till the committee convenes to present your evidence, such as it may be. By the way, third? I thought you were faster than that."

"I couldn't keep my mind on the race. What happens if the committee says I'm guilty?"

"No doubt you'll be expelled and not allowed to graduate."

"That means I'll lose my scholarship."

"More than that, you'll be denied admission to college. No institution is going to enroll a student with that kind of black mark on their record."

"But I'm innocent."

"Like I said, I can't discuss it. It'll be a shame though. You have a real aptitude for working with computers. You could've gone far."

Adam stared at his faculty advisor with disbelief. "Your mind is already made up."

When Adam imagined his future, he saw his hopes and dreams evaporating like mist in the wind.

As Coach Green turned away, three of Adam's friends—Theo, Bud, and Humphrey—came running up. The four boys had known each other since grade school and collectively had begun calling themselves the Four Horsemen, as in the four horsemen of the apocalypse.

"Dude, we've been looking for you," Theo said, still breathing hard. He was small for his age, but quick in his movements and endowed with excellent reflexes.

Bud, whose real name was Robert Martin Taylor, said, "We have good news."

"Let me tell it," Humphrey pleaded. Christened Michael Llewellyn Bogart, he had been awarded the nickname Humphrey when *Casablanca* had been rereleased. He was a lanky teenager of medium height and a thin build. The other children used to tease him by claiming that a high wind would blow him away.

"Go ahead," Theo said with a scowl, but he smiled when he turned to Adam. "You're going to love this."

"We've solved your dilemma," Humphrey declared. "You're off the hook."

A sense of foreboding arose within Adam. "What have you guys done?"

Humphrey continued, "You must've heard about the prank that happened last week the same day you were supposed to have been with Jenny?"

"Who hasn't heard about it?" Adam chortled despite himself. "They're still finding sex toys in some of the classrooms. The dildo those pranksters left on Mr. Lassiter's desk was humongous. [Mr. Lassiter was Clearwater's principal.] I heard that when he switched it on, it vibrated so violently, the sound waves knocked paint off the walls."

Humphrey beamed a broad smile at Adam. "We told them we did it and that you were with us. We also said that we were carrying out our nefarious deed at the very time Jenny claimed you were with her."

"You told them? Who's them?"

"The committee. The people doing the investigating."

"And they believed you? What if the real culprits come forward? You guys will be in as much trouble as I am."

Again, Humphrey grinned broadly."The real culprits have come forward. It was us. We pulled off that prank. The three of us. It was Bud's idea."

"Where did you get the…eh, items you left lying around?"

Bud spoke up. "Do you remember the adult emporium that went out of business about six months ago? When it went under, a lot of unsold merchandise was left behind, all of which was stored in an old warehouse south of town. Nobody spoke up to claim the goods, apparently because nobody wanted to be associated with that kind of paraphernalia. Anyway, we borrowed a few things."

Adam felt slightly offended. "You did this without including me?"

Theo shrugged. "You would have said no and tried to talk us out of it. By the way, where were you that evening?"

"Like I keep telling people, I was at home."

"Did anybody see you there? Your mother, Rachel?"

"No. They went to see a movie."

"Excellent. That means nobody can disprove what we told the committee." Theo glanced at the now nearly vacant field, most of the meet's attendees having already departed. "Are you done here?"

"I am."

Theo slapped Adam on the back. "Good. Let's go celebrate."

The Four Horsemen headed off to see what mischief they might create.

*   *   *

Casey seemed upset. "I'll bet you were relieved. Whether they are true or not, allegations like that can haunt a man for the rest of his life. People can be so judgmental—eager to believe whatever bad things they hear. That's how reputations get ruined. You can shout that you're innocent, but who's going to listen? It's not right. So you were cleared of all charges?"

"The charge of sexual assault was dismissed, but the four of us were each given a month's detention for the prank. However, when word got out that we were the perpetrators, I think it actually bolstered our reputation. For a time afterwards, I kind of wished that I had participated in the stunt."

"That cheerleader, what was her name?" Casey swept a lock of hair away from his eyes. The gesture again made me hope that he would cut it. A shaggy mane was not a good look for a prospective lawyer.

"Jenny Vaughn."

"I gather she was hot?"

"Very much so."

"When she came on to you, why didn't you…you know? Sounds like she was willing."

I sat quietly for a time, considering my reply. Casey waited while I collected my thoughts. At length, I said, "Perhaps the most compelling reason was I was afraid she would get to know the real me. I couldn't allow that. It would have been too demeaning."

Casey frowned. "I don't understand—"

"Neither did I at the time. It took years to piece together how my upbringing shaped my self-image. Inwardly, I felt inferior, a failure, worthless. No matter how hard I tried, no matter how much effort I put forth, in my own mind, I never measured up. Wherever I went, I carried this nebulous burden of guilt. I couldn't let people get to know the real me."

"I still don't see—"

"Perhaps the dynamic will become clearer as we move forward. That's what I'm hoping." We had stumbled on one of the reasons I had chosen to share my life story with my grandson.

Casey sat back on the leather couch, signaling that he was willing to wait. "This Jenny person, what happened to her? Was she ever held accountable?"

"Not directly. An ugly rumor was started that she had contracted gonorrhea. She moved away not long after. I haven't seen or heard from her since. I did, however, take my revenge on the Sexual Misconduct Committee in a different sort of way."

"Really?" It became apparent that I had attracted Casey's full attention.

*　　*　　*

June 1997

The nation had just fought the first Gulf War. The Soviet Union was in the process of disintegrating. Los Angeles was being ravaged by the Rodney King riots. And a renewed commitment to the sanctity of free, unfettered speech was sweeping the nation.

Clearwater High School, in particular, was profoundly influenced by this latest cultural trend. To show their support for the free speech movement, the school's administrators had proposed an enhancement to the graduation ceremony. Their recommendation was that one student, selected by lottery, should be allowed to deliver a speech, not more than five minutes in length, that could deal with any topic whatsoever. The choice of subject matter would be entirely up to the student.

Both the faculty and the student body gave the suggestion their enthusiastic backing. Faced with a tidal wave of support, the school board had ultimately consented, and to encourage participation, they had declared that there would be no repercussions for anything that was said, unless of course the orator advocated violence or outright sedition. Another rule adopted by the board was that the speaker would not be required to seek prior approval for his or her subject matter. The intent was that the presentation should be as unregulated is possible. They would later come to regret their decision.

On a whim, Adam registered for the drawing and was astonished when his name was pulled from the hat.

*   *   *

When graduation day rolled around, Adam was ready. He had memorized his speech and repeatedly rehearsed, presenting it until his delivery was crisp and precise. Waiting backstage for his turn to go on, he peeked out from behind the curtain. The auditorium was full. More than three hundred friends and family members had come to watch their son or daughter graduate.

As Adam stood waiting, his mind was mainly on his speech, but his thoughts were also on the graduation gift his mother had given him, a desktop computer running Windows NT 4.0. How she could afford such a prize, he had no idea. Briefly, he had thought about returning the gift and getting her money back, but he had promptly decided against parting with such an essential tool. He had already determined that his future would somehow be linked to computers. That he knew for sure. After all, a guy named Bezos had just founded Amazon, an online shopping service. *If he can do it, so can I,* Adam told himself.

A sudden urge to urinate overtook Adam. He needed to go, but he felt he should wait. Besides, it was a brief speech and would be over soon.

After consulting the clipboard she carried, the stage manager whispered to Adam, "Five minutes."

Great, Adam thought, *just enough time. I can make it if I hurry.* "I'll be back," he said to the stage manager as he bounded toward the restroom. She tried to stop him, but he was already gone.

When Adam finished his business and started to zip up his pants, the zipper got stuck. Tugging on the stringers failed to loosen the snagged teeth, and the slider would not budge. He tugged harder until, without warning, the zipper came apart. Try as he might, he could not fit the separated parts back together. To make matters worse, that morning he had forgone wearing underwear since every pair of boxers he owned was in the wash.

Adam was in a pickle. He couldn't go on stage with his fly gaping open and nothing showing but his privates.

Then an idea came to him. He had prepared a single sheet of notes, just in case he forgot his material. He had folded the paper and tucked it away for safe keeping. After digging the page out of his shirt pocket, he unfolded it and held it in front of his broken zipper. By checking himself in the mirror, he discovered that if positioned just right, the page would protect his modesty.

Feeling his tension release slightly, Adam returned to where the stage manager was anxiously waiting. He was just in time. As he stepped up, she signaled that it was his turn.

Holding the sheet of paper discreetly in front of him, Adam strode onto the stage. To his immense relief, he realized that there was a podium he could hide behind. He had failed to take note of it before. Positioning himself for minimal exposure, he gazed out upon his audience. After pausing for effect, he launched into his oratory, deliberately emphasizing certain words and phrases.

"Board members, teachers, fellow students. Today is a momentous occasion. I am honored to appear before you as a proud graduate of Clearwater High School. There can be nothing finer than to stand erect in the presence of so many notable personages.

"Before I begin, there are several special people here today, people with whom I've recently had the opportunity to engage in social intercourse. I'd like to acknowledge the members of the Sexual Misconduct Committee. They have a tough but important job. Serving on the committee is a major responsibility, and I'm sure that putting out the effort has been hard on them.

"Coach Green, I'm glad you're here. For those who don't know him, he coaches basketball and track. Usually, he's in the gym, shooting his balls at the hoop. Coach, you do good work, you know. You're always there for the team. Personally, I think you have the right policy, keeping each and every jerk off the team and not letting every Harry, Dick, and Tom play. It's uplifting to realize that the school has such a huge athletic supporter on its faculty.

"And Ms. Fisher, our English teacher, did you know you are much admired by your students? You teach. You don't just pay lip service to the curriculum. More than that, you hold yourself open to receive new ideas.

"And then there's Mr. Banks, our band director. I gotta tell you, folks, his band rocks—really gets you moving. When they play, the entire student body can feel the vibrations in their bones. You guys should feel especially proud of your music. I mean, y'all got spunk.

"Lastly, there's Mr. Lassiter, our principal. I was worried that he might not come this evening. Usually, he's either whacking balls at the driving range or at home polishing his flute. He's a talented player, you know. He can really blow it. It's true that from time to time he's been a bit prickly, but it's not his fault that he sucks as an administrator. After all, he's a nice guy and certainly not a weenie. Did you know he almost single-handedly raised the money to build our memorial, that glorious erection out in front of our school?

"Anyway, here's to the Sexual Misconduct Committee, truly a group of dedicated professionals. I'm sure the school board will, whenever you need help, make giving you a hand job one.

"As for the rest of you guys out there, remember this: stay healthy, work hard, and have a wonderful life."

With that, Adam bowed and stepped away from the podium.

As Adam walked off the stage, he forgot to carry his notes in a decorous manner. All along the front row, he heard gasps of embarrassment.

It took almost two whole minutes for his speech to sink in, but when it did, the student body erupted in peals of laughter.

He had his revenge.

*　　*　　*

I looked at Casey, who seemed to be stifling the impulse to laugh out loud. "You actually gave that speech?" he said with a snicker.

"I did."

"What did they do to you?"

"Not a thing. The rules they'd adopted prevented any retaliation. I graduated just as if nothing had happened, but the following year, they dropped that segment from the program."

"I would imagine so."

I glanced at my watch and yawned. "It's getting late. Time for this old man to go to bed."

"You're not going to tell me more?"

"Not tonight. Let's save the rest for a later day, that is, if you wish to continue? You're under no obligation, you know. You can call a halt at any time."

"I wouldn't think of it. I had no idea your childhood was so…" He seemed at a loss to find the right word.

"Conflicted?" I suggested.

"I was thinking harsh or perhaps troubled."

"It has been interesting."

Casey rose to his feet. "I'm beginning to understand what you mean by that."

I escorted my grandson to the front door. En route, we agreed that he would return in two days, which suited me fine. In recounting my tale, I had been reminded of a bit of unfinished business I needed to attend to. It was a matter I should've handled years ago.

45

3

A DEBT TO BE REPAID

The morning after my first meeting with Casey, I awoke early. Rather than roll out of bed right away, I lay still for a time, reviewing our conversation. I felt pleased with the way things had gone. As far as I could tell, my grandson was genuinely interested in hearing my story.

However, a long-forgotten memory had surfaced during the telling, and I could not dismiss it from my mind. While describing my father's funeral, I had recalled the commitment my mother had made to Mr. Robinson, president of the Missoula Savings and Loan. She had promised to repay my father's debt, but to the best of my knowledge, she never had. The fact that the debt was still outstanding troubled me considerably. After all, a promise is a promise.

When I did climb out of bed, my joints were stiff, and the pain in my lower back reminded me that I was no longer young, as if I could forget.

I rose to my feet, put on my robe and slippers, and trundled downstairs to make myself a cup of coffee. The more I thought about the defaulted loan, the more certain I became that like it or not, it was my responsibility to set the matter right. Leaving the debt unrepaid would forever stand as a blot against my family's reputation, at least in my own mind.

Motivated by a newly formed sense of purpose, I hurried through my morning routine.

*   *   *

The drive across town was stop and go. The Missoula Savings and Loan was located just west of the town's primary mall. Monday morning shoppers eager to secure the day's best bargains were already filling the mall's parking lots as I drove past. When I finally reached the Savings and Loan, its doors were just being opened.

Not bad timing, I thought, *even if I do say so myself.*

I stepped inside and looked around. This was my first visit. From the bronze statue on a side table to the oil paintings on the wall, each element of the Savings and Loan's modern decor spoke of understated affluence.

My intent was to speak with the man in charge, meaning I would have to make it past his secretary first.

I approached the most strategically placed desk. The lady seated at the desk appeared to be in her late middle years. Donning an affable smile, I said, "I'm here to speak with Mr. Robinson, president of this fine institution. Is he available?"

The woman stared at me as if I was a ham sandwich short of a picnic. "Mr. Robinson died more than forty years ago."

I gave a dismissive wave of my hand. "Of course he did. I was just testing your familiarity with this institution's history. Actually, I was wondering if I might speak with your current manager?"

The woman eyed me suspiciously. "That would be Mr. Fields."

"Do you think he's available?"

"Let me check." The woman's demeanor told me that the odds were strongly against my being granted an audience. She dialed a number and then engaged in a muted conversation. After hanging up, she stated, "I'm afraid Mr. Fields is busy. Perhaps if you'd care to make an appointment?"

"Tell him, please, that I wish to repay the money I owe—in full."

A subtle change of bearing overtook the woman. After another brief conversation, she actually smiled. "If you'd care to wait, Mr. Fields should be available shortly." She indicated a row of uncomfortable-looking chairs against a side wall.

"Thank you." I crossed the room and sat down.

An hour later, a middle-aged man emerged from the corner office. He wore a three-piece suit. His striped tie stood out against his charcoal gray vest.

I rose to my feet as he drew near.

"I'm Mr. Fields."

We shook hands. His grip was firm, befitting a man in charge.

I introduced myself and returned the handshake with equal vigor.

"Please." He gestured toward his office, which was also lavishly appointed. He sat down behind his oak desk.

I took the facing armchair.

Without preamble, he said, "What can I do for you?"

Right to the point, I thought. *Time is money.* "I'm here to repay a loan."

"Any of our clerks would be happy to help with that."

"I'd be surprised if they could. You see, this isn't an ordinary debt. The loan is rather old. My father borrowed the money in 1990."

Mr. Fields snorted. "That was sixty years ago. And you're just now proposing to clear your obligation?"

"I am. You see, my father died not long after borrowing the money. My family first learned about what he had done after his passing. I must tell you, it came as quite a shock. You see, he left so many debts, and—well, money was in short supply. The matter kind of got shoved aside and forgotten. Only recently was I reminded that his debt is still outstanding. Now I'm here to set things right." I nodded smartly to emphasize the point.

"How much money are we talking about?"

"$5,000."

"You're here to pay back a $5,000 debt that's sixty years old? Incredible."

"It was a lot of money at the time."

"I'm sure it was." Mr. Fields steepled his fingers. "By any chance, Mr. eh…?"

"Masters. Adam Masters."

"Mr. Masters. Right. By any chance are you a Missoula native?"

"I am. I've lived here all my life."

"The reason I ask is you might recall that a fire destroyed the old Savings and Loan some thirty years ago."

"The incident does sound familiar, now that you mention it."

"I'm afraid any records pertaining to your father's loan were lost in the fire. There is no way we can validate what you're saying."

I bristled. "You don't need to validate. I'm telling the truth."

"I meant no offense. The rub is that without documentation, we can't credit your repayment to the proper account."

"How about putting the money into a general fund or something of the sort?"

"Under what designation? No, I'm afraid that's not possible."

"Label it 'Restitution of an Undocumented Default'?"

"That wouldn't work either. Sorry." Mr. Fields picked up a pencil and began tapping its eraser on the desk's surface. "Why is it so important that you repay the loan after all these years? I would've thought—No, let me rephrase that. Most people would consider the matter a stroke of good fortune. They'd be overjoyed not to have to repay the loan."

"I'm not most people. The money is owed, and I intend to pay it back."

Mr. Fields stood up. "I'm afraid I can't help you. Why don't you donate the money to charity? That might ease your conscience."

It was apparent that the man wanted me to leave. I stood as well and said, "It looks like there's nothing to be done. I appreciate your taking the time to speak with me."

We shook hands again.

Mr. Fields tilted his head and regarded me with a quizzical expression. "You're not going to let the matter drop. Are you?"

"Nope." I turned and left the president's office.

Not by a long shot, I told myself as I exited the Missoula Savings and Loan.

*   *   *

Theo Lane was my best friend. The one thing I admired most about him was his razor-sharp intellect. He had an uncanny ability to cut through distractions and get to the heart of a problem. If anyone could help me with my conundrum, it would be Theo.

Theo lived in a four-bedroom, two-bath home that was nearly as spacious as my current residence, not that we were competing. Still, I often felt a tiny twinge of pride whenever I paid him a visit. His father had worked as a high-level executive for a major trucking company. His mother had made her fortune as a successful real estate agent.

Fresh out of high school, Theo had gone to work for Tranco, an auto parts company. As the Internet had flourished, so had his company's profitability. Blessed with a winning personality, Theo had steadily climbed the corporate ladder until, ultimately, he had been named northwestern regional manager. Always an optimist, he had invested wisely rather than squander his money on expensive hobbies. By his mid-forties, he had doubled the fortune he had inherited from his parents.

My lifelong buddy was still in his pajamas when he answered the front doorbell. He looked haggard, but then I had just awakened him from sleep. I knew he was in pretty good shape—for a septuagenarian.

"Mickey Mouse?" I pointed to the caricature on his pajamas.

Theo shrugged and invited me in.

As usual, we wound up in the kitchen where I offered to help fix breakfast.

"Let me understand this," Theo said as he scrambled the eggs. "You intend to repay a debt that no longer exists?"

"That's the scope of it."

"And you want to do this why?"

"'Cause it's the right thing to do. I looked it up. Matthew 5:23 basically says that if you remember that your brother or sister has something against you, you should leave your offering at the altar and go and be reconciled to them. I think that passage sort of applies."

"Perhaps, except for a couple minor points. For one, you're not offering a gift at the altar. Two, you're dealing with a savings and loan, not your brother or sister. And three, nobody has anything against you, which is kind of the point."

"Still, the principle would seem to apply. We're told to settle our debts before doing anything else. At least that's my take on the Scriptures."

"All right, let's say I get where you're coming from. How can I help?" Theo divided the eggs into two portions, which he transferred onto our plates. After adding a couple strips of bacon and an English muffin fresh from the toaster, he placed the plates on the table along with two glasses of orange juice.

I set out a jar of orange marmalade. "You are well-connected. In your years as a venture capitalist, you got to know a great many people."

"I was hardly a venture capitalist. All I did was invest what my parents left me."

"Be that as it may, I'd bet good money that you know someone at the Missoula Savings and Loan."

Theo handed me a napkin and a fork and then joined me at the table. "As a matter of fact, I do. At least I think she's still there. Last time we spoke, she was a senior teller. What is it you're asking?"

"I need her to find me a loan that has been in default for years. It must have an unpaid balance greater than $5,000, and it must be flagged as uncollectible."

"That's fairly specific. Let's say she finds such a loan. What would you do with that information?"

"Why, I'd make an anonymous payment, of course."

"A payment of $5,000?"

"Precisely."

"And this would soothe your ruffled conscience?"

"It would. The important thing is, if your friend is willing to do this, she has to keep the matter secret. If Mr. Fields were to find out, he'd quash the deal."

"The person who actually borrowed the money, what are you going to tell him, assuming it's a male?"

"Nothing."

"Do you think that's wise? When the guy hears about the repayment, don't you think he'll start asking questions? If he speaks with Mr. Fields, who doesn't strike me as being especially dull-witted, he'll see the coincidence. First you stop by, asking about an ancient $5,000 loan, and then $5,000 gets paid into an uncollectible account. He'll figure out where the money came from, and he still could quash the deal."

"Good point. Perhaps I'll send the borrower a note suggesting that they keep their mouths shut and simply accept the gift."

Sarcastically, Theo said, "Now that isn't going to raise any eyebrows, is it?" He tilted his head back and stared at the ceiling. "You know, this might work if the borrower was dead."

"You're not suggesting…?"

"Of course not. We're not going to start bumping people off. What I meant was, your plan would work better if the borrower had died from natural causes, and that's why the loan was in default."

I grinned. I knew there was a reason I had needed to speak with Theo.

My best friend brought his head down again. "Very well, let me see what I can do. I'll get back to you by this afternoon."

I knew it was an iffy proposal. For the plan to work, several things had to fall into place: Theo's contact at the Savings and Loan had to still be alive and in a position of trust. There had to be an outstanding loan that fit our parameters. And we had to find a way to make the payment without anybody noticing.

We ate our breakfasts at a leisurely pace, all the while reminiscing about the good old days, which, in retrospect, weren't all that good. When I took my leave, I prayed that Theo would succeed in his mission. It seemed an elegant solution. The bank would get its money. My father's debt would be repaid. And some lucky corpse would receive an unexpected gift. As far as I could tell, it was win, win, win.

I felt more than a little pleased as I drove home.

*   *   *

Early that afternoon, Theo called to say that we had hit the jackpot. His friend had turned up an unpaid debenture in the amount of $27,562. The debt had been deemed uncollectible for more than nine years. Apparently, the borrower had died in a rafting accident without leaving any heirs. The Savings and Loan had maintained the note on the books, hoping that a beneficiary would eventually step forward to claim the estate, against which it had already filed a lien.

It was a perfect fit. The loan met all our criteria.

An hour before closing time, and anonymous person made a cash deposit as partial payment against the defunct loan. Dressed in a nondescript overcoat, sunglasses, and a floppy hat that covered his forehead down to his eyebrows, the customer could not be identified. Despite the payment, the loan remained in default and was eventually returned to the uncollectible bin.

That evening, I called Theo to thank him. "I owe you one," I said.

"Are we still keeping score? I thought we had dispensed with that long ago."

"Yes, we did. Anyway, thank you."

"You're more than welcome, compadre. Sleep tight."

He didn't know that I would stay awake most of the night rehearsing what I would say to Casey, who was expected to come over the next evening.

4

WANT VS. NEED

Tuesday afternoon, my doorbell rang. I checked my watch: 4:30 p.m. *Good lad*, I thought. *Right on time, as usual.*

Until that moment, I'd worried that Casey might cancel our meeting. In a youth-oriented culture, old folks like me tend to become superfluous and easily ignored—more of a burden than a resource. Needless to say, I was relieved when I opened the front door and found my grandson standing on the stoop.

"Good. You made it." I ushered him in.

"Did you think I wouldn't?"

"Not for a moment. What's this?" I gestured toward the gift box Casey carried in the crook of his arm. It seemed about the proper size for a bottle of wine.

"I figured it was my turn to provide the refreshments. I hope you don't mind. The guy in the liquor store swore this was a good vintage."

"I'm sure it will be splendid. Come with me, and we'll try it out."

We opened the bottle in the kitchen and poured two glasses. Taking the bottle with us, we moved to the library where we resumed our previous seating arrangements: Casey on the leather couch, me in my favorite armchair.

I took another sip of wine. "This is good." I set my glass down on the low coffee table. "I'm not a connoisseur, but I know a robust pinot noir when I taste one."

"I hoped you would like it."

"It has a mellow bouquet. Say, I heard something on the local news this afternoon, and I thought of you. The commentator was discussing the spate of recent burglaries. Apparently, the police now believe they are somehow tied to the university."

"Seriously?"

"I guess they're basing their theory on the fact that nearly all of the victims were faculty members. They think it's more than a coincidence. Have you heard anything on campus?"

"No, I haven't," Casey replied tersely, as if adverse to pursuing the subject.

I flexed a kink out of my back and said, "Well, no matter. So have you had a chance to think about what we discussed last time? What's your opinion of what I told you?"

Casey's brow furrowed. "What do you mean?"

Rather than back off, I pressed my grandson for his opinion. "Tell me truthfully. Having heard my life story, what do you think?"

Casey hesitated.

"Go on," I said. "Tell me what's on your mind."

"Since you asked, I'd say you had an appalling childhood."

"True, but that's not the point, is it? It's what comes after that matters. One of life's greatest challenges is learning to cope with the emotional traumas we suffer in our youth. The damage done can have lasting effects. As the sapling is bent, so grows the tree."

Casey blanched, indicating that he had caught my meaning.

I continued, "Mending character flaws takes a long time and a lot of hard work. Most people can't do it on their own, but rather than ask for help, they go on making the same bad choices, doing the same wrong deeds, and the hole they are digging gets deeper and deeper. All the while they keep repeating, 'It's not my fault. The devil made me do it.'"

Thinking about my past, I felt a pang of regret.

"Oftentimes, the damage done isn't even their fault."

Casey eyed me suspiciously. "Is this your way of preparing me to forgive you for choices you made, Grandfather?"

With sincerity, I admitted, "That is one of my goals."

"You have more than one?"

"The second is a bit more complex. I'm hoping to prove that, with help, it is possible for an individual to overcome even the most serious it is possible character flaws, even the ones that aren't self-made."

Casey toasted me with his wineglass. "This I would like to hear."

"Then I should get on with it, but first, there's more background I need to share, and that brings us to the saddest day of my life…"

*   *   *

October 1997

The Blackford Mortuary was deathly quiet. Adam sat in a folding chair backed up against one wall. He sat with his hands in his lap as he stared at his mother's closed casket. The injuries Lizzie had suffered in her automobile accident had been deemed too severe to allow for an open casket. As a rule, the funeral home preferred that its clients commune with their departed loved ones in the lavishly appointed viewing suite.

Adam's unpleasant memories of his father's funeral had spawned his request to be allowed to wait in a different space. The holding room, where the unaccompanied dead were stored pending their disposition, was like an oversized closet. In a way, it mirrored how Adam was feeling inside: confined, bleak, and devoid of those elements that remind us of our humanity.

The shock of his mother's passing had hit Adam hard, and he had not yet come to grips with the enormity of his loss.

Adam could hear the ebb and flow of his own breathing as he stared at his mother's plain casket and thought about nothing much at all. Somewhere in the back of his mind, he wondered why he wasn't replaying old memories, picturing his mother going about her customary routines. Perhaps because a blanket of sorrow had smothered all other thoughts. He felt there was a void inside him that swallowed any remembrances that might have brought a modicum of comfort.

Rachel sat beside her brother. As was her nature, she had said very little since arising that morning. When addressed directly, she had answered cryptically and then returned to her cocoon of silence.

Adam looked at his sister. "Are you okay?"

Rachel nodded. Ever since their father's passing, her reluctance to express how she was feeling had troubled Adam. Now he was even more concerned. No human can function normally if they bottle everything up inside. He feared that his sister might withdraw so completely into herself that she would be unable to find her way back.

A knock sounded at the door. Then it opened slightly. Deputy Garcia, a member of the Missoula County Sheriff's Department, poked his head in and looked around. After pausing a moment, he said softly, "Sorry to bother you." Deputy Garcia had been first on the scene at Lizzie's accident. "I'm just checking to see if there's anything you guys need?" The badge on his chest reflected a golden glow in the muted light.

Adam shook his head. "We're okay."

"That's good." The deputy seemed unconvinced. "If there's anything we can do—Here, let me give you my card." He eased forward with a business card in his outstretched hand.

Adam accepted the card and slid it into his breast pocket.

The deputy nodded and retreated to the door. "Call me if you need to."

As Deputy Garcia started to leave, Adam exclaimed, "Wait!" He rose and crossed the room. Under his breath, he said, "I need to know more about what happened."

The deputy glanced at Rachel and then motioned for Adam to follow. "Why don't we talk outside." They stepped into the hallway and closed the door behind them.

"What do you want to know?" the deputy said.

"Details. The officer who came to tell us, all he said was that she'd driven off the road and crashed into a tree."

"I'm sure he would have told you more, but the investigation was ongoing. He was limited in what he could say. Your mother was working the swing shift at the Roadside—a greasy spoon diner on the outskirts of town. She'd gotten off at eleven thirty at night and was headed home. An early cold snap had settled in across the county. It was a bad night. There were patches of black ice on a number of roads. She wasn't speeding. There was no alcohol in her blood. Our investigation revealed that she hit a stretch of ice heading into a curve. She was doing about fifty-five when she slid off the road and struck the tree. The coroner concluded that she had died instantly. She didn't suffer. When the paramedics arrived on scene, there was nothing they could do.

"Me and the guys in our department, we are truly sorry for your loss. I knew your mom. She was an upstanding lady. Her life wasn't easy, but she's in a better place now."

"Do you think so?"

"I know it." Deputy Garcia spoke with conviction.

A frown spread across Adam's face. "Hold on. Now I remember you. You came to our house. It was years ago. I was younger, maybe twelve at the time."

"You're right. I was answering a domestic disturbance call. Your father—"

"He's dead, you know. He died six years ago."

"I read that in the investigation report."

What Adam didn't mention was that he also remembered that the deputy had brought him home late one night after he had decided to run away. The incident had occurred a year and a half after his father's death and had been written off as teenage angst.

The deputy didn't mention the incident either. Instead, he said, "Have you decided what will happen with your sister? I assume Child Protective Services has been in touch?"

"They said that because I'm eighteen, I can petition the court to be made Rachel's guardian. She'll be staying with me in our family home. I'm going to look after her."

"Do you have any other relatives, someone who could help care for her?"

"We have an uncle, my father's brother. He lives somewhere back east, but we haven't communicated in years. I doubt he would be willing."

"Rearing a thirteen-year-old, that's a lot to lay on a young man's shoulders."

"I'll manage."

Deputy Garcia regarded Adam with a penetrating gaze, as if sizing him up. "I'm sure you'll do your best. By the way, do you guys have a ride home?"

"We came with Maggie Sullivan. She's our next-door neighbor. I assume she'll be giving us a lift."

"Okay then. I'll be getting back to work. Again, we're sorry for your loss."

"Thanks for your concern."

The deputy departed, and Adam returned to the holding room.

During his mother's memorial service, Adam listened attentively. He paid particular attention to the pastor's eulogy and tried to soak in every nuance. However, he repeatedly found himself distracted by worrying about what lay ahead. A mountain of responsibilities had been dumped at his feet. Deputy Garcia was right, raising a thirteen-year-old would be difficult, to say the least. And then there was the house to maintain, the mortgage to pay, groceries to buy, and heaven knows what other bills would be coming his way. He nearly broke down. Instead, he willed himself to remain impassive as he stifled a quiet sob.

Something the pastor was saying caught Adam's ear. He refocused his attention. The man wore a suit and tie rather than the traditional vestments generally associated with the clergy.

The pastor gestured by bringing both hands together in front of his chest and declaring, "Scripture teaches us that if we draw near to God, He will draw near to us."

How do you draw near to God? Adam wondered. *Besides, does God really exist, or is He a figment of society's imagination?* At first blush, the question seemed detached from the immediacy of his needs, but the more he thought about it, the more relevant it became. Similar uncertainties had haunted him after his father's funeral. This time, he resolved to seek an answer, though he had no idea where to begin looking.

When the sermon was over and the service ended, people pressed forward to express their sympathy and offer condolences. Adam was startled by the number of people who had taken the time to attend. Many of the mourners who shook his hand and wished him well were unknown to him. Some were thoughtful enough to share how they had come to know his mother. Others simply assumed that he was familiar with their history. The contrast with his father's funeral was blatant.

Adam became aware of a tugging on the back of his shirt. He turned around to look his sister in the eye. She announced, "I want to go home." Adam sensed that the throng of mourners surrounding them was making her feel trapped.

He leaned closer and whispered in her ear, "Rachel, we have to go to the cemetery first. Do you think you can hang in there a little longer? It's important that we give Mama a proper goodbye." If he'd had a choice, he would've taken his sister home right then and there.

Rachel shrugged, which was her way of saying she would try. Had she objected, she would have responded with an angry outburst.

"Good." Adam reached out to tousle his sister's hair, but she shifted her head out of reach.

Adam looked up to find himself face-to-face with Madeline Gardner, Olivia's mother. Olivia was the teenager who had helped supervise his fifth birthday party. He almost didn't recognize either of them. The years had not been kind to Madeline. Olivia, on the other hand, had grown into a fine-looking woman. Mrs. Gardner said, "Adam, tell me honestly, how are you two doing?"

Putting on a brave face, Adam replied, "We're coping."

Mrs. Gardner lowered her voice. "What about financially? Money, or a lack thereof, can cause major difficulties in times like these."

What business is that of yours? was what Adam wanted to say. Instead, he adopted a solemn demeanor and replied, "We're doing okay for now. Mother left a small life insurance policy, plus there's the settlement for the car. Also, come Monday, I'll be heading out to look for work."

The funeral director appeared at Adam's elbow. He leaned in and said, "Adam, I'm sorry to interrupt, but it's time to go. There's a car waiting to take you and your sister to the graveyard."

"We're ready," Adam announced, though in his heart, he knew he wasn't. "Excuse me," he said to Mrs. Gardner, "we have to go." He then turned and, together with Rachel, followed the funeral director to the side entrance.

The graveside service was mercifully brief. The October cold front that had settled in was still lingering over the region. Those mourners who hadn't dressed warmly enough were soon headed back to their cars. By the time Adam and Rachel were on their way home, they were chilled to the bone.

Adam was still shivering when he sat down at the kitchen table and began pondering what to do next. As he wrote down a list of tasks, not all his shivers were from the cold.

*   *   *

Casey reached for the wine to refill his glass. He then offered to pass me the bottle. "Friends are the legacy we leave behind," he declared

"I like that." I shook my head to decline his offer. "Did you read that somewhere?"

"I just made it up."

"Impressive."

"Thank you. You know, I was thinking, Adam was—I mean, you were…It's strange hearing you talk about yourself in the third person. It throws me off."

"I warned you it would seem funky. What about Adam? Me?"

"Well, it's just that when you think your life is about to get easier, it doesn't."

Abstractly, I agreed. "There always have been and always will be challenges to overcome. That's for certain."

"The last time I was here, didn't you mention that you were planning on going to college and even had a scholarship?"

"My mother's death kicked that dream out of reach." A wave of regret washed through me as I recalled how sad I had been. Rather than lament prior disappointments, I said stoically, "I had more urgent needs to attend to. The most pressing was finding gainful employment. Rachel's future, and mine, depended on my bringing home a regular paycheck. It took nearly two weeks of searching, but I finally landed a position at Townsend Electronics. At the time, I had no idea my getting hired would launch an entire career."

*   *   *

November, 1997

One November afternoon in 1997, after pounding the pavement all day looking for work, Adam was about to pass by the retail outlet for Townsend Electronics. On impulse, he stopped in to inquire if there were any openings. His expectations were so low that he had almost given up hope of finding work. However, in that moment, he was blessed by a stroke of good fortune. Just that morning, a computer repair technician had quit without warning. A shipping clerk with hardly any experience in working with computers had been promoted to fill the vacancy. That had left the store one shipping clerk short.

Adam had bluffed his way through the interview and had been hired on the spot. Since it was late in the day, he had been instructed to report back the following morning, ready to work. The problem was that he had lied about his age and his qualifications. He had no idea what a shipping clerk was supposed to do.

Upon returning home, Adam immediately parked himself in front of the narrow table in his bedroom where he had set up his desktop computer. With diligence, he searched the Internet, seeking information on how a shipping department was supposed to function. This was the year of Google's inception; YouTube had not yet been invented. Only a few references were available online. He did learn, however, that a clerk's duties included keeping and verifying records, determining the best shipping method, preparing items for shipment (which basically meant packaging delicate and very expensive stuff so it wouldn't break), and attaching the appropriate shipping labels.

Sticking labels on boxes seemed easy enough. It was the part about determining the best shipping method that troubled Adam. To perform that function, he would need a working knowledge of procedures, rates, and routes, none of which were familiar. That night, he stayed awake till dawn, visiting websites and tracking down online manuals. When the sun came up, he still felt unprepared, but at least he had learned to distinguish between FedEx, UPS, and USPS.

* * *

February 1998

Three months later, Adam was seated in the break room at Townsend Electronics, enjoying his brown bag lunch and shooting the breeze with Humphrey, who had just been hired as a custodian.

"Thanks for putting in a good word for me." Humphrey rummaged through the contents of his lunch pail, as if ranking each item's suitability for human consumption. He still lived at home, and Adam suspected that his mother had packed the lunch for him.

Graciously, Adam replied, "Not a problem."

Although still a probationary employee, the store manager had been impressed by Adam's diligence. When the time had come to hire a new custodian, his recommendation had counted toward the outcome.

"After all, what are friends for?"

Snippets of conversation drifted in from around the room. A middle-aged woman at an adjacent table exclaimed, "Isn't it horrible? I still can't believe Princess Diana is dead. She was such an elegant woman."

Strange, thought Adam. *Death and dying are always with us, hovering just out of reach.* The thought made him feel uneasy.

Humphrey bit into his peanut butter and jelly sandwich and then mumbled, "I've been wondering, how are you getting to work?" It was mid-February in Montana, meaning it was still winter.

Adam downed a sip of soda. "When the snow's not too deep, I ride my bike. Otherwise, I walk."

"Ever thought about buying a car?"

"I'd love to, except that after I pay the mortgage, put food on the table, and take care of Rachel, my paycheck is pretty well shot. I've learned to tell the difference between want versus need. It's a simple rule. You can't have the things you want if you can't afford the things you need. It seems like there should be an axiom: needs expand to soak up the money that's available. You'd be surprised how expensive a younger sister can be. I've been thinking I should look for a second job."

"How is Rachel, by the way?"

"I guess you'd say she's stable. Her desire to be left alone is pretty much the same as it has been. I keep hoping she'll get out and mingle with people, but she says she's not interested. I spoke with her teachers. They say she's doing okay in school, turning in her homework on time and such, but I don't know. It's hard to imagine what goes on inside her head."

Humphrey took a last bite of the dill pickle his mother had included for variety. His teeth crunched as he chewed. "Have you taken her to see someone?"

"You mean like a psychiatrist?"

"Yeah."

"I've thought about it, but I can't afford that level of care. I'm looking into maybe a social worker or a community-based support group as an alternative, but so far, I haven't found anything that feels right."

Humphrey blotted his mouth with a napkin. "I know a guy who has PTSD, which kind of sounds like what Rachel has. I think he gets his care through the VA. Though I doubt Rachel would qualify to be treated there."

"I'm pretty sure she wouldn't. It's been discouraging. Nevertheless, I intend to keep looking."

Humphrey watched as two women got up and left the break room. They pointedly ignored him as they passed by. Offhandedly, he said to Adam, "What's it like being a shipping clerk? Do you enjoy the work?"

"It's okay, once you get the hang of it, but you have to stay sharp. If you lose focus, you can screw up big time."

"I imagine it's not like being a custodian. All we have to remember is to dump the trash, mop the floors, and make sure the restrooms are clean and the stalls have toilet paper." Humphrey's face scrunched up like he was straining to have a bowel movement. Then he grinned and took on a look of relief. "You ever had a fart get stuck in your butt cheeks?"

"I don't believe I have." Adam chuckled.

"Let me tell you, it's quite a sensation. I kind of like it. It's like carrying one around, being ready to let loose at precisely the right moment." Humphrey fashioned a mischievous grin.

"Sounds uncomfortable."

A young woman near to Adam's age stepped up to the table where the two friends sat. She carried a lunchbox in her hand. "Hi," she said. "Mind if I join you?" She had a pleasant smile and was reasonably good-looking, not pretty, but her features blended together well. Her most noticeable attribute was her cobalt blue eyes.

"Sure." Adam started to rise from his chair.

The woman gestured that he should stay seated. "Your mother raised you well, I see."

"Hello, gorgeous," Humphrey mumbled around another bite of peanut butter and jelly sandwich. "How you doing?"

"I'm doing fine. How are you?" The young woman sat down and began taking food out of her lunchbox: apple slices in a baggie, carrot spears, a packet of raisins, and a small plastic bin containing celery sticks smeared with peanut butter.

"Eating healthy, are we?" Adam gestured toward the woman's lunch.

In return, she gave him a look that said, "And you're not?" Then she smiled. "I'm Alice Cunningham. I work in accounting."

Humphrey swallowed hard and declared, "Nice to meet you. I'm Michael Bogart. Everybody calls me Humphrey. I just got hired. I'm a custodian."

"That explains the uniform." Alice popped a raisin into her mouth. She cast a glance across the table at Adam. "Is it true you read repair manuals during your break time? Is that what you call fun?"

"I don't plan on staying in the shipping department forever. When I learn enough, I'll apply to become a repair technician. They make half more than I do."

"A man with a plan. Smart." Alice tapped her temple several times.

Humphrey checked his watch. "Damn. Gotta go. Don't wanna be late getting back to work again."

"Take care, bro," Adam said. "We'll talk to ya later."

Alice nodded her goodbye but said nothing.

After Humphrey departed, Alice leaned closer and asked quietly, "What's with your freaky friend?"

"He's not freaky when you get to know him."

"He's been on the job less than a week, and he's already scoping out the girls in my department."

"That's horny, not freaky."

"If you say so."

A moment of silence followed, and then Alice perked up. "I'm curious. What do you really do for fun? I'm sure it's not reading boring repair manuals."

Adam chewed his last bite of hard-boiled egg and washed it down with another swig of soda. "These days, repair manuals have to suffice. I used to be into MMORPG. I was a huge fan, but now I don't have the time."

"Into what?"

"Massively multiplayer online role-playing games, like *Knight Commander* or *The Devil's Spawn*."

"Sounds gruesome."

"It's only make-believe—not even close to real life."

"Tell me, Mr. Role-Playing Warrior, do you have a girlfriend?"

"Now that's fairly direct."

"Well, I want to know more about you. I've heard that you're still living with your family."

"That's true, except it's just me and my sister. She's thirteen going on twenty. I'm doing my best to raise her. I inherited the responsibility after my mother died."

"I'm sorry. I didn't know—"

"No harm done. By the way, who's been telling you about me?"

"The grapevine, of course."

"Oh, really?"

"You'd be surprised at the kind of information that gets passed around. You were hot news from the moment you applied for the shipping clerk's position."

"Should I feel flattered?"

"I suppose that would depend on what's being said. Aren't you the guy that shipped a GBX model 73 processor to Williamsburg, Pennsylvania, instead of Williamsburg, Virginia?"

Adam flushed. "Yep, that was me. The order ticket was blurry, so I checked online to see where Williamsburg was located. I guess I picked the wrong state."

"It took our department a week to straighten out the billing, but don't worry, everybody screws up from time to time." Alice smiled coyly. "Just don't do it again."

"I don't intend to."

"So, Adam, MMORPG warrior, what do you say? Do you think you might want to get together sometime?"

Taken aback, Adam stammered, "I don't know. I, eh…let me think about it."

"Don't take too long. Another hot hunk might come along, and you'd lose your opportunity."

Adam blushed in lieu of offering a reply. He stood and gathered up what was left of his lunch, which he tossed into the trash. As he said goodbye to Alice, he noticed that most of her lunch was also uneaten.

On his way back to the shipping department, he considered her invitation. He hadn't been on a date since his senior prom. Even then, his reason for going had arisen more from a sense of duty than from any feelings of attraction for his date.

Hot hunk? For real? Adam squared his shoulders and stood a little taller. Then after giving the matter a second thought, he told himself, *I'm going to have to watch myself around that one.*

When Adam entered the shipping department, the senior clerk pointed to the clock on the wall. Adam signaled that he understood and promptly went back to work.

*   *   *

I sat back and looked at my grandson.

When he realized I was studying him, he said, "Things seem to be going pretty well at this point."

"So it would seem."

"Seem? I'd say you're doing okay. You've got a job. You're learning a trade. You're taking care of Grandaunt Rachel. What am I missing?"

"Doesn't it bother you that I lied to get hired?"

"Not really. You made up for it by studying hard and working your tail off. It turned out all right in the end, didn't it?"

"You can judge that for yourself as we go along. For now, let's get something to eat. I'm hungry. How about you?"

"Now that you mention it."

I had planned a more substantial meal than the one during his initial visit. We had meatloaf, mashed potatoes, peas, hot dinner rolls, and ice cream for dessert. Both of us were feeling a bit stuffed when we returned to the library.

"Where were we?" I asked, sinking into my favorite armchair.

Casey consulted his memory. "You'd just made a new friend. Alice, I think her name was."

"Right, Alice Cunningham. She was a sweet girl. She didn't deserve what happened to her, especially since it was my fault." I sat quietly for a while, reminiscing.

"Go on," Casey said, clearly anxious to hear what was coming next.

"Before continuing, there's something else I should tell you, though I'd rather not. While I was studying to become a computer repair technician, I was also building my own machine." Then again, I remained silent for a time.

"And?" Casey said, impatient to be moving on.

"It's something I'm not proud of, and I've never told this to another living soul. In my days as an online gamer, I used to covet the high-end computers used by the best players. They were truly awesome machines, and I had always dreamed of having one. Working for Townsend Electronics, I saw my opportunity. Bit by bit, I began assembling a kick-ass piece of computing hardware. The CPU was overclocked at

3.2 GHz. It had eight core processors and a 256-bit main bus. The hard drives were state-of-the-art and configured to run in a RAID 2 array. The graphics subsystem was mind-blowing."

"Sounds really cool, but I have no idea what you're telling me."

"Let's just say that for that day and age, it was a rather impressive computer."

"So what's the problem?"

"The problem is this: I never could have afforded those parts, not on my salary, not if I wanted to pay the bills. The only way to lay my hands on such expensive components was to steal them. Working in the shipping department, it was actually easy to do. I would wait until an order came in for a part I needed. Then, rather than ship the part to the customer, I would set it aside to take home later—secretly, of course. Next, I would fill out a damaged item form, declaring that the part had been destroyed in the mail. Lastly, I would requisition a new part and send it to the customer. It was a simple scheme, and it worked beautifully. No one ever caught on, except I knew that what I was doing was wrong, and I did it anyway."

Casey seemed appalled. "If you knew stealing was wrong, didn't your conscience tell you to stop? I get craving a fancy computer, but I never took you for a thief. What was going through your head?"

"Looking back, I guess the best explanation is I felt like the world owed me a debt, and I intended to collect. It didn't matter where the payment came from. Yes, my conscience bothered me, but I ignored it. The truly sad part is, this was not the worst thing that happened while I was working at Townsend Electronics."

"There's more?"

"There is, and it involves Alice Cunningham. Do you remember my mentioning that I'd been thinking about taking on a second job? Well, I did. I hired on as a part-time night clerk at a local motel. It meant that Rachel was on her own more than I liked, but it gave us just enough extra income that we could start putting money aside for things like a car, new clothes, and other sundries.

"Normally, my shift at the motel ran from 7:00 p.m. to 11:00 p.m. One night I got off early. On my way home, I remembered that I had left a very valuable item in my locker, so I decided to stop by Townsend Electronics to retrieve it."

*   *   *

March 1998

Two hours past dinnertime, Adam pulled into the parking lot in front of the electronics store. Except for one other car, the lot was deserted. Adam chose the space nearest the main entrance. After racing up the front walkway, he began banging on the glass. Eventually, the night watchman answered his summons.

"Let me in!" Adam shouted loudly enough to be heard inside the building. "It's important." It took some doing, but he finally convinced the guard to unlock the door.

"I'll be right back," Adam said to the guard as he sprinted off into the interior of the building. The employees' lockers were around the corner from the break room. Adam was surprised when he turned down the next-to-last corridor. The ceiling lights were on. Normally, they were turned off after everyone had gone home. When he rounded the final corner, he was astonished by what he saw.

Alice Cunningham was standing in front of his open locker.

A dozen thoughts raced through Adam's mind. The one that captured his attention was that he needed to document what he was seeing. He quickly ducked out of sight and rushed back to get the security guard. Together they ran back to the employees' lockers just as Alice was securing his locker.

"You saw that, right?" Adam said to the guard. "Tell me you did."

"I saw it, yes, sir. You best check your locker and see if everything is okay."

Alice startled when Adam stepped forward. "What are you doing here?" There was a look of surprise in her eyes.

"I could ask you the same thing. Excuse me." Adam elbowed his way past Alice to stand in front of his locker. That's when he noticed that his padlock was in its proper place and securely latched. "How did you get my locker open?" he demanded.

"I don't know what you're talking about," Alice protested defensively.

"I'm talking about the fact that you were just rummaging through my stuff. I want to know why."

The guard stepped forward. "You best answer the man, Ms. Cunningham. If you don't, we'll call the police and let them handle this. I suspect that if they search you, they'll find a master key in your purse."

Alice threw up her hands and, with an air of resignation, said, "All right. You got me. I broke into your locker. It was supposed to be a surprise. I'm throwing a party this coming weekend, and you're invited. I put your invitation in your locker. It was supposed to be a puzzle for you to figure out, trying to explain how it got there. But now you've ruined it."

Adam fished in his pocket for his own key and opened the locker. He immediately discovered the invitation Alice had mentioned. It was lying in plain sight, but the item he needed to find wasn't there. He searched a second time with the same result.

Spinning around to face Alice, Adam demanded, "What did you do with it?"

"Do with what?" Alice seemed genuinely at a loss to know what Adam was talking about.

"My mother's diamond necklace. It's a family heirloom and worth a great deal of money. It was the only piece of jewelry she owned. Where is it?"

"I have no idea. I never saw a necklace or anything else of value."

"Ms. Cunningham," the guard said, "I'm going to have to ask you to wait here until the police arrive. They're going to want to talk to you."

*   *   *

Late the next morning, Adam and Alice stood in Mr. Bingham's office. Neither would speak to the other. Mr. Bingham was the regional manager for Townsend Electronics. He had driven over from Helena just for this meeting. The police had conducted a thorough investigation. The necklace was nowhere to be found. Without actual proof that Alice had taken the item, there was nothing they could do. Mr. Bingham, on the other hand, was governed by a different set of rules.

Looking up from his desk, he addressed his two employees.

"I've reviewed this matter thoroughly. I've spoken with the police sergeant who led the investigation. I've interviewed our night watchman. And I've read both your statements. This is not the first theft we've had. Other items have gone missing from people's lockers. However, this is the first time there were witnesses.

"Ms. Cunningham, I don't know if you stole the necklace or not. But I do know that you were seen rummaging through a fellow employee's locker without their permission. That's probable cause enough for me. If it was up to me, I'd throw the book at you, but unless the police turn up new evidence, it's unlikely that you'll be prosecuted. There is something I can do, however. You're fired. Clean out your desk and your locker and leave this store immediately. We'll mail you your severance pay."

Alice opened her mouth to protest.

Mr. Bingham cut her off by declaring forcefully, "I mean now."

After a moment's hesitation, Alice spun on her heel and departed.

"As for you, Mr. Masters, the next time you have anything worth more than a few dollars, why don't you request that we lock it in our safe. That way we can avoid situations like this. Now, maybe you should go back to work."

"What about the insurance claim?" Adam said before leaving.

"Yes, yes," Mr. Bingham said dismissively, as if wanting to be done with the matter. "I checked with our underwriter. Our policy will cover your loss. Now go."

That evening, as Adam was preparing for bed, he threw his dirty clothes into the hamper in his closet. About to add the soiled jacket he had worn the previous day, he felt something hard in its pocket. It turned out to be the jewelry box that held his mother's diamond necklace. With a start, he suddenly remembered removing the necklace from his locker to bring home. How could he have forgotten? Such a lapse seemed impossible, but there it was. The proof was right there in front of him. He felt profoundly mortified.

Adam stood unmoving for quite a while as he pondered what he should do. He had two clear choices: call Mr. Bingham and confess his mistake, or stay silent and let things stand as they were. He settled on doing nothing. *So what if Alice lost her job?* he reasoned. *She'll find another.* On the other hand, if he were to confess his error, there was a small but real possibility Mr. Bingham might sack him for all the trouble he'd caused. Also, there was the issue of the insurance payment. If he kept his mouth shut, he would wind up with both the necklace and the money. It seemed an easy enough choice, but it was one that would haunt him for many years to come.

*   *   *

I avoided making eye contact with my grandson. "Once again, no one ever found out, but I've had to live with my sins all these years. See what I mean about making choices? It's not always clear who's in charge: me or the things that surround me. Sometimes, forces beyond our control influence us more than we know."

"But you said you knew what you were doing. You made the choices you made of your own free will."

"A man can justify almost anything to himself."

"What happened to the necklace?"

"I still have it. I keep it as a reminder."

"And Alice? What happened to her?"

"I don't know. I wish I had an answer. I'd like to think she came out of the kerfuffle okay, that she landed on her feet. She deserved better than she got."

"Another question. Why did you take the necklace to work in the first place?"

"I'd planned on having it appraised before selling it. I'd intended to stop by a jewelry store after work. Instead, Rachel had a minor meltdown, and I got distracted. By the time I got home to check on her, I'd forgotten the necklace was in my pocket."

Casey shook his head. He seemed legitimately disappointed. "All these misdeeds, and there were no consequences for your actions."

"I wouldn't say that. There are always consequences. It's just that they don't always present themselves as we think they should. And sometimes, it takes a while for the wheel to come around full circle."

*   *   *

August 1998

Adam decided he would take Rachel to church.

The organist sounded the hymn's final note as the choir and the congregation finished their song. The interior of the church became as silent as a tomb, except for the footfalls of the preacher as he climbed the dais and stepped into the pulpit. He gestured with both hands. "You may sit down."

Dutifully, fifty-odd people, most of them elderly, did as directed.

Adam slid his well-worn hymnal into the rack on the back of the pew in front of him. When he sat down, the wooden seat felt hard against his backside, causing him to consider how long he might have to endure the discomfort. Would the sermon be short and to the point, or would the preacher ramble on for an eternity? *Only time will tell*, he thought. *Wait and see.*

Rachel watched Adam stow his hymnal, and then followed his lead. She too sat down.

When Adam had initially broached the idea of going to church, Rachel had refused, but after being cajoled, she had reluctantly consented.

To the best of Adam's recollection, this was his sister's first time attending a Sunday service. When she had asked what church would be like, he had advised her to keep an open mind regarding what she would see and hear, mainly because he himself did not know what to expect.

Why did I decide to come to church? Adam asked himself. *And why insist on bringing Rachel along?* The questions intrigued him. *Could it be because it had seemed the proper thing to do, being Rachel's guardian and all?* One thing was for certain. It wasn't because of some deep-seated spiritual yearning, at least none that he recognized. At nineteen years of age, he hadn't even begun to ponder such matters.

He had picked the Presbyterian Church near the center of town because the building's imposing edifice fit his mental image of what a religious institution should look like.

The preacher, Rev. Aloysius Comstock, began reading a list of announcements. He had a dry, brittle voice. Rather than pay attention, Adam opened the bulletin he had been handed on his way in—one bulletin for both him and his sister. *Probably trying to cut down on expenses.* As he scanned the order of service, he saw that they were to sing another hymn, and then the pastor would deliver his sermon entitled "The Pros and Cons of Fasting."

Fantastic, Adam thought. *That's precisely what I need right now, learning how to do without food. Heck, it's easy to fast when you have no money.* He began questioning the wisdom of giving up a Sunday morning to be regaled with useless information.

Rachel fidgeted.

Adam leaned over and whispered to his sister, "What's wrong?"

She answered in a voice a shade too loud. "My butt hurts. Can't they afford cushions for these wooden seats?"

The woman seated behind them laughed.

Adam shushed his sister and then consulted the bulletin again. "If I'm reading this right, after he finishes the announcements, we'll sing another hymn. That means you'll get to stand up."

Rachel made a sour face. "Can we do something fun after we're done here?"

"I was planning on surprising you, but I might as well tell you now. We're going out to lunch."

Rachel brightened a bit. "Really?"

"Really really. The Four Horsemen are getting together. Today it'll be the Four Horsemen plus one."

"I'd rather it was just you." Rachel pouted.

"You like the guys, and they're always asking about you. It'll be a good time."

"Where are we going to eat?"

"That Italian restaurant near the mall. We've been there before. You liked it."

Just then, the pastor invited the congregation to stand. About to offer a comment, Rachel instead breathed a sigh of relief.

Adam reached for his hymnal. His sister did the same. They began singing hymn number 163, "The Old Rugged Cross."

As they sang, Adam suddenly found himself vexed by an unpleasant memory still fresh in his mind. Less than a month had passed since the locker incident. As he pictured the look on Alice's face when Mr. Bingham had fired her, a fresh surge of guilt swelled up within him. He had done a very bad thing. Previous attempts to rationalize his actions had done nothing to ease his conscience. Even worse, he had gotten away with it. Transgressions require punishment. That axiom had been beaten into him since early childhood.

Is that why I've come? Adam wondered. *Was I subconsciously looking for someone who could forgive me?* Later, he would learn that what he actually wanted was to learn how to forgive himself.

The hymn ended, and the congregation took their seats. The pastor gazed down from the pulpit and began his sermon, which turned out to be as droll and as lengthy as Adam had feared. Eventually, the sermon ended, and then they were ready to depart, but before leaving, Rachel announced that she needed to use the restroom. While Adam was waiting in the hall for her to return, a young woman approached him from behind and tapped him on the shoulder. He startled.

"Oh, sorry," she said. "I didn't mean to alarm you. I saw you when you first came in, and I was wondering if you're new here."

The woman, who looked to be near his own age, had a very pleasant voice and a quiet demeanor. Not only that, she was extremely good-looking. She wore a pale-yellow blouse and an Irish green skirt. Her belt and pumps were white.

"My name is Victoria Wayne. What's yours?"

"Eh, Adam. Adam Masters. My sister's name is Rachel. I'm waiting for her. She's…" With a head gesture, he indicated the ladies' room. "Yes, this is our first visit."

"What did you think?"

"What an exciting message, I mean—wow. I never imagined there was so much to know about fasting."

"I know, right? Pastor Comstock has such a way with words. On occasion, his messages are utterly thrilling."

Adam looked closely to see if he was being teased. For a moment, he believed that she was dead serious until a faint upturning at the sides of her mouth gave way to a sunny smile.

"Gotcha," Victoria said brightly.

"Yes, you did. I'll admit it."

"Actually, Pastor Comstock is a very nice man, but he's getting on in years. You wouldn't believe it to look at him, but he's nearly eighty years old."

"I'd believe it," Adam said earnestly.

"Sometimes we call him Pastor Corn Stock, but I guess he's heard that name so often, it no longer bothers him. We keep thinking that one day soon he'll retire, but he keeps on plodding on like an old racehorse."

"I gather you come here regularly?"

"Every Sunday."

"Do you come with your family, or is there someone else?" Adam flushed when he heard himself speak. The question had sounded a little too forward to ask a stranger. But then he had precious little experience interacting with the opposite sex.

"Sometimes I come alone. Mostly it's with my dad. He's not well. I help take care of him. Say, are you staying for our potluck lunch? It starts in about twenty minutes."

"Actually, we have another commitment. Some guys I've known since high school are getting together. Otherwise, Rachel and I would have been glad to stay."

Rachel emerged from the restroom and moved to join her brother. Adam introduced her to his new acquaintance.

"How old are you, Rachel?" Victoria said.

"Fourteen." Rachel turned to her brother. "Why do people keep asking me how old I am? What difference does it make?"

"They're being polite. It's a good way to get to know you." With an apologetic shrug, Adam said to Victoria, "It's her first time in church, ever. She's… That is, she's not used to it."

"I was much the same myself, at first." Victoria gave Rachel a welcoming smile. "We're glad you came."

Rachel looked away.

Adam glanced at his watch; it was time to leave. The thought of leaving made him unexpectedly sad. "I'd like to stay and chat, but we have to go. We have people waiting for us."

"It's been nice speaking with you. Will you be coming back, do you think?"

"I'm sure I will, probably next Sunday." Adam dipped his chin for emphasis, and then to himself said, *And next time, I'll leave my little sister at home.*

* * *

The waiter served Rachel a six-inch pepperoni and cheese pizza. He then placed a plate of cannelloni with Alfredo sauce in front of Adam. Theo got the pasta primavera, and Bud got the lasagna. Humphrey had ordered a hamburger, medium rare, with cheese and no pickle. The Four Horsemen plus one began consuming their lunches with gusto.

The conversation at the table had ranged among various topics, including the transfer of the governance of Hong Kong from the United Kingdom to China. Theo had brought up the subject because of his strong feelings about how wrong it was that a communist dictatorship be allowed to suppress a fledgling democracy.

"Britain should never have given in to China's demands." Theo reached for a breadstick.

"Enough with the geopolitical crap already." Bud looked around the table. "It's good to see you guys. We should make it a rule that we get together at least once every year."

Humphrey nodded in agreement. "I can't believe it's been nearly two years since we graduated."

"It doesn't feel that long, does it," Theo agreed. "But you're right. Let's talk about something else. Rachel, what about you? How are you doing?"

"I'm doing okay."

"You're what, fourteen now, right?"

"She just started her freshman year in high school," Adam boasted with a touch of pride.

Theo said, "I remember when you were born. Your dad had to rush your mom to the hospital. She had the nerve to go into labor right in the middle of Adam's fifth birthday party. Those were interesting days, weren't they?"

About to take a bite, Rachel put down her slice of pizza and sat back in her chair. Rather than speak, she stared at her hands in her lap.

Adam understood that being reminded of their father had triggered her reaction. *Some memories never fade away*, he thought. "I have good news," he said to counter the sudden change in mood that had descended upon the gathering. "Two pieces of good news, actually."

Bud said, "Really? What would they be?"

"There's an opening in the service department at Townsend Electronics. I put in an application, and I'm pretty sure I'll get the job. I'm about to become a computer repair technician."

"Good for you!" Theo exclaimed.

"And the second piece of news?" Bud said.

"I've enrolled in an online degree program. It's offered by Ridgecrest College. When I finish, I'll have a bachelor of science in information technology."

"How long will that take?" Bud asked.

"Anywhere from two to three years, depending upon how hard I push myself. It'll probably be closer to three years. Even with a raise, I'll have to work two jobs to stay afloat. Let me tell you, it used to be a whole lot easier when I wasn't the one worrying about money. These days, it seems like I spend an awful lot of time trying to sort out the difference between want vs. need."

"You'll do it," Theo declared with conviction.

"You always were the ambitious one." A hint of envy hardened Humphrey's voice. He chomped a large chunk out of his cheeseburger.

Adam looked around the table. "What about the rest of you? What are you guys doing with your lives?"

Theo was first to speak up. "As you may or may not know, I've taken a job at Tranco Auto Parts. They're small now, but I'm convinced that they're going to grow rapidly. If I'm right, I should be able to move up the corporate ladder rather quickly."

"Invest where you find opportunity, right?" Adam said. "Isn't that what you're always telling us? And what about you, Bud? What does your future look like?"

Bud swallowed a mouthful of lasagna. "I'm thinking I'd like to be an accountant, like my dad. He says it would be good for us to go into business together."

"Is that how you feel?" Humphrey said.

"Yeah, I suppose. It's either accounting or…I don't know, play professional soccer. I'd rather play football, but I'm not big enough for the NFL."

"Taylor and Son Accountants," Adam commented. "Sounds good. How long will it take to get a degree?"

"Four years. Three and a half, actually. I enrolled at MSU last fall."

"Last I heard," Theo said, "you were working as a security guard?"

Bud nodded. "Nights and weekends. The pay is good, and I can study if things are quiet."

"Good for y'all." Humphrey seemed inexplicably bothered by what he was hearing. "Everybody's got their future all mapped out."

"Well, what about you then?" Adam said in a conciliatory tone of voice. "Do you have any plans?"

"Me?" Humphrey pointed to himself. "I'll probably be a custodian for the rest of my life. Hell, I might even open my own business—Bogart's Janitorial Services. How about that? Does that have a nice ring?"

"By the way, Adam," Theo said after an uncomfortable silence. "I found something the other day that might interest you. I was looking for new start-ups with unique business models. I came across a company called Challenge Gaming. They're brand-new and looking to expand, and apparently, they're thinking about opening a gaming franchise here locally. If they do, they're going to need a manager to run their salon—that's what they call their retail outlets."

"A gaming franchise?" Adam echoed with interest.

Theo arched an eyebrow. "I knew that would catch your attention. Apparently, the way it works is Challenge provides a high-speed Internet connection and top-of-the-line hardware so gamers can play online any game they want. They bill by the hour. For a reasonable fee, customers can feed their gaming addictions with the fastest setups available. The company plans on organizing tournaments. They'll have a national leaderboard. Prizes will be awarded to the top players. Some of the prizes sounded pretty sweet, like a Hawaiian vacation or a trip to

Europe. With your MMORPG background, I thought you might be interested. After all, you know all about that online stuff."

Adam swallowed his last bite of cannelloni. "It does sound intriguing. I'll check them out. Challenge Gaming, you say?"

"Yeah, I'll email you their URL."

When the meal ended, the Four Horsemen agreed that they should get together on a regular basis, at least every six months. Rachel, for her part, was clearly glad to be heading home.

What am I going to do about you, little sister? Adam thought as he escorted Rachel from the restaurant. *There has to be something that will cheer you up, put a spark of joy in your life.* He tried to think what that something might be, but came up short. Optimistically, he told himself, *It'll come to me, if I give it time.* He certainly hoped that was true.

*   *   *

Casey stood up, stretched, and then covered his mouth with the back of his hand as he stifled a yawn.

"Was I boring you?" I said teasingly.

"Far from it. Sorry. It's just that I haven't gotten much sleep this last week."

"Why is that?" I stood as well. The pain in my lower back reminded me that it was almost bedtime.

Casey commented, "Finals are coming up." When he spoke, I detected an undertone of tension in his voice.

"I should've figured," I said mildly. Again, I had the nagging suspicion that there was more to my grandson's angst than a bunch of exams that were still a month away. There was something he wasn't telling me, but again, I elected not to force the discussion of a topic he obviously wished to avoid.

Instead, I suggested, "Do we need to stop for a while, maybe come back after you've taken your tests?"

"Not at all. I'm honored to share your life story."

"It's not what you expected, is it?"

"I doubt anybody gets through this life without messing up now and then."

I took hold of Casey's upper arm for support as I accompanied him to the front door. En route, I said, "By the way, your applications to law school, have you heard anything?"

"I should've said something. I've been accepted to Baylor."

"Congratulations. Are they a good law school?"

"They're number forty-eight out of the top fifty. I'm not keen on living in Texas. I'd prefer something closer to home. I have other applications that are still pending. Maybe another option will turn up."

I gave Casey's arm a squeeze before releasing my grip. "You'll make the right decision, I'm sure. So, when should we get together again?"

Casey consulted the calendar app on his phone. "Today is Tuesday. I'm meeting with my study group both tomorrow and Thursday. How about Friday?"

"Same time?"

"Works for me."

"What would you like for dinner? How about Chinese takeout?"

My grandson put on his jacket. "Isn't it my turn to buy?"

"You worry about your studies. I'll worry about feeding us."

I watched Casey walk to the street and climb into his car. *Lord,* I thought, *please make it be that he comes to understand the message we're about to impart.* There was so much more I intended to say, and a great deal of it would be both humiliating and appalling.

5

A CHANCE TO SET THINGS RIGHT

Early Wednesday morning, the day after my second session with my grandson, I went to see Theo again. To my surprise, he was already awake and attending to his morning chores. Generally, Theo has an upbeat personality and a perpetual optimism. This morning, however, he was in a sour frame of mind. When he greeted me at the front door, his gruff "Good morning" was accompanied by a scowl.

"Get up on the wrong side of the bed, did we?" I instinctively headed toward the kitchen. "What you need is another cup of coffee."

Theo trailed behind. "I've already had two."

"It wasn't enough."

Theo brews his dark roast blend in a single-serving coffee maker. I prefer a percolator myself. He claims his machine is more efficient, and he's probably right. I just like the sound mine makes when it's percolating away.

Theo sat quietly at the kitchen table while I brewed both of us a mugful. Lifting his mug up, I said, "Cream? Sugar?"

He shook his head no.

"It must be something serious," I said, "for you to take your coffee unadorned. What's going on? Why so glum?"

"I went to see the doctor yesterday. My cholesterol is up. He put me on a statin medicine."

"Good grief!" I exclaimed. "You're seventy-four years old. Who gives a damn what your cholesterol is?"

"It's the principle of the thing. I've never taken medicines for anything in my life. Why should I start now?"

"Theo, you're one of the healthiest people I know, especially for your age. You're going to be in fantastic shape when you die. Let it go. Worrying isn't going to change a thing, except it'll ruin your day."

"I suspect you're right. Besides, who wants to live forever? Right?" He pointed to the headline sprawled across the top of the newspaper lying on the kitchen table. It read "New Wave of Immigrants Hits Southern Border."

"Do you see that?" Theo tapped his finger on the newspaper. "They're coming across in droves. I say it's intentional. The government wants more illegal aliens to flood into our country. You know why? They dilute the labor market. They compete for the low-end jobs, thereby keeping wages down. Businesses don't have to pay as much for unskilled labor. I say our immigration policies should be merit based, period—except of course for a small number of humanitarian cases where people's lives are truly in danger."

During our lifelong friendship, on innumerable occasions I'd listened to Theo pontificate on this subject or that. Generally, a political theme underlay his tirades. This morning, however, I wasn't in the mood to be lectured. So I interrupted him. "Theo, immigration isn't why I'm here."

"Oh. And here I thought you just wanted to shoot the breeze. What's up?"

"I have an issue, and I could use your help. Last night, as I was talking with my grandson, our conversation dredged up another bad memory."

Theo cut straight to the chase. "Tell me."

I explained about Alice Cunningham and my mother's diamond necklace. I left nothing out and took full responsibility for how I had mishandled the situation.

Theo listened attentively and interrupted only once to ask a question I hadn't considered before. "Did Alice actually throw the party she mentioned?"

I gestured to indicate my ignorance. "Why would that be relevant?"

"It speaks to the strength of her defense. If there actually was a party, and she'd been planning it for a couple weeks, that would support what she told you—her reason for being in your locker. If there was no party, then the invitation was bogus, and you could judge her to be a liar."

"I never thought of that." Again, I was impressed by Theo's ability to cut through extraneous distractions and get to the heart of a problem.

With his elbows resting on the kitchen table, Theo steepled his fingers in front of him. "What do you want from me?"

"I want you to help me find her."

"Do you know if she's even alive?" He did some quick calculations in his head. "That was fifty-two years ago. The odds are she's dead."

"Then I'll try to find her closest living relative."

"Seems like a lot of effort for a long-forgotten misdeed."

"All I know is I have to try."

"For the same reasons you paid back your father's loan?"

"Precisely. It's a matter of principle. What good is it to read the gospels if you don't do what they tell you to do? Loving one another involves more than paying lip service to your faith. You need to live it, and that means trying to undo the wrongs you've done, if you can. Will you help me?"

"Where do we start?"

*   *   *

By 9:00 a.m., we had exhausted every online resource we could think of. I was astounded to learn how many Alice Cunninghams there were nationwide, far more than I had imagined. None of them, however, satisfied the criterion for what I had come to regard as our manhunt.

Theo knuckled an eye. "That's it. There are no more online resources to review."

We'd visited a slew of person-finder websites, combed through any number of white-page directories, Google-searched using various combinations of her first and last name, and consulted several genealogy research services. In desperation, we had even picked through a handful of obituary databases, such as they were. I was as worn out as my friend.

"Let's get a late breakfast," Theo suggested. "I need to get up and move around."

"There has to be someplace else we can look. I'm not willing to give up yet."

"I don't see what more we can do. We've exhausted every online resource."

"Maybe we're looking in the wrong place. What if there's someone who knew her, somebody who worked with her at Townsend Electronics, and what if they stayed in touch?"

Theo shook his head. "That's a whole lot of what-ifs."

"Do we have any other options? I can't think of any," I said, answering my own question.

We returned to the kitchen where we each had yet another mug of coffee. After several sips, I set my mug aside. I was beginning to experience a lightheaded buzz—too much caffeine. As I sat there, I racked my brain to recall the names of some of my coworkers. I came up with several, but only one had worked with Alice in the accounting department. When we looked her up in a white-pages database, we found that she was still living in Missoula, about a mile from my home.

"Maybe our luck is about to change." I copied her name and address into the notebook app on my phone. "Now about eating—"

Theo shrugged. "I know, I know. You're on a quest, and you can't be distracted."

"What I was going to suggest is that we pick up some takeout and eat it on our way to her house."

"You're on. Let me get my coat."

Theo closed and locked the front door, but then stopped to look at me apologetically. "All that coffee, and now I've got to pee."

I laughed but then decided that I should probably go too.

*   *   *

Mabel Buchanan lived on East Sycamore. Her back was stooped, and her shuffling gait was slow, but her cheeks were rosy, and her mind was sharp. She invited us in and offered us cookies and coffee, both of which we refused.

"Yes, yes, I remember Alice," Mabel said. "She was a sweet girl. I was sorry to see her go."

"That's why we're here," I said. "We're trying to find her. You wouldn't happen to know where she is now, would you?"

"No, I surely wouldn't. The day she cleaned out her desk, that was the last time I saw her. Say, why are you two looking for her? It wouldn't have anything to do with her getting fired, would it? I never for one minute believed she was a thief."

I was impressed by Mabel's powers of deduction. "You remember that incident, do you? Well, actually, yes. This does have to do with that event. Anyway, if you can't help us, we'll be going. Thank you for your time."

Theo and I stood and were about to leave when Mabel said, "I do remember something that might help. I remember her telling me once that she was from a small town in Kansas where she had a passel of relatives. Maybe one of them could help you."

"Do you remember the name of the town?" I held my breath while Mabel rummaged through her recollections.

"Let's see, it was like…Piney—no, Aspen… No, that's not right. I'm sure it was the name of a tree."

"Ash? Oak? Dogwood?" Theo suggested

"Shush," Mabel snapped. "Let me think. Let me think."

"Cedar!" she exclaimed after a while with a satisfied grin. "That's what it was. Cedar Shores, Kansas. That's where she was from. Lordy, who says I'm getting senile?"

We thanked our hostess and quickly departed. On our way back to Theo's house, I used my phone to look the town up on Google Maps. It lay in the south-central portion of the state. By the time we pulled to a stop in his driveway, I had already booked an early afternoon flight to Kansas. In a rush, I said goodbye to Theo and drove straight to the airport. I figured I could pick up whatever personal items I might need once I got the Cedar Shores.

*   *   *

After landing in Wichita, I rented a midsized sedan and then drove the fifty-three miles to Cedar Shores. It was a beautiful moonlit night, and the countryside, mostly farmland, was eerily pleasing to behold, though the topography was a little too flat to suit me. As far as the eye could see, there was no change in elevation greater than five hundred feet. I much prefer the grandeur of the Rocky Mountains and the surrounding forests.

When I reached Cedar Shores, it was far too late to do anything other than check into a motel.

Thursday morning, I again rose early and began canvassing the town. I had discovered that the population was near twelve thousand souls, and by my estimation, there were from three to four dozen businesses clustered within a five-mile radius. With determination, I plodded from one to the next, block after block.

After giving the matter considerable thought, I had come up with no better plan than to randomly ask complete strangers if they knew anybody with the last name Cunningham. Consistently, the answer was no.

By 10:00 a.m., I was already tired and starting to get depressed. I had canvassed more than a third of Cedar Shores with nothing to show for my efforts. That's when I noticed a diner at the end of the street. Suddenly, I was hungry as well as tired. I figured I would take a break and have a late breakfast.

When I entered the diner, I noted that half a dozen customers were seated at the counter or in booths along the walls. On impulse, I advanced to the center of the room and loudly cleared my throat. "Excuse me," I said. "May I have your attention? Excuse me… Good, thank you. I'm trying to track down a woman who grew up here many years ago. It's important that I find her. I'm looking for anyone with the last name Cunningham. Is anyone here aware of someone by that name? Cunningham, does it ring a bell?"

Nobody spoke up.

Feeling disappointed, I said, "Well, thank you for your attention."

I was about to take a seat at the counter when an older woman in a back booth called out, "I used to deliver mail for the post office. I remember a Cunningham family that lived on a farm a mile or two out of town."

I crossed the room to stand beside the table where the old woman sat. "Would you happen to know if anyone by that name still lives there?"

"As I recall, there was a daughter who stayed on after her parents died. When she got married, she and her husband continued to work the place. Her married name is Richardson, I think, Rose Richardson. The husband passed away, but far as I know, she still lives there. That's all I can tell you."

"Thank you so much." I reached for a napkin and retrieved a pen from my shirt pocket. "Could you draw me a map to her farm please?"

Ignoring my hunger, I rushed from the diner. Map in hand, I returned to my car, which was parked several blocks away. Soon, I was headed out of town.

* * *

Rose Richardson turned out to be a short heavyset woman in her late fifties. Strands of thin gray hair lay tangled on her shoulders. She wore a food-stained apron over her gingham dress. When she answered the front door, she took one look at me and declared, "We don't countenance peddlers around here. You best git."

The Great Dane on the other side of the screen door snarled a warning.

"Easy, Duke," Rose said. "He don't take to peddlers."

The dog snarled again.

"I'm not a peddler," I said politely. "I'm looking for someone, and I was told that you might be able to help me. It's important that I find her. I understand that your maiden name is Cunningham. Is that correct? The person I'm looking for is Alice Cunningham. I was told that she grew up in Cedar Shores. Do you know anybody named Alice Cunningham?"

"Alice Cunningham? Aunt Alice? What do you want with her?"

"So you do know her. Is she still alive? Where can I find her?"

"I asked you why you're looking for her?"

"Many years ago, we worked together at Townsend Electronics. Regrettably, her time there didn't end well. I know this sounds odd, but I'd like to make things right for her."

"I remember Aunt Alice speaking of being employed there." Rose scratched a patch of eczema on the side of her neck. "That was ages ago. She said it was the only job she ever got fired from, but she never mentioned why she was laid off."

"It's an unhappy story, and I regret to say that I was part of the reason for her termination."

"I see. Well, you best come in and tell me what this is all about." Rose held the screen door open.

Rather than enter directly, I regarded the Great Dane with uncertainty.

"He'll leave you be," Rose said as if reading my mind. "Just don't make any sudden gestures."

Moving very slowly, I stepped inside.

*   *   *

When I had the information I had been seeking, I concluded my visit with Rose and took my leave. On my way back to Wichita, I briefly considered changing my reservation and flying straight to Swiftwater, Alaska, which, according to Rose, was where Alice was currently living with a friend named Tracy Yang. The problem was that a change of itinerary would force me to miss my Friday session with Casey, which I was loathe to do.

Feeling frustrated by the delay, I begrudgingly conceded that my reunion with Alice would have to wait, at least until the weekend or shortly thereafter, depending upon what travel arrangements I could manage.

I was in a pleasant mood when I returned my rental car to the airport lot. I was right on schedule to catch my 5:19 p.m. flight back to Missoula. I had accomplished the goal for which I had come to Kansas. There were still hurdles to overcome, but at least I was further along than when I'd first thought of reconciling with Alice. I was moving in the right direction. Hopefully, my good fortune would continue.

One step at a time, I reminded myself. *One step at a time.*

Before heading into the terminal, I paused for a moment and allowed the cool afternoon breeze to wash over me.

6

EVIL IS FOR REAL

When Friday afternoon rolled around, rather than settle for Chinese takeout, I called Casey to suggest that we dine out instead. He heartily agreed, and together, we decided to try the new French restaurant that was earning an excellent reputation.

I picked Casey up at his apartment and drove to the restaurant, intentionally arriving more than an hour early. After confirming our reservation with the maître d', we headed for the bar, which wasn't at all crowded. A table in the far corner looked like just the place to converse without being overheard.

When the cocktail waitress stepped up to take our orders, I was pleased that Casey asked for an iced tea rather than something containing alcohol. His selection suggested that he wanted to stay sharp. I decided to follow his lead and requested a club soda.

Rather than ease in with small talk, Casey began by saying what was on his mind. "I've been troubled by something you shared the last time we met. You said that on several occasions, you did things that you knew at the time were wrong. Did I hear you correctly?"

I nodded. "You did. As you probably can imagine, I'm not proud of some of the things I've done."

"The question that keeps bugging me is why? If you knew what you were doing was wrong, why do it? Why not go in a different direction and do the right thing?"

"I can give you an answer, but I'm not sure it's the one you want to hear. Mainly, I behaved the way I did because I wanted to. I know it's no excuse, but I was young and naïve concerning the ways of the world.

At the time, the choices I was making seemed perfectly reasonable. Only later did I begin to appreciate the magnitude of the wrongs I had committed: stealing from my employer, bearing false witness against a fellow employee, lying to get ahead."

"Didn't you worry that you would be found out?"

"Of course I worried. I could've been fired…or worse."

Casey seemed deeply bothered. "But you went ahead anyway. That's what I don't understand. Sometimes I think it's almost as if we want to get caught. How sick is that?"

I suppose I should've picked up on his use of the pronoun *we*, but I didn't. Later, the implications of his statement would become clear. Instead, I continued with the line of thought I had been pursuing. "Back then, there was another factor to consider. I didn't believe in evil. I held to the philosophy that every individual should be guided by his or her own moral compass. What might be right for some could be wrong for others. I guess you'd say I lived by a code of relativistic morality. Whatever was expedient, whatever worked was right. Whatever was imprudent or didn't work was wrong.

"Besides, I had a goal I wanted to achieve. I was determined to succeed in the workplace, and I was willing to do whatever was needed to reach that goal, consequences be damned."

"In those days, did you believe in God?"

"I did, but I had a different concept of who He was."

"Weren't you worried that God would judge you for what you were doing?"

"Honestly, I didn't think He would notice, or if He did notice, I didn't think He would care. After all, back then, God and I weren't exactly communicating with one another."

"Do you still believe in God?"

"Wholeheartedly. As I've experienced more of life, it's become impossible to deny His existence. Wherever you look, you see evidence of His handiwork. For atheists to claim that God doesn't exist, they must intentionally ignore the myriad proofs that surround us."

"I know people like that," Casey confided. "They go to great lengths to justify what they have already decided to believe. They tell themselves that God isn't real, and to support that belief, they ignore all the evidence to the contrary."

"To their detriment, sadly."

Casey let out a sigh. "Last time when we left off, you were telling about your reunion with the Four Horsemen."

"That was a good get-together. I think I also mentioned meeting a young lady in church—Victoria Wayne. For days after our first encounter, I kept seeing her in my mind's eye. When the next Sunday rolled around, I made certain that I was again seated in a pew at the Presbyterian Church. Likewise for the Sundays that followed.

"After several weeks of exchanging pleasantries, I finally mustered the nerve to ask Victoria out on a date. I was astonished when she accepted my invitation. I never imagined that she would. In fact, I was so sure that she would turn me down, I hadn't given any thought to what we would do on our date, but Victoria was cool. After considering various alternatives, we decided to go bowling. As first dates go, we had a really good time, and we thoroughly enjoyed each other's company.

"Around 9:00 p.m., I drove to Victoria's house and dropped her off and then headed home where I was greeted by a legitimate emergency."

*   *   *

October 1998

Adam was in high spirits after his date with Victoria. Normally shy and hesitant around women, he was grateful for her ability to make him feel at ease. She was a good listener. When he spoke, she would pay attention as if every word mattered, and because he knew she was actually listening, he found himself talking more than usual and about subjects he normally would avoid. As he unlocked his front door, he was already imagining the next time they would get together.

"I'm home!" Adam called out as was his custom.

There was no reply.

"Rachel? Did you hear me?"

Still no answer.

When Adam strained his ears to listen, all he heard was the faint electric hum common to modern houses.

Just then, Maggie Sullivan came striding up the front walk. She startled when she saw Adam standing in the open doorway. "Oh, hello," she exclaimed. "You're home. I thought you'd be out until at least eleven." Adam had hired Mrs. Sullivan to babysit Rachel, despite the fact that Rachel had pleaded to be left on her own. To Adam, leaving a fourteen-year-old to fend for herself had seemed like a bad idea.

"I ran home for just a second," Mrs. Sullivan explained, "to let Fritz out." Fritz was a yippy little Boston terrier. He and Adam were not the best of friends. Mrs. Sullivan was a widow, and the obnoxious little Fritz was her constant companion. She would have brought the dog with her while babysitting, had Adam allowed it.

"It's okay," Adam replied mildly, still standing in the entryway. Mrs. Sullivan was a good woman, and he trusted her sense of duty. He called out more loudly, "Rachel? Did you hear me? Answer me."

"She's probably asleep in her room," Mrs. Sullivan suggested when there was no reply. "I'll go check."

"I'll go." Adam headed for the stairs before Mrs. Sullivan could respond.

Rachel wasn't in her room, nor in the bathroom, nor anywhere else that they looked. It was a small house, and there weren't that many places where a teenager could hide. It soon became apparent that Rachel was gone.

After completing their search, Adam and Mrs. Sullivan wound up in the hallway in front of the stairs.

"I was only gone for a couple minutes," Mrs. Sullivan protested. She seemed on the verge of tears.

"I'm sure this is not your fault."

An ugly foreboding struck Adam, and he left to check the latches on the back door and the windows, looking for signs of forced entry. Thankfully, he found none. Likewise, Rachel's room seemed undisturbed. Her bed was made, and nothing appeared to be out of place, until he noticed that her purse and her school backpack were missing. The fact that both were gone made it more likely that his sister had departed on her own volition.

"What should we do?" Mrs. Sullivan asked plaintively.

"Call the police."

Adam's thoughts scattered in different directions. He believed that he knew most of Rachel's friends, but not their telephone numbers. Otherwise, he would've been on the phone immediately. He tried to guess where his sister might've gone, but then found himself wondering why rather than where. Could it be because of his date with Victoria? Had she felt threatened somehow? Or jealous? The idea seemed ludicrous, but who could know the workings of a teenage brain? He also considered climbing in his car and setting out to search the immediate vicinity and surrounding neighborhoods. But then he remembered that the police would be arriving shortly, and they would expect a full account of recent events.

An even more ominous thought came to Adam. Was it possible that his sister had actually been abducted? The very notion sent a wave of terror rushing through him. Such a horror could push his sister over the edge, given her fragile psyche. He thrust the thought from his mind, but it refused to leave.

And then the guilt set in. In recent weeks, he had spent time satisfying his own needs while ignoring his sister's. He had pursued a relationship with Victoria, devoted himself to his online studies, striven to excel in his new position at work, and—the list seemed disconcertingly long. *How could I have been so selfish? What kind of a big brother thinks only of himself and ignores his sister's needs?*

*　　*　　*

Twenty-four hours later, there was still no word—no message from Rachel nor from any assailant. Theo had come over to support his friend. His main contribution was to remind Adam to stay calm and not to continually imagine the worst. He had also prepared a light meal and literally forced Adam to eat.

Deputy Hector Garcia from the county sheriff's office had been detailed to stand watch in the Masters' house in case Rachel's abductor should call with a ransom demand. Thus far, however, Adam's cell phone had rung not even once.

Alerts had been broadcast to all law enforcement agencies within a two-hundred-mile radius. Officers had spoken with Rachel's friends and her teachers at school. A missing person bulletin had been posted on the sheriff's website. Earlier, Adam had been on the verge of setting out to search for Rachel on his own, but Deputy Garcia had dissuaded him.

"Let the cops do their job," the deputy had said. "We have a lot of officers out looking for your sister. They'll find her soon. I'm sure of it."

Despite the stress of having a cop in the house, Adam was grateful for the deputy's presence, in that he had been providing ongoing updates on the status of the investigation, like the one around noon when a possible sighting had been reported. The tip had proven to be bogus.

Adam's history with the deputy had helped him feel more comfortable than he might have with a stranger. Yet occasionally, he sensed that the deputy was watching him, monitoring his behavior. *Am I a suspect?* he wondered. *How could they possibly think I would harm my own flesh and blood?*

Adam stood by the living room window, peering out between the blinds. "Theo, do you know what's worse than knowing that she's missing?" he said over his shoulder

"No, what?" Theo had chosen the straight-back rocker.

"It's not knowing. It's wondering if some pervert is doing something unspeakable."

"Worrying like that doesn't help. Come, sit down." Theo patted the armrest of the couch beside the rocker.

Adam continued to stare into the night.

*　　*　　*

On the third day after Rachel's disappearance, the search for her was beginning to lose steam. The generally accepted presumption was that she had run away on her own accord, another unhappy teenager convinced that she would be better off on the streets than with a sibling who loved her. Adam wasn't buying the conventional wisdom. He felt certain that something bad must have caused her to leave. No matter how depressed she might have been, she never would have abandoned him without a word.

Townsend Electronics had granted Adam a week off, calling it personal time. More than half had already elapsed. At the insistence of the sheriff's department, he had stayed home to be available, should the need arise. He would much rather have been out searching for his sister. Patiently waiting, hoping that the phone would ring, had weighed heavily on his nerves. Eventually, the strain of doing nothing had reached a tipping point.

"That's it," Adam declared to Deputy Garcia. "I'm not going to sit on my ass any longer. You guys might be giving up, but I can't. I can't. Do you understand?"

"I hear you." Deputy Garcia polished off the English muffin and the glass of orange juice Adam had served him. Offering the deputy a light breakfast had become part of Adam's morning routine. As the day wore on, he and the deputy would spend time talking, playing cards, staring at the ceiling, or doing whatever just to make the hours pass more quickly. This morning, however, Deputy Garcia had announced that he had been reassigned and would be leaving.

As he sat back in his chair, Deputy Garcia looked up at Adam. "I can't stop you from searching, but remember to stay alert. On the streets, anything can happen."

"That is precisely why I need to get out there and start looking. Hell, I should've been there already."

The deputy shoved his breakfast plate aside. "What about your meeting this afternoon? You're not going to skip it, are you?"

"I'd like to, but I don't think I should." Being reminded of the meeting he had scheduled for later in the day caused Adam to feel seriously conflicted. He loved his sister and wanted to do all he could to bring her home. At the same time, he recognized that he was being handed an opportunity that might never come along again.

The recruiter for Challenge Gaming had reviewed Adam's application for employment, and there was a real possibility that he might be made general manager of the local franchise. The recruiter had scheduled an interview to evaluate Adam's qualifications in greater detail. The man was staying in a local hotel and would be available for only a few hours. Adam understood that this was his big opportunity, and he had resolved not to blow it.

"Whatever you decide, I wish you well." Deputy Garcia folded his napkin and laid it on the table. He stood up and turned to face Adam. "I've seen how hard this has been for you. I wish we had better news, but at least—well, sometimes no news really is good news. I still believe that if we don't find her first, one day she'll walk through your front door and announce that she's glad to be home."

"I pray to God that you're right," Adam said. "Mind if I call you from time to time? I appreciate the way you've kept me up to date."

"You have my number. If anything turns up, I'll call you." The deputy departed, and the house became intolerably quiet. It was time for Adam to hit the streets, but first, he had a meeting to attend.

Adam grabbed his jacket. The seasons were turning cold again. In a month or so, snow would begin falling. The thought renewed his determination to find his sister.

As he drove to the hotel where the recruiter was staying, rather than work on how he would present himself, he tried to logically plan how he would conduct his search.

* * *

October 1998

Adam triggered his staple gun to tack a leaflet to his sixty-first telephone pole—he'd been keeping count. He'd had a hundred flyers printed up and was determined that each should be displayed where it would do the greatest good. Spiraling outward from the center of town, he had gradually invaded the seedier neighborhoods. As he continued his search, he would boldly approach people he encountered, hand them a flyer, and ask, "Have you seen this girl?"

Universally, the answer thus far had been no. To Adam, it seemed as if his sister had fallen off the planet.

While plodding along the sidewalk, Adam reflected upon his meeting the previous day. From his perspective, the interview had gone quite well. The recruiter had seemed satisfied with the answers he had received. One thing he had repeatedly stressed was that the person they hired would have to be totally reliable. Challenge Gaming would only employ people they could depend on.

Another bit of good news had slipped out during the interview. After eighteen months on the job, Adam would be eligible to purchase his own franchise. Financing could be made available. *Opening a franchise, that's where the real money's to be made*, he remembered thinking. *One day, I'll be the boss.*

However, as with Townsend Electronics, Adam had lied to the recruiter about several details. He had claimed he was twenty-one when in fact, he was only nineteen. He had stated that he was nearing the end of his online studies when in fact, he wasn't even a quarter of the way through his quest for an IT degree. Most serious of all, he had presented himself as having had significant managerial experience, as if holding down an after-school paper route would qualify. He had rationalized his falsehoods by telling himself they were merely little white lies—hardly worth mentioning.

Midmorning sunlight shimmered off the asphalt ahead. While pounding the pavement, he thought about Victoria, about how she smiled, the way she moved, the way her blonde hair flowed down her back when she turned her head. He thought about the way they had discussed the most mundane things as if they were actually interesting. The bottom line was he enjoyed being with her. It had only been five days since their date, but it seemed longer.

Maybe I'm in love. If it's not love, it's something akin to it. Either that, or I'm coming down with something awful.

When he arrived at the telephone pole on the corner of the street he had been trekking, Adam positioned another flyer in preparation for stapling it to the rough wood.

Without warning, something hard was pressed against the base of his neck. "Don't move," said a gruff voice. "Give me your money, or you die. I ain't messing around, man. You do as I say."

Startled, Adam lost his grip on the stapler. It slipped out of his hand. He went to grab for it, but then froze. Instead, he let the stapler fall to the ground with a metallic *thunk*. "My wallet's in my hip pocket."

"Take it out slowly—two fingers only. Now hand it to me over your shoulder, and don't do nothing stupid."

Adam did as he was told.

The person standing behind him snatched the wallet out of Adam's hand and shoved it into his jacket pocket. "What else you got?"

Adam said with a quaver in his voice, "My IDs and some pictures that mean a lot to me are in that wallet. They won't do you any good. Could you take the money and leave me the rest?"

"Shut your face," the voice commanded. "I asked you what you got. Don't be giving me no lip."

Adam thought he had detected a Hispanic accent, but he wasn't sure. "Nothing. I have nothing that would benefit you."

"Oh yeah? You got a watch, don't you? Let me see it."

Without looking behind him, Adam slid up his sleeve and raised his forearm above his shoulder. "It's a cheap watch, not worth more than a couple bucks."

"Give it to me. No fast moves, remember?"

As Adam unbuckled the watch from his wrist, his fingers were shaking so badly, he lost his grip. This time, he grabbed for the watch as it began to fall. As he reached down, the barrel of a gun slammed against his temple. He was knocked to the ground, stunned. He landed on his side, but then rolled onto his back. His head spun, his vision blurred, and a wave of nausea flowed through him. He tried to rise but was too dizzy.

"I told you, no fast moves." Adam's assailant drew back his foot and delivered a vicious kick to his rib cage.

Adam heard a snap like the breaking of a twig. A searing pain shot through his chest. He let out a cry of agony. The pain flared anew when he took in a deep breath.

"Dumb bastard. Why don't you bitches ever listen?"

The sun was in Adam's eyes as he lay on his back looking up. He tried to make out his assailant's features, but the man's face was obscured by a pair of dark sunglasses and a baseball cap pulled low on his forehead. There was a wisp of a goatee on his chin, but that was all Adam could see.

The attacker drew back his foot, as if to deliver another kick, but then turned away and sprinted down the sidewalk.

Adam lay on the cold hard pavement until his head stopped spinning. Then he rose up on one elbow to look around. There was nobody in sight. Apparently, there would be no witnesses to the mugging.

Adam gingerly touched the side of his head. He felt something sticky, and his fingers came away bloody. He then became aware of the trickle of blood that had run down the side of his face. He pulled a tissue out of his front pocket and pressed it against the sore spot on his temple. Maybe it would stop the bleeding.

Adam sat up but did not try to stand. Instead, he picked up his watch and, after looking it over, decided it was still functional. He strapped it on his wrist. Sitting there, he considered what to do next. He knew he needed medical care, but there was no way he could afford an ER visit. As he considered other alternatives, a thought came to him. There was someone he could call upon. Maybe she would help him.

The wind caught the leaflets Adam had been carrying, scattering them along the sidewalk. Before standing, he reached for the stapler. It looked to be scratched, but was otherwise undamaged.

With care, Adam rose to his feet and began trudging back to his car parked half a mile away. By the time he got there, the pain in his head was better, but his ribs were hurting even worse. Very cautiously, he climbed in and drove to Victoria's house.

*　*　*

"Good lord!" Victoria exclaimed when she opened the door to find Adam standing on her front porch. "What happened?"

"I got mugged. I was out looking for my sister, and some thug attacked me. He stole my wallet. It had my driver's license, insurance card, credit cards, and stuff in it. It's weird, but losing my IDs makes me feel like I've ceased to exist."

"You poor thing. Look at you." Victoria reached out, but stopped short of actually touching the side of Adam's face. "Come in." She stepped aside and allowed Adam to enter.

He winced as he crossed the threshold. "The jerk kicked me in the chest. I'm pretty sure he broke a rib. Let me rephrase that. I know he broke a rib."

"We should get you to the hospital. Are you hurt anywhere else?"

"Just my pride, and I'll have to say no to the hospital. I can't afford a trip to the emergency room."

"But what if there's internal damage?" Victoria seemed genuinely concerned.

"Except for the rib and the side of my head, I'm okay. I was a little lightheaded at first, but that went away. I was hoping you could patch me up, if it's not too much trouble. If it is, just say so, and I'll head home."

"It will be no trouble at all. Come with me. All our first aid stuff is in the bathroom cupboard."

"I apologize for intruding like this. You're not in the middle of something, are you?"

"I was ironing laundry. It'll be good to take a break."

Adam followed Victoria to the master bathroom. On previous visits, he had only been as far as the living room. Along the way, he noted that the walls were decorated with watercolors and what appeared to be original oil paintings. "Nice artwork. Very colorful."

"My father used to paint. Most of these are his."

"He has quite a talent. I like the landscapes. He's not painting anymore?"

"Not since his prostate cancer flared up."

"How is your dad doing, by the way?"

Victoria shook her head. "He tries to put on a brave face, but I can see he's in pain."

"Is there anything they can do? I mean in way of treatment."

"He takes medication to ease pain. That's about it. The cancer is already in his bones."

"Is he home?"

"He went to the store to fetch a few items. We're out of milk, and we're getting low on eggs and butter. Here we are." Victoria stepped inside the bathroom and opened the cupboard door. From a plastic bin on the second shelf, she gathered up cotton swabs, a couple rolls of plastic tape of different widths, iodine solution, gauze pads, and a bottle of rubbing alcohol. She arranged the items on the counter beside the sink and turned to Adam. "Take your shirt off. Let's see what damage has been done."

After unbuttoning his shirt, Adam went to slip it off, but the effort caused him to grunt in pain.

"Let me help you." Victoria moved closer and gently slid the shirt off Adam's shoulders.

With her standing so close, Adam could smell the scent of her hair. It smelled like lilacs. For a moment, he forgot about his injuries, that is until she touched the side of his chest where a bruise was forming. "Ouch!" he exclaimed.

"Sorry. Let's tape that. It's not a cure, but it'll help stabilize the rib."

"You were right," Adam said after she had finished applying four strips of two-inch tape. "It does feel better."

"Now for the bloody parts." With a cotton swab soaked in rubbing alcohol, she began dabbing dried blood away from the area of injury on his temple and down the side of his face. When she finished, she commented, "It's a small wound, maybe half an inch. I can close it with Steri-Strips, but that means I'll have to shave some of your hair."

"I'd rather you didn't. I'm kind of vain that way. I'm sure it will heal just fine even if you don't."

"It could get infected. The wound needs to be closed. I could put in a stitch or two."

"With what?"

"A needle and thread. My grandma used to do it all the time when a farmhand would hurt himself."

"Do what you think best."

Victoria left the room, but soon returned with a straight needle and a spool of black thread.

Adam grit his teeth as she began sewing, but was soon relieved to discover that the needle didn't hurt as much as expected. With admiration, he said, "You're pretty good at this. I suspect you've done it before?"

"I volunteered as a candy striper for two years in high school. We got to see a lot of gruesome stuff in the emergency department. That's why I'm saving up to go back to school. I want to be a nurse someday."

"Really. Well, I'd say you're off to a very good start."

Victoria backed up a bit and stood facing Adam with her hands on her hips. She looked him up and down. "Not bad." A mischievous grin crinkled the corners of her eyes.

For a moment, Adam wondered if she was referring to her handiwork or to his physique. When he noticed the grin, he felt a sensation of warmth rise in his cheeks. "Could you help me put my shirt on?"

"If I must." Victoria seemed disappointed.

Adam heard the sound of a car pulling into the garage and then the sound of a door opening into the kitchen. "Vicki, honey," called out a male voice. "I'm home."

"I'll be right there, Dad." Victoria lowered her voice and said to Adam, "Say, are you hungry? Would you like some lunch?"

"Thanks, but I should head home and change into clothes that aren't so bloody. Then I need to get back on the streets to look for my sister."

"I assume that means there's still no word?"

Adam shook his head. "Nothing yet."

"I'm so sorry for what you're going through, but she'll turn up. I've been praying for her safe return."

"Me too. Really, I have."

"I'm glad to hear that," Victoria said with obvious sincerity.

On his way out the front door, Adam said hello and goodbye to Mr. Wayne.

As the door closed behind him, he could hear Mr. Wayne exclaim, "Good lord, Vicki, what did you do to that poor fellow?"

"It's a long story, Dad. Come help me fix lunch, and I'll tell you all about it."

*   *   *

When Adam's week of personal time was used up, he was forced to return to work. He would have continued searching for his sister, but there really was nowhere else to look. Not only had he canvassed the likely neighborhoods where she might have gone, he had crisscrossed the county numerous times, pursuing every possible lead until there were no more leads to follow. At length, he had been forced to concede that Rachel had probably left the area. One possibility was that on the very first day she had hitched a ride and was now in another state. The one thing he could not bring himself to admit was that his sister might be dead.

For the most part, Adam's coworkers at Townsend Electronics refrained from mentioning Rachel's disappearance. Only a few broached the subject, and then only to offer their sympathies. Adam appreciated their thoughtfulness, but even though he wasn't being repeatedly reminded of his loss, he still couldn't get Rachel out of his mind. In his heart, he knew she was alive, but there was nothing more to be done to bring her home.

While standing at his repair bench, attempting to resurrect an unresponsive hard drive, Adam finally came to the realization that his only option going forward would be to wait and hope. The problem was that waiting and hoping felt a lot like giving up.

Adam removed his cell phone from his back pocket and laid it on the repair counter. Maybe the sheriff would call, or maybe the flyers he had posted all over town had attracted somebody's notice. Either way, he didn't want to miss the call when it came in.

Adam soldered a loose power connector back into place. When he fired up the hard drive, it responded appropriately. *Job done*, he thought. *What's next?*

He was about to begin tearing apart a computer with a bad video board when a receptionist from downstairs entered his workspace. For a moment, he thought she intended to talk about his sister, but instead she apologized. "I wanted to get this to you earlier, but I got distracted. I took a message on your behalf. It was from a guy who works for Challenge Gaming. He said you would know who he was. He gave me his name, but I forgot it before I could write it down."

"Thorpe? Gary Thorpe?"

"Yeah, that sounds about right. Thorpe. Anyway, the guy said he wants to offer you a position. He asked if you could meet him at the airport. He's flying in just to see you, and he'll have a forty-five-minute layover. His outbound flight leaves at 11:17 a.m." She handed Adam a standard message form. "Sorry I didn't get this to you sooner, but it's been totally crazy this morning. And now I've got to be getting back." She turned and hurriedly walked away.

Adam took a moment to process what he had just been told. As he stared at the form in his hand, the gist of the message finally sank in. He was about to be offered a position, which he could only assume would be general manager of the local franchise. This was the break he had been hoping for.

He looked at his watch, which still seemed to be working normally. It showed that the time was 10:47 a.m. He had exactly thirty minutes to get to his Jeep, drive across town, park at the airport, and find the recruiter before his flight took off. It would be extremely tight, but if he drove like a maniac, he could make it.

Without even putting his tools away or cleaning up his workspace, Adam dashed for the exit.

Midmorning traffic was light, and he was making good time. He could see the airport in the distance when suddenly, the engine in his Jeep Renegade began to knock and sputter. The car lurched forward when he stepped on the gas, but then quickly lost power. He was barely able to pull over to the side of the road before the engine died. *It's not that old*, he said to himself in disbelief. *It's got less than 125,000 miles on it.* Several times he tried starting the engine, but the starter could barely turn the engine over. Eventually, all it did was make a clicking sound. It was no use. Something mechanical had gone horribly wrong.

Adam consulted his watch—twelve minutes left. He wasn't going to make it. Though he could see the airport, he would never get there in time, not even if he flat-out ran. He reached back to fetch his cell phone out of his hip pocket. He would call the recruiter—he still had the man's number—and explain what had just happened. Then he remembered. His cell phone was lying on his workbench back at Townsend Electronics.

Twelve minutes later, while stranded by the side of the road, Adam watched a plane take off and slowly bank to the east, presumably headed for Cincinnati, Ohio, home base for Challenge Gaming.

*   *   *

"Your table is ready, sir. If you'd care to follow me." The maître d' had approached so quietly that I hadn't noticed him until he was at my elbow.

The aroma of the restaurant's French cuisine reminded me how hungry I was.

Casey and I followed the maître d' into the dining room. En route, Casey commented, "Those must've been difficult times. How did you cope with all that stress? I mean, Grandaunt Rachel vanishing like she did. That alone would have been horrible enough, but to be mugged, have your car vandalized, and lose a major business opportunity—how did you feel when all that was going on?"

"About like you'd expect." When we came to our table, I sat down and gathered my precisely folded napkin off the dinner service in front of me. Opening it, I spread it on my lap. "At the time, I viewed my misfortunes as nothing more than a run of bad luck. In these later years, however, I've come to think of them as essential elements in a larger narrative."

"What do you mean?" Casey also placed his napkin on his lap.

The maître d' handed me my menu.

I looked up at him and said, "What's good tonight? Is there something special you would recommend?"

"Everything is good, certainly, but the beef bourguignon would be an excellent choice, or perhaps the coq au vin."

"I'll have the bourguignon," I declared.

"And I'll take the coq au vin." Casey sipped ice water from his crystal goblet. "This is a fancy place."

The maître d' smiled as he walked away.

Casey smoothed a wrinkle out of the linen tablecloth. "What did you mean a larger narrative?"

"It's kind of like a zen thing. I've come to believe that seemingly random events are all somehow interconnected and that everything has a purpose."

"Divine ordination. Is that what you're saying?"

"In a manner of speaking, I guess."

"Seriously?"

"Absolutely. Haven't you noticed there's a trajectory to your life? One thing follows another until something comes along to nudge you in a different direction. And then later, when you look back, you see that you've been molded by forces beyond your control."

"How does that relate to the story you just told me?"

"Take Rachel's disappearance, for instance. Who knows what my life might have been like if she hadn't disappeared? As it was, I was no longer responsible for her upbringing. I was free to pursue other objectives. Don't get me wrong. I missed Rachel terribly. I would have given anything to have her come home safely, but that wasn't the course my life was destined to follow."

"How do you know her vanishing wasn't just a terrible but meaningless tragedy? Why read something more into it? Do you know what I mean?"

"To me, it's become clear that her being gone was in fact a lesson I was supposed to learn. Her absence taught me to cherish what I have because who knows when the things you care about might be taken away."

"What about the mugging? Did you learn anything from that?"

"I learned to be more aware of my surroundings. For example, our maître d' is packing heat. If you look closely, you'll notice that his right pant leg has a slight irregularity. He's wearing an ankle holster. And the woman seated at the bar, she never once touched her drink. Instead, she was watching the young couple seated in the booth by the kitchen. I'm pretty sure she's conducting some sort of surveillance."

"And the mugger? Did they ever catch the guy?"

"Not to my knowledge. I'd like to believe that his misdeeds carried with them their own punishment."

"You mean 'Live by the sword, die by the sword'?"

"Precisely. Every action has consequences. I wouldn't be at all surprised if it turned out that he tried to rob someone skilled in self-defense and was severely punished for his transgressions."

"Your car dying like it did? Are you saying that wasn't a coincidence, that God trashed your engine to keep you from being hired as a general manager?"

"Actually, I know for certain it wasn't a coincidence, but then neither was it an act of divine providence. It turned out that someone poured sugar into my gas tank. Months later, I found out who that someone was. The engine was a total loss. I had to borrow money from Theo to have a rebuilt motor installed."

"For real? Your sister goes missing. You're the victim of a brutal mugging. And then some heartless villain sabotages your car? That's low."

"Yes, it was, and you'll be even more disgusted when I tell you who did it, but let's not get ahead of ourselves."

"Was it Alice Cunningham? Was she out for revenge?"

"No, it wasn't Alice, but for now, that's all I'm going to say."

"So once again, I have to wait?"

"I'm afraid so."

"Okay, you're the storyteller. Then tell me this: all these bad things, did anything good happen, or were all your experiences negative?"

"There were several good things. For one, my relationship with Victoria was growing stronger. We'd been going to the Presbyterian Church, but neither of us were particularly enthralled with the Sunday sermons. So we decided to change churches. We began attending early worship services at the Capstone Chapel. Mostly I was going to be with Victoria."

"What else was good?"

"I made a new friend. When I was out posting handbills and searching for my sister, I came across a stray cat, a calico. He followed me for several blocks, meowing and trying to rub against my ankle. When I couldn't stand it any longer, I bundled him into my car and brought him home. I named him Jinx because that was the way I was feeling at the time—jinxed. He turned out to be a really good cat. He lived with me for almost a decade, and then he too just disappeared. I think he simply wandered off to die."

Leaning forward, Casey braced his forearms on the table. "All the bad things that happened, taken together, how would you interpret them? What lessons did you learn?"

I paused to consider my reply. "I suppose I'd have to say that they taught me firsthand that evil is for real, and sometimes, it lives inside of us. Every man fights a battle that's as old as humanity. We get to choose between doing what's right or doing what's wrong. Sometimes we choose to do the right thing, other times we don't. Either way, it's our choice. But when we make a choice, for it to mean something, there must be legitimate alternatives to choose between. If our choice is between good and evil, then not only must good exist, but evil must exist as well. Evil isn't simply an absence of good any more than darkness is an absence of light."

Casey stroked his chin while he pondered for a moment. "Let me see if I can summarize the point you're making. You're saying it's up to each of us to choose between good and evil. Pardon me for saying so, but that seems fairly simplistic."

"That's because your summary is only part of the equation. It doesn't take into account the sin nature of man. There's something inside us that wants to choose evil. We can't help ourselves. It's who we are."

"Do you think that's why we do things we know are wrong?"

"Absolutely. By the way, it's not an excuse, but it is a reason. The good news is we can change."

Casey brightened up a bit. "Do you really think so?"

"If we sincerely want to, we can learn to overcome our sin nature and consistently choose good, not evil. But to accomplish this, we need help."

Out of the corner of my eye, I noticed a waiter approaching carrying a tray of food. "For now, it looks like we'll have to suspend this conversation till after we eat."

The waiter served our dinners.

During the meal, Casey and I chatted about his plans for the future. Again, I sensed that my grandson was troubled when our discussion touched upon how he felt about enrolling in law school and what kind of lawyer he would be.

When we'd finished eating, we headed back to the bar for an after-dinner aperitif. On our way, we passed by a table upon which lay a newspaper. The headline read, "Fairmont Remembered," which reminded me that it was the six-month anniversary of that horrible massacre.

Casey tapped the newspaper. "See that? Isn't that what you've been saying? Those two killers chose to do something undeniably evil. They slaughtered sixteen people, including themselves."

"Indeed. In fact, I would say that if their actions don't qualify as irrefutable evidence for a sin nature, I don't know what would."

"And you're telling me they could have changed their nature before they committed those murders?"

"Not without help, but yes. That is what I'm saying. Any one of us can change our character if we truly want to, but we need help to get it done. I hope this will all become clearer as we go along."

"Me too." Casey led the way back to the table we had previously occupied.

7

A GLIMPSE OF THE DIVINE

March 1999

Five months after losing his chance to work for Challenge Gaming, Adam found himself sitting in what he had come to regard as Humphrey's office at Townsend Electronics. The space was, in fact, a tiny room that served as the custodial staff's base of operations. Stout metal shelves lined three walls. Arrayed on the shelves according to function was an assortment of cleaning supplies and implements. One of Humphrey's principal duties was to make sure that the shelves remained fully stocked.

The small desk at which Adam sat was principally used for filling out requisition forms, organizing work schedules, keeping the daily logs, and similar duties that ensured that the Townsend Electronics Custodial Department was functioning properly.

"How much longer do you think you'll be?" Adam began idly fingering a rubber plug that looked to have been a stopper for a jug filled with this or that solvent. "It's twenty minutes past quitting time. Let's get a move on." Even a casual observer would have gathered that Adam was anxious to be on his way.

"Just one more task to complete." Humphrey continued gathering the supplies he would need and arranging them on the wheeled cart he would take with him. "There's an ink spill in the billing office on the second floor. One of the girls was replacing a printer cartridge. Somehow, she managed to break it open."

"I thought you had to hit those things with a hammer to get them open."

"I don't know how she did it, but there's a puddle of ink on the floor. I have to get it cleaned up before it leaves a permanent stain. Fifteen minutes, okay?"

"We're going to be late to Bud's party. You'd best get a move on."

Humphrey snapped, "What does it look like I'm doing? It's not like I can wave my magic wand and have messes mysteriously disappear. You computer jockeys, you have no appreciation for what it takes to maintain a clean environment."

"Easy. I wasn't criticizing. I know you work hard. It's just you—well, you know me and how I hate being late." Adam remembered his own birthday party. He had just turned twenty. To celebrate, the other three Horsemen had arranged to throw him a surprise party. However, a sudden influx of busted computers had held him up for two hours past quitting time. His tardiness had cast a wet blanket over the rest of the evening, even though it wasn't his fault.

As Humphrey was about to guide the wheeled cart into the hall, he stopped and turned around. "You know what you could do, if you're willing? My jacket is in my locker. If you would grab it for me, it would save a little time getting out of here."

"I can do that." Adam rose from the swivel chair and stepped closer, hand out, palm up. "I'll need the key to your padlock."

Humphrey fished in his pocket for a key ring that held half a dozen keys. He removed the smallest one and flipped it to Adam. "It's locker 127. If you see my Grizzlies baseball cap, bring it too. I don't remember whether or not I wore it this morning."

Humphrey and his wheeled cart disappeared down the corridor, and Adam headed off to fetch the requested items.

As Adam climbed the stairs to the second-floor break room, he reflected on his time with the company and how he had risen from shipping clerk to lead repair technician. He was proud of what he had accomplished, but there was a problem. His career had stalled. His only option, if he wanted to move ahead, would be to transfer to administration and become an executive. There was no other way he could earn a promotion. His online coursework at Ridgecrest College was still on track, but progressing slowly. It would take another eighteen months to earn his bachelor of science degree.

When Adam reached the bank of lockers that spanned the back wall of the break room, he quickly found number 127 and unlocked it. Humphrey's gray windbreaker was hanging on a hook, but the baseball cap was nowhere to be seen.

As he was about to close the locker, Adam noticed a sprinkling of white substance on the shelf at the top of the locker. At first, he imagined it to be some sort of cleaning powder or perhaps salt, but when he looked more closely, he noted that the white substance had a rougher, more granular consistency. In fact, it looked like sugar. He was again about to close the locker when curiosity got the better of him. He moistened the tip of his index finger and gently touched it to the white substance. Carefully he put a few granules on the tip of his tongue. It tasted sweet, like sugar. It was sugar.

Why, he wondered, *should there be a residue of sugar in Humphrey's locker?*

Adam's first inclination, because of his compulsive neatness, was to brush the locker clean. However, it was Humphrey's locker, not his, and he decided to leave well enough alone. Instead, he closed the locker and reset the padlock. As he descended the stairs and turned down the main corridor, an unpleasant thought popped into his mind.

"No, it can't be." Adam stopped dead in his tracks. "He couldn't have. There's no way he would have…"

Adam resumed walking, but much more slowly. By the time he returned to the custodial office, he knew what needed to be done.

Ten minutes later, Humphrey came back from his cleaning chores on the second floor. "Well, that's it. Done for the day. We're out of here."

"You go ahead. I'll catch up with you at Bud's house. Something has come up, and it can't wait."

"You sure? I don't mind waiting."

"No, I'm sure. You go on. Tell Bud and Theo that I might be a little late."

"Okay, if you say so." Humphrey slipped his jacket on over his custodial work shirt and then departed.

Adam listened as Humphrey's footfalls faded away in the distance.

When he was sure that Humphrey had gone, he headed for the security office. After knocking on the door, he opened it without waiting and stepped inside. Greta Marsh, the security officer on duty, sat on a wheeled office chair looking up at a bank of flat-panel displays. On some screens, the view was static; on others, the image shifted every fifteen to thirty seconds.

Greta wheeled herself around when she heard the door opening. "Hey there, Adam. What's up?"

"Hi, Greta. I was wondering, the data you collect from the surveillance system"—he indicated the bank of monitors—"how long do you keep it?"

"At least six months. Sometimes longer. Why?"

"And these cameras, they see everything, including the parking lot?"

"Yes, they do. They're positioned for maximum coverage. If you want to know if your shoelace is untied, we can tell you."

"What about a particular day, say, approximately five months ago? I'd like to see what you have for the north parking lot. It would've been early in the morning, sometime between eight and ten thirty. Is that doable?"

"I assume this is important?"

"Would I bother you if it wasn't?" Adam grinned broadly.

"Your masculine charms won't work on me. Would you like to share the reason for your request?"

"I have a hunch about something bad that happened that day. I'm hoping you can help me disprove my theory."

"I see. The archive is next door in our storage room. Wait here. Oh, and keep an eye on these monitors. If you see anything suspicious at all, give a holler."

"Got it."

"Good. I'll be right back."

When Greta returned three minutes later, she was carrying a video disc in her hand. "I assume this is the date you were looking for." She slipped the CD into a player and hit the Play button.

Adam watched the screen above the player for a bit and then said, "Can you fast-forward about half an hour?"

The image zipped by at double speed until Adam exclaimed, "Stop!"

The image froze.

He pointed to the screen. "Back up two minutes, and zoom in on that spot if you can. Good. Now play it forward, slowly. Good. But now, it's kind of fuzzy."

"Let's see what happens if I adjust the contrast and maybe make it a little brighter. There, that's better." The image on the screen became sharper and easier to make out.

"I'll be damned," Adam said under his breath. "I never would've believed it." A wave of disgust rose up in his gut.

Greta peered closely at the screen. "Who is that? Do we know him?"

"We thought we did. Now I'm not so sure."

"What's he doing? I can't see from this view. Perhaps one of the other cameras got a better look. Let me check." The guard started to rise from her chair.

Adam rested a hand on her shoulder. "There's no need. We know what's happening, don't we?"

Greta studied the screen again and blinked. "Is that…?"

"Yes, it is. Tell me, would one of these discs play in a standard DVD player?"

"Sure, unless it's a genuine antique."

"Would you mind if I took this disc with me? I need to show it to some friends."

"I'm really not supposed to—"

"This truly is important. Besides, if you do me this favor, I'll bring you a nice homemade cherry pie."

"You scoundrel. You know how much I love cherry pie."

"What do you say? Will you let me borrow the disc?"

"Oh, go ahead. Just be sure it comes back in the same condition it's in now."

"I'll take extra special care." Adam crossed his heart and held up three fingers in a Boy Scout salute.

"Just make darn sure it doesn't come back erased." Then Greta said more to herself than to Adam, "Though I can't remember the last time anybody wanted to review one of our archive discs."

"Don't worry. I'll be exceedingly careful."

With the DVD safely stored in a protective sleeve, Adam headed for Bud's birthday party. On his way out the door, he asked himself, *Why didn't I think of scanning the video archives when the sabotage first happened? Am I that witless?* Then he remembered the stress that had been heaped upon him: Rachel's disappearance, the mugging, losing the use of his car. *Okay, you're forgiven*, he thought as he fired up the Jeep's new engine and drove away.

*　　*　　*

During the drive to Bud's apartment, Adam had time to think about Humphrey's betrayal, and the more he thought about it, the darker his mood became.

Bud Taylor lived in a fourplex. His was the upstairs apartment on the east side. With only one bedroom and one bath, it was modest, even by working-class standards, but for Bud, it was most satisfactory since he was independent and living on his own.

Nearly six months had passed since the Four Horsemen's most recent reunion. Rather than wait another six months for the next scheduled get-together, Bud had decided to host his own birthday party.

As Adam climbed the outside stairs, he heard music playing, a pop tune from his high school days. After ringing the doorbell, he drew his coat tighter around his chest as a March breeze carrying the last of winter's chill flowed past.

When Bud opened the door, he was wearing a fez-shaped party hat. Several paper leis hung around his neck. He also had a beer in his hand and a smile on his face.

Bud was by far the beefiest of the Four Horsemen and the most athletic. In high school, he had excelled in both football and baseball. When he saw Adam standing on his front landing, he clapped him on the back and invited him in. "You're late, as usual. Grab yourself a beer. There are snacks on the kitchen table, and you're welcome to anything you find in the fridge." When he saw the DVD in Adam's hand, he pointed and said, "Will you look at that. Adam brought us some adult entertainment?"

"Not exactly." Adam crossed the threshold. "But I think we should watch it together, the four of us." When Adam glanced around the apartment, he startled when he noticed there was a young woman present. She appeared to be in her late teens or early twenties. A brunette by nature, she had strands of purple hair and a nose piercing.

"Oh, right," Bud said when he noticed that Adam was staring at the young woman. "This is Ellie. She's a friend. I hope you don't mind, but even if you do, she stays. We kind of like each other."

"How you doing?" Adam said politely, and then thought, *I hope her being here isn't going to be a problem.* He had visualized what he intended to do and several of the scenarios that might subsequently unfold.

Ellie nodded her response.

"Welcome, compadre," Theo called out from the corner of the room where he lounged on a large throw pillow, hippie style. He too had a beer in his hand.

Humphrey, also lying on pillows on the floor, spoke up. "I see you made it." Adam detected an edge of disappointment, but maybe it was his imagination. Humphrey continued, "I thought maybe you'd decided not to come."

Reflexively, Adam balled his fists. "And miss a chance to put things right?"

Humphrey ignored the challenge. Instead, he said, "By the way, Bud, how goes the college experience? Are they treating you okay at MSU?"

Adam advanced farther into the room but remained standing. He tried hard not to stare at Humphrey for fear the rage smoldering within him might provoke him to do something rash. *Violence isn't the answer*, he told himself. *Instead, I will heap a full measure of shame and loathing upon my adversary's brow.*

"It's going well enough," Bud replied, "though my schedule is kind of rough. I'm in school five days a week, and I work nights and weekends. I don't get a lot of self time or sleep time for that matter."

"You're still working as a security guard, aren't you?" Theo's words were slightly slurred.

"I am. It's good work. The pay's okay, and I can study when everything is quiet."

Humphrey said, "Imagine, only three more years to go."

Bud made an unhappy face. "Thanks for reminding me."

Adam moved closer to Bud and said in a quiet voice, "Do you still have your DVD player?"

"Yes, sir. It's even hooked up to the TV. I assume you're asking because you want to play that disc in your hand."

Adam realized that the moment of truth was at hand. He could play the DVD and expose Humphrey's betrayal, forever ending their friendship, or he could slip the DVD back into his pocket and go on as if nothing had happened—but that would require forgiving his duplicity, something he was unwilling to do. It took Adam only a couple seconds to make his decision. He extracted the DVD from its sleeve and handed it to Bud. "I want all of you to see this. Even you, Ellie."

At the mention of her name, the young woman brightened.

Bud inserted the DVD into the player and pushed the Play button. The surveillance video sprang to life on the TV screen.

"Could you fast-forward a bit?" Adam said to Bud. "I'll tell you when to stop."

Bud did as asked, and a short time later, Adam exclaimed, "Now! Stop. Go back. Rewind just a little. Right there. This is what I want you guys to see." He pointed to the screen. "See that? That's my Jeep. Now watch."

A man wearing a gray windbreaker came into view. He walked about halfway along the driver side and stopped just in front of the rear fender. The video clearly showed that he was carrying two things. One was a funnel and the other was a bulging paper sack. The man looked around, as if to make sure no one was watching.

Adam glowered at Humphrey. "Do you recognize yourself? That is you, is it not? Come on, man. Admit what you did. Tell these guys how you betrayed me."

Bud peered closely at the screen. "Humphrey, that sure looks like you. I recognize the way you move and the way you toss your head to get the hair out of your eyes."

"Now here it comes," said Adam, still staring daggers at Humphrey. "Pay attention."

The man in the video stooped down. It could be clearly seen that he was doing something to the car, but because of the camera angle, it wasn't clear exactly what.

"Why did you do it?" Adam snarled, his voice filled with loathing.

"What are you accusing him of doing?" Bud said, suddenly alert.

"The stuff in the brown paper bag is the sugar he poured into my gas tank. Not only do I have this video, I found traces of sugar in his locker where he must've spilled some." Adam pointed directly at his adversary. "Come on, Humphrey, man up. You sabotaged my car. You know it, and I know it. Now admit it."

Theo's look of disbelief announced that he was having a hard time accepting what he was hearing. "Is this true? Did you really sabotage Adam's Jeep? Are you the one who cost him his chance to work for Challenge Gaming? Was it you?"

Humphrey seemed to shrink into himself.

Adam pressed his attack. "For once in your life, take responsibility. Don't be a coward! Tell us the truth!"

Something seemed to snap inside of Humphrey. "I am not a coward!" he yelled as he surged to his feet and lunged at Adam.

Adam was ready for the assault. He slipped to the side and delivered a vicious right hook into the center of Humphrey's abdomen. Humphrey yelped in pain and collapsed to his knees. He groaned as he wrapped both arms around his midsection.

Adam stood over Humphrey, his fists at the ready. "Are you going to tell them the truth, or do you want some more?" He drew back his right arm as if preparing to deliver another blow.

"All right. I admit I did it. I'm sorry. I was angry." He gave Adam a pleading look. "Ever since high school, you're the one who gets all the breaks. All I get is the dregs. You think I like being a custodian? Not on your life. You're always first, and I'm always second. Man, I hate that. It's like I'm forever in your shadow."

With obvious revulsion, Theo said, "And that gives you the right to vandalize his car? You cost him $3,700 for a new engine, not to mention missing out on a major opportunity. How could you do such a thing? You were his friend. Man, you need to pay him back."

"You always did take his side," Humphrey muttered under his breath.

"Not without good reason," Theo shot back.

Adam gave a dismissive wave of his hand. "I don't want a thing from you. In fact, I don't even want to know you. As far as I'm concerned, either you quit the Four Horsemen, or I will. I mean, how could you betray me like you did? We've been buddies since high school. And then you keep quiet all these months and let me wonder who did that to me? How could you?"

Suddenly, Adam thought of Alice Cunningham and how he had kept silent and let her be falsely judged. A gush of shame arose within him.

Theo spoke up. "I agree with Adam. As far as I am concerned, you're out of the group."

Bud backed up a pace, as if to distance himself from Humphrey. "As much as I hate doing this, based on your own admission, I concur."

"I guess that makes it unanimous." Humphrey stood up and brushed himself off. "I won't stay where I'm not wanted. You know, you may not believe this, but I was going to tell you. I'd planned on confessing one day when you were less tender about what had happened. Honestly, I was."

Humphrey squared his shoulders and exited the apartment.

The remaining Horsemen mutely stared at one another. When Adam glanced at Ellie, he was embarrassed to see that she was visibly shaken by what had just transpired.

*   *   *

August 2001

Two years and five months after Humphrey was banished from the Four Horsemen, Adam and Victoria were walking hand in hand among the carnival sideshows at the Western Montana Fair. Missoula's midsummer temperatures had begun to recede from their July highs. A canopy of stars shimmered in a cloudless sky. The mood throughout the country was generally optimistic. In January, George W. Bush had been inaugurated president, and the tragedies of 9/11 had yet to occur. Internationally, the news was equally benign. Also in January, an earthquake in India had killed more than twenty thousand people and left more than a million people homeless. Otherwise, there had been surprisingly few catastrophes of note. All in all, it seemed a divine night for a date.

"I really am proud of you," Victoria said, continuing a line of conversation that had begun shortly after their arrival at the fair. "Yes, I know it took a long time, but now you have a bachelor's degree. That should make you feel good about yourself."

Adam had at last completed his online coursework at Ridgecrest College and had passed his final exams. That morning, his diploma had arrived in the mail—bachelor of science in information technology. He had proudly framed it and hung it on his wall.

"Slow and steady wins the race," Adam declared, quoting one of his mother's favorite sayings. "It was frustrating taking one course at a time. I often felt like I was spinning my wheels, going nowhere fast, but that's what it took to hold down a full-time job while going to school."

"Now you can look for a better job, if you choose to do so."

"I've already sent out a few résumés. The demand for information technologists is low right now, but I imagine something will turn up—eventually."

"You won't have to move away, will you?"

"And leave you? Not a chance."

Victoria seemed greatly relieved. "Oh, look!" she exclaimed. "Cotton candy. I love that stuff. Come on. If you buy me some, I'll pay for your next game." She indicated the carnival booths that surrounded them.

Victoria took Adam's hand and dragged him toward the cotton candy vendor.

Rachel would have loved this. The thought had come to Adam out of the blue. No trace of his sister had yet been found, and he had nearly given up hope that she was still alive. *It's sad that she can't be here.* He put the thought out of his mind, as he had done so many times before.

"Two, please," Victoria said to the cotton candy vendor. He spun up two cones and handed them over. She passed one to Adam, who paid the man. When Adam took his first bite, he wound up with a chunk of cotton candy stuck to his chin. Victoria laughed as she gently plucked the sugary confection off his face and then popped it into her mouth. She then licked her fingers.

As they strolled off to explore the carnival, Adam studied Victoria out of the corner of his eye. She seemed happy, with an almost childlike delight. Although animated by a sunny disposition, she could be single-mindedly stubborn when it came to defending a cherished position. There was no telling when her obstinacy might emerge. Also, she had a tendency to latch on to some of the most peculiar notions or defend some of the strangest points of view. Still, over the four years they had been dating, his affection for her had grown exponentially.

After subjecting themselves to several of the fair's rides like the bumper cars and the Viking Ship—a pendulum ride—they needed a break from the kinetic attractions. As they strolled around a bit, they found themselves in front of the ring toss.

"I'll bet you can't land all three," Victoria teased. "Go ahead, it's my treat." She dipped her hand into her purse and pulled out a dollar bill, which she passed to the carny manning the booth. In exchange, he started to hand her three rings, but she pointed to Adam. "Those are for him."

Adam gently tossed the first ring, and it encircled the neck of a milk bottle.

"Very good," Victoria said with a show of encouragement.

The second ring also found its mark.

Victoria clapped her hands. "Excellent. Only one to go. Steady now."

"Let me concentrate," Adam chided. He took a deep breath and lightly tossed the ring. It missed.

"Oh, what a shame," Victoria said with mock sorrow. Then she giggled.

"Sir, your prize." The carny gestured toward the back of the booth. "You can pick one from the second shelf."

"I'll take that one." Adam pointed to a bobblehead hula dancer. He looked at Victoria. "I'm going to put this on my dashboard to remind me of you." It was his turn to laugh.

Victoria swayed her hips to and fro. "What should we do now? Are you hungry?"

"I've already eaten too much. I don't think there's room for anything more."

"Well, what about another ride?"

"You're on. Lead the way."

Victoria briefly surveyed the fairgrounds and then headed in the direction of the Tilt-a-Whirl. "I used to love riding this when I was a kid. We'd get it spinning around and around. I got so dizzy, I thought I'd be sick."

"That sounds like a lot of fun. You know, I read an article about this ride not that long ago. It was invented by a man named Herbert Sellner." Adam recited from memory: "'The spinning car you sit in is attached at a fixed rotational point to a disk which also spins.' Old Mr. Sellner called his ride controlled chaos. To me, it looks like a great way to rid myself of the food I've eaten."

Victoria gave Adam a wry smile. "You know some of the oddest things. How can you remember all that stuff?"

"I don't know. I read, and it sticks with me."

"I wish I had your talent."

Looking ahead as they approached the ride, Adam suddenly stopped dead in his tracks. "I'll be damned."

"What's wrong?" Victoria said, halting beside him.

"Let's go find another ride, why don't we? I don't think this is the one we want."

"Why not?"

Adam turned away and hooked a thumb toward the ride behind him. "You see that fellow over there, the guy running the ride? I know him. You may not remember, but I told you about him a couple years ago. His name is Bogart, Humphrey Bogart—"

"For real?"

"It's a nickname. His real name is Michael Bogart. He used to be my friend, that is, until he betrayed me."

"What did he do?"

"He deliberately scuttled my chance to land a great job, a job that would've been perfect for me, a job I really wanted. The short of it is he destroyed our friendship. Let's go find a different ride."

Adam was about to walk away when an all-too-familiar voice stopped him. "Adam? Adam Masters? Is that you? Come on over here and say hi. Bless my soul. It's been, what?"

"Not long enough," Adam muttered under his breath. With a sigh of resignation, he turned and approached the ride where Humphrey stood waiting. Victoria followed.

"Man, how have you been?" Humphrey extended his hand.

Adam ignored the gesture. Instead, he replied flatly, "Doing well enough."

"Still carrying a grudge, are we?"

"We're celebrating," Victoria interjected brightly, as if hoping to change the mood. "Adam just earned his bachelor of science degree in information technology."

"Is that right? It took you long enough." Humphrey grinned. "Just teasing. Congrats. I can appreciate how much effort that must've taken."

Adam shoved his hands into his pockets. "So this is where you're working now? I wondered what happened to you." Forty-eight hours after being banished from the Four Horsemen, Humphrey had quit his job at Townsend Electronics and dropped out of sight.

"Six months now. Do you want to ride? I'll let you on for free."

"No thanks, Humphrey. I don't think we will."

"It's Michael now. I've gone back to using my given name. Nobody calls me Humphrey anymore." Humphrey/Michael tilted his head, as if sizing Adam up. "Are you still working at Townsend?"

"I am, but now that I have my degree, I'll be looking to move into something more challenging."

"Good luck with that."

Adam felt his body tense up. "What's that supposed to mean?"

"Nothing. It didn't mean nothing." Humphrey/Michael turned his attention to Victoria. With a lustful grin, he said, "Who's your friend?"

"Somebody you don't know." Adam took hold of Victoria's arm and gently turned her away. "Come on. We need to be somewhere else."

Humphrey/Michael seemed offended. He called out, "Hey, don't go away mad."

Adam and Victoria continued walking. Victoria seemed perplexed. "After all this time, and you're still mad at him?"

Adam clenched his jaw and remained silent.

When they were out of sight of the Tilt-a-Whirl, Victoria stopped and turned to face Adam. "I don't think I've ever seen you this upset. It's not healthy. You need to learn to forgive him."

"I thought I had, but seeing him in person, all I feel is this deep-seated loathing."

"You remember what Pastor Hudson says about forgiveness?"

"I remember. If we want to be forgiven, we must forgive. Someday, maybe, but not yet."

"That's not a good attitude. We're supposed to love our enemies—do good to those that harm us."

"How do you love a snake who deliberately ruined your life?"

Victoria placed her hands on her hips and looked Adam up and down. "Your life doesn't look ruined to me."

"You know what I mean. He betrayed me. That's one of the worst things you can do to a person. If I forgive him, it would be like it never happened. No. I'm not going to give him the satisfaction of thinking everything is all right because it's not."

"You don't forgive him for his benefit. You forgive him for yours." Victoria turned and began walking, dragging Adam along with her. "Come on. Let's go play."

Thirty yards farther on, she stopped and again turned to look into Adam's eyes. "Adam Tiberius Masters, do you know that I love you?"

"Yeah, I think you've mentioned it a time or two."

"I'm serious."

"I know."

"What I'm trying to say is, I want you. I know we agreed to wait, but now, I'm not so sure. What I mean is, when you're ready, so am I."

"Are you sure? We talked about this."

"I know, but… Look, you don't have to be afraid. There's nothing that's going to hurt you. I'll be gentle. I promise." Victoria chuckled.

"I'll think about it. It's the first time—it's a big step."

"It's a step we can take together. Just let me know."

"I will." Adam wondered how much longer he could keep his girlfriend at arm's length. He didn't want to lose her, but at the same time, the thought of having sex terrified him. It wasn't the physical intimacy he feared. In fact, he was strongly attracted to Victoria. It was the possibility that as his lover, she might come to know him as he really was, a battered, worthless individual who could never truly measure up. Repeatedly demeaned and belittled as a child, whatever self-esteem he might've clung to had been beaten out of him, leaving behind a worthless loser, and he needed to make sure that person stayed locked away inside.

Victoria slipped her arm through Adam's arm, and together, they turned toward the giant Ferris wheel.

*   *   *

July 2002

Eleven months after the Western Montana Fair, Adam and Victoria had two new reasons to celebrate. Gunnar Manufacturing had just hired Adam to manage its in-house computer networks, plus it was Adam's twenty-third birthday. In recognition of both occasions, the couple decided to throw their own private party.

Adam had driven straight from work to Victoria's apartment. He rang the doorbell, and when Victoria answered, she was wearing a plaid blouse, a pair of old jeans with holes in the knees, and well-worn cross trainers.

"You're early," she said as she stepped aside to let him enter. "I was going to change into something more alluring before you got here."

"I left early. I couldn't wait to see you." Adam edged closer so he could wrap one arm around her waist. He planted a quick kiss on her lips.

Victoria smiled. "You're forgiven. Why didn't you let yourself in? You have your own key."

"In case you had something special planned, I didn't want to ruin the surprise."

"I doubt you could ruin it if you tried," Victoria said coyly.

Adam wondered, *What is that supposed to mean*? He sensed it would be wrong to ask. He removed his shoes. The plush carpet felt good against his feet. "You've been here three weeks. How do you like the place so far?" He indicated the boxes still stacked in the corners and the oddly arranged furniture.

"To be honest, I miss my home, but selling was the right thing to do. With Dad gone, it was just too much house to care for."

"You've hung several of his paintings. They look nice. The walls aren't so bare."

"They remind me of him." An aura of sadness came into Victoria's eyes, but passed quickly.

"You miss him."

"Of course I do."

"Please don't take offense, but why aren't you more distraught? I mean, you seem to be coping extremely well."

"I have my faith to sustain me."

Over the years they had been together, the subject of faith had come up many times, usually following their Sunday morning visits to Capstone Chapel. Adam was still undecided as to how he felt. Rather than invite another discussion that would again challenge his spirituality, he steered the conversation to a different topic. Pointing to a watercolor hanging on the wall beside him, he said. "That is you, isn't it, holding that fish? You look to be, what? Seven?"

"Eight actually. That was the first fish I ever caught. I was so proud. Dad had taken me camping on the Clark Fork River. It was just the two of us."

In that moment, Adam realized just how much he envied her pleasant memories of her father.

Victoria turned toward the kitchen. "So how was your first day? Are you going to like working for your new employer?"

Adam trailed behind. "I think so. So far, the people I've met seem nice enough, but there's an awful lot to do. Most of it is really technical. I'll need to keep my wits about me. It makes me wish I had put more effort into studying for my degree."

In the kitchen, Victoria reached up and brought a bottle and two glasses down from a cupboard shelf. She poured two fingers of scotch into each glass and handed one to Adam. Raising her glass, she said, "A toast to your new job. May you do well and prosper thereby."

They clinked glasses, and Adam took a healthy sip. The amber liquid burned going down. "Whoa. I'd forgotten how strong that stuff is."

Victoria took a small sip and then set her glass down on the counter. "What will be your responsibilities, precisely?"

About to sit down, Adam noticed that the kitchen table—an assemblage of tubular chrome and glass—was new. He gave Victoria an inquisitive look.

"I bought it at a garage sale. It appeared to be in good condition, and the price was right."

Adam decided he approved; the kitchen could do with a touch of modern. "My official title is network supervisor. It's my job to keep Gunnar's in-house networks up and running."

"After you mentioning that Gunnar is a 3D printing company, I found a video of 3D printing online. It's fascinating the way they can craft intricate three-dimensional objects one thin layer at a time."

Adam downed another swallow of his scotch and again made a wry face. "In a nutshell, that's what they do. Gunnar's specialty is fabricating one-of-a-kind items. Take the project the team was working on today. A company called Free-Flow Plumbing builds sump pumps. One of their employees came up with an idea for a new valve assembly. Free-Flow took a look at the employee's idea and decided his valve would almost certainly make their pumps more efficient, but to test their theory, they needed a prototype. So they came to Gunnar."

"How do you fit in as a network supervisor?"

"Well, the process goes something like this: The client creates a blueprint that includes dimensions, orientations, and tolerances, plus a precise description of how the movable parts are expected to function. Based on the blueprint, a data table is drawn up and given to Gunnar's engineers. The engineers design a three-dimensional CAD rendering, which can be rotated, twisted, turned, resized, or viewed from any angle. When the graphical model is perfect, it's sent back to the customer for final approval.

"If the customer signs off on the design, the engineers then turn the project over to the programmers who translate the rendering into a set of algorithms. The algorithms are then passed on to the print technicians, who oversee the operation of one or more 3D printers. The end result is a complex valve assembly that would have been nearly impossible to build by hand.

"And to answer your question, the way I fit in is I'm supposed to maintain the networks that allow the customer, the engineers, the programmers, and the print technicians to communicate with one another. If the network breaks down, the entire process grinds to a halt, and since some of Gunnar's projects are time sensitive, that can be a real catastrophe. A network outage can cost the company thousands if not tens of thousands of dollars." Adam sipped his scotch again. This time, it did not burn quite so much.

"I can understand why you have to stay alert." Victoria refreshed Adam's drink. "I hope you're up for a home-cooked meal?"

"What are we having?"

"Meatloaf, sweet potatoes, and black-eyed peas. I baked a rhubarb pie for dessert. We can have it á la mode with vanilla ice cream."

"Count me in. By the way, how was your day? Are you still having fun bossing people around?" Adam grinned. Victoria had recently been promoted to supervisor in Outbound Sports Wear's customer service department.

"I do very little bossing. Yes, I enjoyed my day, but not as much as I'm going to enjoy my night."

Again, Adam wondered what she meant but again decided not to ask.

Rather than elaborate on her statement, Victoria moved on. "I ran into Rev. Hudson in the hardware store the other day." Rev. Peter Hudson was Capstone Chapel's senior pastor. "He asked about you."

"No kidding? What did he say?"

"He wanted to know how you feel about being in church."

"What did you tell him?"

"That you were coming along…slowly."

"Tell me something, and be honest. Why do you believe all that Jesus stuff?" Too late, Adam realized that he had just broached the topic he had hoped to avoid.

Victoria stopped stirring the black-eyed peas and turned away from the stove. "Because I believe the Bible, and the Bible tells me that Jesus was sent by God to save us."

"But you hear so many different things. It's hard to know what to believe."

"Maybe you should talk to Pastor Hudson."

"Sometimes, I think pastors are like used car salesman."

"Don't be so closed-minded. Just talk to the man."

"We'll see."

Victoria opened the oven and removed the meatloaf pan using a pair of potholders. She then collected the sweet potatoes from the microwave and the black-eyed peas from the stove. After dishing up both dinners, she set their plates on the table and opened a bottle of red wine.

Their conversation during the meal was relaxed and free of contention.

After the dinner dishes had been washed, dried, and put away, Adam and Victoria settled next to one another on the loveseat in the living room. Rather than turn on the TV or stream a movie, at Victoria's suggestion, they had chosen to listen to music. As an instrumental ballad played softly in the background, Adam realized he was feeling more than a little relaxed, the scotch and the wine having combined to make him somewhat tipsy.

"This is nice," Victoria mewed as she snuggled closer. She then reached for the wine bottle to add to Adam's glass.

"No thanks," Adam protested. "I have to work tomorrow."

"Tomorrow is Saturday, silly." She filled his glass more than halfway full.

Rather than appear impolite, Adam sipped his wine and smiled.

Adam wrapped one arm around Victoria's shoulders. In return, she angled her body so she could lay one leg over his. Then she pressed close against him. With her lips near to his ear, she whispered, "You do know that I love you, don't you?"

"I do. You keep telling me often enough."

"I don't want you to forget."

On impulse, Adam turned his head and kissed Victoria on the mouth, a long, passionate kiss. She responded by running her fingers across the back of his neck and into his hair. He pulled her closer, and she obliged by shifting her body. Before he knew it, his hand was inside her blouse. Her skin felt warm and soft. An erotic fullness began in the pit of his stomach. He could feel himself responding physically.

Rather than rebuff his advances, Victoria moved in subtle ways to encourage him.

Almost before he realized what was happening, Adam found himself making love to Victoria right there in the living room. The sensations he experienced, especially the moment of climax, were nearly indescribable.

When they finished, Adam lay back with Victoria nestled against him, a soft blanket covering their naked bodies. Staring up at the ceiling, he exhaled a deep sigh. "Wow. I had no idea it would be like that."

"Think of all the time we've wasted," Victoria chided softly.

"I know. Still, I kind of wish we had waited until we we're married."

"What did you say?" Victoria raised her head off Adam's chest. "Did you just ask me to marry you?"

Adam stammered, "I, eh—yeah. I suppose I did. It just kind of slipped out."

"Well, Adam Tiberius Masters, if that's the best you can do at proposing, all I can say is…I accept."

"Really?" Adam was genuinely surprised.

"What did you expect? I keep telling you that I love you. Maybe that should have been a clue."

"I know, but…Wow."

Victoria smiled. "I'd say that sums it up nicely."

An hour later, they had cleaned up and put on enough clothing to be decent. Adam found himself alone on the couch while Victoria was in the bathroom fixing her hair. Suddenly, he sat up straight, having been overtaken by a thought. *She set me up: the scotch, the wine, the home-cooked meal, the cozy environment, and soft music. She set me up.*

But then he asked himself, *Even so, how do I feel about being engaged? Did I just make a huge mistake?* The answer that came to him was an emphatic *No! I don't think so.* But then a tiny voice in the back of his mind spoke up. *Are you going to let her see you as you really are? Are you prepared for that?*

"I guess I am. I mean, she has to have an idea already—"

"An idea about what?" Victoria emerged from the bathroom wearing only panties and a bra.

"About what happens next," Adam said hastily. He was astonished to learn that he had been thinking out loud.

Victoria sat down on the couch beside her new fiancé and snuggled in. "Well, tomorrow being Saturday, we should go shopping for an engagement ring. Nothing fancy, but nothing cheap either."

"An engagement ring, huh? I should have thought of that."

"This was a spur-of-the-moment thing. I think you're off the hook."

Adam reached across and touched a hand to Victoria's cheek. Gently, he turned her face toward him so he could give her another long, passionate kiss. When they parted, he said, "Where do we go from here?"

"You mean after we make love again? We get to plan a wedding. That's what couples do when they intend to marry."

An engagement ring and a wedding. It's a good thing I have a new job that includes a raise in pay. I suspect I'm going to need it.

Victoria perked up. "What do you think? Victoria Wayne Masters—it has a nice sound to it, doesn't it?"

Adam nodded and then said, "Well, Ms. Soon-to-Be Victoria Wayne Masters, how about you? Do you know that I love you?"

"I do."

It occurred to Adam that a moment would soon come when her "I do" would take on a very special meaning. As he reflected upon recent events, he found that he was both excited and apprehensive. It would take time to sort out the rest of his emotions, but for the time being, they would have to wait. Right then and there, he had more important things to attend to.

"About that lovemaking you mentioned?"

The last thought that passed through Adam's mind as they came together again was *It's true. She set me up. She did. She actually set me up.*

*   *   *

August 2002

Adam sat in the Rev. Peter Hudson's office and tried not to fidget. For more than three years, he had sporadically attended worship services at the Capstone Chapel, but this was the first time he had talked directly with the senior pastor other than to say good morning. To his surprise, he was even more apprehensive than anticipated. Victoria had assured him that premarital counseling would strengthen their relationship, but he was beginning to suspect that a secondary agenda was in play.

From behind his desk, Rev. Hudson sat facing Adam. He was a well-proportioned, athletic-looking man. Adam assumed he could probably take care of himself if push came to shove. He looked to be in his middle years, somewhere between thirty-five and fifty. It was hard for Adam to tell. He had a full head of light brown hair with patches of gray at the temples. His hazel eyes communicated goodwill and a mild temperament, but Adam suspected they could freeze a wayward parishioner in his tracks, should the need arise. Only a few wrinkles populated his face.

Rev. Hudson took the initiative and began. "I'll bet you're wondering why you and I are meeting together without Victoria. The answer is I wanted to get to know you. It's amazing the inhibitions a woman can evoke. So don't be afraid to speak freely."

Just how much did Victoria tell you about me? Adam's reluctance to open up was one of Victoria's pet peeves, and she had pressed the issue on more than one occasion.

"Another reason I wanted to meet with you alone is to see what questions you might have about the church, the Bible, or other spiritual issues." A period of silence ensued until the Rev. Hudson spread his hands in front of him. "Well?"

"Well what?" Adam said, unsure how to respond.

"Questions. Do you have any?"

"None that I can think of."

"Come now. You've been attending our worship services for quite some time, and yet you don't have any questions? I must be slipping. Usually, I leave my parishioners with a dozen or more." Rev. Hudson laughed, a deep, robust laugh that rolled out from the center of his chest.

"I thought I was here to discuss my getting married and stuff like that."

"You are."

Here it comes. Beginning to feel even more uncomfortable, Adam shifted in his chair. "Actually," Adam said with a hint of sarcasm, "now that I think about it, I do have one question. When Victoria and I get married, do I have to wear a tux?"

Again, Rev. Hudson laughed. "You get to wear whatever she tells you to wear, and knowing Victoria, you might as well get used to it. By the way, how old are you?"

"Twenty-three."

"And you're working as a network supervisor? I think that's what Victoria told me."

Like I suspected. She probably gave him my entire biography. "Yes, sir."

"Now I find that interesting. To have landed such a specialized job at such a young age, you must have a well-defined work ethic."

"I'm just trying to put food on the table."

"Oh, I suspect you're going to be doing far more than that. You have the look of a man who's driven to succeed. Am I wrong?"

"I strive to do the best I can—if that's what you mean?"

"Your parents, are they still alive?"

"No, they're both deceased."

"Any other relatives who will be attending the wedding?"

Adam thought of Rachel. *Has it really been four years and still no word?* "No, sir. Just me."

The reverend sat back and waited. When Adam failed to speak up, he eased forward again. "Why don't I ask a question on your behalf? I suspect I know what's on your mind."

"Go ahead." *This should be interesting.*

Rev. Hudson studied Adam with a piercing gaze. "The question I think you would like to ask but are reluctant to do so is, is this Jesus stuff for real? How can people actually believe that he is the Son of God? Am I right?"

"So you have been talking to Victoria. Yes, it's true. I've had those thoughts, but I don't see what that has to do with my getting married."

"Adam, if you're going to wed a fine girl like Victoria, you're going to need all the help you can get. And I'm here to tell you that the greatest source of help you will ever find is Jesus Christ."

For the next ten minutes, Rev. Hudson laid out God's plan of salvation.

Adam listened politely and tried not to look too bored. When the reverend finished, he asked, "How do we know any of what you said is true?"

"Because the Bible is the most thoroughly documented record in the history of humanity. The validity of the text has been verified in innumerable ways, such as its agreement with church records, archaeological excavations, and ancient manuscripts like the Dead Sea Scrolls. Let me assure you, Jesus Christ is Who He says He is, and He can do what He says He can do. What troubles you the most about His gospel?"

"I'd have to say it's the resurrection. It's impossible to imagine that any human being can be dead for three days and then come back to life. It sounds like science fiction."

"I admit, I had the same reaction when I first heard the Good News." Rev. Hudson smiled. "But consider the facts: Hundreds, if not thousands, of people alive at the time of Jesus were willing to endure persecution and torture—even death rather than renounce their belief in the legitimacy of the resurrection. The Bible tells us that more than five hundred eyewitnesses testified to seeing Jesus alive after He was crucified. Do you think the apostles—twelve independent souls—would have willingly suffered and died to perpetuate a hoax? I don't think so. More than that, had Jesus simply died, the Jews would've produced His body and ended all debate then and there, but they couldn't because He was risen."

Adam sat for a minute, searching for a way to poke a hole in the reverend's arguments, but he found none. "All right, I have another question since we're on this topic. Why is it so important that I believe in Jesus? If I say I believe, does that validate your way of thinking? Is that why you so actively proselytize for the Christian faith?"

"The reason we proselytize is for the benefit of those who will one day have to stand before God. The only remedy for our depravity is the sacrifice Jesus made on the cross. He paid for our sins with His life so that we don't have to."

"I don't feel like a sinner," Adam protested. "Admittedly, I make mistakes, but I do the best I can."

Rev. Hudson stabbed a finger at Adam. "Let's test that defense and see how it plays out. Have you ever lied, perhaps even a little white lie that you felt was immaterial?"

"Maybe."

"Have you ever stolen anything?"

"Maybe."

"Have you ever killed anybody?"

"No."

"Let me rephrase that. Have you ever thought harshly about someone and wished them harm?"

"Maybe."

"Have you ever committed adultery?"

"Not yet." Adam gave a nervous laugh. "And I don't intend to."

"These questions and dozens more are the ones you'll have to answer when you stand before your maker. One wrong response marks you as a sinner and makes you unworthy to remain in God's presence. Now I've said my spiel, and I hope you will at least think about what I've said. I mean seriously think about it. Now, with regard to getting married, let's talk about the duties of a husband."

* * *

September 2002

Five weeks after meeting with Rev. Hudson, Adam found himself in the honeymoon suite of the Rushmore Hotel, gazing out of an eleventh-story window. Downtown Los Angeles lay spread out below. Behind him, Victoria was unpacking their bags and hanging up their clothing to prevent wrinkling. They had chosen the City of Angels as their honeymoon destination, though the drive from the airport had prompted Adam to consider that they might have made a bad choice. Negotiating rush-hour traffic in a rental car had been nerve-racking.

Adam watched throngs of people scurry about their business. A declaration the reverend had made came to mind: "All men are sinners." Looking down, he thought, *I wonder, how many of you are destined to go to hell? Is God so vindictive that He would condemn multitudes to eternal damnation?* Then he remembered something Victoria had said: "God doesn't send anybody to hell. Rather, people end up in hell because they refused to choose to go to heaven." These and similar thoughts had plagued Adam ever since his premarital counseling session.

Enough of this. He turned around to watch his new wife as she dealt with their luggage. "Well, Mrs. Victoria Wayne Masters, you're right. It does have a nice ring to it."

"I think so."

"What do you want to do today?"

Victoria glanced up from refolding a sweater. "What are my options?"

"Well, let's see." Adam retrieved the travel guide that was lying on the bureau. He thumbed through it for a moment and then said, "According to this, we have a number of alternatives. There's the La Brea Tar Pits or the Griffith Observatory. Or we can go shopping, maybe take one of the Hollywood tours. Or I suppose we could just stay here and—"

Victoria became suddenly serious. "Adam, sweetheart, there's something you should know."

He crossed the room to stand in front of his wife, and then smiled as he said, "Yes. I do know that you love me." He kissed his new wife tenderly on the cheek.

"I am so glad, but that's not what I was about to say. I need to tell you something that neither of us expected, at least not this soon."

"You should go ahead and tell me. I'm not very good at guessing games."

"Sweetheart, I'm pregnant."

"What?" Adam needed a moment to appreciate what he had just been told. When the message finally sank in, his face lit up in a wide smile. "For real? You're not pulling my leg, are you?"

"The tests were positive. I checked three times. We're having a baby."

"Well, I'll be damned. Instant family." As the implications started to register, Adam had the distinct impression that the forward rush of his life had just accelerated, and he was no longer driving the train. He stepped back to inspect his wife. "You don't look pregnant, unless you count that slight glow in your cheeks."

"Fear not, I'll look pregnant soon enough."

"I've been thinking. I was going to bring this up later, but now seems like a good time. If I'm going to support this family, I'm going to need a better-paying job, and that means I'll have to get my master's degree. How do you feel about that?"

"I will support you whatever you decide. I trust your judgment."

"Okay then. I'll register as soon as we get back to Montana."

"I suppose this means you'll have your nose in a textbook whenever your home?"

"I can't learn if I don't study."

"It's all right. Like I said, I'll support your decision."

Adam picked up one of Victoria's bras from off the bed. He held it up. "Something tells me you're going to need a bigger size." He fashioned a lecherous grin.

Victoria reached for a pair of her panties. "I'm going to need a bigger size in these too."

"A baby? I can't believe it. Do we know if it's a boy or girl?"

"Not yet. I'll have my first ultrasound in a month. We should know then."

Adam's mind reeled. *Will the child be healthy? What will we name him or her? As a parent, how will I cope? Will I know the right things to do?* This last thought triggered a memory of his father tainted by a sense of revulsion. *I will not be like him. I swear I won't. My child will be loved and cared for.*

Another thought jolted Adam. *Where are you now, Dad? Did Jesus pay for your sins, or are you paying for them on your own?* The notion sent chills racing through Adam. *Rev. Hudson was right about one thing. Every man chooses the trajectory of his own life.*

Adam turned to watch his new bride. He hadn't counted on being a father, certainly not so soon, but the more he pondered the news, the more the prospect excited him. As he tried to imagine how his life would unfold, he found that there were too many unknowns. *One step at a time*, he told himself. *One step at a time.*

One thing Adam could not foresee, one thing that would pain him severely, was that within three weeks, Victoria would miscarry, and it would be an additional fourteen months before she would get pregnant again.

*   *   *

The maître d' stepped up and tapped me on the shoulder. "Excuse me, sir, I apologize for interrupting, but we're closing now." He shrugged and indicated the cleaning crew. "They need to—"

"Of course. What time is it anyway?" I had been so engrossed in telling my story that I had forgotten where we were.

Casey checked his cell phone. "Almost midnight."

"My goodness, Casey. Why didn't you let me know it was so late? Here I've gone and kept you up past your bedtime."

We stood up and headed for the exit.

Casey yawned. "I was listening to what you were saying, not thinking about the time. You and Grandmother Victoria, it sounds to me like you hit it off right from the start?"

"We did. She was a very special woman."

"So what went wrong?"

"I did, to put it bluntly. I screwed up big time, but that's—"

"A story for another day. I should have guessed." Casey held the door open for me to exit.

Out on the street, we stood beside my car. I unlocked the door with my key fob but did not open it. Instead, I paused to take a good look at my grandson. To my mind, he was a ruggedly handsome lad, though I might be accused of being slightly prejudiced. I truly loved the guy, but what worried me was his character flaws that had recently begun to emerge. There was so much I wanted to say, to warn him about the consequences of choices he was making. I was especially concerned about his love of money and his relationships with members of the opposite sex. My profound hope was that I would get to finish my narrative and that he would hear every word. However, we were done for the evening. The rest would have to wait.

Casey said, "So, Grandfather, what are your plans for this weekend?"

"Believe it or not, I'm flying to Alaska."

"Alaska?" Casey snugged his windbreaker close around his chest. "What's in Alaska?"

"I'm on a manhunt of sorts, you might say. There's someone I'm hoping to find, someone I knew years ago."

"How long will you be gone?"

"I leave early tomorrow morning. If all goes well, I'll be home early Tuesday afternoon."

"Good. When do you want to get together again?"

I tilted my head and looked him in the eye. "Aren't you tired of listening to the ramblings of an old man?"

"Not at all."

"Well then, how about Tuesday evening, say around five?"

"That sounds fine, but won't you be exhausted?"

"I'll sleep on the plane." I sincerely hoped that what I just said was true.

"As you wish." Casey laid a hand on my arm. "This time, why don't you come over to my place? I'll fix dinner."

"It's a deal."

My grandson grinned. "I hope you like tuna casserole. It's the only thing I know how to cook."

"Whatever you serve will be fine."

As I drove away, I could not help but feel a twinge of gratitude. My grandson was at least tolerant enough to listen to my story. Whether or not it was having any impact, I would just have to wait and see.

8

THE SEARCH CONTINUES

A little after 6:00 a.m. on Sunday, I landed in Nome, Alaska. Having just completed a nineteen-hour flight, which included long layovers in Seattle and Anchorage, I was exhausted. En route, I had managed to sneak in a thirty-minute nap, but that was all.

After renting a midsize sedan at the airport, I headed straightaway south along the Nome Council Highway. There was no need to wait for my luggage. All I had packed was a small carry-on. My destination lay twenty-two miles away. Swiftwater was a tiny fishing village on the shores of the Bering Sea. A slight dusting of snow had fallen during the night.

Fortunately, the road was mostly devoid of traffic, primarily because it was the weekend and most of Nome was still asleep. Through the trees to my right, I could make out the expanse of the ocean, which seemed to disappear into a fog bank hanging less than a mile off the coast. I tried not to think about what driving would be like if that pea soup haze were to suddenly wash ashore, especially at night.

Worrying about road conditions reminded me of my conversation with Casey and when I had mentioned my Los Angeles honeymoon and the traffic snarls Victoria and I had endured. The noise, the pollution, and the strain of stop-and-go driving had convinced me that I never wanted to live in a major population center. But then, even Missoula had grown to the point that it suffered from some of the same shortcomings.

But there was also the opposite extreme. Living in an untamed wilderness might be equally daunting. To the east, I saw nothing but miles and miles of virgin forest, illuminated by the rising sun just peeking over a line of mountaintops.

Thinking about LA traffic brought to mind an image of Victoria as she sat beside me in our rental car. I remembered how deeply in love we had been and how bright the future had seemed. Both of us had assumed our marriage would endure forever. *It's surprising how wrong you can be sometimes.* And then I thought, *I wonder how she's doing? It's been so long.* I told myself, *Maybe you should give her a call since you're obviously in the fence-mending business. After all, isn't that why you're on your way to Swiftwater?*

When I came upon my destination, I very nearly missed it. The village was so small that if I hadn't been paying attention, I would've driven straight through. Finding Tracy Yang's house turned out to be a straightforward affair; there were only half a dozen possibilities to consider. Her home, I discovered, was a two-story Tudor at the end of Main Street.

I rang the doorbell. It was a little after 7:00 a.m.

Rather than call ahead to announce my visit, I had resolved that I would simply show up. I wanted my reunion with Alice to be a surprise. That way, if she refused to see me, she would have to tell me to get lost face-to-face.

I rang the doorbell again. There was still no response. A third press of the button produced a similar result.

Have I come all this way for nothing? The possibility worried me.

Rather than set off to search for Tracy, I decided to wait. I climbed back in my car, which I had parked in front of her house. To pass the time, I turned on the radio. Regrettably, there were only two choices: a country western station or a Christian church service. I switched the radio off and settled back in my seat. My fatigue must've caught up with me because the next thing I knew, it was early afternoon, and a woman with Asian features was knocking on my window.

When I checked my watch, it told me that I had been asleep for almost seven hours. I rolled down the window.

"Sir, are you okay?" The woman appeared to be in her mid-sixties. She was of medium height with a thin angular build.

I blinked and tried to clear my mind. "By any chance are you Tracy Yang?"

"Yes." The woman regarded me with suspicion.

It suddenly occurred to me that they probably didn't get many visitors in Swiftwater. Had I lived there, I imagine I might have been suspicious too. "Hi, my name is Masters, Adam Masters. I've come a long way to speak with you and your friend, Alice Cunningham. Would you mind if I—" I opened the door and started to step out of the car.

Tracy backed up with a look of alarm.

I froze with one foot on the pavement. "It's all right. I only want to talk. I'll stay in my car if it makes you more comfortable." I shifted my weight to sit back down, but did not close the door.

Tracy looked like she might take off running. "Do I know you?"

"I would doubt it. I've never been to Alaska before. I'm here because I need to talk with Alice. Is she available?" In anticipation of what I assumed would be Tracy's next question, I said, "I knew Alice a long time ago. We had a disagreement over an incident at work. Something unfortunate happened, and she was fired. It was my fault, and I've come to apologize."

"I don't understand. When did you say you knew her?"

"Back in 1998. I was nineteen at the time. We both worked at Townsend Electronics. She was in the accounting department."

"1998!" Tracy exclaimed. "That was—"

"Fifty-two years ago. Yeah, I know. There's been a lot of water under the bridge since then."

"And you're just now getting around to apologizing?"

"It's a long story. Let's just say that in my elder years, my conscience has begun hounding me. I've been trying to set to right some of the wrongs for which I am responsible. Alice is one of those wrongs. Tell me, is she here?" I looked toward the house. I still could see no sign of life inside.

Tracy seemed reluctant to answer. But then again, I would've been too, given my outlandish explanation. At length, she said, "No, Alice isn't here. She's gone."

"Gone? She's not dead, is she? That would be most unfortunate."

"She's not dead."

"Then is there some way I can get in touch with her?"

Tracy didn't answer. Instead, she eyed the front door of her house as if calculating how long it would take her to get inside. Tracy didn't answer. Instead she

"Look, I'm not here to harm either you or Alice. I wish there was some way I could put you at ease. All I want to do is to set things right."

I sat quietly and held my breath. If the woman chose to clam up, there would be nothing I could do, and my trip would have been for naught.

Eventually, much to my relief, some of the tension seemed to leave her body. "I apologize," she said. "I'm forgetting my manners. Visitors are scarce around here, and often they don't mean well. Living alone this far from civilization, we need to be cautious about who we trust. I'm sure you can understand."

"I do understand. There are evil people in the world, but again I assure you, I mean you no harm."

After a moment of reflection, Tracy announced, "I believe you."

"Thank you. You've made the right choice. Would you mind my asking, what persuaded you?"

Tracy grinned. "No villain would ever dream of using a fifty-two-year-old apology as an excuse for a visit. Would you like to come inside? You look like you could do with a cup of tea and perhaps something to eat."

"That would be fantastic." I climbed out of the car, shut and locked the door, and followed Tracy inside.

* * *

Tracy Yang had one of the most spartan homes I had ever seen. A bonsai was bathed in sunlight that fell through the living room window. A crucifix hung above the door that led to the garage. A Salvador Dali print decorated one wall in the living room. That was all there was. There were no photographs, knickknacks, or mementos. The one thing Tracy did have in abundance was books. Several floor-to-ceiling bookshelves were filled with volumes. There were stacks of books beside the easy chair in a corner of the living room and on the coffee table in front of the sofa.

Tracy set out a cup of Earl Grey tea and a tuna salad sandwich on the oak table in the dining nook. Only after taking my first bite did I appreciate how hungry I was. Rather than talk with my mouth full, I gazed out the window. Beyond the trees, I could barely make out a patch of blue-gray water. After swallowing, I said, "What's it like living this close to the ocean? I'm from Montana. We're a landlocked state. All we have is some pretty spectacular lakes."

"It can get a little blustery when the storms roll in, but most days it's beautiful. I often go down to the shore and watch the sunset. What do you do in Montana?"

"Oh, I retired years ago. I used to be in the computer industry. In fact, that's what I was doing when I met Alice. I was a repair technician. By the way, you still haven't told me how I can get in touch with her?"

"That's because I don't know how. She was here, but she got a phone call, and the next thing I knew, she was gone. I could only hear her side of the conversation. Apparently, a friend of hers from high school is gravely ill. Alice volunteered to help take care of him. She's like that, always doing for other people."

"This friend of hers, would you happen to know where he lives, or what his name is, or a telephone number—anything? Sorry, I don't mean to be so pushy. It's just that it's been a long journey, and I'm tired."

"It's all right. No, I don't know his name, and I don't have a telephone number, but I remember overhearing that he lives in Omaha, Nebraska. I'm pretty sure that's what Alice said."

"You say they were in high school together?"

"I got the impression they were high school sweethearts. I think that's why she left in such a hurry."

"Did she happen to leave a contact number or a forwarding address?"

"Nope. Just a note saying goodbye and that she would call later to explain everything. So far, I haven't heard a word."

"How long ago did she leave?"

"She flew out Friday afternoon."

I felt an upwelling of disappointment. *So close.* I wondered if in Seattle or Anchorage we might have passed each other and not even known it. "How is it you know Alice, if you don't mind my asking."

"When I was five, my parents emigrated from Japan. They both died from influenza in that same year. That was 1990. Alice's mother took me in as a foster child. Alice and I were like sisters. Over the years, we've stayed in touch. She's been up to see me half a dozen times. I think the world of her. She's one of the good people."

"I'm getting that impression from the folks I've talked to."

"I'm curious, how did you learn that Alice was here?"

"I spoke with Rose Richardson, her niece."

"Of course. How is Rose? Does she still have that horse she calls a dog?"

"You mean Duke? Yes, she does. I'd hate to have him mad at me."

While I finished my sandwich and drank the last of my tea, we spoke about what it was like living on the edge of the wilderness and how resilient people needed to survive. Clearly, frontier life was unlike the big cities where everything you might need could be purchased within a thirty-mile radius.

When I consulted my watch, I discovered it was later than I thought. I stood up to take my leave. Rather than simply bid me farewell, Tracy suggested, "It gets dark early this far north. The road to town can be treacherous, especially if the fog starts rolling in. It should clear off by tomorrow morning. You're welcome to stay the night if you'd like. I have a guest room you can use. You'd have your own bathroom."

"Thank you, but I really do have to be getting back. I have an early flight out in the morning. By the way, if you hear anything from Alice, I'll leave my name and number. Please give me a call if you would."

"How about I have her call you?"

"That would ruin my surprise."

"What surprise?"

"Like I said, I want to set things right. Don't worry, I'm not planning anything nefarious. Please, just call me if she gets in touch."

"All right. I will."

"Oh yeah. One more thing, just to confirm. It was Cedar Shores, Kansas, where you lived with the Cunninghams, right? I know that's where Alice grew up."

"That's correct. We lived on a small farm outside of town."

"Would you happen to remember where Alice went to high school?"

"Sorry, I don't. I was so young at the time, and I didn't speak English very well. But it was a small town. There probably was only one high school."

"Of course."

We said goodbye. I thanked Tracy for her hospitality and soon was back on the road, headed north. The sunset, which otherwise might've been spectacular, was obscured by the fog bank that had rolled in closer to shore. All the way to Nome, I kept one eye on the ocean, hoping against hope that the fog would stay put, which it did. Thankfully.

I had told Tracy that I was flying out in the morning, when in fact, my flight wasn't until late in the afternoon. Truth was, I would have felt uncomfortable staying in a house with a woman I didn't know.

Needing a place to sleep, I set off to search for a motel and soon found one that would do.

My visit to Swiftwater wasn't a success, but then it wasn't exactly a failure either. All I had to do to move forward was learn the name of Alice's high school boyfriend who was now living in Omaha. *Piece of cake*, I thought. The question was, where to start?

* * *

Upon awakening the following morning, I noted that although it was nearly nine o'clock, it was still dark outside. Then I remembered that Nome was much farther north than Missoula. When I thought about how my day would go, I realized I had almost ten hours to kill before I had to check in at the airport. With that much time, it occurred to me that I could pursue my investigation online without feeling rushed.

After setting up a virtual private network, I connected my laptop to the motel's Wi-Fi. A Google search indexed on Cedar Shores, Kansas, produced a number of citations. I narrowed the search by focusing on the town's educational resources and confirmed that Tracy had been right. Only one high school was within a reasonable driving distance from the center of town.

Another quick search led me to the Cedar Shores High School's website. It contained the usual info pages: a mission statement, a listing of faculty members, a calendar of upcoming events, a Contact Me page, and similar items of note. However, no student records were available, nor was there any mention of the school's history.

On a different website, I found a brief history of the Cedar Shores Township, and although the site seemed devoid of information that would suit my needs, I jotted down its URL for later reference anyway.

After four hours, I had exhausted my online resources. Once again, I had come up dry. *You would think*, I complained to myself, *what with all the information on the web, I'd find something I could use.*

I sat back and tried to think. *Who would know the names of students who had attended Cedar Shores High School ages ago?* The only logical answer was the school itself. So I returned to the school's website and navigated to the Contact Me page. An extension number for the school's administrative offices was listed near the top.

A woman who I presumed was the school secretary answered my call with businesslike efficiency. In a husky voice, she said, "Cedar Shores High School. This is Helen. How may I help you?"

I introduced myself and explained my reason for calling: that I was trying to track down a student who had attended Cedar Shores a long time ago. I refrained from mentioning that I was actually seeking the boyfriend of a girl named Alice Cunningham.

Helen's immediate response was "I'm sorry, but we do not give out information regarding our students."

As persuasively as possible, I countered by explaining the reasons for my inquiry, but to no avail. After several minutes of futile haggling, Helen said flatly, "I would like to help you, but there is nothing I can do. We have ironclad rules against divulging student information. Look, if it's historical material you're after, you might speak with Gladys Purdue. She's Cedar Shores's historian. She knows virtually everything there is to know about the town."

"Would you happen to have her number?"

Helen begrudgingly looked up the number, read it to me, and then hung up.

My expectations were low as I dialed Gladys, but I figured, *What the heck. I might as well call and see what happens. It's not as if I have something better to do, nor do I have any other leads to follow.*

A woman with a pleasant voice answered the phone. When I mentioned the reason for my call, that I was seeking historical information, she seemed genuinely disposed to be of assistance. Gladys asked, "What sort of information are you after?"

"I need to track down a student who attended Cedar Shores High School sometime around 1990."

"Do you have a name for this student?"

"I don't. That's where I'm hoping you can help me."

"And the reason you're trying to find this person is…?"

Rather than slog through a tortuous explanation that might or might not prove efficacious, I elected to take a more expeditious approach. I crossed my fingers and said, "Because my aunt, who passed away last week, specified in her will that if we could locate her friend, he would stand to inherit a tidy sum of money. You see, my aunt had Alzheimer's, and all she could remember about her friend's identity was that he had attended Cedar Shores High School in the early nineties. Apparently, they were romantically involved for a time way back when. I promised my aunt that I would at least make an effort to track him down."

To my amazement, the ruse seemed to work. Gladys said, "I see. Well, that is a long time ago, but I may be able to help. We have copies of the school's yearbooks dating back almost one hundred years. My grandfather began collecting yearbooks the first year they were published. He was the school's first principal and was very proud of his collection. Our family has continued the tradition of setting one aside for posterity ever since."

"How incredibly fortuitous. Is there any possibility I might borrow several of those yearbooks, say from 1988 to 1992? I'll take excellent care of them, and I'll reimburse you for your time and effort."

"I don't know. We've never loaned them out before. I'd hate for something to happen. That would break up the set."

"I can certainly understand your reluctance, but I promise, I'll treat them like the prized possessions they are. You have my word."

After several minutes of pleading and begging, Gladys finally acquiesced and agreed to express ship the yearbooks to Montana. Rather than deliver them to my house, I gave her Theo's address. I figured that if I was delayed getting home, he at least would be there to receive them. I also provided her with my address, my telephone number, and the other bits of biographical data she requested. In return, I promised to send her a money order in the amount of two hundred dollars to cover her expenses.

After hanging up, I did some rough calculations. The high school's average class size was approximately three hundred students. Assuming a 10 percent turnover rate per year, I'd be looking at somewhere between 400 and 450 names to evaluate when I got home. It would be a tedious but not impossible task.

I was still in the game.

I packed my bags and headed for the airport.

9

THE ROOTS OF SIN

I drank the last of my club soda and polished off my tuna casserole, which was surprisingly good. I suspected that Casey was a better cook than he let on.

As scheduled, my flight home had landed early Tuesday morning, and I was bushed. I felt like I'd been ridden hard and put away wet, to quote a cowboy saying. Yet rather than go straight home and fall into bed, I had driven to Theo's house to check on the status of the yearbooks Gladys had shipped. I was greatly pleased to learn that not only had the yearbooks been delivered, but Theo was busy compiling a list of names for us to evaluate. With the radio blaring to keep me awake, I drove home from Theo's house.

Freed from worrying about the yearbooks, I could finally relax and catch up on my sleep. Rather than take the time to undress, I lay down on top of the bed, and it was lights out within less than a minute. Five hours later, I awakened feeling the effects of jet lag, but much refreshed nevertheless.

By the time five o'clock rolled around, I had showered, changed my clothes, and driven to Casey's apartment. He answered the doorbell after the second ring.

Our dinner fare was simple but filling. During the meal, I delivered a brief synopsis of my trip to Alaska. I could tell my grandson was more than curious, but rather than regale him with a full account of the reason for my trip, I simply stated that my manhunt was moving forward, albeit slowly.

Like many impoverished students, Casey's one-bedroom apartment was furnished in a style that might be described as ultramodern cheap. There was a bookshelf made out of cinder blocks and boards and a desk cobbled together from sheets of plywood. Everything in the apartment looked utilitarian. There were, however, two anomalies that stood out. One was a high-fidelity music system. The other was a large flat-screen TV. Both looked expensive. I wondered how Casey had procured them—perhaps with a portion of his student loans. Otherwise, there were very few knickknacks and only those two luxury items. Such was the life of a struggling college senior.

There was, however, one item I recognized right off—the ivory and ebony chess set I had given my grandson for his thirteenth birthday. I had subsequently taught him the rules of the game.

"Do you still play?" I said as I studied how the board was laid out.

"When I get the chance," Casey said. "Mostly I play against myself."

For a time, I stood there inspecting the arranged pieces then said, "Knight C3 takes Bishop."

"Pawn E6 takes Knight," Casey countered.

"Rook to E5. Mate in four."

"No. That won't—wait a minute. I'll be damned. Do you know how long I've been working on that puzzle?"

"Keep at it. It takes time and lots of practice."

When we finished eating, we cleared away the dinner dishes and then returned to the kitchen table. Sitting on poorly padded chairs that faced one another was preferable to sitting side by side on a lumpy couch in the living room.

Casey produced a plate of Oreo cookies for dessert. "I've been thinking about last time, in particular your meeting with Rev. Hudson. Did you give much thought to what he told you about Jesus?"

"Not then, but later I did. I gave it a lot of thought. Why?"

"Nothing, really. I've just been wondering."

"About whether or not you should believe?"

"Yeah, basically."

I could tell my grandson was troubled, but rather than deviate from the chronology I had prepared, I said, "Maybe if I continue my narrative, some of your questions might get answered."

"I'm ready," Casey announced with a nod.

"I believe when we left off, I had just mentioned Victoria's miscarriage. Upon looking back, I've come to regard that tragedy as a turning point in my life. To say I was devastated would be a gross understatement. Losing a child, even an unborn child, can have a profound psychological impact. I'd have to say that my principal reaction was anger—anger and resentment. I felt cheated. I wanted to lash out, to attack something, but there was nothing to vent against. Instead, those emotions festered inside me, leaving me depressed and vulnerable to doing something I never should have done.

*   *   *

July 2003

Adam had been invited to a Fourth of July party hosted by his boss, Rudolph "Rudy" Gunnar. As founder and CEO of Gunnar Manufacturing, Rudy was a self-made millionaire. Like Adam, he too had started working with computers at a young age. Rudy, however, had been intrigued by their ability to control peripherals rather than reckoning them as mere information processors. With the advent of 3D printers, he seized his opportunity. By mortgaging everything he owned, he founded the company that now bore his name.

As was his tradition, Rudy's party included a barbecue and live music with dancing. The food service was handled by a local company, Tasty Catering, whose specialty was servicing high-end affairs. No expense had been spared. A full-size pig was roasting on a spit, and there was a seemingly endless supply of booze. A majority of Rudy's guests were either drunk or well on their way to being drunk, and that included Adam.

Unlike his coworkers, however, Adam was in a somber mood. The lingering stress of work was a contributing factor. Not only did he put in long hours under tight deadlines, but the people he worked with often failed to appreciate the demands placed upon him as a network supervisor. There were operational protocols to follow, diagnostic algorithms to run, equipment to service, and firewalls to maintain. Twice, he had requested an assistant, but had been turned down because of the expense.

Another factor responsible for Adam's sour disposition was Victoria's miscarriage. The loss of their first child had severely strained their relationship. Although there was no evidence whatsoever to suggest it was true, Adam could not help but wonder if his wife had done something to end her pregnancy. He recognized that the idea was irrational, bordering on paranoia, but it would not leave his mind.

The combination of alcohol, an oppressive mental funk, and Victoria's decision to stay home after their latest argument had left Adam vulnerable. His defenses were down when Jolene McDermott approached him with a smile and a simple request.

"Could you give me a hand?" Jolene said with a slight Southern drawl. "I have a couple cases of liquor in my car, and I need a strong man to help me carry them to the bar. Mr. Gunnar was afraid we might run out, so he sent me to fetch some more."

Rather than refuse her request, Adam gallantly consented. As he followed Jolene to her car, he could not help but notice the sway of her hips and the way party lights painted highlights in her auburn hair.

"I don't think I've seen you at work before," Adam said.

"That's because most of the time, I'm not there. I'm Jolene, Mr. Gunnar's personal assistant."

"I'm—"

"I know who you are. I've had my eye on you for some time. You're a hard worker. I admire that." Jolene opened the trunk of her BMW, and Adam noticed three cases: one of scotch, one of bourbon, and one of vodka.

Jolene said, "We need to take those"—she indicated the cases—"over there." She pointed to the outdoor bar fifty yards away. "If you can carry two, I can carry one. Or we can make two trips. What do you say?"

"Let's do it in one trip. What's the worst that could happen?"

"We could end up breaking thirty-six bottles of booze."

"Is that like thirty-six bottles of booze on the ground, thirty-six bottles—"

"Stop!" Jolene laughed. "I'll never get that song out of my head."

When their task was done, they rewarded themselves with a round of drinks. After fifteen minutes of small talk and another couple shots of liquor, Jolene grabbed a half-full bottle of scotch and said, "Follow me, I have something I want to show you." She led the way into the house and up the stairs to the second floor. Adam had the impression that she knew where she was going. When they came to one of the house's four guest bedrooms, she took hold of Adam's hand and pulled him inside. She closed the door and spun around to face him.

Before Adam could respond, she kissed him full on the mouth. Pressing her body against him, she kissed him again.

Adam was still sober enough to know that he should not walk but run away—as fast as possible. Instead, he hesitated, and that was all it took. The alcohol, his emotional chaos, and his male urges combined to determine what happened next.

When they had finished making love and were putting their clothes back on, Adam was suddenly besieged by a new emotion— remorse. He had betrayed his wife's trust. The weight of his infidelity pressed down on his already fragile psyche.

"I shouldn't have done that," he said.

"Relax, you sweet boy. You did just fine."

"I don't even know your last name."

"It's McDermott, Jolene McDermott."

"You won't tell, will you? If my wife finds out—"

"Don't worry. Your secret is safe with me. Now what say we get back to the celebration."

Adam followed Jolene out into the backyard, but rather than remain at the party, he got in his car and drove home to his three-bedroom cottage on Springwood Lane. Rather than purchase a new house together, Victoria had agreed to move into the house he had inherited. Worrying over what he would say to his wife blunted the effects of the alcohol. By the time he reached his destination, he felt nearly sober.

"You're home early," Victoria said.

"I missed you." As the words came out of Adam's mouth, they felt like a lie. "I'm sorry I was harsh earlier. I hate it when we quarrel. Can we put the whole thing behind us?"

Victoria seemed to let go of her bitterness. "Sure."

Adam stepped forward to kiss her, but she pushed him away. "You smell like a brewery. Go take a shower."

On his way into the bathroom, Adam belatedly realized that his wife might have detected some of Jolene's perfume on his body. If she had, she hadn't given any sign.

In the shower, he lathered vigorously three times and tried to dismiss the memory of his infidelity from his thoughts. Yet no amount of soap could wash away the guilt that haunted him.

Five weeks later, he would suffer the lingering consequences of his moral lapse.

*   *   *

August 2003

Adam was engaged in doing system maintenance in the server room at Gunnar Manufacturing when he heard a noise behind him. He had just finished swapping out an errant network card and was bringing the restored computer back online. Without looking to see who had entered, he said "I'll be with you in a second. Let me just plug this in." The network cables snapped into place, and he switched the machine on. The red light on the status display turned green, indicating that the network was functioning properly. Adam said as he turned around, "Now, what can I do for you? Oh, it's you."

"Sweet boy, I thought you'd be glad to see me again." Jolene McDermott stood in the doorway, silhouetted by the lights in the corridor. The chic pantsuit outfit she wore made her look very businesslike.

"What are you doing here?" Five weeks had elapsed since the Fourth of July party, and Adam had done his best to forget his transgression.

"Technically, I'm working on a feasibility study for a new project Mr. Gunnar has in mind. Actually, I'm here to see you."

"If you're hoping for a rematch, forget it. What we did was wrong. I still can't believe I let you seduce me."

"As I recall, it wasn't that hard. I mean, getting you into bed wasn't hard. As for the other—well, you were there."

"What do you want?"

"Houston, we have a problem."

"What sort of problem?" Adam said with suspicion.

"I'm pregnant."

"What do you mean you're pregnant?"

"As you will recall, we didn't use protection. That was my bad, I suppose."

"I just assumed you were on the pill!"

"I don't like taking them. They make me retain fluid. I get all puffy."

"So you decided to chance it?"

"Pretty much, yeah. It was close to my time of the month, and I thought I'd be safe. Oops."

"Are you sure?"

"Of course I'm sure. The damn thing turned pink, didn't it?"

"I meant are you sure I'm the father?"

"I won't dignify that question with a response."

"How do I know you're telling the truth?"

"Well, we can wait nine months and do a paternity test."

The gravity of the news struck Adam hard. Again, he worried that his wife might find out. "What do you want?"

"I'll tell you what I don't want." Jolene touched a hand to her abdomen as if subconsciously acknowledging the new life growing inside her. "I don't want this baby. I'm not ready for a family. Not yet."

"You're thinking of having an abortion?"

"That's the plan."

Adam had always considered himself to be pro-life, but his enthusiasm for the cause was more a matter of endorsing an abstract concept rather than being moved to action by a firm commitment to the sanctity of life. "What do you want from me?"

"I need twenty thousand dollars to get it done, and since this is your fault, I figure it's your responsibility to get me the money."

"My fault?" Adam snarled with indignation. "You're the one who came on to me."

"Yes, but you're the one who got me pregnant. Besides, you wouldn't want your wife to find out, would you?"

Adam felt the color drain from his cheeks. "You wouldn't…"

"Not if you give me what I need, but don't take too long. I only have a couple weeks to get it done legally."

"I don't have twenty thousand dollars."

"That's your problem. Either pay me, or I ring up Victoria and tell her what a sleazebag her husband is." Jolene turned to leave. She called back over her shoulder, "Two weeks. Got it?"

What am I going to do? Adam wondered as he watched her go. Immediately, he set to work searching for a solution.

*   *   *

Six days later, Adam sat in the bar at the Grand Oak Hotel in downtown Missoula. Refrains of an instrumental ballad competed with traffic noises outside. Out of the corner of his eye, he scanned the room. Other than himself, the man seated across the table, and the bartender, the bar was deserted. Not even a two-for-one happy hour could draw in customers, which was one reason Adam had chosen that particular bar as a place to meet. It wasn't popular, and therefore, the chance of bumping into someone he knew would be negligible.

Adam glanced across the table at Roger Freeman and attempted to assess his mood. Other than a slight tension in the muscles at the angle of his jaw, the man seemed at ease. Roger earned his living as a midlevel executive for Tidal Aquatics. To the best of Adam's recollection, they had met in person only once before, at a chess tournament several years back.

The scotch on the rocks Adam had ordered sat untouched on the table; it was mainly for show. "It's good of you to meet with me on such short notice," Adam said.

"Not a problem. You piqued my curiosity with your cryptic message." Roger was an average-looking fellow wearing an average-looking sport coat and average-looking slacks. Adam was aware, however, that there was nothing average about his intellect. He was an excellent chess player and a shrewd businessman.

"As I mentioned in my text, I have something that might be of interest to your company." Adam tapped the thumb drive lying on the table between them.

"What would that be?"

"The schematics for a variable pitch propeller. It's a 3D rendering that details the propeller's mechanics and operational characteristics, plus a complete set of manufacturing algorithms."

"What's so special about that? Propellers with variable pitch blades have been around since the 1920s."

"But not with this design. This entire mechanism is created by 3D printing. It's fabricated as a self-contained unit. Almost no assembly is required, which substantially lowers production costs. The control linkages have a life expectancy of twenty-five years, and virtually no maintenance is needed. Hell, this propeller could be manufactured so cheaply, you could install one on every boat you sell."

Roger seemed impressed. "Where did you get that? A self-contained unit, you say. And it doesn't need someone to put it together?"

"Not only that, using modern thermoplastics, the finished product will be lighter and more resilient. Actually, we're on the verge of building a prototype."

"Seriously?"

"That's why time is of the essence."

Roger leaned back in his chair. "Why come to me?"

"Because I want to sell you this design."

"For how much?"

"Twenty thousand dollars—cash."

"Let me ask again, how did you get this?" Roger reached for the thumb drive, but Adam snatched it away. Roger gave Adam a look of skepticism. "How do I know the design is genuine?"

"You'll know the first time you fire up the graphics. Correct me if I'm wrong, but it's my understanding that boat makers dream about upgrading their watercraft with the latest and best innovations."

"That's true. Anything that increases efficiency and reduces fuel consumption. Also, there should be a huge military demand, especially for submarines. Variable pitch propellers reduce the risk of cavitation, which decreases the boat's acoustic signature, making them stealthier. But you still haven't answered my question."

Adam pictured himself returning to the office late the previous evening. He had cajoled his way past the night guard by claiming a network emergency. Working swiftly, he had downloaded a copy of the simulation onto the thumb drive, finishing just before the guard passed by on his rounds. "As you may know, Gunnar Manufacturing is a 3D printing company. This sim is one of our work products. You might say I borrowed it from our printing lab."

Roger steepled his fingers in front of him. "Let's pretend that Tidal Aquatics might be interested. How would your schematic do us any good? If the design is complete, I'd think that your work product would soon be on its way to your client, which I presume is Lincoln Marine. Correct?"

Adam nodded an affirmation.

"I thought so. With the schematics in hand, Lincoln would have a huge advantage in bringing the product to market."

"Not if they rely on the schematics I substituted. I added a couple minuscule but fatal flaws. Their design won't work. You would be the ones with the major head start."

"I'll have to think about this," Roger said.

"You have as much time as it takes for me to get up and walk out the door. I need your answer now. This offer expires when this conversation ends."

Roger said nothing. Instead, he stared across the table at Adam.

Adam tried not to fidget while he waited. A great deal was riding on Roger's decision. After a time, Adam's impatience finally got the better of him. He stood up. With profound disappointment, he said, "I guess I have your answer." He slipped the thumb drive back into his pocket and started to leave.

"Wait," Roger said. "I need time to get you your money."

"I'll be here this time tomorrow. If you don't have it by then, the deal is off." Adam stuck out his hand.

Rather than return the handshake, Roger scoffed, "What good is a handshake from a man who would betray his own employer? If I find out you're scamming me, there will be consequences."

"I would imagine so. I'll see you tomorrow." Adam turned on his heel and left the bar.

The next evening, Adam exchanged the thumb drive for twenty thousand dollars in hundred-dollar bills, which he in turn gave to Jolene to pay for her abortion. In Adam's mind, the transaction put an end to the whole sordid affair, that is until five weeks later, when Victoria returned home after a shopping trip to the mall with friends.

* * *

October 2003

Seated on his living room couch at home, Adam was trying to solve the daily puzzle offered by the chess app on his cell phone. It was Sunday afternoon. Technically, he was off work, though he could be called in at any moment for a network emergency.

He heard Victoria enter through the kitchen. He listened as she deposited her purse on the counter beside the radio. Her key ring jangled when she returned it to its hook on the wall. Next, she hung her coat in the entryway closet. After thirteen months of marriage, Adam recognized each of the familiar sounds, but this time they seemed different. He couldn't put his finger on what was abnormal, but he sensed that something was wrong.

"How was shopping?" he called out. "Find anything interesting?"

"No." Victoria entered the living room. It was obvious to Adam that she was dealing with something distressing. Victoria remained standing. Looking down at her husband, she announced, "I ran into somebody I hadn't seen in ages, Pauline Newman. Do you remember her? She's the event planner for Tasty Catering. They hosted that Fourth of July party you went to a couple months ago."

Upon being reminded of Rudy Gunnar's shindig, Adam felt a hollow open in the pit of his stomach. "I don't recall her." Hoping to change the subject, he quickly added, "Was the mall crowded? I'll bet the decorations were macabre. They always are around Halloween."

Victoria refused to be distracted. "Pauline mentioned that she knows a woman named Jolene. She's your boss's personal assistant. Apparently, this Jolene person helped plan the party. Do you know her?"

"Jolene? I can't say that I do. It was a big party. There were lots of people there. I'm sorry you decided not to go. I think you would've had a good time. By the way, did you remember to pick up a nine-volt battery for my spotlight? It's getting darker earlier, and I'm going to need it."

"It's in the car. I forgot to bring it in."

"I'll go get it." With alacrity, Adam rose to leave the room.

Victoria stopped him. "Wait. There is something I need to know. It's important. Please, sit down."

Adam sank into a corner of the couch. Victoria remained standing. Adam could tell she was on the verge of tears. The hollow sensation in the pit of the stomach grew more intense.

Standing in front of her husband with her arms wrapped around her midsection, as if holding herself together, Victoria said, "Pauline told me that you were with her, that she saw you two go upstairs together. Is this true?"

"I have no idea what Pauline is talking about."

"Did you sleep with her?"

"No."

"Don't lie to me. Pauline was there. She saw you. Did you make love to this Jolene woman? I need to know."

Adam felt the full weight of his betrayal come crashing down on his conscience. The secret he had tried so hard to conceal was being exposed, and there was nothing he could do to stop it.

"Man up," Victoria demanded. "Tell me the truth. At least care for me enough to admit what you did."

"All right. Yes. It's true, but it wasn't like it sounds. I didn't plan it. It just happened. I was drunk. I was angry. You and I had just had a row—"

"Don't you dare make this my fault. I've been angry with you plenty of times, but I've never gone out and cheated on you."

"I know."

"How could you? I thought we had something special."

"We do. All I can say is I'm sorry. I truly am. I wish it had never happened."

"Is this the only time you've been unfaithful, or were there others?"

"It was the only time, I swear—a one-off thing. You have to believe me. I love you. Honestly, I do. I don't know what came over me. Under other circumstances, it never would have happened. I am so, so sorry."

"Have you seen her again since then?"

"No," Adam lied. "Not once."

Victoria wiped a tear from her cheek. "It's weird. I want to believe you, but I don't think I can trust you."

"How can I make this up to you? What can I do?"

"Honestly, I doubt there's anything you can do."

The genuineness of Victoria's statement caused Adam to recoil with alarm. He sensed that the damage to his marriage was worse than he had anticipated. There was a real possibility that their relationship was irreparably harmed. "Am I going to lose you?" he said with foreboding.

"I don't know. We'll see how I feel after I've had a chance to think about this. For now, it would be best if you found someplace else to sleep tonight."

Adam patted the couch cushion beside him. "I'll be okay right here."

"No. I mean you need to leave. Go check into a motel or something. I don't want you around."

"I understand. This is hard for you, but we can work it out. I'll make it up to you. I promise."

"I said go. Either you leave, or I will." The flash of anger in Victoria's eyes warned Adam not to press the issue.

Resigned to his fate, Adam capitulated, "I'll get a room, but sometime soon, we'll need to talk. I do love you, and I don't want to lose you. If you give me half a chance, I know I can make this right." He stood up and went into the bedroom to pack a bag.

As Adam was driving away from his house, he suddenly realized that Victoria hadn't mentioned Jolene's pregnancy, her abortion, the twenty-thousand-dollar payment, nor his theft of the 3D simulation from Gunnar Manufacturing. *Maybe things aren't as bad as they seem. Please, God. May she never find out.*

Adam checked into a local motel. That night, no matter how hard he tried, he could not fall asleep, and for the next week, he felt truly miserable. But then, Victoria decided to give him a second chance. In the months that followed, he worked hard to rebuild their relationship, but not to the level of intimacy they had once enjoyed. Something precious had been lost from their marriage. Adam understood that the thing that had gone missing was unconditional trust. Yet their affection for one another was restored to the point that shortly after the start of the new year, Victoria became pregnant again, and then nine months later, Charles David Masters, Casey's father, was born.

As for Jolene and that whole sordid affair, they weren't mentioned again.

*   *   *

"Twenty thousand dollars for an abortion?" Casey exclaimed. "I don't think so."

"I agree. It was extortion, pure and simple. I doubt she was even pregnant, but I could not afford to chance not paying her."

Casey shook his head. "One problem sure snowballed into a bunch of problems, didn't it?"

"Yes, it did."

"I've heard it said that for us men, sex is the bane of our existence."

"For women too, I would imagine. Sex is one of the few activities where we humans can be both perpetrator and victim at the same time."

"I remember Father mentioning that Grandmother Victoria used to complain that he'd been a difficult delivery." Casey stood up from the kitchen table. "Excuse me, but I've got to take a leak."

When Casey returned, I said, "She's a strong woman, your grandmother. She can be stubborn when her mind is made up. She was in labor for twenty-three hours. Twice, her obstetrician advised her to have a cesarean section, but she wouldn't hear of it. Instead, she forced herself to tough it out and deliver her baby naturally. Had I been there, I might've been able to convince her, but as it was, I nearly missed the birth."

About to sit down, Casey remembered his manners and said, "Can I get you anything?"

"No, I'm fine. Thank you."

Casey again took his place at the kitchen table. "What do you mean you nearly missed it?"

"I had enrolled in a chess tournament. Some of the best players in the state were there. I felt privileged to be among them. I'd played well all the way up to the quarterfinals. Midway through my quarter-final match, the referee slipped me a note informing me that my wife was in the last stages of labor.

"When I read the message, I wanted to leave then and there, but to do so would have meant forfeiting my game. I could tell I was winning, so I decided to hold on a little longer. But then my opponent made a strategic move that seemed to come out of left field. Suddenly, I was in jeopardy of losing my queen. I sat back, took a deep breath, and refocused on playing the game. In so doing, I put my wife's labor out of my mind. For more than an hour, we battled back and forth. My opponent turned out to be a much better player than I had been led to believe. I eventually managed to capture his bishop, but he responded by taking my rook. Shortly thereafter, he won. In fact, he went on to win the tournament.

"By the time our game ended, Victoria was well along in her delivery. When I finally put on a gown and slipped those paper covers over my shoes, Victoria was in the delivery room preparing for a final push. I made it just in time to see your dad come into the world."

"That must have been something special, welcoming a new life you helped create. One day, I hope to see my own son being born." Casey eyed the last Oreo on the plate and then looked at me.

I pushed the plate in his direction. "Go for it. It's yours."

"You must be one lucky dude," Casey muttered around a mouthful of Oreo.

"How so?"

"Twice now, you've gotten away without getting caught: once when you pilfered parts for the computer you were building, the other when you stole the 3D rendering to sell."

"I didn't get away with it, as you say. That's a fallacy in the way we think. It was just that I didn't get punished."

"They sound pretty similar to me."

"There is a huge difference. All these years, I've had to live with knowing that I'm a thief. More than that, I caused irreparable harm. Stealing those computer components like I did, that was virtually the same as taking money out of my employer's pocket. Not only did I wrong my employer by delivering a flawed simulation to our client, I nearly put an unsuspecting company out of business. When Tidal Aquatics began installing variable pitch propellers on all their watercraft, they gained a huge market share. Lincoln Marine was hard-pressed to compete and nearly went under.

"Worst of all, I paid Jolene to get an abortion. At the time, I tried to rationalize my decision by thinking I was doing what was best for both of us, but since then, I've come to believe that abortion is legalized murder. Every day I've had to live with the fact that I paid someone to murder my unborn child. I don't call that getting away with it."

I sat quietly, staring into space. When I looked, I noticed that Casey had an odd expression on his face, as if dealing with a queasy stomach.

I commented, "It's not easy being forced to see yourself as you truly are. And then twenty-one months later, the same thing happened again."

"I was hoping you two would have patched things up."

"We did, for a time, but that wasn't the end of the story."

"What went wrong?"

"I'll tell you, but first, there are a couple things I should mention first." I took a deep breath and continued. "After your father was born, I devoted myself to my work. It took nearly two years, but I ultimately earned my master's degree in computer science. In the spring of 2005, I got a job offer from Bit-March Systems, which included a substantial increase in pay. Overnight, I went from network supervisor to computer programmer. It turned out that I really enjoyed that line of work, and I was good at it. So much so that within four months, I was promoted from programmer to project manager, and that's when the real troubles began, but before we get to that, it's my turn to use the restroom."

When I had again settled in at the kitchen table, I took up where I had left off. "As project manager, I was tasked with overseeing a team of software development specialists. There were five people on my team: me, Kelly, Tug, Sean, and Alexander. Each of us had our own unique capabilities, and for the most part, we worked well together, but as sometimes happens with talented people, we could get on each other's nerves. This was especially true of Kelly. She seemed particularly vulnerable to the stress of working alongside headstrong males.

"Don't get me wrong. Kelly was no slacker. She was a bright, hardworking employee with excellent coding skills, especially for someone fresh out of college. Kelly was four years younger than me, and I was twenty-six at the time. The problem was that her conflicts with other team members began affecting her work.

"As project manager, my job was to make sure that interpersonal disputes didn't interfere with our productivity. Therefore, it seemed incumbent upon me to speak with Kelly, but not at work. I wanted her to be able to vent what was on her mind without worrying that another employee might overhear. For that reason, I decided to call upon her at home after dinner one night."

1 0

LIFE AMONG THE THISTLES

May 2006

It was a clear star-speckled evening in the middle of May 2006 when Adam called upon Kelly Stafford at her home. This was his first visit to her residence, and he was surprised that she lived in an upscale four-bedroom house. He later learned that Kelly came from money; her father had made his fortune working as the CFO for a major oil exploration company.

As Adam approached Kelly's front door, he detected the scent of lilacs. It had rained earlier in the day, and he could smell wet earth as well.

When Kelly opened the front door and saw her boss standing in front of her, she reacted with a look of surprise.

"I'm sorry," Adam said. "I probably should have called ahead. I hope I'm not interrupting. I just want to talk, if that's okay?"

Kelly quickly recovered her composure. "It's fine. I just wasn't expecting anyone. Sure, come in. I was doing some light reading—the new Thurston Delacroix novel, *The Hangman's Daughter*."

"Sounds gruesome." Adam stepped inside. The house had an open, uncluttered feel to it. He could hear soft music flowing out from an all-purpose room just off the kitchen. Through a large plate-glass window at the rear of the house, he noted a swimming pool in the backyard—a rarity that seemed unusual. In Montana, swimming pools tended to freeze in winter.

"It's not as horrific as you would think," Kelly said with a smile. "It's actually a medieval love story. The heroine is an independent, self-sufficient woman who is trying to make a life for herself, but everywhere she goes, she has to cope with her father's reputation. But then she meets a man whose father is an assassin for the king, and the story goes on from there. But please, come in. Can I get you something? I'm having a glass of wine. Would you like one?"

"Yes, thank you."

Adam and Kelly carried their wineglasses into the all-purpose room where he noted a novel lying open-faced on the end table beside a leather recliner. He assumed that was where Kelly would choose to sit, so he selected the sofa instead. Looking around, he saw that the room was tastefully decorated. There were fresh-cut flowers in a vase on the credenza. An oil painting, very likely an original seascape by an artist he did not recognize, hung on the wall beside a built-in floor-to-ceiling bookcase.

Adam leaned forward with his elbows on his knees. "The reason I'm here is because I want to talk to you about how things are at work."

A look of concern came into Kelly's eyes. "Is there a problem?" As anticipated, she chose the recliner, but rather than settle in, she sat erect with her hands clasped in her lap.

"Frankly, yes, there is, but it's not a huge problem. I've noticed that your output has started to fall off, and I'm wondering if it's because of the friction you've been experiencing. I've seen that certain members of the team can get under your skin. It worries me that you might not be happy with your work environment."

"Why does how I feel worry you?" Kelly had on a pair of designer jeans and a loose-fitting sweater that gaped open at the neck to reveal a couple inches of cleavage. She was also barefoot. Adam found the combination extremely alluring.

"Because you're an excellent programmer. You have good instincts with regard to how code should flow. Also, because I like you. I would hate to lose you. You brighten up my day, as they say." When Adam heard himself speak those words, he sat back in amazement. He had intended to keep their conversation impersonal. Instead, unbidden, his feelings had just sort of slipped out. "I apologize. That was forward of me." *But it's true*, he thought. *That's how I feel.*

"It's all right. I feel the same. Sure, I've had some disagreements with other team members, especially Tug, but we'll work out our differences. I'm not as fragile as I look."

"I'm sure you aren't, and I also believe that you can handle the conflicts on your own. I just want to see if there was anything I could do to ease the situation. It's important that you're happy in your work."

"Thank you. That's very kind. Have you spoken with Tug?"

"Not yet. I wanted to visit with you first. Are there areas where you think I could improve your office environment?"

For the next half hour, Adam and Kelly discussed job-related routines, work assignments, conflict resolution, and other issues relative to her employment. Eventually, they agreed that Kelly should, for the time being, be allowed to deal with the disagreements on her own. In exchange, she promised to let Adam know if the office tension got out of hand.

But then, rather than call an end to his visit, Adam stayed on, and they switched to discussing more personal topics.

When the subject of Kelly's childhood came up, she fetched a scrapbook to share her early memories. Instead of returning to the recliner, she sat down beside Adam on the sofa, close enough that he could feel her body move as she turned pages and pointed to this or that photograph. After a time, he discovered that he was no longer paying attention to what she was saying, but was instead focusing on her mannerisms and the way she expressed herself.

Adam perceived that there was an innocence about Kelly that he found highly attractive. She had an inherently pleasant personality that drew him in. The longer he remained in her presence, the more enamored he became. In addition, he sensed that she felt the same, perhaps because of the way she laughed at his silly jokes or because she stayed in close physical contact rather than open a space between them after they had finished with the scrapbook.

Whatever the reason, Adam found himself being physically stimulated. His pulse had increased, his palms were moist, and he felt a pressure rising in his loins. Gently, he reached out and touched a hand to Kelly's cheek. She did not pull away. Instead, she responded by turning her face so she could gaze directly into his eyes. Without haste, he leaned closer and kissed her, tenderly at first, but then with greater passion. Soon, it seemed that they could not get enough of one another. She allowed his hands to explore her body, touching her in places that sent thrills rushing through her. She then reciprocated in kind.

Later, lying in bed after making love, Adam suddenly grasped the magnitude of what he had just allowed to happen. With Jolene, he had been blindsided by her aggressiveness. With Kelly, he had essentially orchestrated their encounter. *How can I be such an idiot?* he thought. *I have to work with this woman.* The truth was, if he was being totally honest with himself, that he had wanted things to work out the way they had, though he had originally refused to believe it. *This was my fault. I set myself up. I'm the one who's responsible.* But then another much more distressing thought came to him. *What am I going to do now? Or more to the point, what am I going to tell Victoria?*

His previous transgression had revealed how deeply wounded Victoria had been because he had attempted to keep his tryst secret. If not for bumping into her friend Pauline, she might never have known. There would have forever remained an unspoken secret between them, a gulf tearing them apart.

So what am I going to tell my wife? Adam asked himself. After a moment of reflection, he had his answer. *Nothing. I'm not going to tell her a thing.*

Still lounging in bed, Adam rolled on to his side and placed his hand on Kelly's abdomen. "I realize it's kind of late to bring this up, but we didn't use any protection."

Kelly chuckled. "Don't worry, I'm on the pill."

Adam exhaled a huge sigh of relief. "In that case…" As he moved his hand farther down, he felt Kelly respond.

* * *

July 2006

Nine weeks after beginning his affair with Kelly Stafford, Adam was a miserable wretch. His conscience refused to cease hounding him about his infidelity and reminding him that he had blown it once again. Despondent and filled with regret, Adam desperately needed someone to talk to. Unannounced, he had called upon his friend. As always, Theo had welcomed him, albeit with dismay, having sensed the moral soul-searching that lay ahead.

Upon crossing the threshold, Adam had declared, "You know, Theo, your friendship is the one thing I can always rely on. I love you, man."

"Have you been drinking?" Theo had replied.

"Not yet, but I intend to."

"This is going to be a long night," Theo muttered under his breath. "So what's bothering you? Come into the den and tell me all about it."

Twenty minutes later, Theo sat in an armchair opposite his friend. He was still nursing his first gin and tonic. He had kicked his shoes off, but then had thrown a small blanket over his lap. "What makes you say that?" Theo asked, continuing their conversation.

Adam rose and stepped to the mini bar where he helped himself to his third scotch. "Because it's true. I am a lousy father. Victoria thinks so. She says I don't spend enough time with Charlie, and she's right. I'm either at work, or worrying about work, or working at home. Besides, how do you spend time with a two-year-old? He's only recently learned to talk, and who can know what he's trying to say. When I can, I get down on the floor and help him play with his toys. Talk about boring. Was I that uninteresting when I was two? I don't remember."

"What else do you do with him?"

"I bought a pair of tickets to take him to a Grizzly football game, but Victoria put the kibosh on that. She felt he wasn't ready. I told her it would be good for him to socialize, but she seemed to think that being around a bunch of drunk fans wasn't the right venue. Go figure."

"What about taking him to a park? Maybe he could play on the slide or ride on that thing that goes around and around."

"A merry-go-round?"

"Right."

"And have some pervert abduct him right from under my nose? No way."

"Well then, think of something else. What did you do when you were two years old?"

"Honestly, the only thing I remember is slamming my thumb with a hammer. Man, did that hurt."

"That doesn't sound like fun. I doubt Victoria would approve," Theo said dryly.

"I suppose not."

Theo took a small sip of his gin and tonic and then gave Adam a shrewd look. "Do you want to tell me why you're really here?"

"What makes you think I haven't?"

"Because I know you. Something is on your mind, and it isn't Charlie."

"You're right. I screwed up again. This time it's serious."

"Not like last time, when your wife kicked you out of the house?"

"Well, yeah, but this time it's worse."

"Don't tell me. You didn't."

"Actually, I did. I've been seeing this girl—wait, they don't like being called girl, do they? This female—this young lady. She worked with me at Bit-March Systems. She was on my development team."

"She's one of your subordinates?" Theo said with incredulity.

"Yeah. Why?"

"We'll come back to that. Go on with what you were saying."

"I'd been seeing her for about two months, and then I made a mistake. While I was outside working in the yard, Victoria found her number in my cell phone and called it. The young lady—"

"You might as well tell me her name. It's not like I'm going to do anything with it."

"It's Kelly. Her name is Kelly. Anyway, Kelly must've recognized my number and thought it was me calling. She answered and began talking dirty like we sometimes do. Victoria hit the fan. When I came inside, I thought she was going to kill me. I've never seen her so mad. Not even after the first time. She kept screaming at me to get out. Theo, I'm worried. I'm afraid this time there may be no coming back from this."

"This Kelly person, she isn't pregnant, is she?"

"Not that I know. She kept assuring me she was on the pill. By the way, what did you mean when you said we'll get back to that? What's on your mind?"

"Kelly works for you, right? You're her boss."

"Worked for me. She quit when I ended our relationship."

"She walked off the job? That's even worse. When did all this happen?"

"This last weekend. That's when everything started going to hell in a hand basket. What do you mean it's worse?"

"Don't you see what you've done? You've set yourself up for a massive sexual harassment lawsuit. She'll claim she had to leave because you made her work environment intolerable. She'll probably sue you, your employer, your team, and the postman who delivers your mail."

"I think you're being melodramatic. We had a sincere thing going. We actually cared for one another."

"Are you familiar with the expression 'Hell hath no fury like a woman scorned'? That saying is still with us because there's a lot of truth behind it. It will be a miracle if she doesn't come after you, but for now, I suspect the bigger question is what are you going to do about Victoria?"

"I'm not sure what I can do. I suppose I'll give her time to cool off and then see if there's anything left to salvage. You know, there are times when I really hate myself. I mean, I don't just dislike me, I loathe who I am. I do things I never imagined I would do. I behave in ways that I find disgusting. I love Victoria. Why in the world would I put our marriage at risk? Just for a casual fling? It makes no sense. I'm an utter fool."

Theo downed another sip of gin and tonic. "If you expect me to disagree with you, I don't. On the other hand, you're no different than the rest of humanity. We all do things we don't want to do, and we don't do the things we know we should. It's the way we're wired. Hopefully, Victoria can understand that. It will help her let go of her anger."

"I can't tell her. She won't listen to me. Would you speak with her?"

"Me? You want me to talk to your wife about your infidelity? I'm your friend, but that's really pushing it."

"Maybe if we give it a few days, she might calm down enough to listen. What do you say?"

"On the other hand, if I approach her on your behalf, she might think you're too much of a coward to face her."

"She'd be right about that."

"You know, there's another saying that seems to apply to your situation: A bear never shits where it eats."

"I know. Believe me, I know." Adam stood up and moved to the sidebar to pour himself another drink.

*   *   *

September 2008

A small flow of water splashed into the catch bucket Adam had strategically positioned under the kitchen sink. The cold water's shut-off valve was old and hadn't been used in a while. Even though he had tightened its handle firmly, the valve hadn't closed completely. Nevertheless, he reasoned that if he worked quickly, he could replace the faucet and reconnect the water lines before there was too much of a mess.

When it came to home repairs, Adam wasn't much of a handyman. Small jobs like nailing up loose fence boards or gluing wobbly chair legs were within his range of abilities. Larger jobs, especially those that involved any type of plumbing, were usually left to the professionals. Over the previous six weeks, he had completed more home repairs than during any other period. In the back of his mind, Adam regarded the projects as nest building, similar to when a male bird assembles a nest for his mate.

The impetus for his flurry of handyman projects was that Victoria had finally agreed to let him move back in on a trial basis. It had taken two years of agonizing, pleading, begging, and many, many tears, but on his birthday, she had relented. "Every scoundrel deserves a second chance," she had declared forcefully, "and, buddy, you've had yours. Cheat on me again, and we are done." The strength of her declaration had left no question in Adam's mind that she meant what she said. So for the past month, he had been walking on eggshells and looking for ways to win back his wife's affection.

With the new faucet firmly bolted to the metal sink and all the rubber fittings properly in place, Adam was about to attach the cold-water line when the front doorbell rang. *Who would be calling on a Saturday?* he wondered. *Probably another pair of Jehovah's Witnesses.* Victoria had taken Charlie and gone to the grocery store. He was alone in the house. He put down his wrench and went to see who was at his front door.

For more than two years, Adam had expected to hear something from Kelly Stafford ever since the day he had ended their affair, but so far, there had been not a word. When he thought about it, he considered that to be a good thing. Not only was a clean break preferable to an ugly schism, he figured that the more time that passed, the less likely it was that she would sue. *Please don't let this be her*, he prayed as he opened the front door

The sight that greeted Adam literally took his breath away. When he had recovered sufficiently, he exclaimed, "Rachel? Is it really you? You're alive!" He very nearly refused to believe his eyes. Rather than the fourteen-year-old girl he remembered, a mature twenty-four-year-old woman stood facing him, though she was thin, almost emaciated, and she wore a haggard expression. Crow's feet at the corners of her eyes and several small scars on her cheeks marred her sun-weathered complexion. Her clothes were soiled in places and torn in others.

When the shock of seeing his sister alive began to fade, Adam stepped forward to give her a joyful hug, but she drew back.

"I gather you still don't like being touched," Adam commented. "No matter. Please, come in. How are you? How have you been? How could you leave like that without a word? I was worried sick. How could you do that to me?"

"So many questions." Rachel stepped inside and looked around. "Hasn't changed much." She focused her attention on her brother. "Neither have you. You doing okay?"

"I've had my ups and downs, but things are getting better." As he closed the front door, Adam scanned the street. No cars were parked in front of his house. "How did you get here?"

"I hitched a ride. They dropped me off on Broad Street. I walked from there."

That was when Adam noted the pack on his sister's back. "That looks heavy. Would you like to stash it in the closet?"

Rachel shed the backpack and handed it to Adam, who tucked it into a space beneath his winter coat. After closing the closet door, he turned to face his sister. "Why did you leave? I need to know. Was it me? Did I do something to drive you away?"

"It wasn't you. There were just too many memories to deal with. I knew you wouldn't let me go if I asked, so I just left."

"You could've said something—told me where you were going."

"You would've come after me."

"Yes. I would have."

Rachel turned toward the kitchen. "Have you got anything to eat?"

Adam followed. "Sure. How about a bowl of tomato soup and a grilled cheese sandwich? I'd offer you something more substantial, but Victoria isn't back from the grocery store yet."

Rachel stopped and turned around. "Who's Victoria?"

"My wife. Oh, that's right. You don't know. I'm married now—have been for six years."

"Six years? Has it been that long?"

"Actually, it's been ten since you left—1998. I was thinking about you the other day, and I did the math."

"Married? Is that right? I wasn't sure that would ever happen. You were never very comfortable around women, as I recall," Rachel turned and continued on toward the kitchen.

"Not only am I married, I have a son. He's four years old. His name is Charlie. Well, that's what we call him. His full name is Charles David Masters. He's your nephew."

When they entered the kitchen, Adam noted that an expanding puddle was forming on the linoleum.

* * *

September 2008

When Victoria and Charlie returned home, Adam and Rachel were in the living room, catching up on their ten years apart. Adam had learned that his sister had traveled widely, never staying in one place for more than several months at a span. To support herself, she had worked odd jobs, mostly waitressing, like their mother. She had confessed to having had several boyfriends, none of whom had been interested enough to stick around for long. Reading between the lines, he had also gleamed that Rachel probably had a substance abuse problem, most likely cocaine or perhaps heroin. He wanted to ask if she'd ever been to rehab, but was afraid he might antagonize her.

When asked about her plans for the future, Rachel had deflected his questions with questions of her own. His presumption was that she had fallen on hard times and was running out of options. On hearing the news that she was homeless, Adam had volunteered, "Of course you can stay here. We have a guest bedroom. It's yours for as long as you need it."

Just then, Victoria entered through the kitchen. When she noted the new faucet and that the floor had been recently mopped, she called out, "Good job. I didn't think you would finish so quickly."

From the living room, Adam replied, "It was easier than I thought. It's a simple task if you have the right tools and the correct fittings."

When Victoria entered the living room with Charlie trailing along behind, she took one look at Rachel and immediately tensed up. "Who is this person?" she demanded. "I'm gone a couple hours, and this is—"

Adam lurched to his feet. "Victoria, I'd like you to meet my sister. This is Rachel." To Rachel, he said, "This is my wife, Victoria."

"Oh!" Victoria exclaimed. "You're his sister? We thought you were—"

"Dead?" Rachel chuckled. "Yeah, I've heard that before. I've come close, let me tell you, but, well, like they say, close calls don't count."

Adam spoke up, "You two should get to know each other. I imagine there will be plenty of time for that because…" He looked to his wife. "Sweetheart, I've invited Rachel to stay with us for a while. She's down on her luck and has nowhere else to go. Can you believe that she's alive? And here she is. I didn't think I would ever see her again."

Charlie toddled over to where Rachel sat. With the innocence of a four-year-old, he stood looking up into her face. Rather than reach down to pick him up, Rachel sat quietly and gazed at her youngest relative. For a time, they simply stared at one another.

Victoria turned to Adam and said in a modulated tone of voice, "I have several bags of groceries in the car. Could you give me a hand?"

When they were outside, Victoria spun around to confront her husband. "You invited her to live with us without asking how I felt about letting a stranger into our home?"

"You weren't here. It was a spur-of-the-moment thing."

"You have a cell phone. You could have called me."

"I didn't think you would object. She is my sister, my blood relative whom I haven't seen in ten years. Besides, Rachel is not a stranger. She's family."

"She's a stranger to me. We don't know anything about who she is or what she's been doing. She could be on the run from the law for all we know. By the look of her, she might even be a druggie."

"That thought had occurred to me," Adam admitted, "but that's all the more reason we should take her in. Just look at her. Can't you see that she needs our help? In 1 Peter chapter 4, the Bible says we are to offer each other hospitality."

"Now you're quoting Scripture to me? Too bad you didn't quote it to yourself when you were out tomcatting around."

"Hey, I thought we were supposed to put the past behind us?"

"Sorry, it's just that being told that a stranger—I mean, a new family member will be staying in my home caught me off guard. I apologize. I shouldn't have brought it up."

"No, you're right. I should have thought about what the Bible says. Next time I'll do better."

"Next time?" Victoria snarled with a flash of hostility.

"Next time I'm tempted. Trust me, it won't happen again."

"I do want to trust you." Victoria opened the back hatch of her SUV and handed Adam two bags of groceries, but then paused. "I guess I'm just not ready, nor am I convinced that I ever will be."

"At least you're honest. I just wish there was something more I could do or say to hurry the process along."

"The one thing you can do is keep your wick in your pants."

About to protest, Adam recalled how severely he had hurt his wife. *Of course she's upset*, he thought. *Wouldn't I be, if the shoe was on the other foot?* So he said nothing. Instead, he turned and carried the groceries into the house.

*   *   *

May 2009

Smoke from the barbecue drifted upward into an azure sky. Earlier, an advancing weather front had threatened rain, but the storm clouds had dissipated. To Adam, it seemed like the perfect Memorial Day, except eight months had slipped by since Rachel's unexpected return, and she hadn't landed a job, nor had she found her own place to live. Her lack of initiative was one reason Adam strongly suspected she was doing drugs, but he hadn't been able to prove it. And without proof, any talk of enrolling his sister in a rehab program was destined to go nowhere.

The three-bedroom cottage on Springwood Lane had been spruced up expressly for the occasion. Adam had fertilized and watered the grass until it was verdant green. The brown patches had been filled in with fast-growing grass seed. He had painted the fence and weeded the flower beds. Small American flags decorated the yard out front. The house too had also attracted his attention. He had repaired and painted the shutters and window frames. The bedroom door that wouldn't close had been planed to its proper size. Clogs of leaves and debris had been removed from the gutters and downspouts.

"You've been busy," Bud Taylor commented, having noted the improvements. "The place is looking good." He raised his beer in a toast to his wife Charlotte, who smiled at him from across the yard. They had been wed nearly six months but were still in the honeymoon phase of their marriage. Charlotte Taylor was a pleasantly plump woman with a dimpled smile. She and Bud had first begun dating after he had helped prepare her taxes. Bud's father was fast approaching retirement age, and it was widely expected that Bud would soon take over their family accounting business.

"That's what happens," Theo said sagely, "when the landowner is sufficiently motivated." He gave Adam a sly wink.

Adam did not respond to the unspoken commentary. Theo had mostly been kept up-to-date regarding the Masters family's ongoing saga, but Bud had been excluded from the confidential briefings, and at that moment, Adam had no desire to take the time to fill him in.

Theo was still unmarried, and there were no prospects that his bachelorhood might end anytime soon. On the other hand, his relationship with Tranco Auto Parts was flourishing, him having recently been named general manager of the local outlet.

Other guests who had been invited to the Memorial Day celebration included Madeleine Gardner and her daughter Olivia, who, like Theo, was still unmarried; Rev. Hudson from Capstone Chapel; Tug Vasquez from Adam's team at Bit-March Systems (Sean Faulkner and Alexander James had been invited, but both had declined); and Maggie Sullivan, the Masters' next-door neighbor. Victoria and Charlie were inside the house, as was Rachel. No one had even considered inviting Humphrey/Michael, who, as far as Adam knew, was still working as a carny.

Bud polished off his beer and said, "I think I'll grab another." He sauntered off to be with his new bride.

When Bud had moved beyond earshot, Theo said, "So how goes the war on the home front?"

Adam checked a hamburger patty by testing its sponginess. He then set it to the side, away from the hottest part of the grill. "I think we have what might be referred to as an uneasy truce. Sometimes, the tension is so thick you could cut it with a butter knife. Rachel doesn't say much, but then she never has. Victoria, on the other hand, has no problem vocalizing her sentiments, sometimes with complete disregard for other people's sensibilities."

"That means they're not getting along." Theo chuckled.

Adam seemed offended. "Isn't that what I said?"

"What about you and Victoria? Has there been any progress in that regard?"

Adam sighed. "My sister's being here hasn't helped. I'm sure Victoria and I would be further along if Rachel hadn't dropped in like she did. At least I'd like to think so." A frown spread across Adam's face.

Theo took note of his unspoken commentary. "I gather there's more?"

"There is something that troubles me. I've been writing it off to Victoria's having been blindsided by my…eh, issues, but now I'm not so sure. She seems changed. She's not the same person I married. That person was kind and pleasant to be around. Now she's snappy and hypercritical. Maybe the best word to describe her attitude is bitchy. It almost seems as if she doesn't want to move on. I hate to say this, but I think she likes being the wounded wife, that somehow victimhood suits her.

"The worst part is, I can't help thinking I'm responsible. Maybe having to deal with the mess I created changed her, made her…angrier inside? I don't know. All I do know is that I want my old Victoria back. I'd hate to believe I've permanently destroyed something beautiful."

"What about counseling? Have you guys given any thought to seeking professional help?"

"We've talked about it, but Victoria refuses to air our dirty laundry in front of other people. I doubt I'd ever be able to talk her into it."

Theo's mien became more serious. "What about Kelly? Have you heard from her?"

"Not a word."

"That's good. I just hope she doesn't show up on your doorstep with a toddler in tow."

"Don't even think that," Adam said with a shiver. "Victoria would come unglued."

The sound of raised voices filtered into the backyard from the kitchen. Adam could not make out the words, but from the sound of it, there was a heated argument going on. He handed Theo the spatula and said, "Mind the burgers. I best go see what that's all about."

Just as Adam entered the kitchen, Rachel spun on her heel and stormed out of the room. A short time later, he heard an upstairs door slam shut.

Victoria stood by the sink, a heavy metal spoon in her hand. She held it like a weapon. A large glob of potato salad had spilled onto the floor. Her face was flushed. "I swear I'm not going to put up with this any longer."

"What happened?" Adam said.

"She has the nerve to criticize me for the way I run my household. She's the one who can't keep a boyfriend, much less a husband. And then she goes and tells me I'm a lousy mother, as if she would know what it takes to raise a child."

"My sister said that?"

"Not in so many words, but her meaning was clear. She also said I'm too unkind, and she doesn't like the way I treat you. If she only knew what I've been through." Victoria fumed, "I can't believe the gall that woman has. I'm done. She has to go. Either she leaves, or I do." There was an air of finality to Victoria's pronouncement, though she continued, "Do you know what else? I had almost a hundred dollars set aside in a coffee tin in the cupboard. Now it's gone. She's the only one that could have taken it. I know Charlie didn't. And I assume you didn't either?"

"No, I didn't. I didn't even know it was there."

"I was saving up to buy our son something really nice, but now I can't because the money is gone."

"Did you accuse Rachel of taking the money?"

"No, but I asked if she knew anything about it. Of course she would deny she'd taken it. Not only is she a thief, but she's a liar as well."

Adam chose not to continue the discussion for fear of making matters worse. Instead, he said, "Let me go talk to her. Maybe we can straighten this out. It's not like her to be so assertive."

"That's right. Stand up for your sister. Ignore how I feel."

"I'm not ignoring you. I'm just trying to figure out how we can get past this. And please, keep your voice down. We have guests, remember?"

"What? You don't want me to embarrass you in front of your friends? Fine. I'll play the dutiful housewife, but not as long as your sister is living under our roof. Like I said, either she's gone, or I am."

The door to Rachel's bedroom was closed when Adam climbed the stairs. He knocked softly, but there was no response. "Rachel, honey, it's me, your brother. I'd like to talk to you."

He knocked again, but heard no sounds coming from inside the bedroom, not even a whimper.

"Rachel, please, open the door." He tried the doorknob, and to his surprise, it was unlocked. He opened the door slowly. Rachel wasn't inside. Nor was she in the other bedrooms or the bathroom when he looked.

Returning to the guest bedroom, he sat down on the edge of the bed. That's when he noticed that Rachel's meager possessions were missing. The closet was empty when he checked, and so were the dresser drawers. The vanity had been cleared of all its little knickknacks

Obviously, Adam thought, *she must have slipped out of the house immediately after leaving the kitchen. That means she was already packed. And that means she had planned to leave all along.* When the ramifications of what had just happened became clear, Adam silently wailed. *No! No. No. This can't be happening. Not again.*

As he descended the stairs, he asked himself, *What do I tell our guests if they ask? Tell them she's running an errand, and we're not sure how long she'll be gone? And what do I tell Victoria? Tell her nothing, just that the problem is solved.*

When Adam entered the kitchen, Victoria was on her hands and knees, angrily scrubbing the potato salad off the floor and muttering to herself.

It occurred to Adam that maybe his sister's leaving was a blessing in disguise, but then he thought, *When will I see her again? In another ten years? Maybe never?* The possibility distressed him severely. Then another even more disturbing notion came to him. He looked down at his wife and wondered, *What if this is what I have to contend with for the rest of my life?*

*　　*　　*

I'd been watching Casey during my narrative, trying to assess his mood. It hadn't been easy baring my soul, especially in front of someone whose opinion I valued. Thankfully, I had detected only a modicum of disapproval. Truthfully, I had expected more, at least to the level of disdain I had for myself. It's one thing to admit the wrongs you've done. It's quite another to confess them to someone you care about. I could only hope that he would learn from my mistakes and conduct himself accordingly.

Casey folded his arms across his chest and sat back in his chair. "If you don't mind my saying so, it seems to me that your greatest adversary was yourself, at least when it came to managing your relationships with women."

I gave a nod of concurrence. "That is rather astute. Perhaps life's greatest challenge is learning how to deal with the opposite sex. Untold numbers of men have been brought low because they let their little head think for their big head, if you catch my drift. Do you have a girlfriend?"

Casey tipped back in his chair and balanced on two legs. "Not exactly. There is someone I enjoy being around. We seem to get on well together."

"What's her name?"

"Chloe."

"Her last name?"

"Rasmussen. Chloe Rasmussen."

"Are you fond of her?"

"I am, but I'm not sure how far that fondness goes. I mean, we're just friends."

"Do yourself a favor. If you care for her at all, don't mess around. Be with only one woman at a time. That's some of the best advice I can give you."

Casey blushed. "We haven't—you know, done anything yet."

"You're still a virgin?"

"Yeah," my grandson admitted sheepishly.

"Good for you. I would strongly recommend that you keep it that way until you meet the one you're destined to spend the rest your life with. If you do, you'll save yourself a whole lot of grief. Trust me in this."

"I hear what you're saying. By the way, when do you want to meet again? I assume there's more to your story?"

"Much more. Today is Tuesday. Early tomorrow morning, I'm flying to Omaha. I should be home in a couple days. How about Friday?"

"Friday is fine. Same time?"

"At 5:00 p.m.?"

"Sounds good." Casey laughed. "My place or yours?"

"Mine, I guess. It's my turn to fix dinner. Any requests?"

"Dealer's choice. I'll eat whatever you set before me."

"That's what I like, an easy date."

We both laughed.

A moment later, Casey asked, "What's in Omaha?"

"Hopefully, the resolution to a problem I've carried around for many years."

"Oh yeah?" Casey perked up with obvious interest. "Does this involve the manhunt you've been conducting?"

"It does."

"Want to tell me about it?"

"Not tonight. You may not be tired of listening to me talk, but I am. I need to go home and throw this old body into bed. I've got an early flight out in the morning."

As I drove back to my house, I reflected upon how our times together were progressing. Casey's attentiveness pleased me. I figured that one or two more sessions would allow me to hammer home the message I wanted him to absorb.

1 1

REDEMPTION

In order to make my 6:36 a.m. flight to Omaha, I'd had to be at the Missoula airport by 4:30 a.m., which meant I'd rolled out of bed at 3:00 a.m. After an hour-and-a-half layover in Denver, our Boeing 737 finally touched down at Eppley Airfield at 12:38 p.m. Wednesday afternoon.

The first thought that came to me as I deplaned was *I really am getting too old for this. Hopefully, this will be my last junket.* As with previous flights, I had packed only a small carry-on bag, so I headed straight to the rental car counter. Twenty minutes later, I was in another midsized sedan cruising toward the center of town.

Theo and I had worked out a game plan to expedite my search. From the five yearbooks Gladys Purdue had loaned me, we had identified four candidates that fit the criterion that would lead us to Alice Cunningham's friend: all were male, all lived in or around Omaha, and all had the same name as a student who had attended Cedar Shores High School between 1992 and 1998. One of our four candidates had already been eliminated because of his social media footprint. The student's yearbook picture showed that he was white, but the candidate's Facebook page indicated he was black—same name, different race. The other three candidates had virtually no social media footprints.

As before, I had determined not to call in advance, but rather, I planned to show up unannounced on each candidate's doorstep. That way if I did find Alice's friend, and she was with him, she would have a hard time refusing to speak to me.

My biggest fear was that all three candidates would turn out to be the wrong person with the right name. My apprehension was fueled by remembering the number of Alice Cunninghams Theo and I had identified when we had launched our manhunt.

A troubling thought came to me as I drove toward the first address on my list. *Theo and I had assumed that Alice's friend was male. What if he was a she? I mean, it wasn't totally outside the realm of possibilities. Even in the early nineties, same-gender relationships weren't entirely unknown. I simply hadn't considered the likelihood.* I decided that if my current search came up dry, I'd redo our yearbook evaluation using revised criteria.

The first name on my list was Robert Allendale. His online profile showed that he lived on the north side of town in a residential community that turned out to be a warren of twisty streets and cul-de-sacs, each having the same name followed by Street, Place, Lane, Drive, Road, or Trail. After more than a few wrong turns, I finally located his residence.

I rang the front doorbell five times, but nobody answered. Feeling downhearted, I was about to leave when I heard what sounded like someone digging with a shovel. The sound came from the backyard. I followed the noise around the side of the house where I discovered an older man approximately my age tilling a modest-sized garden.

From a dozen feet away, I called out, "Hello? Excuse me? Hello there." The man did not react. I called out louder. "Hello? Can you hear me? I'm sorry to bother you, but—"

Startled, the man abruptly stopped digging and turned to face me straight on. The shovel came up defensively in front of him. "Who are you, and what do you want?"

"I'm sorry to bother you, but I'm looking for someone, and I hope you may be able to help me. Is your name Robert Allendale?"

"Who wants to know?"

"I apologize. I should have introduced myself. My name is Adam Masters, and I'm wondering, did you attend Cedar Shores High School?"

"What?

"I'm trying to locate a man named Robert Allendale who attended Cedar Shores High School in Cedar Shores, Kansas. Might that man be you?"

"I'm Robert Allendale, but I don't know nothing about Cedar Shores or whatever."

"So you don't know a woman named Alice Cunningham?"

"What in tarnation? Who are you?"

"I'm sorry. My name is Adam Masters. I'm trying to track down a friend of mine. Her name is Alice Cunningham. I've heard that she's possibly visiting a man she knew in high school. That man's name is Robert Allendale. Could you please just tell me if you attended Cedar Shores High School in the early nineties?"

"Not me. I went to Glendale High in Phoenix, Arizona."

"Then you don't know Alice Cunningham?"

"Nope. Ain't never heard that name before."

"I see. Well, thank you for your time. I'm sorry to disturb you. Looks like you've got a pretty nice garden going there."

"It's a lot of work, let me tell you." Mr. Allendale went back to tilling the soil while I returned to my car and headed out to find the next name on the list.

*   *   *

Mr. Bruce Thurgood was recorded as living in the suburbs west of town. I followed Dodge Street until it turned into West Dodge Road, and then I veered off onto surface streets. After a brief sojourn through middle-class neighborhoods, I located what I thought was his house. The place seemed to have fallen on hard times. The grass needed mowing, paint was peeling off the front porch, and a cardboard patch had been taped over a broken bedroom window.

Nevertheless, I ascended three steps to the front door and pushed the doorbell. I didn't hear it ring, so I knocked loudly. A short time later, an older woman cracked open the door and peeked out. "Yes?" she said.

"Hi, my name is Adam Masters, and I'm looking to find a friend of mine." I rambled on through the entire explanation while the woman listened patiently.

When I finished, she said, "Yes, Bruce Thurgood lives here, but I don't know where he went to high school. I'm his cousin from Pittsburgh. I'm house-sitting until the place sells." She pointed toward the front yard. I visually tracked in the direction she had indicated and saw a real estate For Sale sign that I had failed to notice. I looked at the woman and said, "And your name is…?"

"Beatrice Thurgood. I'm Bruce's cousin."

"From Pittsburgh, right? Well, Beatrice, is Mr. Thurgood available? Might I speak with him?"

"You could try, but I don't think it would do you much good. He has senile dementia. We had to put him in a nursing home. He hardly remembers me anymore."

"Is there any way we could find out where he went to high school?"

"I don't know how. All I can tell you is he grew up in Pasadena, California. Probably he went to high school somewhere near there. I don't think he's ever been to—where was it?"

"Cedar Shores, Kansas."

"No, I don't recall him ever mentioning that place. I wish we could help you."

"Thank you. I appreciate your taking the time to speak with me, and I hope your cousin gets better soon."

"Oh, he's not going to get better. It's just a matter of time till his body gives out like his brain has."

"If that's the case, I wish him well nevertheless." I waved goodbye as I climbed into my car. *Two down. One to go.* I headed for the third name on the list. The odds of my trip being a success were rapidly diminishing.

* * *

Online, Samuel P. Burke was recorded as living in an upper-class section of town a quarter mile from the Missouri River. His three-story home had gabled windows and a wide circular driveway. I pulled in and parked.

A middle-aged woman wearing wire-framed glasses above a broad nose answered the door. Her prematurely gray hair was done up in a bun. "May I help you?" she said.

I introduced myself and said, "I'm looking for Mr. Burke, Samuel P. Burke. Is he at home?"

"Yes, but Mr. Burke is not receiving visitors." That was when I noticed that the woman was wearing a modified nurse's uniform consisting of a crisp white blouse and an A-line white skirt. She also had on clean white shoes. An analog watch was safety-pinned to her lapel. From her apparel, I concluded that she was probably a private duty nurse.

"I've come a long way, and this won't take long. I just need to ask him a couple questions."

"I'm afraid Mr. Burke is indisposed. Like I said, he's not receiving visitors."

"Is there a problem, Annie?" The female voice had come from someplace out of sight on the other side of the door.

Over her shoulder, the nurse replied, "Some gentleman is asking after Mr. Burke. I told him the man is not available.

The woman who had spoken stepped forward. She was of medium height and build, perhaps 5'6" tall and 135 pounds. She looked to be in her late sixties or early seventies. Her neatly combed silver hair glinted when a beam of afternoon sunlight caught it. The most noticeable thing about her was her cobalt blue eyes. When she looked at me, I thought I saw a flash of recognition.

I certainly recognized her.

I exclaimed, "Alice!? I don't believe it. It's really you? Man, you are one hard lady to track down."

Alice cocked her head as if struggling to pull a name out of a dusty memory archive. "And you are…?"

"Adam Masters. We worked together at Townsend Electronics. I've come a long way to find you."

"Adam Masters—oh, yes." Alice's eyes narrowed. "I thought I recognized you. After all these years, what do you want?" Her mild voice had taken on a flinty edge.

I had hoped that Alice was no longer harboring a grudge. However, that was apparently not the case. "I need to speak with you. There's something I need to tell you. Is there someplace we can talk? Please? Like I said, I have come a long way."

Alice seemed on the verge of flat-out refusing, but then relented. "Very well. Come in, but like Annie told you, Mr. Burke is not available, and please keep your voice down. We wouldn't want to disturb him."

I stepped inside. "Actually, the reason I wanted to see him was to ask how I could get in touch with you. Now that's not necessary. You're looking healthy. Are you well?"

"Well enough." Alice led me to a nicely furnished parlor just off the entryway. We sat down facing one another, a low coffee table between us.

Alice crossed her legs, her elbows close by her sides. "You indicated that I was a hard lady to track down. What did you mean by that?"

"It's a long story. I'd be glad to tell you, but first, there's something I need to ask. That day at Townsend Electronics when we first came upon you, the guard and I, you said you were placing an invitation in my locker. Later, did you go ahead and have the party to which I'd been invited?"

"After all these years, that's the question that's been burning a hole in your brain? I don't believe it."

"Please, I need to know. This is important."

"I can't imagine why, but very well. Yes. I did have the party. Only a few people showed up. It was a real downer. Satisfied?"

"Yes. Thank you. I had hoped that would be your answer. Now there's one more question I would like to ask you."

"Seriously?"

"Alice Cunningham, will you do me the honor of having dinner with me tonight? If you will, I'll explain everything. I promise."

I could tell that I had piqued her curiosity. After a moment of reflection, she said, "Why not tell me now?"

"I will if you insist, but I think it would be much more pleasant if we could talk quietly. I promise, I will behave myself."

"I don't know. Sam isn't doing well—"

"Please. It will only be a couple hours, and I'm sure you'll find it worthwhile."

Despite her obvious skepticism, Alice said, "All right. What time?"

We agreed that I would pick her up at 6:00 p.m., and she would get to choose the restaurant.

*   *   *

The Casa Blanca Mexican Restaurant was crowded when we arrived. Most of the customers seemed to be in a jovial mood, probably because happy hour had just ended. Since we didn't have a reservation, we were forced to wait approximately half an hour. To pass the time, we slipped into the bar. All tables were occupied, so Alice snagged a chair at the bar. I stood beside her.

During the ride over, Alice had refrained from asking any questions, instead leaving it to me to address the issues I knew she had on her mind. Rather than jump right in, there was a topic that had been in my thoughts since my visit to Swiftwater, Alaska. I leaned closer so that she could hear me above the din. "Your friend, Mr. Burke? I gather he's not well?"

The bartender came over to take our orders. Alice asked for a club soda. I wondered if maybe she wanted to avoid drinking alcohol because she didn't trust me, or maybe she was a teetotaler. I resolved to find out later. Rather than imbibe on my own, I told the bartender I would stick with ice water. Alice gave me a curious look, but rather than commenting, she said, "Sam has a number of health issues. His main problem is advanced kidney failure. He was on dialysis until last week, but because he also has metastatic prostate cancer that's progressing, the decision was made to stop his treatments.

"That's why he called me. He understands that he will soon die. We've been friends since high school. People thought we were boyfriend-girlfriend, but we weren't. We were just two people with interests in common, like a fondness for fine jazz and an appreciation of early American history.

"Sam's been enrolled in hospice care for the past five months. We don't expect him to live more than another week or two. Mainly, I came here so that he wouldn't die alone."

"That's extraordinarily kind of you. Thank you for sharing. I wasn't going to ask."

"No, but I could tell you were curious."

"Speaking of which, I did promise you that I would explain why I am here."

"I'm listening." Alice angled her body on the barstool so she could face me more directly.

I began by summarizing how Mabel Buchanan had sent me to Cedar Shores, Kansas, where I had contacted Rose Richardson, Alice's niece, and how Rose had referred me to Tracy Yang in Swiftwater, Alaska. From there, my search had again focused on Cedar Shores, where, with the help of Gladys Purdue's high school yearbooks, I had identified Samuel Burke, the classmate I was seeking, who now lived in Omaha, Nebraska. I finished up by saying, "And tracking him down led me to you."

"Wow." Alice seemed impressed. "You've put a lot of time and effort into finding me, but the question you haven't answered is why?"

"I was coming to that. Some years ago, I accepted Jesus Christ as my Lord and Savior. Allowing him to rule my life began to change me. I started seeing things from a different perspective, and reading the Scriptures reshaped my conscience. Things I had previously tolerated, even embraced, I could no longer abide. The more refined my moral code became, the more pressure I felt to go back and set things right. One of the misdeeds that has haunted me is how I treated you. Exodus chapter 20 verse 16 says, 'Thou shalt not bear false witness against thy neighbor,' which is precisely what I had done to you.

"I accused you of stealing my mother's diamond necklace out of my locker. Although there was no proof, my accusation was largely responsible for your getting fired."

"I remember."

"What you don't know is that when I returned home that evening, after you were terminated, I found the necklace in my jacket pocket. I'd forgotten I'd put it there to bring home. When I found it, I could have spoken up. I could have cleared your name, perhaps even gotten you your job back, but I said nothing, and that failure to act has stuck with me all these years. I remained silent because I was a coward. I was afraid of losing my own job on account of the ruckus I'd caused.

"What I'm trying to say is…I'm sorry. What I did was wrong, or rather what I didn't do. I'm aware that for all these years, you've had to live with the knowledge that you were falsely accused. That must have been especially difficult, but I'm asking you now is there any way you can forgive me?"

To my utter amazement, Alice laughed, a hearty, full-throated laugh. Eventually, she said, "Not only can I forgive you, but I need to thank you." She swallowed some of club soda to clear her throat. "Getting fired from Townsend Electronics was perhaps one of the luckiest things that has ever happened to me. Had I continued working in the accounting department, I never would have become a wildlife biologist. You see, getting fired forced me to rethink my career path. That's when I decided that what I really wanted was to be out of doors. I wanted a job that would let me spend time in the natural world. That never would have happened had I continued working for Townsend. So I'd say we're even. Sometimes, you win by losing."

"We're not quite even. There's something more I need to do. This is mostly for my benefit, not yours." I reached in my pocket and pulled out a small gift-wrapped box. I placed it on the bar. "Please accept this as a token of my sincerity. I would really like you to have it."

At first, I thought Alice would refuse my gift outright. But again, her curiosity seemed to dictate her response. She picked up the box and carefully removed the wrapping, exposing a slightly beat-up jewelry case. When she opened it, she discovered my mother's diamond necklace. She gasped in amazement.

"Please, don't say no." I gently placed a hand on her arm. "I need to do this. If you choose not to wear it, that's perfectly fine. You can sell it. I'm sure there must be something worthwhile you could do with the money. Consider this a token of my redemption. It would mean a lot to me. What do you say?"

"I don't know what to say. I'm stunned, literally. Perhaps I'll just say thank you."

"Very good. Now let me go see how much longer before we get a table. I don't know about you, but I'm hungry."

During our meal, I got to hear Alice's life story and how she had followed her passions. I learned that she had been widowed at a young age and had never remarried, but instead had reverted to using her maiden name. I also learned that not only was she a fan of jazz and American history, she enjoyed visiting new and interesting places, as did I. The subject of the necklace did not come up again. However, as I listened to her speak, a tremendous sense of relief filled me, as if an anchor I'd been hauling around had suddenly been cast off from my soul.

It was nearly midnight when I returned Alice to her friend's house and said good night. By then, it was too late to seek out a motel. So I drove straight to the airport. Once again, my return flight home was scheduled to leave bright and early. Hopefully, this time, I would be able to sleep on the plane. If not, I feared that I would be a frazzled mess when I next met with my grandson to begin my final round of storytelling.

1 2

ALL THE WRONG CHOICES

"You cook good Chinese, Grandfather," Casey mumbled around a mouthful of takeout.

"Glad you like it." Rather than fix dinner as I had initially planned, I had given in to my fatigue and ordered our meals from the Lotus Blossom, a Chinese restaurant a little over a mile from my house. I had chosen shrimp lo mein, beef with broccoli, pork foo young, and combination fried rice.

Casey said, "We don't have to do this, you know. You look worn-out."

"It's been a hectic week." Once again, I'd had trouble sleeping during the plane ride home. *Maybe next time you should take a sleeping pill*, I told myself. As I considered the notion, another thought occurred to me. *But then you'll arrive all drugged up and groggy. No, thank you.* I cracked open my fortune cookie.

"What does it say?" Casey reached for his.

I chuckled as I read it. "'He who laughs last is laughing at you.' I like that one. It's good to stay humble, keeps things in their proper perspective. What does yours say?"

Casey smiled. "'You will soon prevail in your quest.' I hope that's true, since I'll be taking my finals in three weeks."

"Sounds to me like the fortune cookie genie expects you to pass. How are your studies coming along, if I might ask?"

"I'm plodding through them."

"You don't sound very confident," I said with concern. "Should I worry?"

"It's just that there's so much to remember. Sometimes, I fear my brain will explode."

I nodded in agreement. "I used to feel the same when I was younger, but usually the morning after a wild cocktail party. Seriously, is everything all right? What about between you and Chloe? Are you two getting along?"

"Oh, we're fine. No problems there. Besides, we're just friends."

"So you've said. Still, something is going on. I can tell. Do you want to share what it is?"

Casey looked away rather than make eye contact. "I'd rather not."

"Hey, I've shown you mine, now it's time for you to show me yours. What's getting you down?"

"If you must know, I've done something I shouldn't have done, but it's nothing you need to worry about. I'll work it out."

"Are you sure? It might help to talk."

Casey stood his ground. "I'll be fine. By the way, you haven't mentioned how your manhunt turned out. Did you find the person you were looking for?"

"It took some doing, but yes. I did. In fact, it was a far bigger success than I had hoped for." I considered telling Casey the whole story, but decided that it would be better if I returned to my ongoing narrative. "If you're done eating, we should pick up where we left off."

"Let's do it."

We cleaned up our dinner messes and headed for the library.

*   *   *

March 2011

Almost a year after Adam had begun working for Aurora—an up-and-coming software development company—an opportunity came along that could substantially advance his career. He was thirty-one at the time, and competition in the workplace was fierce. There was always a push to see which employee could kiss their bosses'…

*   *   *

"Hold on," Casey interrupted. "I thought you were going to talk about Grandaunt Rachel. Wasn't it late in 2009 when she disappeared the second time? I want to know what happened to her."

"I wish I could tell you, but like the first time, she simply disappeared. It wasn't until much later that we had any word at all, and we'll come to that eventually."

"So we do know what happened to her?"

"We do, but—"

"Let me guess. I'll just have to wait…again."

"Bingo."

*   *   *

As I was saying, Adam had been working for Aurora for about eleven months, and competition among his coworkers was fierce. His fellow employees were constantly looking for ways to move up the corporate ladder, usually at someone else's expense. This confrontational mindset made for a difficult work environment, but the company's leaders wanted it that way. They felt that active rivalries were good for productivity. The most effective staff members would stay alert and focused. Sluggards were in danger of being swept aside.

Adam had been hired as a senior project supervisor. He was responsible for bringing to market as quickly and cheaply as possible whatever software package management felt could turn a profit. Since being hired, he had worked hard to do his job properly, and for that reason, he was surprised when one morning, he was summoned to Mr. Duckworth's office. As Aurora's senior vice president for software development, Roger Duckworth was Adam's boss. *I wonder what I've done wrong this time?* he thought.

Adam saved the subroutine code he had been editing and promptly reported as ordered. Mr. Duckworth's door stood partially ajar, so he knocked softly and poked his head inside. "Yes, sir. You wanted to see me?"

"Aw, yes, Masters. Come in. Take a chair while we wait."

"Wait for what?" Adam wanted to say, but he remained mute. It turned out that he didn't have to wait long. He startled when Elias Hayes also knocked on Mr. Duckworth's door and stepped inside. Like Adam, Elias was a project supervisor and, therefore, Adam's primary competition. In the short time Adam had worked for Aurora, he had learned through the grapevine that Elias had a reputation for being both capable and ruthless, especially when it came to making himself look good.

"Gentlemen," said Mr. Duckworth, "I've summoned you here because I intend to change your assignments. Our lawyers have finally finished their negotiations. The contracts have been signed, and we have two new projects that are ready to launch. Both of these projects are top drawer. If we can bring them in on time and on budget, it will transform Aurora from a startup to a major player in the industry.

"That's where you two come in. Adam, you're relatively new, but I believe you have potential. I know you haven't had a chance to really get your feet wet, but I want to see what you can do with this assignment. Elias, I know you. You're effective when it counts, and you can get the job done."

Mr. Duckworth looked from man to man.

"Adam, I'm giving you the Downlink Project. You'll be working with the same team you have now. They are to drop what they're doing and pivot to this new package as quickly as possible. Elias, I'm giving you the Long Wire Project. You too will keep your current team with one exception. I'm going to swap Markham for Greig. I need Greig to help sort out a glitch in the Fairfield Project."

"Sir," Elias protested, "Greig is one of my best programmers. I really would hate to part with her."

"Markham is good too. You'll just have to make do. Gentlemen, let me remind you of the importance of these new assignments. Succeed, and Aurora's future will be assured. Fail, and you may not be here next year, nor will any of us.

"As a special incentive, and because so much is riding on your performance, the first team to bring their project to completion will earn each member a substantial bonus and their supervisor a special reward."

"What sort of reward?" Elias asked.

"I'm not at liberty to divulge that at this time, but trust me, it will be substantial." Mr. Duckworth picked up two manila folders off his desk. He handed one to Adam and one to Elias. "These are your project requirements. Inside you'll find design specifications, interface parameters, performance targets, and operational goals. Both of you are talented programmers, so let's see what kind of software packages you can bring me. Any questions?"

"One, sir," Adam said. "What's our time horizon?"

"Six months. However, for every week that we're early, there will be a bonus, and for every week that we're late, there will be a penalty, so let's not be late. Anything else?"

"Yes, sir," Elias said. "What about teams 3 and 4? Will they be participating?"

"They're going to stay with their current assignments. Which reminds me, you are not to discuss your projects with anyone who's not on your team. Both of these projects are classified and have national security implications. Anything more?"

"No, sir," Adam said.

"No, sir," Elias echoed.

Both supervisors rose and left the room together. In the hallway, Elias turned toward Adam and extended his hand. "Best of luck. This should be fun."

Adam returned the handshake. "May the best man win." As his competition walked away, Adam looked down at his hand to make sure all his fingers were still attached.

Without delay, Adam returned to his office in what the programmers called the boiler room, a large central space that hosted sixteen cubicles. There were four teams with four programmers on each team. A supervisor's office was located in each corner of the boiler room.

Seated at his desk, Adam began reviewing the information he had been given. The Downlink Project seemed fairly straightforward. With the world's increased reliance on satellite communications, there was an immediate need for improved data transmission metrics, especially with regard to speed and accuracy. The Downlink team was being tasked with creating a brand-new satellite communications package, which he presumed would require brand-new algorithms that had never existed before.

Piece of cake, Adam facetiously told himself. It was one thing to write new code for well-tested algorithms. It was a different matter entirely to have to design the algorithms first.

As Adam thumbed through his manila folder, he came upon a spec sheet outlining the Long Line Project. He assumed the summary had been included so that he would appreciate what he was up against.

The Long Line Project shared similar goals, but would require a different implementation. Elias's team was being tasked with building communication software that would service undersea telecom cables. Boosts in both speed and accuracy were the critical endpoints to be achieved.

Adam reached in a desk drawer and took out a tablet of lined yellow notepaper. He straightaway began breaking his project down into manageable segments. It soon became apparent that the first thing his team would need to accomplish would be to design a new suite of algorithms. Everything else hinged on that.

*   *   *

"Come on, Billy," Adam said to his lead programmer, "we've tried that. It doesn't work. That old encryption routine is a dinosaur. It slows down the entire throughput. What we need is something faster, something more elegant, maybe something based on an entirely new concept."

Billy Johansson leaned back in his chair and laced his fingers behind his head. "You're right, but where we're going to find such a routine, I have no idea."

In frustration, Adam barked, "Work with me on this." For more than three months, his team had been chipping away at their primary obstacle. What they needed was a refined set of algorithms. Yet thus far, they had very little to show for their efforts. They had achieved several small victories, but the main obstacle of data encryption/decryption still lay ahead of them.

One thing that seriously worried Adam was that every time his team had achieved a small breakthrough, Elias's team had not been far behind, and frequently with an identical solution to the problem. In Adam's mind, the similarities could not be explained by random chance. He was beginning to suspect that somehow Elias had gained access to his team's in-house network or to the secure folders where their data was stored.

"All right, team," Adam said, "let's call it a night. We're all tired, and we're not thinking clearly. Go home. Get some sleep. Come back tomorrow ready to work."

Adam waited until his team had departed, and then locked down the network, making their online resources inaccessible.

By the time he finished, Adam was exhausted, and on the drive home, he found it difficult to concentrate. For some reason, the image of a meat grinder kept returning to his thoughts. He pictured meat being torn apart as it was squeezed through an array of small holes. In some respects, that process paralleled what happened during encryption. Blocks of data were broken apart, transmitted through the air, and then reassembled. The problem was that it took time on both ends to do the breakdown and the reassembly. *What if there was a way*, he thought, *to take the ground-up meat, squeeze it back through the array of small holes, and have it come out of the grinder in its original form—reverse sausage making? But how to do that?*

A light bulb switched on inside Adam's brain.

What if you turn the sausage maker around?

He steered his Jeep into a tight U-turn and rushed back to Aurora.

An hour before sunrise, Adam had his answer. The solution was to fragment the data stream into manageable packets, encrypt each packet, and then transmit that packet's decryption instructions ahead of the packet itself. That way when the encrypted data was received, it would be immediately reconstituted into its original form. *It's like turning ground meat back into steak.*

When he ran a simulation to test his theory, he noted a 20 percent improvement in both speed and accuracy. He had his answer.

Adam was about to save his new algorithm online when he recalled his concerns regarding Elias and the possibility that his nemesis had somehow gained access to his team's network.

Another idea came to Adam. Working quickly, he reconfigured his algorithm to include a nasty surprise. Anyone who tried to run his modified algorithm would unleash a worm that would chew through their data storage in milliseconds.

By the time his team was ready to begin their day, he had prepared assignments that would set them on the road to fulfilling the Downlink contract.

*   *   *

April 2011

One month later, Adam and Elias found themselves back in Mr. Duckworth's office. They sat facing their boss.

From across his desk. Mr. Duckworth said, "Congratulations, Adam. Our client has tested your software package and found it acceptable. I guess that means you win."

"Thank you, sir. It was certainly a challenge."

"I imagine it was. As for you, Elias," Mr. Duckworth said, "I'm disappointed. I expected you to be much farther along by now."

"Yes, sir. Me too. I'm not sure what happened. Somehow, we lost more than half of our resource files. It took almost a week to rebuild our code library."

Adam smiled inwardly, but let nothing show on his face.

Mr. Duckworth stood and stepped around from behind his desk. "Elias, I want you and Adam to work together. If you use his algorithm, you should still be able to complete your project on time."

Elias seemed crestfallen. "Yes, sir."

"Now as to the reward I promised. In one month, I'm going to retire. That means that Aurora is going to need a senior VP for software development. Adam, the job is yours if you want it. You're what? Thirty-two now? Impressive."

"Yes, sir. I mean, thank you, sir. It will be an honor."

"Don't thank me. I should be the one thanking you. Have you checked Aurora's stock price recently? Since news of our contract fulfillment leaked out, our shares have gone through the roof. I'm going to retire a rich man, and you haven't done too badly either. I've been monitoring the shares you've been squirreling away in your IRA. That was a wise move, investing in your own company. Again, congratulations."

Both men stood.

"Thank you, sir," Adam said as he left the room.

"Yes sir," Elias said as he too departed.

In the corridor outside, they stopped to face each other. Adam said, "Give me an hour to get my stuff together, and I'll come over to help your team work on their design."

"You set me up, didn't you?"

"I don't know what you're talking about." Adam smiled inwardly again.

"I won't forget this."

To himself, Adam thought, *In a month, it will be 'I won't forget this, sir or boss,' whichever you prefer.* Out loud, he said, "No, I imagine you probably won't."

*   *   *

September 2012

A year and a half after his promotion to senior vice president, Adam pulled into the driveway of his home on Springwood Lane. It was a little after 3:00 a.m., and he was drunk, although not as drunk as he had been several hours earlier. Rather than attempt to park his Jeep in the garage, he switched off the engine and climbed out. *I should get myself a more appropriate ride*, he thought. *Something that matches my status in life. Maybe a Lexus or a Mercedes? Or at least a new Jeep. A Grand Cherokee Limited might do.* After fumbling with his keys, he managed to unlock the front door and step quietly inside.

The house was dark.

Good. That means Victoria is asleep.

He began tiptoeing toward the bedroom when a voice behind him spoke up. "Do you have any idea what time it is?"

"Dark and early," Adam snickered. He pressed an index finger to his lips. "Shhh. You'll wake my wife." Then he laughed again.

Victoria switched on a light in the living room. "How dare you come home in such a state."

Adam blinked against the brightness. When he looked at his wife, he had trouble focusing. "It's not my fault."

"What do you mean it's not your fault?"

"You should've been there with me. You could've been my conscience." Adam started to turn away, but then hesitated. "Or maybe that's wrong. Maybe I would've drunk even more. Anyway, I'm going to bed."

Victoria stepped forward. She was wearing a bathrobe over her pajamas and fuzzy slippers on her feet. Her hair was done up in curlers. "I warned you not to go to that office party. I told you what would happen. Now look at you. You're a mess. Have you no dignity at all?"

"You know," Adam said with an air of long-suffering, "you really are a shrew."

"I'm a shrew?"

"That's what I said. Not only that, you have a real knack for making my life miserable." It was easy to see that the barb had wounded his wife, and for a moment, Adam felt a twinge of remorse. *Why can't I keep my mouth shut?* he wondered. *I should have just let it go.* Still, it was how he felt.

"This is rich." Victoria punched her hands to her hips. "You come home three sheets to the wind in the wee hours of the morning and accuse me of ruining your life. You are one of the most insensitive people I have ever known. I've been sitting here worried that something might have happened to you. You could've called me or sent me a text— something. No, you just go out and have yourself a high old time and forget about me."

"I tried to, but we ran out of booze."

"That would suit you, wouldn't it? To pretend that you're not married, that you don't have a family? Would it hurt you to show a little tenderness every now and then?"

"How much more do you want from me? I put a roof over your head, clothes on your back, and food on your table."

"And you think that's enough? You used to make me feel special. Now all I feel is disgust. Am I so awful that you won't even hold me?"

"Perhaps I would if you weren't so frigid."

"And whose fault is that?" Victoria shrilled. "You treat me like I'm a pariah, like you want to be rid of me, and then you expect me to put out when you're in the mood. Forget how I feel. I can't even remember the last time we had a romantic evening."

"Keep your voice down. You'll wake Charlie."

"So now you care about our son? Most of the time, you just ignore him, unless I demand that you act like a father should."

"I love my boy. You can't say I don't."

"If you love him, why is it you never show it? Mostly it seems he's an inconvenience you have to endure."

"Enough of this. I'm going to bed. I have to work in the morning."

"Stop," Victoria commanded as Adam turned away again. She stepped closer and reached out to touch his collar. "What is that? Is that makeup?" She leaned her head closer to his body and sniffed the air. "Is that perfume I smell?"

"Don't be ridiculous. You're imagining things."

"Am I? I don't think so. You've been with another woman, haven't you?"

"No."

"Yes, you have. Don't lie to me." Victoria looked him up and down. "It's written all over you. You swore you would never cheat on me again. I can't imagine why I ever thought I could trust you. You're a liar and a cheat."

"That's not true—"

"Yes, it is!" Victoria screamed. "It's as plain as day! And you don't even have the guts to admit it. You're pathetic!"

"All right. It happened. But she came on to me. It's not like I set out to have an affair."

"Who is this person? What's her name?"

"Honestly, I don't remember. She was a friend of one of my team members. I'd never seen her before, and I'll never see her again. Look, it was just sex. It didn't mean a thing."

"It means something to me," Victoria declared with an icy hardness to her voice.

"Mommy?" Charlie emerged from his bedroom wearing his pajamas. He knuckled an eye.

Victoria kneeled down to comfort her son. "It's okay, Charlie. Go back to bed. Daddy is leaving. We won't disturb you anymore. You can go back to sleep."

Adam asked, "What do you mean Daddy's leaving?"

Still kneeling, Victoria looked up and said, "I warned you what would happen if you cheated on me again. You and I are finished. In the morning, I'm going to hire a lawyer and file for divorce. Now get out."

"Mommy?" Charlie said again.

Victoria rose to her feet and took hold of her son's hand. "Come on, Charlie, let's put you to bed."

"I can make it up to you," Adam protested.

Victoria took a step toward Charlie's room. "No, you can't. Not this time."

"I'm not leaving," Adam declared flatly. "We can work this out. In the morning, things will look different. We both need a good night's sleep, what's left of it."

Victoria stopped and spun around to face her husband. "I told you to leave. We're done. This marriage is over. You will not spend another night in this house. Are you too thick to understand what I'm telling you? We're finished. Now get out."

"And I said I'm—"

"Go away!" Victoria shrilled at the top of her lungs. "Just leave."

"Fine. If that's how you feel!"

Victoria glowered at her husband, jaw clenched, hands balled into fists. She said nothing, but her silence was more telling than if she had picked up a dagger and thrown it at his chest.

Adam departed through the front door, the same way he had come in.

After climbing into his Jeep, he drove off, destination unknown. He wound up in the parking lot at the Montana Natural History Center beside the Clark Fork River. Bundled into the back of his Jeep, he tried not to think about his predicament as he struggled to fall asleep.

*　*　*

"Those must have been tough times," Casey said, interrupting my train of thought. "I must say I'm surprised."

"Surprised by what?"

"By how badly you screwed up. You really didn't manage your relationships with members of the opposite sex very well at all. No offense."

"None taken."

"I'm not judging you, you know."

"But I am judging myself. If my confessions keep you from making the same mistakes I did, it will be worth it."

"Actually," Casey said with a laugh, "I plan on making a whole bunch of brand-new mistakes."

"Let's see if you're still laughing when you do." In spite of myself, I laughed too. "Wise guy. Anyway, there's more you should know."

When I looked at my grandson, I saw that I had his complete attention. I went on to explain.

"Toward the end of September 2012, Victoria filed for divorce. Several times I tried to reconcile, but she would have none of it. Her mind was made up, and she refused to budge. Our relationship soon became so contentious that she stopped speaking to me altogether and insisted that whatever I had to say, I could say to her lawyer. The divorce proceedings were a messy affair. What might have been as simple as saying goodbye and wishing each other well turned into a battle royal that seemed to drag on for months.

"There were three major areas of dispute: ownership of the house on Springwood Lane, the division of capital assets, and custody of Charlie. Of course, Victoria got the house. That was almost a given, as was the fact that I was ordered to pay child support. The other two issues were more problematic. By this time, I had become a modestly wealthy man. Having a large chunk of my fortune awarded to my wife hurt, but not as much as Victoria being granted sole custody of our son. I was guaranteed visitation rights, but it wasn't the same. In fact, being legally estranged from Charlie taught me just how much I loved my son and how much I regretted not having spent more time being a dad.

"It was during this period that the quality of my life began to slide downhill. In August 2013, I was convicted of DUI, driving under the influence. In addition to a $500 fine and having to spend a long weekend in jail, my license was suspended for six months. Being forced to either beg rides from friends or ride my bicycle in the dead of winter reminded me of my early days at Townsend Electronics.

"Eventually, I started to pull myself together. In March 2014, I moved into a newly constructed five-bedroom, three-bath mansion on Poplar Court. At least it felt like a mansion, given that I had been living in a one-bedroom apartment since my divorce. Soon, however, the place began to feel more like a mausoleum than a home. One night, not long after moving in, my depression became so intense that I feared I might do myself harm. In desperation, I called Theo, who agreed to come over right away."

*   *   *

May, 2014

Adam was in the library when Theo let himself in. Seated in the lushly padded armchair he had recently purchased, Adam raised his glass of scotch in a toast and said, "Welcome, friend. Nice of you to drop by." His words were slurred, and a two-day growth of stubble darkened his chin and jaw. The twill dress pants and long-sleeve shirt he wore looked to have been slept in. His eyes were bloodshot, and his hair uncombed.

"From the looks of you, it must've been one hell of a party." Theo stepped fully into the room. He looked around as if familiarizing himself with Adam's new abode. This was his third visit. His first two had been brief.

"Excuse the clutter." Adam indicated the boxes stacked in the corners and the piles of books waiting to be arranged on the bookshelves. "I haven't finished unpacking. Maybe I'll get to it tomorrow. Wait a minute." He glanced at his watch. "This is tomorrow. My, how time flies."

Theo's gaze landed on the pistol lying on the end table next to the armchair. Being unfamiliar with guns, he could not discern its make or model. He pointed and said, "Is that loaded?"

"Wouldn't be much use if it wasn't."

"Mind if I take a look at it? I've been thinking maybe I should get one, for self-defense, you know."

"Of course you have. You who won't even set a trap to get rid of a mouse. Like you're going to shoot somebody. No. It's okay. Go ahead." Adam gestured toward the firearm. "Just don't shoot yourself in the foot."

Theo crossed the room and picked up the pistol, handling it gingerly as if at any minute it might explode.

Adam raised an index finger. "There's only one rule you need to remember: the end with a hole in it, never point it at anything you don't want to kill."

"Sounds simple enough. Tell me, how do you unload this thing?"

"Give it here, I'll show you."

"Why don't you just tell me? I need to learn how."

"I know what you're doing."

"Humor me."

"Why not? See the button on the side? Push it."

Theo did as instructed. The magazine dropped out and landed on the hardwood floor. He bent down to pick it up.

"Now rack back the slide," Adam said.

"Do what?"

"Hold the top part of the gun and push it back toward the hammer, firmly." He gestured with his hands. "Just don't squeeze the trigger, or things could get messy."

Again, Theo did as he was told. On his second attempt, a bullet popped out. He retrieved it as well. "Why don't we put this over there?" He crossed the room to lay the pistol on an empty bookcase shelf. The bullet and the magazine he slipped into his jacket pocket.

"You can keep 'em," Adam said. "I've got lots more ammunition."

Theo moved to the couch and sat down. "You want to tell me what's going on here?"

"They're gone." Adam's voice trembled with sorrow.

"Who's gone?" Theo said with concern.

"Victoria and Charlie."

"It's been a year and a half since you moved out."

"Yeah, but the judge just issued his final decree."

"I thought your divorce was finalized months ago?"

"It could have been, but we've been haggling over how to divide up my money. Actually, I was the one who was stalling, hoping that she would change her mind. Now it doesn't look like that's going to happen."

"Maybe it's time to move on?"

"To what?" Adam snapped. "My life is a shambles. I live alone in a huge house. I'm going nowhere at work. I have a criminal record—"

"It was only a DUI. It's not that big a deal."

"That's what you say. Do you know how close I came to getting fired? If they had put me in jail for more than three days, Aurora would've let me go."

"But they didn't."

"The truth is, I'm no use to anybody." Adam rose and moved to the built-in bar beside the bookcases. He started to fix himself another drink, but then said over his shoulder, "I'm forgetting my manners. Can I fix you something?"

Theo shook his head. "What I don't need right now is alcohol, and neither do you. How would you like a cup of coffee instead?"

Adam thought it over for a moment, and then shrugged. "Whatever you say, boss. That's another thing. I drink too much."

"I won't argue with that. Now if you could point me in the direction of the kitchen…"

"It's this way." Adam left the room, and Theo followed.

When they returned to the library, each man carried a steaming mug of coffee. Theo again took his place on the couch. Adam remained standing, though he seemed a little wobbly on his feet.

Theo said, "What did you mean you're going nowhere at work? I thought you held an important position at Aurora? Not many people get to be a senior vice president."

"My promotion was the result of one good idea three years ago. Since then, all I've done is push papers around. If I don't get my act together, some hotshot is going to come along and take my job. The sad thing is, I don't give a damn. It was exciting at first, but more recently, it's been a drag. I will admit that the company is doing some good stuff. We're working on projects that will make a difference in people's lives, but somehow, it isn't enough. I feel like something is missing from my life, something more than just not having my family around. Theo, I've thought about this—a lot. I have a bad case of the uns. I'm unsatisfied, unfulfilled, and unhappy. Did you know I even joined a country club?"

"No, I didn't know that. Which one?"

"Rancho Cantata. It's south of the city, in Brookhaven. Very swank. Very expensive. And very snobbish. I mean, you would think that people would have more to do than sit around and talk about the dandelion infestation in other people's yards or how much more horsepower their SUV has than so and so's. They define the word *boring*."

"I thought I saw you driving a new Jeep the other day."

"You noticed, did you? It's a great car, but it didn't help. That's another thing. I buy stuff I don't need because I think it will help me feel better. But it doesn't. It makes me feel worse for having squandered my money. What am I going to do?" Adam turned toward the bookshelf. "Maybe I should take that pistol and—"

"Don't even think it." Theo cradled his mug in his hands as if soaking in its warmth. "I have two questions: What do you think the reason might be that your life is the way it is? And what can you do about it? What are your options?"

"Isn't that what I asked you? What am I going to do?"

"What I asked you was what can you do, not what are you going to do. They are not the same. But first, tell me why things are the way they are."

"That's easy. They are the way they are because I am the way I am."

"I'm very glad you can see that. That will save a lot of time. Now tell me what you can do about it?"

Adam thought for a moment, but then shrugged his shoulders. "I've told you what I've tried so far. Nothing has worked. I don't know where else to go or what else to do."

"The obvious answer is if things are the way they are because you are the way you are, then to change the way things are, you must change who you are. Does that make sense?"

"I see what you're saying, but my question for you is how? A leopard doesn't change its stripes."

"Spots. Leopards don't have stripes."

"Whatever. The question remains. How do I change me?"

"I have a suggestion. First off, put yourself in a different environment. Break your old behavior patterns. Do something new."

"Like what?"

Theo sat bolt upright on the couch. "I just had an idea. There's a men's retreat coming up this next weekend. I saw it advertised. You can look it up. From what I read online, I suspect it might be right up your alley. The goal is to provide an opportunity for men to get in touch with their inner self."

"This isn't some of that new age self-actualization mumbo jumbo, is it?"

"It didn't sound like it. That pastor from the Capstone Church is leading it."

"Rev. Peter Hudson?"

"That's the guy. Do you know him?"

"He's the one I went to for my premarital counseling. He preached a whole lot of Jesus at me."

"Maybe that's what you need?" Theo smiled.

"You think so? Do you believe in Jesus?"

"I have for many years."

"I never knew that."

"You never asked. Look, what have you got to lose? It sounds like you've tried lots of things, and nothing has helped. Why not give this a try? Is your computer online? I'll call up the retreat's webpage."

"Is my computer online? I'm vice president of a software development company. What do you think?"

Half an hour later, Adam had signed up for the retreat, and Theo was getting ready to leave. Before departing, he stepped to the bookcase and picked up the empty pistol. "Maybe I'll just take this for safekeeping."

"Go ahead," Adam said. "I have another one."

"You have two? Why do you need a gun anyway?"

"Hello. This is Montana. Everybody owns a gun. Most folks have six or more."

"Sometimes you frighten me."

"Break into my house, and we'll see how frightened you are. Just kidding. By the way, Theo, thank you. I mean that. I don't know what I would've done if I hadn't had someone to talk to."

"You are more than welcome. Call me anytime you need me, and don't worry. We'll get through this. You'll see. And stay off the booze— promise me?"

"As you wish, boss."

After his friend had departed, Adam sat in his plush armchair and stared into space. "I just signed up for a Jesus seminar. I don't believe it. What is this world coming to?"

1 3

A CONFESSION OF FAITH

I stood up and flexed my lower back to take the kink out that had settled in. It had been a taxing week, what with flying cross-country to track down Alice Cunningham. My body was telling me to quit for the night, but my heart was telling me to continue a little longer.

I looked at my grandson. "How are you holding up? Can I get you anything? How about some dessert? When I stopped by the Lotus Blossom Restaurant to pick up our dinners, the receptionist mentioned that they had just made a special treat, dragon's beard candy. I tried one on the way home. They are really good. They're like cotton candy, but without as much sugar. Would you like to try one?"

"How big are they?"

"About the size of a cupcake, but they're mostly air." I made a circle with my fingers.

"Okay, but just one. Since we've been getting together, I've put on four pounds."

A few minutes later, I returned from the kitchen carrying a tray holding two mugs of coffee and six Chinese confections on a plate.

Casey gave me a look of reprimand. "I said just one."

I responded with a wink, "The others are in case you change your mind."

"Hey, these are good," Casey said after sampling one.

"I thought you'd like them. I certainly did. It looks like you inherited my sweet tooth."

Casey reached for another dragon's beard. "Theo has been a good friend to you, hasn't he?"

"All my life." I sat down again. "I hope and pray that you will find someone equally genuine. If you do, protect your friendship with all your might. A solid friend is worth more than gold or precious gems."

"Unless that friend betrays you."

"I presume you're referring to Humphrey? I never could get used to calling him Michael."

"Did you ever get even?"

"No because there was no need."

"You let him get away with what he did. He should have at least paid you back for the damage he caused."

"Actually, I owe him a debt of gratitude. If he hadn't sabotaged me, I wouldn't be where I am today. My life would have taken a different course, and who knows where I would have wound up. A lady I know recently told me, 'Sometimes, you win by losing.'" I pointed to the plate on the tray. "Have another."

"No thanks. Two is my limit."

"Okay then, let's get started. Where were we? Oh yeah, the retreat."

*   *   *

June 2014

The Trinity Falls Bible Camp, located thirty-five miles south of Missoula, sat on a forested plot of ground overlooking the Bitterroot River, not far from the Lee Metcalf National Wildlife Refuge. It was the first week of the month, and the men's retreat was scheduled to run from Friday night through Sunday afternoon. Attendees were expected to bring a Bible, a sleeping bag, a pillow, a towel, a notebook with paper and pencil, a flashlight, comfortable clothing, and personal items such as a toothbrush, a comb, a razor, etc., plus whatever medications they might need. Everything else would be provided, including three square meals a day. Cell phones, radios, and computers were expressly forbidden. The facility's style of camping was generally referred to as glamping or glamorous camping.

Following directions downloaded off the camp's website, Adam arrived twenty minutes before check-in. Rather than stand around waiting, he used the extra time to familiarize himself with the camp's layout.

The meeting hall was at the center of the camp and served as the central point of reference. To the north were four bunkhouses with ten bunkbeds in each—twenty men to a bunkhouse, eighty men in total. The showers and the restrooms were beside the bunkhouses. The staff's sleeping quarters were farther north. The administration office was to the west, as was the infirmary, which was staffed by a full-time nurse. To the south was the dining hall, and a little farther on was the chapel. Looking east, the Bitterroot River meandered through a shallow valley thirty yards below the camp. The range of mountains beyond the river still had snow on their crests.

As Adam explored the campground, he noted that the facility looked to be in good repair and well maintained. When he inhaled, he caught the scent of pine needles and loamy earth.

Upon returning to the check-in station, Adam noted that his fellow attendees had begun arriving in force. Soon, eighty men were milling around, getting to know one another. He scanned the throng to find a familiar face, but there was no one he knew.

Adam's first order of business, after stowing his gear in the locker beside his assigned bunk, was to gather at the chapel.

Night was falling as the group began a time of worship consisting of a brief devotional followed by a round of hymns and evening prayers. Then it was off to bed. Lights out was at 10:00 p.m. Fortunately, Adam had thought to stop for dinner on his way to the camp. Otherwise, he would've gone to bed hungry.

Saturday began with another chapel service followed by a hearty breakfast, and then a series of activities in the meeting hall where the group was divided into eight-man teams. Competitions were held to see which team could present the best skit, deliver the most inspirational message, or create what Adam regarded as a fourth-grade arts and crafts project consisting of designing posters and such, which, although childish, was surprisingly fun. It had been a long time since he had enjoyed the fellowship of other men.

Saturday evening after dinner, the group again assembled in the chapel. By this time, Adam had begun to shed some of the cares he had brought with him from the outside world, and time had begun flowing at a less hectic pace. When he learned that Rev. Peter Hudson was to be the keynote speaker for the evening session, he felt somewhat disappointed. Over the years, he had attended a number of the pastor's church services, and having grown accustomed to the man's preaching style, he had hoped for a change of pace.

This evening, however, the Rev. Hudson's message was different. Not only was his delivery more severe and more on target, Adam had the uncomfortable feeling that the reverend was speaking directly to him. In years to come, he would remember the man's exact words.

"Gentlemen, many of you are here because you've made a mess of your lives. You're dealing with bitter failures, broken dreams, and grievous disappointments. You've hurt people, and you've been hurt by them. In fact, you've lost your way, and you are overwhelmed by guilt and feelings of remorse. Even worse, you recognize that you're a sinner, and you are in danger of spending your eternity in hell."

At this point, Adam nearly fled from the chapel. *I don't need some sanctimonious clergyman to remind me of who I am*, he thought. The only thing that kept him rooted in his seat was the fear of embarrassing himself in front of his new acquaintances.

Rev. Hudson continued, "The good news is, I can show you a better way, a way that leads to salvation and eternal life. Many of you have tried to turn your lives around on your own and have failed repeatedly. You've found that you cannot overcome the addiction, or the self-destructive behavior, or whatever it is you're fighting against on your own power. You are up to your neck in sin, and you cannot break free. Some of you have even reached the end of your rope."

Adam pictured his handgun still lying on the bookcase shelf. A shiver raced through him.

The reverend stood tall and pointed toward heaven. "When God created man, he gifted him with free will. However, the first man, Adam, used his gift to sin by disobeying God. As a consequence, his very essence changed. He took on what we refer to as our sin nature. In each of us lies an unrelenting, irresistible compulsion to break God's laws. Every human being since Adam has had to struggle with his or her sin nature." He pounded the podium for emphasis. "The truth, as I'm sure you've already discovered, is it that no matter what you do, no matter how hard you try, you cannot keep from sinning by relying on willpower alone. You need God's help to stop.

"It was for this reason that God sent His only son, Jesus Christ, to live a perfect, sinless life, and then to die on your behalf. He willingly paid the penalty for your transgressions. He died for your sins so that you don't have to. Three days after He died, Jesus rose from the dead, proving that God had accepted His sacrifice. Jesus's death on the cross is the greatest gift we could ever imagine. And right now, this very instant, Jesus is offering you that gift of salvation and eternal life. All you have to do is trust Him and receive His gift. Invite Him into your life. Allow Him to fill you with the Holy Spirit, Who will then empower you to overcome your sin nature.

"Will you accept Jesus into your life? Will you change your destiny from hell to heaven? Will you decide to be with Jesus for all eternity? If you are willing to receive His gift, then pray this prayer with me now."

Adam had never heard the gospel preached so clearly. Something inside of him recognized the truth of the message. He could not resist. He felt anticipation mingled with hope and a hint of joy, like standing in a doorway that leads to a glorious realm or being presented with a beautiful present on Christmas Day.

With unabashed sincerity and filled with an inexpressible longing to draw near to God, he repeated these words: "Almighty God, I admit that I have sinned against You. I am sorry for what I have done, and I humbly ask for Your forgiveness. Jesus, I believe that You lived, that You died, and that You rose again. I believe that You paid the price for my sins as a gift for my salvation. I accept Your gift and invite You to come into my life. Fill me with Your Holy Spirit. I welcome You as my Lord and Savior. Amen."

Rev. Hudson finished up by saying, "If you prayed this prayer with me, we'd like to speak with you. Please remain behind, and one of our counselors will come to you. Otherwise, gentlemen, good evening. Please remember to keep silent until you are outside the chapel."

Adam stayed seated, unsure what would happen next. A soft instrumental hymn was playing in the background. He became aware that he was trembling.

The rest of that evening and the following days seemed to pass as a blur. Later, he would remember the storm of emotions he had experienced: joy, relief, gratitude, anticipation, and a spark of hope. Intertwined with these, he felt uncertainty, a shade of doubt, and a fair amount of confusion. The counselor had recommended that he begin his Christian walk by faithfully studying the Scriptures. He had also suggested that Adam attend church on a regular basis and that he join a small group of like-minded believers as soon as possible.

In deference to the counselor's recommendation, Adam made certain that he was in attendance at Capstone Chapel's 10:00 a.m. worship service the following Sunday.

* * *

June 2014

As parishioners gathered for Sunday morning worship, Adam had the odd sensation that the church seemed to resonate with religious energy. Several men who had participated in the weekend retreat were members of Capstone's congregation. Most were still keyed up from their spiritual experience.

Adam had intentionally arrived early so he could quietly slip in and take his seat rather than mingle with people he hardly knew. As a brand-new Christian, he had no idea as to how he was supposed to relate to fellow believers, and he had no desire to say or do the wrong thing.

A secondary concern was that he wished to avoid bumping into Victoria. Because they had ceased speaking to one another, he had no idea if she still attended services at Capstone or not. In any event, it seemed prudent to err on the side of caution by keeping a low profile.

"Adam!" called out a man's voice off to his right.

Adam looked to see who had spoken.

Rev. Hudson came striding toward him from across the foyer. "It's so good to see you here." He took hold of Adam's hand with both of his. "We've been praying for you. How are you doing? How was your week? Spirit-filled, I hope."

"A bit overwhelming, actually."

The reverend smiled knowingly. "Do I detect a hint of fatigue? Don't worry. That happens. You were pretty well energized when the retreat ended. We all feel a little let down after our mountaintop experience."

"The truth is what I'm feeling is insecure."

"Are you now?" Rev. Hudson let go of Adam's hand. "Why is that?"

"In a way, things seem different, and yet they're still the same. It's hard to explain. Does that make any sense?"

"The world isn't changing. You are."

"That could be it. Maybe I'm seeing things differently. I don't know."

"Let me guess. You've been wondering what happens next. What you're experiencing is perfectly normal. Look, I'll be in my office after the service. Why don't you stop in? We can talk."

"I would, but I can't today. I pick up my son at noon. This is my day to be with him. By the way, does Victoria still go to church here?"

"I haven't seen her in some time."

Inwardly, Adam relaxed a bit. "Actually, Rev. Hudson—"

"Peter, please. Rev. Hudson sounds so formal."

"Peter, I would like to speak with you. Are you ever available in the evening?"

"I can make myself available. How about tomorrow? I'll be in my office around seven. Does that work for you?"

"I'll be there."

"I'll look forward to it. It's important for new Christians to begin growing their faith right away."

The two men parted, and Adam entered the sanctuary to take his seat. When the service concluded, he hurriedly left the building and drove straight to his old home on Springwood Lane to pick up Charlie.

*   *   *

"Come on in," Rev. Hudson called out when Adam knocked on his door. He stood facing the bookcase beside his desk. He appeared to be searching for a particular volume. "Have a seat. I thought that while I was waiting, I'd work on next Sunday's service. I've been trying to put an odd twist to common sayings like 'A bird in the hand is messy' or 'A penny saved is virtually worthless.' Or my favorite, 'If you can't stand the heat, buy a fan.'"

Adam sat down on the couch. "How about 'One hour in heaven is better than an eternity at the DMV.'"

"That's good."

"Or 'Give a man a fish, and you will feed him. Teach a man to fish and you will never see him again.'"

Rev. Hudson laughed as he sat down at his desk. "I like that. Mind if I use those next Sunday?"

"Be my guest."

The reverend scribbled a note to himself and then sat back. "While we're on the subject of fishing, I gather you're feeling a little like a fish out of water? That's not uncommon. It takes time to get your spiritual sea legs, so to speak. Incorporating the teachings in the Bible into everyday life doesn't happen overnight. The important thing is to keep moving forward. Believers who, instead of following Jesus, wander off to go their own way, we call backsliders."

Adam hunched forward, elbows on his knees. "So what do I do? If I understand what I've learned, God promises that He'll make us into a new creation. How and when is that supposed to happen?"

"I don't mean to be facetious, but it will happen when God says it will happen. That's one of the first lessons a new Christian must learn. God sets His own agenda. He doesn't march to our drummer."

"Okay, but in the meantime, what? I don't imagine that I'm supposed to sit around and wait to be supernaturally reinvented."

"Actually, there are only two rules you need to follow, but you need to follow them explicitly. Number 1, love the Lord your God with all your heart, all your soul, all your strength, and all your mind. Number 2, Love your neighbor as yourself. These two rules are the essence of Christianity. Do them, and you will fulfill every ordinance in the Bible."

Adam thought for a moment and then said, "So is that how I get saved?"

"Not at all." Peter leaned forward. "You are already saved. That happened the instant you took Jesus into your life. It's called justification, and it's a done deal. Your faith alone is all that was required. What we're talking about now is how to live a Christian life. It's a process we call sanctification, which basically means learning to be progressively holy, just as God is holy. Obey these two rules, and it will happen automatically."

"Why do I get the feeling this isn't going to be easy?"

"Because your sin nature is going to war against you. Accepting Jesus as your Savior doesn't take your sin nature away. It's still there. Jesus, on the other hand, gives you the tools you will need to fight against your sin nature until it no longer has any power over you."

"What sort of tools?"

"Primarily the Holy Spirit."

"That's all?"

"For the most part. There's also glorification, but that's a topic for another time. Just remember the two rules: love God, love others, and you'll do fine. Oh, one more thing. We need to get you baptized. How about next Sunday?"

"Why do I need to be baptized?"

"Because it's a sacrament ordained by God. Baptism is a public declaration of our faith in Jesus Christ. Being immersed symbolically represents the reality that we have died to self and have been resurrected to new life."

"Very well. Sunday is fine. I'll reschedule Charlie for a different day."

"Bring him with you," Peter suggested. "That way, he will get to see his dad being born again."

"Let's see how Victoria feels about that."

"I can speak with her if you'd like."

"No, but thank you. I think it's best if I take care of it myself."

"As you wish, but if there's anything I can do, just holler."

After expressing his gratitude, Adam said goodbye and left the office. *Two rules*, he thought. *Didn't there used to be ten?*

*   *   *

June 2014

When Adam arrived at church the following Sunday morning, he was pleased to learn that he was not the only one to be baptized. There would be two others ahead of him. One was a woman possibly twice his age. The other was a boy who looked to be about ten.

The three candidates waited behind a curtain for their turn to be immersed. A baptismal font large enough to accommodate two people had been positioned in the center of the stage. Adam was already shivering, and he hoped the church had thought to use warm water to fill the tub.

"Isn't it exciting?" said the woman. Her enthusiasm seemed genuine.

Adam wished he could feel the same. Instead, what he felt was self-conscious anxiety. The baptismal candidates had been instructed to wear either a bathing suit or shorts and a T-shirt. Not being an outdoor person and having an aversion to spending time in the sun, Adam's legs were as white as a sheet of printer paper. He wanted to wrap the towel he had brought with him around his waist, but that would require removing it in front of the congregation, and that might call even more attention to his pallor.

The instructions the candidates had received had seemed simple enough: Pinch your nose with your left hand. Grab your left wrist with your right hand. Take a deep breath. Relax when you're laid back into the water. Keep your arms rigid when Rev. Hudson brings you back up.

When the worship session ended, the first candidate, the boy, was sent onto the stage. Adam peeked through the curtain to see how it was done. It seemed that Rev. Hudson and the boy engaged in a brief conversation before the pastor lowered him into the water. When the lad was raised again, he shouted, "Hallelujah!"

The older lady's baptism proceeded in the same fashion, except that when it came time for her to be immersed, she said loudly enough to be overheard, "You will bring me back up, won't you?" A wave of laughter rippled across the audience.

Then it was Adam's turn. As he walked on stage, he could not help but look out at the congregation. Scattered here and there, he saw the faces of men he had met at the retreat. All were either applauding or raising their thumbs as signs of encouragement. When he reached the font, holding the handrail for support, he climbed three steps up and then three steps down into the water. To his great relief, the water was indeed warm.

"Adam Tiberius Masters," said Rev. Hudson, "do you believe that Jesus Christ is the son of the living God?"

Distracted by a disturbance on the far side of the stage that had caught his attention, Adam missed what was said to him. "Excuse me?"

The reverend repeated the question, and Adam enthusiastically responded, "I do."

"Do you believe that Jesus died and that God raised Him from the dead?"

Again, Adam answered, "I do."

"Do you now accept Jesus as your Lord and Savior and ask Him to come into your life and guide you by the power of the Holy Spirit?"

For the third time, Adam responded, "I do." A sensation of peace enveloped Adam, and he forgot about the congregation that was watching.

Rev. Hudson declared, "Then I baptize you in the name of the father, the son, and the Holy Ghost." To Adam, he whispered, "Pinch your nose and grab your wrist like they showed you. Good. Take a deep breath. Here we go."

With his left hand supporting Adam's back and his right hand firmly clutching Adam's right wrist, the reverend lowered Adam into the water. A few seconds later, he raised him up again.

"Congratulations. May God bless you and keep you for all eternity."

A feeling of pure joy overtook Adam, and he could not restrain himself. He punched both fists into the air and shouted, "Hallelujah!"

The congregation erupted in applause.

After Adam had toweled off and changed into dry clothes, he quietly joined the audience. Several people wished him well as he settled into an empty seat. *I guess that makes it official*, he thought. *For all eternity, I'm a Christian. Hallelujah. It's sad that Charlie wasn't allowed to be here. It would've meant a lot to him.*

*   *   *

I massaged the back of my neck as I glanced at my grandson, just in time to see him take the last dragon's beard off the plate. I gave him a wink. "I told you they were good."

He responded, "These things are like potato chips. You can't eat just one."

"Or two. Maybe tomorrow I'll go back and get some more. Should I get you some too?"

"Absolutely. I'll pay you back."

"No need. My treat. So what are your plans for the weekend? Doing anything interesting?"

"Not really. Studying, mostly."

"Me neither. I think maybe I'll catch up on my sleep. That reminds me. I heard this the other day. Do you know what the problem is with doing nothing?"

Casey thought for a moment and then said, "No, tell me."

"You never know when you're done." I laughed, and so did my grandson.

Then Casey said, "I thought you were going to tell me it takes a lot of practice to get it right."

"Good one. About next week, should we meet on Tuesday again? Does that work for you?" I stood up, and so did Casey.

"Tuesday is good. Same time?"

"Maybe a little earlier. What about three thirty? Is that too early?"

"It's not a problem for me. I'll be here anytime you say."

"Excellent." I laid my arm across my grandson's shoulders. "I've prepared a small surprise. I think you'll like it. Until then, behave yourself, and remember to make good choices. I'll walk you out."

"Wait a minute. That's it? You're saying we're done?"

"Only until next Tuesday." I removed my arm and studied my grandson with confusion. "Am I missing something?"

"You're not going to try to convert me? I thought that was what this was all about."

"I'll try if you want me to, but that wasn't my intent."

"Isn't that what you've been leading up to for all these sessions, to get me to become a believer?"

"As I told you before we first began, I wanted to tell my tale so I could review my life from the proper perspective. Talking is a lot easier when there's a live listener rather than trying to converse with an empty room. If you happen to glean something from my story that will benefit you, so much the better, but that is a secondary consideration. As it is, when we finish, I'd like nothing better than to wrap my narrative into a neat package and put a bow on it."

"Then you really do plan to go on?"

"Oh, we're not at the end. Not by a long shot." I cocked my head to look at my grandson. I could tell he was troubled. "All right, you've been acting strange since you got here. What's going on? You look as if there's something on your mind. Out with it."

"Grandfather, I've gotten into something that's not good, and I can't figure out how to get free of it. Do you remember telling me how you felt when you did something wrong, and nobody knew but you? How you had to live with the guilt? That's how I feel."

"Would you like to tell me what you've done?"

"I can't, not yet. I have to think it through."

Clearly, my grandson was distraught. I was dying to know why, but I feared that were I to press too hard, he would clam up entirely. Instead, I sensed that the most prudent way forward would be to hold off and allow him to open up on his own. "As you wish, but remember that I'm here anytime you need me."

Casey hesitated as if about to comment, but then shrank in upon himself and said, "All right then." More brightly, he added, "It'll be interesting to see where we go from here."

"Indeed it will. And next Tuesday, bring your appetite."

"Would that have anything to do with the surprise you've planned?"

"We'll see."

After Casey had gone, I settled into my favorite armchair and picked up the book I had been reading. Before opening the book, I said a short arrow prayer: *Lord, I'm worried. When my grandson and I meet again, open my mind and give me the words to say. Please be with both of us as we move forward. Amen.*

1 4

AN UNEXPECTED CONSEQUENCE

Philately is a hobby I have enjoyed for many years. I am an avid stamp collector. Early Saturday morning, the day after meeting with Casey, I was in my library admiring my collection. My favorite stamp, an 1851 Benjamin Franklin, had caught my eye. It was undoubtedly the most valuable stamp I owned. Originally, it had cost a little more than $7,000, but was currently worth at least twice that amount. I was admiring its blue color and its slightly blurred frame when the front doorbell rang. I carefully put the stamp away and went to see who might be calling at such an hour.

I was astonished when I found Alice Cunningham standing on my doorstep. Taken aback, I blurted out, "What are you doing here?"

Alice chuckled. "Obviously, I've come to see you. I hope I'm not interrupting something important?"

Recovering my composure, I said, "Not at all. Please come in." I stepped aside and allowed her to enter. She was wearing a pair of chocolate brown pants, a pale blue blouse, and comfortable-looking shoes. It was the sort of attire a woman might find suitable for traveling.

Alice gave me a warm smile and said, "I just happened to be in the neighborhood, so I thought I would drop in."

"Well, I'm glad you did. It's good to see you again. So you were in the neighborhood, were you?"

"Actually, I'm on my way back to Swiftwater, and I thought a little detour would be nice."

It occurred to me that if she was traveling from Omaha, Nebraska, to Nome, Alaska, she would have been routed through Chicago. Taking a side jaunt from Chicago to Missoula could hardly be considered a little detour, but I made no comment. Instead, I invited her into the living room.

On the way, I said, "Have you eaten? I was just about to have breakfast. Would you care to join me?"

"That would be lovely, but I don't wish to impose."

"Not at all. It will be nice to have some company."

Rather than settle in the living room, we moved to the kitchen.

After brewing a couple mugs of coffee, I said, "What can I fix you? I can do pancakes, bacon and eggs, an omelet, or french toast. Which would you rather?"

We both settled on the omelet, and I set about to prepare our breakfasts.

"You have a beautiful home," Alice said. Seated at the kitchen table, she seemed quite at ease.

"Thank you, though it's a little much for just one person."

"Have you lived here long?"

"Thirty-six years. Yep, like me, this place is getting older. It seems that every year there's more and more things to fix. It does require a lot of upkeep."

"Why not move into a smaller house?"

"I would, except I never get past thinking about having to pack up all my junk. You know what they say, stuff expands to fill the space available. With five bedrooms and three baths, that makes for a lot of stuff." After laying out strips of bacon on a cookie sheet, I put them in the oven to crisp.

"I find that interesting. It sounds like you and I are exact opposites. I don't have a home, and most of my possessions you could fit into a steamer trunk and a suitcase."

"How do you live? I mean, I know that you stay with friends. I learned that when I was trying to track you down, but can you do that full-time? I don't have any friends who would tolerate me for more than a week at a stretch. Well, maybe one friend."

"I rent an apartment when the need arises, usually on a month-to-month basis. That way, when the travel urge strikes me, I can pick up and go."

I fetched an onion and a bell pepper from the vegetable drawer in the refrigerator and then began chopping them into small pieces. "With that kind of lifestyle, I imagine you've seen a lot of this nation."

"Nearly every state. My favorite is Wyoming. As a wildlife biologist, I helped manage Yellowstone's native ecosystem. That was a good job. I enjoyed it. It was also the longest I ever stayed in one place. Twelve years, can you imagine? For a vagabond like me, that's a long time."

I finished whipping the eggs and poured them into the omelet pan. I added the minced onion and bell pepper and a sprinkling of cheddar cheese. I put four pieces of toast in the toaster.

A thought occurred to me, and without thinking, I said, "How is your friend, Mr. Burke?" Belatedly, I realized that the man had probably died. Otherwise, Alice would not have left Omaha. That being the case, I could've been more tactful.

Alice seemed not to notice my gaffe. With sorrow in her voice, she said, "He passed away. It was for the best. He was in a lot of pain."

I flipped the omelet, making sure it didn't burn. Next, I put butter and jam on the table and fetched two place settings. When the toast popped up in the toaster, I gathered the slices onto a plate and said, "I'll let you butter your own since I don't know how you like it." I poured two glasses of orange juice. Next, I divided the omelet and served each of us a half, along with three strips of bacon fresh from the oven, plus several slices of ripe tomato.

When all was ready, I joined Alice at the table.

As I was about to dig in, I noticed that Alice hadn't touched her silverware. Suddenly, I understood the reason and said, "I'll say grace." I bowed my head. "Heavenly Father, we thank You for this meal and for this time of fellowship. Bless us this day and watch over us. In Your son's name we pray. Amen."

"Amen," Alice echoed. She gazed into my eyes from across the table. "One reason I'm here is because I wanted to thank you in person. I sold the necklace you gave me, just as you had suggested. It brought in enough that it paid for almost all of Samuel's funeral. You did him a great kindness, and I thank you."

"I was glad to do it. As I think I mentioned before, that necklace was a reminder of what I had done wrong. I know you think I did you a favor, but I don't see it that way. That episode may have had a good outcome, but that was in spite of me, not because of me. I'm glad that now we can finally put the matter to rest."

Alice paused and then said, "I have a question, but it's kind of sensitive. If you choose not to answer, I'll understand."

"Go ahead. I promise I won't take offense."

"It's about the insurance money you received for the necklace. I was wondering, did you do anything about that?"

"You mean, did I repay it?"

"Right, you said you were making restitution, and, well, I was just wondering."

"As a matter of fact, I did. I mean, I tried. When the urge to make things right came upon me, I tried to track down the insurance company, but they had gone out of business. There was no one to repay, so I donated the funds to charity."

"I knew it. I told myself that was what you would do. Do you realize that you've helped restore my faith in humanity?"

"I was just trying to do what was right." Moving on to a different topic, I asked, "What are your plans for the day? Are you doing anything special?"

"Actually, my flight out tomorrow isn't until around noon. That means I'm free for the rest of today and tomorrow morning."

"Good. How would you like to go horseback riding? I have a friend who owns a string of horses. He likes it when I ride them so they can get some exercise. What do you say?"

"I love horseback riding. It was one of my favorite things to do when I lived in Wyoming. I'll need to change into something more appropriate. My suitcase is out in the car I rented. Would you mind if I use one of your spare rooms to change?"

"Not at all. In fact, if you haven't already checked into a motel, why not stay here tonight? There's plenty of space, and you'll save yourself the cost of a room."

"Thank you. Once again, you are more than kind."

In anticipation of the day ahead, I dug into my breakfast. It turned out that I had made a pretty decent omelet, not that I'm bragging.

*   *   *

The riding trail wound through a patch of pine forest and then up a gradual rise to open into a wide meadow. A shallow stream wandered across the far edge. Strands of vaporous clouds trailed across the sky, blunting the rays of the midday sun. The Skyline Ranch was a 180-acre spread in the Bitterroot Valley, an hour and fifteen minutes south of Missoula. The ranch's primary industry was raising cattle, which meant they were in the horse business as well.

I had saddled Rufus, a large six-year-old buckskin-colored gelding. Generally reliable, Rufus had a tendency to shy at sudden noises. For Alice, I had chosen Daisy, a medium-size mahogany-colored mare with a gentle disposition.

"How about over there?" I pointed to the far edge of the meadow where a stand of trees provided extra shade.

"Looks good to me." Alice shifted in her saddle.

"You doing all right?" I asked.

"It's been a while since I've ridden. There are parts of me that are unaccustomed to being on horseback."

"I know what you mean. The aches come when I'm in the saddle after going for a while without getting a ride in. Usually, I try to get down here at least once a month. Recently, other things have gotten in the way."

"Like tracking me down?"

"Among other things."

When we reached the far side of the meadow, we pulled up and dismounted. I led both horses to the stream that looked clear enough that I allowed them to drink. I then tied their bridles to a pair of skinny Douglas fir trees and went to join Alice as she sat on a boulder beside the stream.

"How far do you think we've come?" she said.

I eased down next to her. "I don't know, maybe three miles."

"It's a good ride—not too steep and not too dusty. Thank you for inviting me."

"You're welcome. When I tell people I like to ride, they look at me funny, as if an old codger like me has no business on horseback. I tell 'em, 'You're only as old as you feel,' right?"

Alice laughed. "If that's the case, I've aged ten years in the last three miles." She picked a blossom off a plant beside the rock. After crushing it between her thumb and index finger, she put it to her nose and sniffed. "Pineleaf penstemon," she announced. "Hummingbirds like 'em." She tossed the blossom away and looked directly at me. "Mind if I ask you something personal?"

"Go ahead."

"Why, after fifty-two years, would you go to all the trouble to track me down? I know what you said, that it was a wrong you had to put right, but it seems to me there has to be more to it than that."

"The truth is, it was a compulsion I could not ignore."

"But where did that compulsion come from? I can't even remember the people I knew fifty-two years ago, and you and I only knew each other for a very brief period of time. I couldn't have made that big an impression."

"I suppose the reason is because I was hardwired to remember."

"How so?"

"Lately, I've been trying to understand my life. In particular, I've focused on seeking out cause-and-effect relationships. Looking back over a long span has helped put things into perspective. My grandson has been working with me. It's been taxing, but there are a few things I have come to realize about myself. If I tell you what I've learned, promise me you won't think less of me?"

"How can I think less of you for being honest?"

"The first thing you need to know is that my father severely abused me as a child. I was repeatedly taught that every misdeed must be punished. That axiom was literally beaten into me, so much so that whenever I would commit even the smallest infraction, I would expect another thrashing. It got to the point that I needed the beatings to keep from feeling like a wicked person.

"Getting you fired was the first truly bad thing I had done as an adult. The way I treated you was absolutely wrong, and therefore, I absolutely deserved to be punished, but the punishment never came. Instead, the incident stayed with me like the sword of Damocles hanging over my head. I kept expecting the universe to mete out its revenge.

"Over time, I learned to live with that feeling, but when I began my journey of self-realization, all the old memories, all the old emotions came flooding back. Setting things right became something I had to do for my own sanity."

"How horrible that must've been for you."

"It was hellish, but it's not the full measure of what I've endured. There were other consequences I've had to deal with as well. Having been taught that I was never good enough, I've had this lifelong compulsion to excel. Always needing to prove myself has made me an overachiever, which isn't necessarily a bad thing. What is bad is that I never developed the proper socialization skills. When I'm around people, I'm inhibited by a deep-rooted sense of inadequacy. I can never measure up, certainly not in my own eyes. Do you know the real reason I live in a house that's far more than I could ever need? It's to remind myself that I'm not the failure I think I am. It's the same reason I fought so hard to become a senior vice president for software development at age thirty-one."

I fashioned a warm smile. "My compulsive nature has resulted in at least one pleasant though unexpected consequence."

"What might that be?"

"You and I have gotten to know each other. Certainly, that should count for something. There. Now you know as much about me as I know about myself."

"Thank you for sharing. I mean it. Not many men would be so forthcoming."

I looked up at the sky. "We'd best be getting back. Those clouds are starting to thicken up. It could rain soon."

We saddled up and headed back down the trail the way we had come. As we were about to leave the meadow, I guided my horse closer and said, "It's a shame you're leaving tomorrow. I have two tickets to hear a New Horizon at the Wilma Theater. They are a Christian a cappella group. I was going to invite my friend Theo, but I would rather go with you."

"I'd be honored. My ticket to Nome is open-ended, so I accept."

"Excellent."

We arrived at the Skyline Ranch and returned the horses to their stable just as it started to rain.

*   *   *

The next evening, upon returning home from the concert, I unlocked the front door and held it open for Alice. Before entering, she paused to look up and down the street. "This is a nice neighborhood. There are some fine houses here."

"It is," I said. "One of the things I appreciate most is that it's quiet. Usually, there's not much going on."

"The yards are all so neat and tidy. You can tell when people care about their neighborhood. I'll bet they are down-to-earth folks. Am I right?"

"Actually, I only know a few of my neighbors, but the ones I do know seem okay."

"How long have you lived here?"

"Thirty-six years," I admitted with a flush of embarrassment. "It's the poor socialization skills I mentioned before."

"I see." Alice stepped inside.

I helped her remove her coat and then hung it and my own in the hall closet. Mostly out of habit, I headed for the kitchen. Alice followed. I said, "What can I get you? Would you care for a snack?"

"You've got to be kidding. I'm still full from dinner."

Rather than simply enjoy the concert, we had elected to make a night of it. Starting out, we had dined at a small bistro on the west side of town. After the concert, we had treated ourselves to ice cream cones, each with two flavors.

"Well then, how about a nightcap? Maybe some crème de menthe?"

"That would be nice." Alice crossed the room to examine my stove. It was the latest model with an induction cooking surface and a large convection oven. "Food is an important part of your life, isn't it?"

"I suppose. I do enjoy a fine meal."

"I'm surprised that you've been able to maintain such a healthy weight. If I ate as much as you do, I'd weigh three hundred pounds."

"It must be my metabolism." I poured us each a digestif, and we headed for the library. "I had a good time tonight," I commented as I settled into my armchair.

"Me too." Alice curled up on the couch with one leg underneath her. "It's been a long time since I've laughed so much."

"I can't believe all the interesting places you've been. In comparison, I've hardly been anywhere."

"Perhaps, but look at what you've accomplished, especially your outreach ministry. I really would like to learn more about it."

"Of course, but not tonight. It would feel too much like talking shop. By the way, I wanted to apologize for dumping my psychological baggage on you yesterday during our ride. I don't know why I felt the need to unload. You must think I'm a neurotic mess inside."

"Is that how you see yourself? Because I don't. Truly, I was impressed that you would make the effort to sort yourself out. A little introspection is a good thing, right?"

"True, but I have a tendency to live inside my head. Whereas you live in the real world."

"Perhaps you should focus more on letting go."

"It's interesting that you should say that. That's precisely what I intend to talk to my grandson about next Tuesday—letting go. I think it will be our final session."

"Casey, that's his name?"

"Yes."

"He sounds like a good person. Someday, I'd like to meet him."

"You should. I think you would like him. Can't you stay on a little longer? Do you have to go back to Alaska?"

"I'm afraid I do. I have some business to take care of. I'm selling a tract of land. My husband's family was very well-to-do. When he passed away, I inherited his wealth. It's been a mixed blessing. Although it's allowed me to live a comfortable lifestyle, it takes a lot of time and effort to manage properly."

"Do you think you'll be coming back?"

"That depends."

"On what?"

"On how you feel about having me around."

I grinned broadly. "Right now, I can't think of anything I would like better." I toasted her with my crème de menthe.

Twenty minutes later, we said good night. As Alice headed up the stairs, I said, "Time was when I would've invited you to my room."

Alice paused to smile down at me. "Time was when I would've accepted that invitation." She turned and headed back up the stairs. "Good night," she called out over her shoulder.

"Good night," I echoed and then watched her until she disappeared from view. *It's true,* I thought, *life does get easier as we get older. Well, less complicated anyway.*

1 5

NOT BY WILLPOWER ALONE

"Right on time, as usual," I greeted Casey at the front door. I had already resolved that, as before, I would not press him regarding the matter that had troubled him during our previous visit. Instead, I would leave it to him to broach the subject, if he chose to do so. Sometimes, the best way to catch a fish is to cast your line and then sit back and wait.

I formed a warm smile. "Come in. There's someone I would like you to meet." I led the way to the kitchen, where I introduced my grandson to the chef I had employed for the evening. "Casey, this is Françoise Lamarck. He's the senior chef at Café Romano. He'll be fixing our dinner tonight. François, this is my grandson, Casey."

"Very pleased to meet you," Françoise said with a polite bow.

"Likewise," Casey said with a hint of uncertainty. He looked at me as if to ask, "Why is there a chef in your kitchen?"

I explained, "Since this is probably our last session, I felt it would be fun to splurge a little and enjoy ourselves. Françoise's specialty is Italian, but he can cook almost anything."

"This is true." Françoise beamed with pride.

To Casey, I said, "For our dinner tonight, I've asked him to prepare a beef Wellington with rice pilaf, steamed vegetables, and a tossed salad. There will be cherries jubilee for dessert."

Françoise pressed his fingertips to his lips and made a kissing sound. "It will be magnificent."

Casey responded, "And here I was expecting hot dogs and beans."

"If so, they would also have been delicious," Françoise said with aplomb.

I looked at Françoise. "Feel free to rummage through my drawers and cupboards. I think I have everything you'll need. If I don't, just holler." To Casey, I said, "As for you, young man, shall we get started?"

"Lead on." Casey followed me to the library in what had become something of a ritual.

When we had settled in, I said, "Let me think. Where did we leave off?"

"As I recall, you had just become a Christian."

"Ah yes. For nearly six years after my baptism, nothing changed. One day seemed pretty much the same as the next. Looking back, I would have to say that I was drifting, but then the troubles at work began."

Casey raised a hand. "Hold on." He sniffed the air. "Is that perfume I smell? Grandfather, is there something I should know?"

"I had a guest over for the weekend. Is that okay with you?"

"Of course. I meant no offense."

"Sorry. She's someone I met recently. She needed a place to stay. That's all it was."

"All right."

"I mean, we're just friends. It's not like we're romantically inclined or anything."

"No problem."

"After all, can't a man my age make new friends?"

"Sure you can. Nothing wrong with that."

"It was entirely platonic."

"Fine."

"Fine. So where were we? Oh yeah. The troubles at work."

*   *   *

October 2021

Adam sat in his office at Aurora. It was late in the afternoon, and it had been a boring day. He was about ready to pack it in when Lydia Greig appeared in his doorway. She seemed worried. "Boss, we've got a problem. I wouldn't bother you with this, but I think it might be serious."

Lydia was one of Aurora's better programmers. She had come on board three months before Adam had first been hired as a senior project manager. Endowed with the prowess of a long-distance runner, she had a quick mind and a tenacious attitude. Often, she would come in early and stay late when there was an issue to resolve. Adam trusted her judgment, and for her to look so concerned meant that the problem must be significant.

"What's up?" Adam said, his lethargy having suddenly dissipated.

"It's Workforce. There is a logic error, and we can't find it."

Workforce, Aurora's magnum opus, had been under development for sixteen months. It was the most ambitious project the corporation had undertaken. Workforce was actually a suite of programs, each tailor-made to achieve a specific objective related to overseeing employees and meeting their needs. By combining specialized modules such as payroll, scheduling, continuing education, policy compliance, and tax issues, the software could provide everything a business of any size might need to manage its employees. One programmer had referred to the suite as a human resource department in a box, and the appellation had stuck.

"This is not news I want to hear," Adam said. "We are three weeks out from our release date, and we're supposed to begin beta-three testing in two days. What are you seeing?"

"We keep dropping packets." A packet was the equivalent of an electronic folder that contained all the information on a single employee.

"You're kidding."

"Actually, I'm not. We enter data and confirm it's been correctly stored. Later, when we search for that packet, it's not there. Sometimes it comes back right away. Sometimes it takes longer. So far, all the packets have shown up eventually, so it's not a deletion issue, but even if we get the records back, they tend to disappear again. It's maddening."

"Which module?"

"All of them."

"Then it's a core issue."

"You would think so, but we're not getting any error codes."

"Have you tried rebooting? Of course you have. How silly of me." Adam slapped his forehead with the palm of his hand." What about wiping the data cache?"

"Tried it. No joy."

"Do you think it could be a formatting error? Maybe the packets are being misread by one subroutine but not another."

Lydia shook her head. "That seems unlikely. When we do get them back, they're intact. The data hasn't been scrambled at all."

"How long has this been going on?"

"Not long," Lydia said defensively. "I first became aware of the glitch late last week."

"And you didn't say anything?"

"I thought I could sort it out."

"You should've told me. Every minute matters."

"You're right. I'm sorry."

"Nothing to do about that now. Let's go see what's happening." Adam exited his office, closed the door, and headed for the computer lab where the beta-two testing was underway. "Show me," he said as he entered through the doorway.

At 1:00 a.m., the team Adam had cobbled together was no closer to finding the glitch than when he had first been notified.

Adam yawned and said, "That's enough for tonight, guys. Thanks for sticking around. Go home. Get at least a couple hours sleep, and come back in the morning ready to have another go at it."

That night, Adam couldn't fall asleep. At 2:30 a.m., he lay in bed staring into the darkness and trying to imagine what could possibly be wrong with Workforce. His instincts told him it would turn out to be either a simple fix, one they just hadn't considered yet, or a deviously complex error that would be nearly impossible to track down. The latter scenario frightened him deeply. With more than 650,000 lines of code to sift through, it would take even his best programmers more than six months to scan them all. Furthermore, his staff was still being impacted by the Covid-19 pandemic. Missed work days were common, and only a few programmers were functioning at one hundred percent efficiency.

Another factor played on Adam's mind. Not only did Aurora's financial future depend upon his solving the problem, his own financial security was on the line as well. In anticipation of Workforce's release into the marketplace, he had held off selling any of his shares of Aurora. If the company went under, so would he.

With his conversion to Christianity, Adam had adopted a new set of standards. One of his resolutions had been to swear off the booze. However, he was so intensely anxious that he felt a need for something to steady his nerves. Without agonizing over the choice he was making, he poured himself two fingers of scotch, and then another two fingers shortly thereafter.

When time came to get ready for work, Adam was in worse shape than at 2:30 a.m. It was a pattern he would often repeat in the weeks to come, much to his detriment.

*   *   *

One week later, the software glitch was still a mystery. All four teams had been told to stop what they were doing and focus entirely on fixing Workforce. Every diagnostic routine imaginable had been run, but to no avail. The pressure seemed to increase by the hour. Tempers were short, and people were growing weary under the stress.

If the worst should happen and Aurora were to go under, Harold Edward Cruz was one of the few people who stood to lose more than Adam. As CEO and chairman of Aurora's board of directors, not only was he responsible for the smooth functioning of the company, he had shareholders to consider, and his shareholders were not happy campers. In fact, a delegation of disgruntled investors was just leaving Mr. Cruz's office when Adam reported as ordered.

Adam stepped aside to allow the group to depart. Not one of them smiled at him or even acknowledged that he was there.

"Masters, get your ass in here!" Mr. Cruz bellowed when he saw his vice president for software development lingering outside his door.

"Whoa," Adam whispered to Marjorie, Mr. Cruz's secretary, as he passed by her desk.

"Shut the damn door," Mr. Cruz barked as Adam crossed the threshold.

"Yes, sir."

"Sit down. Do you realize that our shares have fallen 30 percent in the last two days? That's 30 percent! If this keeps up, we'll be out of business in a week."

"Even if they don't continue falling, if we miss our deadline, we'll be out of business anyway." Adam's intent had been to express his concern, but belatedly, he realized he should've kept his mouth shut.

"Do you think I don't know that? What I need from you is to tell me what the hell is wrong with my software? You've been at this for a week. Nothing is getting done. All teams have been taken off their assigned projects, and we're falling behind on everything. Why can't you find a simple glitch and get on with fixing it?"

"Because it's not a simple glitch," Adam stated flatly. "If it were, we would've found it by now. We've run every check we can think of. As far as we can tell, our codes are pristine. According to every debugging routine we've run, Workforce should be functioning like a charm."

"But it isn't."

"No, it isn't. That doesn't mean we're giving up. I have half a dozen programmers sorting through lines of code as we speak. The rest are running whatever diagnostics we can think of, some for the fourth and fifth times. Sir, we are trying, but as it stands now…I don't know. Maybe it's time to prepare for the worst."

"I don't want to hear that garbage," Mr. Cruz snarled. "That's defeatist talk. Either you find the glitch and get my software back on track, or I'm going to fire your ass. Do you understand what I'm saying?"

"Yes, sir, I will give it my all, but like I said, I'm not sure what more we can do."

Mr. Cruz rocked back in his chair. "Let me be blunt. If Aurora fails, the blame isn't going to fall on me. I'll make sure that you're the one who takes the heat. It will be your mismanagement that was the cause. No software company will ever hire you again. You'll be lucky to get a job printing flyers advertising bake sales. Do you catch my drift?"

"Yes, sir."

"Good, now get out of here. Go debug my software. And shut the door on your way out."

When Adam exited the CEO's office, he didn't even look at Marjorie for fear she had overheard his dressing down. Upon returning to his own office, he plopped down behind his desk and tried to think. Surely they were missing something, something buried in a place they had yet to look. Try as he might, no new ideas came to him. He was feeling utterly dejected when Lydia again appeared in his doorway.

"How you doing, boss?" she said. "I heard that Harold summoned you to his office. How did that go?"

"About like you would expect. What do you want?"

"Actually, I wanted to see if you had any plans for tonight. You look pretty done in, and I was thinking I would fix you dinner if you're up for it. A change of routine might do you good."

Adam pondered her invitation. Normally he would have refused her offer outright. As he had learned from previous experience, fraternization with employees was a dangerous game. However, fatigue and the lingering effects of the booze had weakened his resolve. "What the hell, why not? What time?"

"Whenever you are done here. Do you like hamburgers? They're one of the few things I can cook."

"Whatever you fix is fine. How about six o'clock?"

"That works for me." Lydia pulled a slip of paper out of her pocket and handed it to Adam. "That's my phone number and my address with a map. I'll see you tonight."

What are you doing? Adam asked himself as Lydia walked away. A twinge of conscience needled him, but he ignored it.

*　　*　　*

The next morning, Adam had an additional thorn in his conscience to deal with. After a couple margaritas and a bottle of wine, Lydia had come on to him. Despite calling up every shred of willpower he could muster in an effort to resist, he had finally relented and slept with her, fully aware that fornication was a sin.

Adam's lapse triggered an avalanche of emotions. More than a few dated all the way back to his childhood. He had done something very wrong. Once again, he deserved to be punished. He was a sinner and therefore worthless. The litany of accusations he leveled against himself inflamed the guilt that had taken root in his mind.

By midmorning, he could no longer stand the accusatory voices ringing inside his own head. He needed a quiet place to get control of himself. Despite knowing how it would look were he to leave in the middle of a crisis, he decided to take off from work and go home.

As Adam stepped out of his office and closed the door, Elias Hayes was just passing by. Adam stopped him. "Elias, do me a favor. Let the teams know that I'm not feeling well. I think I'm coming down with an intestinal bug or something. Tell them that, hopefully, I should be feeling better in the morning. Also tell them to continue with what they're doing. If they have any questions, they can come to you since you're a senior team leader. Got it?"

"Yes, boss. I hope you feel better soon." Adam failed to notice that the corners of Elias's mouth curved upward in a very faint smile.

*　　*　　*

Rather than head directly home, Adam changed his mind and drove to Theo's house instead. Using the key Theo kept hidden under a flowerpot near the front door, Adam let himself in. He knew that his friend would be at work, but decided to wait anyway. Then it occurred to him that one of Theo's watchful neighbors might let him know that a stranger had just invaded his home. To prevent Theo from worrying, Adam sent him a text explaining that all was well.

Twenty minutes later, Adam was surprised, and more than a little grateful, when Theo's car pulled into the driveway. He really needed someone to talk to, but had been too embarrassed to ask Theo to interrupt his workday.

"What's going on?" Theo said as he entered the living room where Adam sat huddled into a corner of the couch. "Man, you look hammered. What happened?"

"I screwed up—again. Not only that, Aurora is in big trouble, and I'm about to lose my job, my 401(k), my life savings, and maybe my house."

"Tell me what's going on. Take your time and start at the beginning. We'll work through this. Nothing is ever as bad as it seems…or as good."

Adam explained about the software bug and about his lapse with Lydia.

Theo listened patiently and then said, "I assume you've started drinking again?"

"Yeah. I tried not to, but I don't have any willpower. With all the stress I've been under, it's the only relief I can get. What am I going to do?"

"Have you tried asking God for help?"

"You mean pray?"

"That's usually what followers of Jesus do when they are in trouble. We can pray right now."

Adam planted both feet flat on the floor and sat up straight. "Okay. You pray."

"Me? It's your problem. You ask Him for help."

"I don't know how. I never really got the hang of it."

"Just tell Him what's on your heart. Tell Him how you feel. He already knows, but He likes for us to ask."

"All right." Adam closed his eyes and said, "Heavenly Father, I've done something You say is wrong. I'm sorry, and I need You to forgive me, please. I've been with a woman who wasn't my wife. Give me the strength not to do this again. Also, I need Your help at work. As I'm sure You're already aware, we're up against a real situation. We need to find the coding error in our software, and we need to find it soon. Please help me. Amen." He looked at Theo. "You think that will do it?"

Theo smiled. "I guess we'll have to wait and see."

"By the way," Adam said, "do you have any acetaminophen? I've got a splitting headache."

"I keep some in the medicine cabinet in the bathroom. If it's not there, there is a backup supply in the utility room downstairs. It's in a plastic bin with other medications. Help yourself."

The medicine cabinet turned out to be a bust. When Adam started down the stairs, he flipped on the upstairs light switch. After finding the acetaminophen and taking three extra-strength tablets, he headed back upstairs. Out of habit, he hit the downstairs light switch. This time the light went out.

Adam stopped dead in his tracks. After a moment of reflection, he climbed the stairs and toggled the upstairs switch again. The light came back on, but this time, the switch was in the up position instead of down. *They're wired in a feedback relationship*, he thought. *The function of one is dependent upon the state of the other.*

A light went on inside Adam's brain. *We aren't looking for one software glitch*, he announced to himself. *We're looking for two. There are two miscodings that interact with each other: light on, light off. That's why the packets disappear and then reappear. And I have a notion where we can find these bugs.*

Adam raced back to the living room.

Theo looked up in surprise. "You didn't get into the ephedrine by mistake, did you?"

"What?"

"Ephedrine is a stimulant—never mind."

"I have to go. I think I know what's wrong with Workforce. I'll give you a call later and explain everything." Adam hurried toward the front door, but then stopped and looked back. "You don't think that…?" He pressed his palms together in the traditional attitude of prayer.

Theo shrugged.

"Really? We need to talk about this after I get things sorted out at work. I'll call you." Adam fled the house and drove like a madman back to Aurora.

*   *   *

October 2021

The boiler room was abuzz with anticipation. All four teams had been assembled at Adam's behest. Most of Aurora's employees were feeling the effects of the challenge that had tormented them. Programmers, software engineers, and support technicians fought to overcome their fatigue and remain alert enough to hear what Adam had to say.

Adam stood at the head of the room, waiting for stragglers to filter in. He had been up all night working on fixing the software glitch. He felt exhausted, but his spirits were high.

Mr. Cruz stood off to one side. He too was showing the effects of the strain the entire corporation had endured for the last eleven days.

Two latecomers shambled in to the room. Adam did a quick head count and said, "Is that it? Are we all here? Good. Let's begin." He turned around and unfurled the large projection screen that hung on the wall behind him. With a nod, he signaled the projectionist at the back of the room. A line drawing materialized on the screen.

"Can you all see this?" Using the long wooden pointer he held in his hand, Adam tapped the screen. "This is a wiring diagram for a pair of two-way switches. Now you might be asking yourself what this has to do with anything. Well, let me tell you, this little sucker is the source of all our frustration."

A wave of murmuring spread throughout the assembly. "He's figured it out," someone said in a stage whisper toward the back of the room.

A programmer to Adam's left asked, "What does an electrical circuit have to do with us?"

"That's what I'm about to tell you." Adam tapped the screen again. "This is a simple but elegant configuration. You have a live wire and a neutral wire that feed current through the circuit. In the middle of the circuit you have two switches. Let's call them switch A and switch B. Both switches have two positions, which we will call position 1 and position 2. When switch A is in position 1 and switch B is in position 1, current flows through the circuit. Likewise, when switch A is in position 2 and switch B is in position 2, current flows through the circuit.

"However, when switch A is in position 1 and switch B is in position 2, current does not flow through the circuit. And of course, when switch A is in position 2 and switch B is in position 1, current does not flow.

"The point is that the function of one switch is dependent upon the state of the other switch. If the switches are in agreement, the light goes on. If they are in disagreement, the light does not go on. That's exactly what is happening inside Workforce. Next slide please."

The image on the screen changed to display a coding algorithm.

Again Adam tapped the screen. "We have two subroutines that are normally independent of one another. The way it is supposed to work is input into subroutine 1 always produces output 1, and input into subroutine 2 always produces output 2. It's a typical 'data in, data out' configuration.

"However, these two subroutines are now linked, making them interdependent. Next slide please."

Again, the image on the screen changed to show a modified algorithm.

"The way it works now is when data comes in to subroutine 1, it queries the state of subroutine 2. If the appropriate flags in subroutine 2 are raised, then subroutine 1 produces output 1. However, if the appropriate flags are not raised in subroutine 2, nothing happens. And vice versa. That's why we keep dropping packets. To fix Workforce's glitch, all we have to do is uncouple subroutine 1 from subroutine 2. This will return the algorithm to its original configuration."

"I'll be damned," breathed a programmer near the middle of the room.

A software engineer raised his hand. "What determines whether or not a flag is raised or lowered in subroutine 1 and subroutine 2?"

"That's a good question, but it's irrelevant for our purposes here this morning. If we uncouple the two subroutines, the flags no longer have any functionality."

Another programmer spoke up. "How in the world did you figure it out? Interdependent subroutines. No wonder we couldn't find the glitch."

Adam chuckled. "I was at a friend's house, and the light suddenly came on, so to speak."

"So that's it then?" Mr. Cruz said with amazement. "Are we good to go?"

"We are good to go," Adam declared proudly. "The good news is, Workforce will be the most debugged program we have ever released."

Someone began clapping, and suddenly, the whole room was alive with celebration.

"However," Adam said loudly enough to be heard above the noise, "the bad news is, these coding changes"—he tapped the screen—"did not happen by chance."

The room fell silent.

"Someone thought up this nasty little booby trap and inserted it into our code."

"You mean we were deliberately sabotaged?" Mr. Cruz seemed incredulous.

"That's exactly what I mean," Adam replied.

"Who could have done such a thing?" Mr. Cruz said.

Adam turned to face a particular employee who was seated halfway across the room. "Elias, would you care to answer that question?"

"Me? How should I know?"

"Because you're the only one who had access to Workforce's core immediately before the glitch first appeared. I went back and checked the activity logs. The glitch was first identified at 8:04 a.m. on Monday the thirteenth. Before that, we know that everything was working smoothly, at least up until 3:45 p.m. on Sunday the twelfth. That's when the last beta-2 run ended. The only person who signed in to the computer lab during the interval between Sunday afternoon and Monday morning was you. Nobody else had access. Why did you do it? Could it be because you were passed over for a promotion? Are you still holding a grudge, even after ten years?"

"You have no proof that I did anything."

"Oh, I'd say the evidence is undeniable. Besides, I think that when we do a forensic analysis of your laptop's hard drive, we'll find a wiring diagram much like the one I just displayed. I'm pretty sure that's where you got your inspiration."

Elias folded his arms in front of his chest. "I have nothing to say."

"Well, I do," Mr. Cruz announced. "Elias Hayes, you're fired." He turned to the woman to his right. "Marjorie, please call security and have Mr. Hayes escorted from the premises."

"You can't do this!" Elias sputtered. "This is wrongful termination. I'll sue you."

Adam smiled. "If you think you can win, go ahead." For the second time in his life, his involvement had gotten someone fired, but this time, it felt really good.

As the meeting broke up and people began returning to their workstations, Lydia approached Adam. It was apparent that she was feeling ill at ease. "Do you have a moment?"

"A brief moment, yes."

"About what happened, we haven't had a chance to talk."

"I didn't think there was a need."

"What I want to say is, I hope that our…being together won't affect us working with one another. Will it?"

"As far as I'm concerned, it was a one-off thing. I think we should behave as if it never happened."

Lydia breathed a sigh of relief. "So we're okay then, you and I?"

"As long as you do your job and I do mine, we're fine."

"Thank you." Lydia pointed to the now-dark screen. "That was brilliant, by the way. If you hadn't figured it out, we never would've found the glitch in time. Aurora would've been toast. If anyone deserves a raise, it's you."

"Actually, I've already been blessed for what I did, though a raise would be nice. Now, perhaps you should get back to work?"

"Right. Again, thank you." Lydia walked away.

Never again, Adam promised himself as he watched her go, though he wondered if he would ever have the strength to live up to his commitment. *Maybe I'll take the rest of the day off. I think I've earned a mini vacation.*

Adam's sanguine mood lasted only until he returned to his office and found a slip of paper on his desk. Apparently, someone had taken a phone message on his behalf. He called the number listed on the paper and was startled when the man who answered said, "Coroner's office. May help you?"

"I'm sorry. Is this…?" He read the number off the slip of paper.

"Yes. What can I do for you?"

"I'm not sure. I got a message to call this number."

"And you are?"

"Masters, Adam Masters."

"Ah, yes. Mr. Masters. Could you hold a moment? Coroner Thurgood would like to speak with you."

"Sure," Adam said with uncertainty, but then continued, "Wait. Where are you located?"

"Sheridan, Wyoming. Please hold." The man on the other end of the line signed off before Adam could respond.

A moment later, a different voice came on the line. "This is Coroner Thurgood. Am I speaking with Adam Masters?"

"Yes. I'm Adam Masters."

"Do you have a sister named Rachel Masters?"

"I do. What's this about?"

"Mr. Masters, I'm sorry to have to tell you this, and I'm especially sorry that we have to do this over the phone, but regrettably, it's my duty to inform you that your sister, Rachel Jane Masters, has passed away. We are pretty sure she died of a fentanyl overdose, but we will be performing an autopsy tomorrow to confirm the cause of death. What I need to discuss with you is what you would like us to do with her remains after we're done."

It took Adam a moment to collect his thoughts. He then promised that he would have a local funeral parlor make arrangements for the transfer of his sister's corpse.

Not Rachel, he thought as he hung up the phone. *Not my sister. It's not fair. She never really had a chance. The deck was always stacked against her.* As the first pangs of grief began to settle in, it occurred to him that they were all gone: his father, his mother, and now his only sibling. Not only that, his wife and his son were as good as dead to him. A profound sense of loneliness overtook Adam. *How has it come to this?* he wondered. Then the answer came to him: *One step at a time. One step at a time.*

1 6

DRAWING UPON THE SPIRIT

With the memory of my sister's passing weighing heavily on my heart, it seemed a good place to take a break. I was learning that her unexpected death had touched me more deeply than I had first realized.

I raised my arms above my head, inhaled a deep breath, and slowly released it as I brought my arms down to my sides. I stood up. "Let me see how Françoise is coming along." I sniffed the air. "Smells like he's making progress."

I returned carrying a plate of finger sausages wrapped in pastry. "He sent some hors d'oeuvres to tide us over." I put the plate down beside Casey and told myself not to eat any because they would ruin my appetite. My grandson didn't seem to have that problem.

After both of us had taken a restroom break, we began again.

I remained standing by the bookshelf nearest the door, my hands clasped behind my back. For a time, I simply gazed at my grandson while I collected my thoughts. *Here we go,* I cautioned myself as I pictured all the time and effort that had gone into preparing for this moment. *We are headed for the final chapter. Don't blow it now.*

Once I felt I was ready, I said, "When we left off, your Grandaunt Rachel had just passed away."

Casey commented, "That must've been a terribly sad day for you."

"It was. The pain of losing her was still fresh in my mind the next time I met with Theo. It was on a Sunday afternoon, a week after Rachel's funeral. I had stopped by his house after church to pay him a visit. The preceding week had proven exceedingly taxing, and I was feeling the need to talk."

* * *

October 2021

Toward the end of the month, the leaves, already well along in their autumnal color change, were beginning to fall from the trees. A northerly wind carried a cold front down from Canada. Bundled against the chill, Theo and Adam sat in folding chairs out on his back deck. Winter would soon be upon them, and despite the falling temperatures, they had decided to visit out-of-doors rather than stay cooped up in the house. They had been discussing Rachel's memorial service.

With a faraway look in his eyes, Theo said, "I thought it was a fine funeral. Rev. Hudson's message was right on point."

Adam cast a sideways glance at Theo. Clearly, something was troubling his friend, and he thought he knew what it might be. "You're wondering if Rachel was a believer?"

Steam rose from Theo's coffee mug as he cupped it in his hands. "Sadly, I was. Yes."

"I know. Me too. I've heard it said that the only tears in heaven will be tears shed over lost opportunities. I often wanted to talk to Rachel about what she believed, but it never seemed to be the right time, and then she up and left—twice. And now I can't say if she was saved or not. That's a heavy burden to bear. I wish I had been more involved in her life."

"Actually, I think you influenced her more than you know, especially when she came to stay with you in 2008. Do you realize that was thirteen years ago?"

"How do you know how she felt?"

"Because she told me. One day, I stopped by to see you, but you were out. Rachel and I had a good conversation. I think your hospitality reached her."

"I wasn't a believer back then."

"No, but you were a seeker. I'm sure Rachel picked up on that."

"It would be great if she had because her visit was a disaster. Victoria and I weren't getting along. I've always imagined that the friction between us was the reason Rachel decided to pack up and leave."

"Speaking of Victoria, have you been in touch with her recently?"

"No. Why?"

"Just curious."

"What's on your mind?"

"Nothing in particular. Since we were reminiscing, I thought I'd ask how she's doing. That's all. What about Charlie? Do you still see him?"

"Not as often as I would like."

Theo sipped his coffee, his unspoken commentary having come through loud and clear.

Seated on a folding chair with a blanket covering him from the waist down, Adam gazed out at the trees in Theo's backyard. They reminded him of a still-life painting done in shades of yellow, orange, and brown. Maybe it was just his mood, but the scene seemed rather melancholy, and it brought to mind the reason he had come for a visit.

"Theo, you've been my friend virtually all my life. As you know, I trust you, and I respect your judgment. You probably know more about me than I know about myself. Can I share something with you that's been haunting me?"

"Of course."

"I don't think I'm cut out to be a Christian."

A deep frown sprang up on Theo's face. Adam could tell that his declaration was not what Theo had expected to hear. Theo asked, "Why would you say that?"

"Because I keep falling short. Take Rachel, for instance. I feel like I abandoned her. After my conversion, I should've tracked her down, but I didn't. I should have shared the gospel with her, but I was too focused on my own issues. Now, I can't even tell you what she believed."

"You can't help someone who refuses to be helped."

"That may be, but I could have tried harder. Then there's the recent crisis at Aurora. I didn't handle that well at all. Instead of supporting and encouraging the people under my authority, I was critical and harsh.

When they came to me with their issues, I sent them away rather than take the time to deal with whatever was bothering them. I was more focused on my own worries than I was on theirs. When they looked to me for leadership, they found a tyrant rather than an advocate.

"Then we finally released Workforce, and an odd thing happened. When word got out that I was the one who'd found the glitch, I got moved up on people's list of celebrities to invite to their parties. You'd think that would be a good thing, but the sad part is that I craved the notoriety. One fortuitous epiphany, and I was right back to climbing the social ladder, pandering to their insipid fawning because their flattery stokes my ego.

"Also, do you remember me telling you about that woman I slept with? I knew perfectly well that fornication was a sin and that what I was doing was a violation of God's will, but I did it anyway. She still works at Aurora. She's one of my subordinates. Recently, she's been coming on to me again—nothing overt, just subtle hints. I can tell she wants me. I keep forcing myself to resist, but unless something changes, it's only a matter of time before I give in.

"And then there's the booze. I can't count the number of times I've told myself to quit, but then I start feeling sad or depressed, angry or frustrated, and I reach for a bottle. When I drink, all my other problems get worse. It's a vicious circle: I drink because I'm mad at myself, and I'm mad at myself because I drink.

"I go to church fairly often, but I don't read the Scriptures, not like I'm supposed to, and I rarely pray.

"Theo, I've lost the joy I had when I first said yes to Jesus. Man, I've struggled to get it back, but it's not there. I feel empty and alone. There's no sense of fulfillment in my life. I'm a mess."

Theo waited to make sure Adam was done. "My word, you can beat yourself up better than anybody I know."

"I'm serious. I'm a sinner, and there's nothing I can do to change who I am."

"Oh, I doubt that's true. I mean the part about changing. You are a sinner. I won't dispute that fact."

"I need to be clear. This is not a sincerity issue. I truly want to live a different life—a more abundant life. That's what Jesus promised. I just can't seem to get there."

Theo steepled his fingers and said softly, "I've been doing some reading, mostly in the Bible, but some commentaries as well. The last time you were here, you started me thinking, and I've developed a theory. You're desperate to solve your problems, but you're going about it in the wrong way."

"How can standing up against sin be wrong?"

"What I mean is your basic premise is incorrect. You assume that you have to fix what's broken on your own, that only you can set things right, but that's not the way it works. You need to call upon the Holy Spirit. The Holy Spirit is one of the three manifestations of God: Father, Son, Spirit. Everyone who receives Jesus receives the Holy Spirit."

"If you're saying I have the Holy Spirit, it doesn't feel like it."

"Because you haven't factored in how you've changed. Look, I'll prove to you that you already have the Spirit within you."

"I'm listening."

"According to Scripture, the Holy Spirit has multiple roles to fulfill in our lives. One role is convicting us of our sins. That distress you feel for being a sinner, in large measure, that's due to the prodding of the Holy Spirit. Another role is guiding us into all truth. When you stand back and ask yourself, 'What do I really believe?' and your honest answer is that you believe in Jesus, that certitude comes from the Holy Spirit. Likewise, the Spirit seals our relationship with God. He stands as a guarantee against the day of our redemption as children of God. Yes, the Holy Spirit is already within you. To prevail, all that's needed is for you to allow him to perform a couple of his other functions."

"And what might they be?"

"First is to reveal the deep things of God. That's akin to gaining wisdom. He helps us understand who we are and who God is. The Holy Spirit teaches us God's truths and helps us grow our faith.

"Second, and probably most important, the Holy Spirit empowers us. It's by the Spirit that we acquire the power to resist temptation. Only by invoking the Spirit can we say no to the things that tempt us. Let me say that again. We can't conquer our sin nature on our own. We need the power of the Holy Spirit to resist temptation. If we ask, He will fill us with the power we need."

Adam suddenly recalled Rev. Hudson talking about similar things during his premarital counseling session. He shared that memory with Theo and concluded by admitting, "At the time, I heard what he was saying but didn't understand."

Theo smiled. "I suspect that's because you were not yet a believer. You hadn't confessed your faith, and therefore, you didn't have the Holy Spirit to aid in your discovery of the truth."

Adam snapped his fingers. "By golly, I think I'm finally beginning to understand."

"There you go, another proof. The Holy Spirit is doing His job."

Adam opened both hands in front of him. "The question now, I would imagine, is where do I go from here?"

"You must learn to invoke the Holy Spirit when temptation comes your way. That happens through prayer. Don't worry, if you can't think of what to say, the Spirit will pray for you. It's your intent that counts. Intercession is another one of His roles. He intercedes on our behalf when we're not sure how to talk to God."

"How many roles does the Holy Spirit fulfill?"

"At least ten. I can give you the scriptural references if you would like."

"Indeed I would like to see them. Do you really think this will work?"

"Search your heart and tell me what you believe."

Adam paused to decide how he felt. After a time, he admitted, "I actually think it might. Thank you, Theo. And I think I see a way to find out if I'm right—three ways actually. I'll let you know."

"God promised that when you were born again, you would become a new man. He meant what He said. It seems to me that you're well on your way."

* * *

Adam drove straight home from Theo's house. Encouraged by his friend's explanation of the roles of the Holy Spirit, Adam decided to conduct an experiment to test his premise. Upon arriving at home, Adam shed his jacket and hung it in the coat closet and promptly headed for the library and the wet bar built into the opposite wall.

Without hesitating, he reached for a half-full bottle of scotch and a glass. He carried both to the coffee table where he set them down. His hand trembled as he poured two fingers of the amber liquid into the glass. He then sat back on the couch and waited.

The longer he stared at the scotch, the more intense his craving became. About to reach for the glass, he suddenly stood up and stepped away. *Something is wrong here*, he told himself. *This isn't a fair test. I forgot to invoke the Holy Spirit. How can I know if He's going to strengthen me if I don't ask for His help?*

Adam got down on his knees on the Persian rug and bowed his head. He closed his eyes and pressed his palms together in front of his chest. "Holy Spirit, I invite You to manifest Yourself within me. Fill me with Your power and strengthen me. Enable me to resist the temptation that is set before me. Let me feel Your presence so that I might know with absolute certainty that You are here. Amen."

Rather than stand up right away, Adam remained kneeling. After a long interval, he queried his body to see how he felt. Detecting no internal change, he rose to his feet and returned to the couch where he sat down again.

As he stared at the glass of scotch, he became aware of a subtle sense of anticipation, which he recognized immediately. The same sensation generally greeted him upon returning home after a harrowing day. There could be no doubt about what he was experiencing; his alcoholic cravings were undiminished.

He reached for the scotch and brought the glass to his lips, but then he paused before taking a sip. *What am I doing? God can't be pleased that I'm putting Him to the test. Besides, I've been behaving as if this is all about me. It isn't. It's not my will that should prevail here. It's His. If He wants me to get drunk, He'll let me know. Until that happens, I should probably ask His forgiveness.*

Adam set the glass down and rose to his feet. This time, he remained standing because his knees still ached a little, though he did close his eyes and press his palms together. "Heavenly Father, forgive me for being presumptuous. I was wrong to assume that You have nothing better to do than to attend to my petty cravings. If there's something You need from me, let me know. Otherwise, I will wait until I hear from You. Amen."

Suddenly, Adam realized that he was extremely tired. It had been a long, arduous day, and he was beyond fatigued. His conversation with Theo had used up the last of his stamina, and at that moment, what he needed most was sleep.

Adam turned abruptly and left the library. Rather than stop by the kitchen to get a bite to eat, he headed straight for the master bedroom. After changing into his pajamas, he lay down on the bed and promptly fell asleep.

The next morning, he awakened feeling refreshed. When he again entered the library, Adam was startled to see the glass with its two fingers of scotch sitting untouched on the coffee table. He cocked his head and stared at the alcoholic beverage. The implications of its still being there gradually became clear.

Is that how it works? he thought. *Did I just discover something profound? My craving vanished only after I subjugated my will to His. What's the take-home message?* Adam pondered the matter, then said to himself, *Maybe it should be "Only after you've emptied yourself by surrendering to God can He fill you with the Holy Spirit."*

One trial done, two to go.

*   *   *

November 2021

Three days after his spiritual victory over a glass of scotch, Adam knocked on Lydia Greig's door. Her apartment was one of a dozen in a residential complex two miles south of the center of town. Two years had passed since their previous tryst, but he still remembered which door was hers.

That afternoon, after months of subtle innuendos and veiled overtures, Lydia had finally mustered the courage to invite Adam to drop by after work. Her supposed reason was that she wished to present her ideas for a new software package.

Adam wasn't fooled. He understood her motives. However, rather than rebuff her advances outright, he had seized on the opportunity to conduct another experiment, one that carried substantially greater risk.

When Lydia answered the door, she had already changed out of her work clothes. Rather than the dress slacks and long-sleeve blouse she had been wearing, she had on a pair of skin-tight leotards and a loose-fitting T-shirt that clearly announced that she was not wearing a bra.

Adam recognized the first stirrings of a sexual urge as he stepped inside. Silently, he prayed, *Heavenly Father, I'm here because I believe this is where You want me to be. Be with me now, and allow Your Holy Spirit to guide me. Give me the strength to resist the temptations that await me. Amen.* To Lydia, he said, "I see you've redecorated. A new sofa and new drapes, if my memory serves me correctly."

"You have a good eye—new carpet as well. Can I get you something? I was just about to pour myself a glass of wine. Would you like some?"

From where he stood in the entryway, Adam could see through the kitchen and into the living room. There he noticed the open bottle and the two glasses sitting on the credenza. As politely as possible, he said, "Actually, I've been trying to cut down on my alcohol intake. If you have a soda, preferably decaf, that would be fine."

Lydia seemed clearly disappointed. "I think there's a couple cans in the fridge. Help yourself."

Adam chose a diet cola and then followed Lydia into the living room. When he sat down, he deliberately took the middle of the sofa so that no matter which side Lydia selected, he could slide away from her if necessary.

Matter-of-factly, Adam said, "So, you have an idea for a new software package?"

"You don't want to talk shop straight off, do you? Let's unwind a bit—get comfortable. Aren't you worn-out? It was a hectic day."

"It was busy. I'll grant you that."

"It was more than busy. Anyone can see that the workload gets to you. You look really tense. How about a backrub to loosen you up? As I recall, you enjoy a good backrub. Take off your shirt and lie down." Lydia sat down beside Adam and reached around to undo the top button of his shirt.

Adam hesitated, but then took hold of both her wrists to stop her. "I know what you're doing, but not this time. What we did before was wrong…for several reasons. I don't intend to make the same mistake twice."

Lydia pulled away. "What do you mean it was wrong? We are both adults. Neither one of us is married. What's the harm?"

"According to God's word, any sex outside of marriage is a sin. The Bible's position on the matter is clear. As far as I'm concerned, that settles the issue."

"I'll be damned. You got religion."

"Not exactly. Religion is man's attempt to reach up to God. My faith is based upon a doctrine of spirituality. I believe that God reached down to me through His son, Jesus. There is a huge difference."

"How can an intelligent fellow like yourself believe in a fairy tale?"

"I'm glad you asked." Seizing the opportunity, Adam shared his testimony. He gave an abbreviated account of his childhood and the struggles he had endured. He then presented the Gospel of Christ and the doctrine of salvation by grace through faith. He finished up by touching upon the progress he was making in overcoming his sin nature.

While he talked, Adam monitored Lydia's reactions. Skeptical at first, even hostile, as he spoke, her body language signaled a change in attitude. When he concluded, she said, "I've never heard the story told that way before. I've always imagined Jesus Christ was a myth."

"I assure you, He's very much alive and will be for all eternity. You can be too, if you allow Him into your life. I can help with that if you wish."

Lydia shook her head. "I need to think about it."

"Will you? Think about it, that is? It will be by far the most important decision you will ever make. Normally, I'd tell you to take your time, but none of us know how much time we have. If you want to talk about this again, I'll be available. Otherwise, why don't you show me the ideas you have for a new software package."

Lydia flushed slightly. "We both know I don't have any. As I'm sure you suspected, it was a ruse to get you here."

"In that case…" Adam stood up. "I'll take my leave, but like I said, I'm available if you have questions or if you want to talk—just talk, that is."

"I'll let you know."

On his way back to his car, Adam thought, *How did I do, Lord? It felt really good. The seed has been planted. Now we'll see if it bears fruit. And thank You for keeping me celibate.*

Two down, one to go.

*   *   *

November 2021

Two days after witnessing to Lydia, Adam sat in his Jeep outside of his old home on Springwood Lane. Of course, the property now belonged to Victoria, as it had for the past nine years, ever since their divorce. Still, it was the only home he had known growing up. Yet since moving out, he had discovered that in truth, he harbored a deep sense of revulsion for the three-bedroom cottage. *Too many terrible memories. That had to be what drove Rachel away. I should've torn the place down when I had the chance.*

He was waiting for his ex-wife to come home. Having heard through the grapevine that she had taken a job as the office manager for a car dealership, he had assumed that her hours were from eight to five, which meant she should be home soon. He had left work early to make sure he would be there when she arrived.

As he waited, Adam reflected on the past nine years. Their divorce had been so contentious and their egos so badly bruised that they had stopped speaking altogether. Whatever communication had been necessary had been shuttled through Charlie or their lawyers.

Thinking about Charlie brought to mind the image of a strapping seventeen-year-old who was on the verge of graduating high school. Adam's relationship with his son had never been robust. Over the preceding two years, it had deteriorated to the point that they had become virtual strangers. His weekly visits had ceased when Charlie had turned fifteen and had decided that meeting with his father was a waste of time. Rather than force himself on his son, Adam had agreed to forego his visitation rights, though their estrangement had wounded him severely.

Gazing through the passenger-side window toward the front of the house, Adam tried to anticipate what meeting his ex-wife face-to-face would entail. Their paths had crossed briefly six years previously, shortly after his conversion. Their chance encounter had taken place at Capstone Chapel. When Victoria had learned that Adam would be attending church there, she had promptly switched to a different house of worship. For two people who resided a mere five miles apart, they might as well have lived on different planets.

Will she still be beautiful, or will she look old and worn out? Will she be healthy or sickly? Will she even speak to me, or will she threaten to call the police? These and a dozen other questions plagued Adam's mind while he waited.

Eventually, a white coupe pulled into the driveway and parked. Adam assumed it was Victoria's car, though he wasn't sure, not until a woman climbed out. Even from a distance, he recognized his ex-wife. She looked pretty much the same as she had, and for that he was grateful.

Adam exited his Jeep. As he did so, he launched another arrow prayer. *Heavenly Father, be with me now. I'm here because You've shown me this is the right thing to do. Help me be charitable and kind and bridle my tongue if I become frustrated or angry. Fill me with Your Holy Spirit, and give me the words I will need to fulfill the purpose for which I have come. Amen.*

Victoria fetched her keys from her purse and started to unlock the front door.

Already halfway across the lawn to the front stoop, Adam called ahead, "Victoria, hello."

Startled, she dropped her keys.

"Allow me." Adam hustled forward and bent down to retrieve the ring of keys.

Victoria instinctively backed up a pace. When he went to hand her the key ring, her fists came up defensively.

Adam froze, the keys dangling from his unmoving hand. Very quietly and very gently, he said, "I believe these are yours."

Hesitantly, Victoria took the keys, but continued to maintain her distance. "What are you doing here?"

"I've come to speak with you, if you will allow it."

"I have nothing to say to you. Go away."

"I will, if that's what you want, but first, there's something I need to tell you."

"What makes you think that there is anything you could say that I would want to hear?"

"Victoria," Adam said with all sincerity, "I need to tell you that I'm sorry. I apologize for treating you the way I did. I need you to know that I absolutely regret cheating on you. That was inexcusable, and I am so, so sorry. I was a terrible husband, and you definitely deserved better. I know that words are virtually worthless, and what I'm telling you now doesn't count for much, but know this: what happened to us wasn't your fault. It was mine, and I will regret what I did to you till my dying day. I know that what I'm about to ask is beyond the pale, but I'm hoping you can find it in your heart to forgive me. If you can't, I will understand. Please accept this apology and know that I mean every word of it." Adam took one step back and waited.

Rather than respond, Victoria stared at her ex-husband as if trying to make sense of what she was hearing.

When the silence became uncomfortably long, Adam spoke up. "I understand. Thank you for letting me say my piece. I won't bother you again." He turned to leave.

"Wait," Victoria said softly. "Where did this come from? Why now?"

Rather than approach the stoop, Adam stayed planted several feet away. "Recently, I was shown the sort of man I was. I'm trying to put things right with you, with the people I've wounded—with God."

"You've lied to me so many times, how can I believe you?"

"You can't, not unless you choose to do so."

"This isn't going to change our relationship." Accompanied by an emphatic hand gesture, she said, "We are not getting back together—ever!"

"I know that. That was not my intent. I simply wanted to say I'm sorry and to have you know that I mean it."

"Is this for real? It's not some sort of sick joke, is it?"

"No. It's not."

"I don't know what to say."

"You don't need to say anything. I won't trouble you again." Adam turned toward his Jeep.

"Wait." Victoria regarded her ex-husband and then said simply, "I'm sorry too."

A moment of unspoken communication passed between them, and then they both nodded, signifying that they had just buried the hatchet.

Without saying anything further, they turned away and went about their business.

Three down. Time to report back to Theo.

* * *

November 2021

Theo switched off the television when Adam entered his den. "I was just catching up on the news. How did it go?"

"It went well, I think." Adam's relationship with Theo was such that he had long since been granted permission to come and go as he saw fit, meaning he almost never knocked. He walked over to the mini fridge in the corner and grabbed a can of iced tea. He popped the top and downed a swallow.

"So tell me," Theo said with obvious anticipation. "What did you learn?" This was their first conversation since their seminal discussion regarding the Holy Spirit, and Theo clearly wanted to be brought up to speed.

Adam crossed the room to sit in the straight-backed chair against the wall. He stretched his legs out in front of him and placed one ankle atop the other. "Actually, I've been trying to sort out what I experienced. Admittedly, it's only three encounters, and obviously I'm not a theologian with a doctorate in comparative religions, but I think I see a pattern."

"Go on. Tell me what happened."

"The first thing I did was to see if I could blunt my cravings for alcohol. I figured that would be easiest to test. I believe I have succeeded, but in an unforeseen way. I expected to lose my desire to drink, but instead of my cravings simply vanishing, they were replaced by an awareness of my relationship with God. I found myself questioning whether or not getting drunk would honor Him, and because it wouldn't, I chose not to do it.

"The second trial was different, but the outcome was similar, in a way. I put myself in a situation where my biological urges would work against me. The stronger the temptation became, the more fervently the Holy Spirit led me to focus on meeting her spiritual rather than her physical needs. I wound up sharing the gospel instead of succumbing to temptation.

"The third encounter was more problematic. By the time I went to see Victoria, my internal conflicts had, for the most part, played themselves out. As you know, ever since our divorce, I've harbored a great deal of animosity. The more I pictured confronting her—something I absolutely wished to avoid—the more convinced I became that it was the right thing to do. And the more I thought about how our relationship had crumbled, the more I was led to acknowledge my own culpability. In essence, I was being fed a huge slice of humble pie. Until I actually faced Victoria, though, I had no idea what I would say, and when the words did come out, there was no mention of her part in our troubles. Go figure. That had to have been the Holy Spirit. Otherwise, I would have unloaded on her with both barrels."

Theo stroked the side of his jaw with his thumb. "Can you summarize what you've learned?"

"I can try." Adam uncrossed his ankles and sat up straight. "The Holy Spirit is a real person without physical form as we know it. He indwells each and every believer. We can acknowledge him and profit from his instruction, or we can deny him and muddle through life on our own.

"The Holy Spirit has many roles to play. One of his principal duties is to focus our attention on God first, other people second, and ourselves third. If we allow the Holy Spirit to reign in our lives, we will manifest the fruit of the Spirit: love, joy, peace, patience, kindness, goodness, gentleness, faithfulness, and self-control.

"The Holy Spirit is a counselor, advisor, teacher, intercessor, guide, comforter, and a guarantor of our salvation. When we empty ourselves, it is by virtue of the Holy Spirit that God is able to fill us with His love and compassion, which we then are to pass on to others. Above all, the Holy Spirit is that part of God that dwells within us."

Theo rewarded Adam with a broad smile. "Well done. Well done indeed. Look at how far you have come. It sure seems to me that you're well on your way to becoming an overcomer."

"A what?"

"An overcomer. As 1 John 5:4–5 says in the NIV, 'For everyone born of God overcomes the world. This is the victory that has overcome the world, even our faith. Who is it that overcomes the world? Only he who believes that Jesus is the son of God.'"

*   *   *

I looked over at Casey just as he consumed the last finger sausage. His lack of restraint concerned me because I knew that François would be offended if my grandson failed to eat a decent portion of his dinner. I said, "Are you sure those aren't going to ruin your appetite?"

"Pretty sure. The fact is, I'm still hungry. I missed both breakfast and lunch today." Casey dabbed his mouth with a napkin. "Grandfather, do you honestly believe the Holy Spirit is real?"

"No. I don't believe the Holy Spirit is real. I know the Holy Spirit is real! There are far too many proofs to think otherwise."

"But how can you know for sure? Nobody can see a spirit, can they?"

"No, they can't, but they can see his footprints."

"What do you mean?"

"When I examine my life—as we're doing now—I can see how I've changed. I'm not the wretch I used to be, and that begs an explanation. My first impression is that the changes are an expression of my own free will. I'm different because I want to be different. Then I remember that I'm incapable of effecting those kinds of changes on my own."

"How do you know you're incapable?"

"Haven't you been paying attention? I spent forty-four years striving to purge sin from my life. It wasn't until I embraced the Holy Spirit and allowed him to reign within me that things began to improve. When I look back at where I've come from, his footprints are obvious."

"You're an accomplished man. You've done many good things. Why believe that your successes are the handiwork of a benevolent entity you can't even see?"

"Because I know me, because I know who I am. Trust me when I tell you that the good ways in which I've changed, they weren't my doing."

"Give me an example."

"Sure, but after dinner. Let's go see how Françoise is coming along. I suspect he's probably close to being ready for us."

1 7

LIFE IN ABUNDANCE

Dinner turned out to be the masterpiece I had hoped for. The beef Wellington had been cooked to perfection. Françoise had definitely earned the exorbitant fee I had paid him, and Casey had proven true to his word. Not only had he finished off the servings set before him, he had asked for seconds. Where he put all that food, I had no idea.

As we again settled into our places in the library, I kicked off my shoes and wiggled my toes against the carpet. We were in the home stretch. I looked at my grandson and silently told him, *Hang in there just a little longer, and all will become clear.*

I said, "As I remember it, you were asking for an example of how I changed in a good way, but not of my own volition. Is that right?"

"Yeah. I want to understand why you think the Holy Spirit was responsible for the choices you made."

"All right. Perhaps my tenure with Aurora and how it came to an end will serve to answer your question."

*　*　*

April 2024

When Workforce's debut was declared to be a spectacular success, Adam felt like he was on top of the world. Sales were strong, and Aurora's shares had doubled in price, and then doubled again. Additional software products had been brought to market, and they too had bolstered Aurora's bottom line.

The upshot was that in a mere span of three years, Adam had become a wealthy man, not to mention that he was highly esteemed in the software industry. There were a dozen companies that would have hired him in a heartbeat had he decided to leave Aurora, which paradoxically was exactly what he was planning to do, though he had no intention of signing on at another software development firm.

The decision to leave Aurora had first been planted in Adam's consciousness during a Sunday sermon at Capstone Chapel. Rev. Hudson had been preaching on obeying God's will and learning how to discern between divine inspiration and self-serving urges. As part of the message, the reverend had pointed out that sometimes, radical changes were unavoidable.

Like a seed germinating in fertile soil, the concept had taken root and then grown until it blossomed into an outright conviction that it was time to move on.

Adam had, at first, resisted the idea of leaving. He was content where he was. The thought of doing something new and having to start all over at age forty-four distressed him. As he repeatedly told himself, *Why leave a position where I'm making six figures a year for doing something I enjoy?*

However, the more he resisted, the stronger the impulse became. The principal argument against quitting his job was that he had no idea where he would go or what he would do. *Change for change's sake alone is never a good idea.* Yet he had pledged to himself that he would follow the Holy Spirit's lead in all things.

Then one day, while cleaning out a junk drawer in the kitchen, Adam came across an old brochure for the men's retreat he had attended. In a flash, he perceived what he was being called to do. He would later describe the experience as being like someone had opened the top of his skull and dumped in a road map for his next ten years. Feelings of elation and anticipation effaced the distress that had haunted him.

For Adam, there could be no doubt that his epiphany had been orchestrated by the Holy Spirit.

The next morning, upon arriving at work, Adam marched straight into Harold Cruz's office and announced that he would be taking a sabbatical and that if the CEO didn't like it, he could fire him. Rather than lose a highly esteemed employee, Mr. Cruz reluctantly agreed to allow Adam to take six months off—without pay.

*　*　*

July 2024

Within three months after being granted a sabbatical from Aurora, Adam had purchased a thirty-acre plot of ground beside the Bitterroot River and had filed the necessary paperwork to form a tax-exempt corporation he named the Abundant Life Fellowship. In addition, he was well along in designing a wilderness retreat modeled after the Trinity Falls Bible Camp. He intended to use the same basic layout. *No sense reinventing the wheel, not when we have one that had worked so well.*

Adam intended to create a nonprofit business that would host spiritual retreats for prominent influencers, people whose lives regularly impacted other people. Basically, Adam planned on targeting corporate officers, teachers, politicians, media types, professional athletes, entertainers, and the like. He reasoned that if he could reach one person who would later touch the lives of many others, he could extend his sphere of influence for the same capital investment.

In the spring of 2025, the Abundant Life Fellowship hosted its first retreat. Rather than employ homegrown orators, Adam had procured the services of professional public speakers and highly regarded spiritual counselors to staff the event. The only requirements imposed upon the fellowship were that every staff member must be a follower of Jesus Christ and that all contacts with the attendees must conform to the teachings of the Bible. Otherwise, the staff was to be guided by the Holy Spirit with regard to their conduct and the material they shared with the attendees.

The retreats were fundamentally a means of spreading the gospel. There were lectures, group discussions, prayer times, counseling sessions, and periods of quiet meditation. The retreats were also a time to relax and enjoy being out of doors. To this end, there were activities such as archery, canoeing, hiking, photography, swimming, and nature walks that highlighted some of the local wildlife.

Word spread rapidly, and the venture prospered. It wasn't long before the weekly sessions were booked six months in advance. In fact, the fellowship became so popular that despite the problems inherent in cold-weather camping, Adam was forced to open up a handful of winter sessions. These too became quite popular.

Within five years, Adam's fellowship had established a second camp, and then another shortly thereafter.

*   *   *

I pointed toward my grandson. "In November 2039, you were born, and that brings us to the present." I put my shoes back on and stood up. The telling had taken its toll. I felt worn out and a little achy. Even so, I sensed that I was near to accomplishing my goal, for which I was tremendously thankful.

I looked at Casey. "You must be exhausted too. What I need right now is a good night's sleep, so I will bid you adieu, but before you leave, come with me. I had François put together a selection of leftovers for you to take with you." I turned and headed toward the kitchen.

"Hold on!" Casey exclaimed. "We're just going to stop? There has to be more."

"Why would you think so?" I turned back with a gesture of uncertainty. "I've told you everything there is to tell. What more would you like to know?"

"What was the point? I mean, don't get me wrong. I liked hearing your history and getting to know who you are, but it feels like there should be…more."

"What do you mean more?"

"I don't know, just more."

"As you may recall, my purpose for sharing my story was to help me make sense of my life. And I have. A number of things are much clearer than they were, and for that, I am extremely grateful. What more could there be?" I held my breath as I studied my grandson with anticipation.

Casey began pacing across the Persian rug. "All these weeks, I've listened closely and thought about what you were telling me. Like you, I've tried to put things into perspective and ferret out cause-and-effect relationships, but it feels like I'm missing something, something I'm supposed to think or do. I just can't put my finger on it…"

And there it was. I reminded myself not to hold my breath. "Maybe it's not a matter of thinking or doing. Maybe it's a matter of identifying what's going on inside you. Tell me how you feel."

Casey stopped pacing and looked directly at me. He pondered my question for a moment. I could tell he was genuinely interrogating his inner self. "Honestly, I'm worried. I feel anxious and scared and maybe a tiny bit hopeful."

"That's an odd combination of emotions. Where do you think they might be coming from?"

Casey threw up his hands. "I have no idea."

"Oh, I suspect you do. Try harder. I get the impression that this is really important. Take your time, and tell me what you feel in your heart. What's troubling you?"

"I can't."

"Yes, you can. You need to do this. It will get better if you do. I promise."

Some of the tension seemed to leave Casey's body, as if he was finally letting go. "All right. I guess I can trust you." Casey looked away as if embarrassed. "Grandfather, do you remember me telling you that I was caught up in something bad? Well, it's true, and I can't figure out how to get clear of it." He paused to collect himself. "Last week, we talked about the burglaries that were taking place in neighborhoods around the university. Well, that was me. I'm the thief—me and a friend of mine. It started out as a lark. My friend is a senior who works part-time for the university. He's in the administration section that oversees the faculty's scheduling, so he knows when professors will be away from their homes.

"At first, we thought it would be fun just to see if we could break in and not get caught. I had the same mindset you did when you were younger: I knew it was wrong, but I did it anyway. The first time, it was a prank. The second time we took some stuff, which we sold. It was easy money. Things escalated from there, and now the police are close to figuring out it was the two of us. They are already talking to people in the administration section where my friend works."

I had assumed that my grandson was struggling with something traumatic, but I had no idea his difficulties were so serious. "I see your dilemma. Now you want to walk away, but you can't."

"The police are going to uncover the truth eventually. When they do, I'll be arrested. Not only will I be prosecuted and sent to jail, I'll lose whatever chance I had of ever becoming a lawyer. And if I turn myself in and confess what I've done, they might reduce my sentence, but otherwise, the outcome will be the same. Either way, my future is screwed."

"What does your friend want to do?"

"He wants to keep on stealing stuff. He believes the police are too stupid to catch us. Of course, he's wrong. What am I going to do?" My grandson's desperation was evident in his voice.

"Obviously, you're going to do what's right."

"No offense, but that's really not very helpful."

"Calm down. Take a deep breath and relax. Think about who you are. The answers you seek are inside you. Tell me what it is you want. You mentioned that you're feeling a tiny bit hopeful. Why is that? What are you seeing? What is the best way to move forward?"

Casey's eyes widened with a look of astonishment, as if a light had come on inside his head. "I know what it is. I want what you have. I've listened to you, and I've watched how you present yourself. You have an aura of peace about you, what I'd call a quiet assurance. There's strength in your convictions. It's more than being self-confident. It's hard to define, but I know it's there, and I want that."

"Where do you think that comes from?"

"I'd imagine from your faith."

"And you'd be right. My relationship with Jesus Christ defines who I am. That quiet assurance you noted, that certainty that things are as they are supposed to be, that's entirely the result of trusting God. And you can have it too. It's yours for the asking.

"I believe that right now, at this very instant, Jesus is calling you. He's the answer to your dilemma. If you will allow Him, He will help you sort out the right way to go. More than that, He's offering you a new life, a more abundant life, a life empowered by the Holy Spirit. The question is, how will you respond? Will you invite Him in, or will you shut Him out? The choice is yours. Will you accept Jesus Christ as your Lord and Savior?"

Casey looked away, as if he was being torn in two directions. The struggle raging within my grandson was painfully obvious. I had witnessed it many times during the retreats: in men and women who were afraid, who were entangled in the cares of the world, or who were simply too stubborn to let go and embrace the truth.

But then Casey's countenance changed. He looked at me, and his face melded into a wide smile. Firmly, he declared, "I will. I want Him to be part of my life. Like I said, Grandfather, I want what you have."

My heart leapt for joy. I wrapped my grandson in a tight bear hug and declared, "Praise be to God." When I finally let Casey loose, I said, "Pray with me now." I got down on my knees. Casey did the same. I placed my hand on his shoulder while we repeated the sinner's prayer. By the time we finished, we were both shedding tears of joy.

We stood up, and I wrapped Casey in another tight hug. When we separated, I cradled his face with both hands. My heart was full. "Grandson, do you know how much I love you?"

"Yes, Grandfather. I do."

"It's going to be all right in the long run. You'll see."

The End

EPILOGUE

Three weeks after confessing his faith and accepting Jesus Christ as his Lord and Savior, Casey Masters was baptized at the Capstone Chapel. A week later, he took his final exams and passed them all.

Prompted by the urgings of the Holy Spirit, Casey turned himself in to the police one week after graduating from college.

When arraigned before the magistrate, Casey pled guilty. Since it was his first offense, and because he had turned himself in, and because, with his grandfather's help, he had offered to make restitution to his victims, the judge had felt inclined to be lenient. Casey was sentenced to five years in prison. With time off for good behavior, he was out in three. As expected, his dreams of becoming a lawyer were never realized.

Instead, after being paroled, Casey joined his grandfather on the board of Abundant Life Fellowship. Over time, his role in managing the day-to-day operations increased until he finally replaced his grandfather as head of the organization.

Adam, for his part, was thrilled to work side by side with his grandson. As age began to take its toll, he was more than happy to step aside in deference to a younger generation.

Adam's friendship with Alice Cunningham continued to flourish. Once a year they made a point of getting together at some unique location, and while they thoroughly enjoyed each other's company, their relationship remained entirely platonic.

Adam's quest to understand his life, to make sense of its ebb and flow, was ultimately successful. In the end, after sorting through the tangled web of his existence, he was left with one unassailable truth: only after you empty yourself by surrendering to God can He fill you with His Holy Spirit. Adam adopted that maxim as the linchpin of the Abundant Life ministry. Its simple message has helped transform countless lives.

9 781966 540410